GOLDEN
BUDDHA

Dear Readers,

A few years ago, while I was writing *Flood Tide*, I realized that Dirk Pitt needed some help on a particular assignment, and so I dreamed up Juan Cabrillo.

Cabrillo ran a ship called the *Oregon*, on the outside completely nondescript, but on the inside packed with state-of-the-art intelligence-gathering equipment. It was a completely private enterprise, available for any government agency that could afford it. It went where no warship could go, transported secret cargo without suspicion, plucked data out of the air—it was the perfect complement to NUMA.

In fact, I had so much fun writing about the *Oregon* and its rakish, one-legged chief that I was sorry to see it sail off when its task was done. I promised myself I'd find a way to bring them back some day—and here, I am pleased to say, they are. *Golden Buddha* is the first in a new series about Juan Cabrillo's merry men (and women!), and I hope you get as much of a kick reading about them as I did creating them.

And who knows, maybe some time they'll cross paths with Dirk Pitt again. . . .

Clive Cussler

GOLDEN BUDDHA

CLIVE CUSSLER
AND
CRAIG DIRGO

MICHAEL JOSEPH
an imprint of
PENGUIN BOOKS

MICHAEL JOSEPH

Published by the Penguin Group
Penguin Books Ltd, 80 Strand, London WC2R 0RL, England
Penguin Putnam Inc., 375 Hudson Street, New York, New York 10014, USA
Penguin Books Australia Ltd, 250 Camberwell Road, Camberwell, Victoria 3124, Australia
Penguin Books Canada Ltd, 10 Alcorn Avenue, Toronto, Ontario, Canada M4V 3B2
Penguin Books India (P) Ltd, 11 Community Centre, Panchsheel Park, New Delhi - 110 017, India
Penguin Books (NZ) Ltd, Cnr Rosedale and Airborne Roads, Albany, Auckland, New Zealand
Penguin Books (South Africa) (Pty) Ltd, 24 Sturdee Avenue, Rosebank 2196, South Africa

Penguin Books Ltd, Registered Offices: 80 Strand, London WC2R 0RL, England

www.penguin.com

First published in the United States of America by The Berkley Publishing Group 2003
First published in Great Britain by Michael Joseph 2003
4

Copyright © Sandecker, RLLLP, 2003
"Foreword" by Clive Cussler copyright © Clive Cussler, 2003

The moral right of the authors has been asserted

Printed in Great Britain by Clays Ltd, St Ives plc

A CIP catalogue record for this book is available from the British Library

ISBN 0-718-14565-8

For my brothers
Larry, Steve, Cliff and John,
and my sister, Dawn,
who never let a busy day
get in the way of a good nap.

FOREWORD

Just so you know, this is not a Dirk Pitt adventure, nor a NUMA Files–Kurt Austin story. This book is based on the old tramp cargo ship *Oregon* that I described in the Pitt tale titled *Flood Tide*.

Beneath her derelict superstructure and rusty hull, *Oregon* is a mechanical marvel of technology and scientific genius. She is crewed by a group of highly educated and intelligent mercenaries who function under the myriad umbrellas of a far-flung corporate conglomerate. They contract with governments, corporations and private interests around the world to fight corruption and challenge the sinister threats of rogue villains in the exotic ports of the seven seas.

Craig Dirgo and I worked together to create an entirely new series of adventures with a cast of characters unlike any ever seen before.

I sincerely hope you will find it an enjoyable departure as well as a fun read.

Clive Cussler

CAST OF CHARACTERS

THE CORPORATION TEAM

JUAN CABRILLO: Chairman of the Corporation

MAX HANLEY: President of the Corporation

RICHARD TRUITT: Vice President of Operations for the Corporation

THE CREW
(in alphabetic order)

GEORGE ADAMS: Helicopter Pilot/Operative

RICK BARRETT: Assistant Chef/Operative

MONICA CRABTREE: Supply and Logistics Coordinator/Operative

CARL GANNON: General Operations/Operative

CHUCK "TINY" GUNDERSON: Chief Pilot/Operative

MICHAEL HALPERT: Finance and Accounting/Operative

CLIFF HORNSBY: General Operations/Operative

JULIA HUXLEY: Medical Officer/Operative

PETE JONES: General Operations/Operative

HALI KASIM: Communications Expert/Operative

LARRY KING: Sniper/Operative

FRANKLIN LINCOLN: General Operations/Operative

BOB MEADOWS: General Operations/Operative

MARK MURPHY: Weapons Specialist/Operative

KEVIN NIXON: Magic Shop Specialist/Operative

SAM PRYOR: Propulsion Engineer/Operative

GUNTHER REINHOLT: Propulsion Engineer/Operative

TOM REYES: General Operations/Operative

LINDA ROSS: Security and Surveillance/Operative

EDDIE SENG: Director of Shore Operations/Operative

ERIC STONE: Control Room Operations/Operative

THE OTHERS

THE DALAI LAMA: Spiritual Leader of Tibet

HU JINTAO: President of China

LANGSTON OVERHOLT IV: CIA Officer who hires the Corporation to free Tibet

LEGCHOG ZHUREN: Chairman of the Tibet Autonomous Region

SUNG RHEE: Chief Inspector of the Macau Police

LING PO: Detective with the Macau Police

STANLEY HO: Macau billionaire and buyer of the Golden Buddha

MARCUS FRIDAY: U.S. software billionaire who agrees to buy stolen Buddha

WINSTON SPENSER: Crooked art dealer who attempts to steal the Golden Buddha

MICHAEL TALBOT: San Francisco art dealer who works for Friday

PRELUDE

THE FLOWERS SURROUNDING the summer palace of Norbulingka were closed but ready to bloom. The parklike setting of the complex was beautiful. High stone walls surrounded it, within the walls were trees and lush gardens, and in the center was a smaller yellow wall, through which only the Dalai Lama, his advisors and a few select monks passed. Here were tranquil pools, the home of the Dalai Lama and a temple for prayer.

It was a sea of order and substance centered in a country in chaos.

Not far away, perched on the side of a hill, was the imposing winter palace of Potala. The massive structure seemed to step down the hillside. Potala contained over one thousand rooms, was populated by hundreds of monks and dated from centuries before. There was an imposing orderliness to the building. Stone steps led from the mid levels of the seven-story palace in an orderly zigzag downward and then stopped at a gigantic block stone wall that formed the base of the behemoth. The precisely laid stones rose nearly eighty feet into the air.

At the base was a flat stretch of land where tens of thousands of Tibetans were assembled. The people, as well as another large group at Norbulingka, had come to protect their spiritual leader. Unlike the hated Chinese who occupied their country, the peasants carried not rifles but knives and bows. Instead of artillery, they had only flesh, bone and spirit. They were outgunned, but to protect their leader they would have gladly laid down their lives.

Their sacrifice would require but one word from the Dalai Lama.

I NSIDE THE YELLOW wall, the Dalai Lama was praying at the shrine to Mahakala, his personal protector. The Chinese had offered to take him to their headquarters for his protection, but he knew that was not their true motive. It was the Chinese from whom he needed protection, and the letter the Dalai Lama had just received from Ngabo Ngawang Jigme, the governor of Chamdo, held a truer picture. After a discussion with General Tan, the Chinese military officer in command of the region, Jigme was certain the Chinese were planning to begin shelling the crowds to disperse them.

Once that happened, the loss of life would be horrific.

Raising from his knees, the Dalai Lama walked over to a table and rang a bell. Almost instantly the door opened and the head of the Kusun Depon, the Dalai Lama's personal bodyguards, appeared. Through the open door he could see several Sing Gha warriors. The monastic policemen lent a terrifying presence. Each was over six feet tall, wore a fearsome mustache, and was dressed in a black padded suit that made them appear even larger and more invincible.

Several Dogkhyi, the fierce Tibetan mastiff guard dogs, stood on their haunches at attention.

"Please summon the oracle," the Dalai Lama said quietly.

* * *

FROM HIS HOUSE in Lhasa, Langston Overholt III was monitoring the deteriorating conditions. He stood alongside the radio operator as the man adjusted the dial.

"Situation critical, over."

The radio operator turned the dial to reduce the static.

"Believe red rooster will enter the henhouse, over."

The operator watched the gauges carefully.

"Need immediate positive support, over."

Again a lag as the operator adjusted the dial.

"I recommend eagles and camels, over."

The man stood mute as the radio warbled and the green gauges returned to a series of wavelike motions. The words were out in the ether now; the rest was out of their control. Overholt wanted airplanes—and he wanted them now.

THE ORACLE, DORJE Drakden, was deep in a trance. The setting sun came through the small window high on the wall of the temple and cast a path of light that ended at an incense holder. The wisps of smoke danced on the beam of light and a strange, almost cinnamon smell filled the air. The Dalai Lama sat cross-legged on a pillow against a wall a few feet from Drakden, who was hunched over, knees down, with his forehead on the wood floor. Suddenly, in a deep voice, the oracle spoke.

"Leave tonight! Go."

Then, still with his eyes closed, still in a trance, he rose, walked over to a table and stopped exactly one foot away. Then he reached down, picked up a quill pen, dipped it in ink and drew a detailed map on a sheet of paper before collapsing to the ground.

The Dalai Lama rushed to the oracle's side, lifted his head and patted his cheek. Slowly, the man began to awaken. After sliding a pillow under his head, the Dalai Lama rose and poured a cup of water from an earthenware pitcher. Carrying the cup back to the oracle, he placed it under his lips.

"Sip, Dorje," he said quietly.

Slowly, the older man recovered and pulled himself to a seated position. As soon as the Dalai Lama was sure the oracle was on the mend, he walked over to the table and stared at the ink drawing.

It was a detailed map showing his escape route from Lhasa to the Indian border.

O VERHOLT HAD BEEN born into his career. At least one Overholt had served in every war the United States had fought since the Revolutionary War. His grandfather had been a spy in the Civil War, his father during World War I, and Langston the third had served in the OSS in World War II before switching to the CIA when it'd been formed in 1947. Overholt was now thirty-three, with a fifteen-year history of espionage.

In all that time, Overholt had never seen a situation quite this ominous. This was not a king or a queen in peril, not a pontiff or dictator. This was the head of a religion. A man who was a God-king, a deity, a leader that traced his lineage back to A.D. 1351. If something did not happen quickly, the communist scourge would soon be taking him prisoner. Then the human chess match would be over.

I N MANDALAY, BURMA, Overholt's message was received and forwarded to Saigon where it was transferred to Manila, then over a secure underwater cable to Long Beach, California, then on to Washington, D.C.

As the situation in Tibet continued to deteriorate, the CIA started to assemble a force in Burma. The group was not large enough to defeat the Chinese, just large enough to slow them down until more heavily armed ground troops could be brought to bear.

Disguised as a front company named Himalayan Air Services, the armada consisted of fourteen C-47s: ten that could drop supplies and four that had just been converted to first-generation gunships. This force was augmented with six F-86 fighters and a lone, fresh-off-the-assembly-line Boeing B-52 heavy bomber.

ALAN DULLES SAT in the Oval Office, puffing on his pipe and pointing out the situation to President Eisenhower. Then the CIA director sat back and let the president think for a moment. Several minutes passed in silence.

"Mr. President," he said at last, "the CIA took the liberty of arranging a first-strike force in Burma. If you say the word, they'll be airborne in an hour."

Since his election in 1952, Eisenhower had faced the McCarthy hearings, the first advisors into Vietnam and a heart attack. He'd had to order ten thousand troops to Little Rock, Arkansas, to enforce integration; witness the Soviets take the lead in space; and have his vice president stoned by hostile crowds in Latin America. Now Cuba had a communist leader only ninety miles from U.S. soil. He was weary.

"No, Alan," he said quietly, after a pause. "I learned as a general that you have to know how to pick your fights. We need to stay clear of this Tibet situation right now."

Dulles rose and shook Eisenhower's hand. "I'll notify my men," he said.

In Overholt's command post in Lhasa, the ashtray on the table near the radio was filled with the stubs of unfiltered cigarettes. Hours passed, with only the confirmation that the radio transmission had been received. Every half hour, Tibetan messengers delivered intelligence. Visual reconnaissance reported that the crowds outside the palaces near Lhasa were growing minute by minute, but the messengers were unable to take an accurate count. Tibetans continued to stream down from the mountains, armed with sticks, rocks and knives. The milling mass would be cannon fodder for the well-armed Chinese.

So far the Chinese had taken no action, but the reports mentioned troop buildups on the roads leading into the fabled city. Overholt had seen this same scenario unfold five years ago in Guatemala, when a crowd supporting the anticommunist rebels under Carlos Armas had suddenly sparked. Chaos had ensued. Forces under President Jacobo Arbenz had begun to fire into the crowd to restore order, and before dawn broke, the hospitals and morgues had been filled to capacity. Overholt had organized the demonstration and the knowledge clouded his mind like a shroud.

Just then the radio crackled.

"Top Hat negative, over."

Overholt's heart skipped a beat. The planes he sought were not coming.

"Papa Bear will okay sweeping the path if critically necessary during extraction. Advise on departure and subsequent travel, over."

Eisenhower said not to attack Lhasa, Overholt thought, but Dulles has agreed to cover the escape out of Tibet on his own, if it came to that. If he worked things right, Overholt thought, he wouldn't need to put his boss's ass on the line.

"Sir?" the radio operator asked.

Overholt was jarred from his thoughts.

"They're expecting a reply," the operator said quietly.

Overholt reached for the microphone. "Acknowledged and agreed," Overholt said, "and thank Papa Bear for the gesture. We'll call from the road. Closing office, over."

The radio operator stared up at Overholt. "Guess that's that."

"Break it all down," Overholt said quietly, "we'll be leaving soon."

*　*　*

I NSIDE THE YELLOW wall, preparations for the Dalai Lama's escape into exile were moving at a blistering pace. Overholt was cleared past the guards and waited to be seen. Five minutes later, the Dalai Lama, wearing his black-framed prescription glasses and yellow robes, entered the office in the administration room. The spiritual leader of Tibet looked weary but resigned.

"I can tell by your face," he said quietly, "no help is coming."

"I'm sorry, Your Holiness," Overholt replied. "I did all that I could."

"Yes, Langston, I am certain you did. However, the situation is as it is," the Dalai Lama noted, "so I have decided to go into exile. I cannot risk the chance of my people being slaughtered."

Overholt had arrived expecting to use all his powers of persuasion to convince the Dalai Lama to flee—instead he found the decision had already been made. He should have expected as much—over the years he had grown to know the Dalai Lama, and he had never seen anything that made him doubt the leader's commitment to his people.

"My men and I would like to accompany you," Overholt offered. "We have detailed maps, radios and some supplies."

"We'd be glad to have you come along," the Dalai Lama said. "We leave shortly."

The Dalai Lama turned to leave.

"I wish I could have done more," Overholt said.

"Things are as they are," the Dalai Lama said at the door. "For now, however, you should assemble your men and meet us at the river."

H IGH ABOVE NORBULINGKA, the sky was dotted with a trillion stars. The moon, only days away from being full, lit the ground with a yellow diffused glow. A stillness, a quiet. The night birds that normally warbled their haunting songs were silent. The domesticated animals inside the compound—musk deer, mountain goats, camels, a single aged tiger and the peacocks that ran loose—barely stirred. A light wind from high in the Himalayas brought the scent of pine forests and change.

From high on a hillside outside Lhasa came the chilling scream of a snow leopard.

The Dalai Lama scanned the grounds, then closed his eyes and visualized returning. He was dressed in trousers instead of robes, a black wool coat instead of a cloak. A rifle on a sling rode on his left shoulder, and an ancient ceremonial thangka, an embroidered silk tapestry, was rolled up and hung over his right.

"I am ready," he said to his Chikyah Kenpo, or chief of staff. "Have you packed the icon?"

"It is safely crated and guarded. Like you, the men will protect it at all costs."

"As they should," the Dalai Lama said softly.

The two men walked toward and through the gate on the yellow wall.

The Chikyah Kenpo was holding a large, jeweled, curved sword. Sliding it into a leather scabbard on his belt, he turned to his master. "Stay close."

Then, followed by a cadre of Kusun Depon, they passed through the outer gate and slipped into the crowd. The procession quickly made its way along a worn dirt path. Pairs of Kusun Depon stepped to the rear and waited to see if anyone followed. After seeing no one, they moved forward to the next pair of guards, who remained until the coast was clear. Hopscotching their way along the path, the guards made sure the rear was covered. To the front, pairs of warriors assessed any danger ahead. Finding it clear, they continued their progression. A handcart containing the icon followed the procession, pulled by a large monk. Hands firmly on the poles, the monk raced along like a rickshaw driver late for an appointment.

Everyone was trotting and the sound made by their feet was like muffled clapping.

The sound of water came with the smell of wet moss. It was a tributary of the Kyichu River. After the party made their way across a series of stepping-stones, they continued quickly ahead.

A LONG THE FAR bank of the Kyichu River, Overholt stared at the radium dial on his watch, then shuffled his feet. Several dozen Kusun Depon who had been dispatched hours earlier were tending to the horses and mules that would speed the escape. They stared at the blond-haired American with neither malice nor fear, only resignation.

Several large ferryboats had brought them all across the water, and now the boats were tied up again on the far shore, awaiting the arrival of the Dalai Lama. Overholt caught a quick flash of light from the far bank, signaling it was safe to cross. In the moonlight, he could see the boats quickly being loaded, then minutes later heard the sound of the oars slapping the water.

The lead boat slid onto the pebbled beach and the Dalai Lama climbed over the side.

"Langston," he said, "did you leave the capital undetected?"

"Yes, Your Holiness."

"All your men with you?"

Overholt pointed to the seven men that made up his command. They stood off to the side with several footlockers of equipment. Reaching the opposite shore, the Chikyah Kenpo climbed from the boat and assembled the lead troops onto horses. Long spears draped with silk banners were placed in the troops' hands. Earlier, their steeds had been covered with ceremonial blankets and adornments. Then, like the honk of a goose on his way south, a sound of a muted trumpet filled the air. It was time to leave.

Overholt and his men were helped onto horses and lined up following the Dalai Lama. By the time the sun rose the next morning, they were miles from Lhasa.

*   *   *

WO DAYS INTO the journey, across the sixteen-thousand-foot Che-
La Pass and over the Tsangpo River, the group stopped for the
night at the monastery at Ra-Me. Messengers racing on horseback
caught up with the party and brought news that the Chinese had shelled
Norbulingka and machine-gunned the helpless crowd. Thousands had
been killed. The news cast a pall over the Dalai Lama.

Overholt had reported their progress by radio and felt relieved there
had been no need to call for help. The route had been expertly chosen
to avoid any conflict with the Chinese. He and his men were exhausted,
but the hardy Nepalese pushed on without pause. The town of Lhuntse
Dzong was behind them, as was the village of Jhora.

Karpo Pass, the border with India, was less than a day's ride.

And then it began to snow. A blizzard with howling winds and low
clouds hunkered down over Mangmang, the last Tibetan town before
the Indian border. The Dalai Lama, already exhausted by the journey
and stressed by the knowledge that many of his countrymen lay dead
and dying, took ill. His last night in his country was torment.

To ease his journey, he was placed on the back of an animal called
a dzomo, which was a cross between a yak and a horse. As the dzomo
climbed the side of Karpo Pass, the Dalai Lama paused to glance at his
beloved Tibetan soil one last time.

Overholt pulled closer on his horse. He waited until the Dalai Lama
glanced his way. "My country never forgets," he said, "and someday
we will bring you back home."

The Dalai Lama nodded, then patted the dzomo's neck and steered
it into exile. To the rear of the column, the monk pulling the cart containing the priceless artifact braced his legs as he crested the pass and
started down the grade. The six-hundred-pound weight, so heavy on the
climb up the pass, now wanted to run free. He dug in his heels.

1

THE PRESENT DAY

EIGHT IN THE evening. From out of the south, like a dark insect crawling over a wrinkled blue tablecloth, a tired old cargo ship pushed her way through the Caribbean swells toward the entrance of Santiago Harbor on the isle of Cuba. The exhaust from her single funnel drifted in a blue haze under an easterly breeze as the sun settled below the western horizon and became a ponderous orange ball magnified by the earth's atmosphere.

She was one of the last tramp steamers, a cargo ship that traveled the sea anonymously to the exotic and far-flung ports of the world. There were few left in operation. They did not follow a regular shipping route. Their schedules depended on the demands of their cargo and its owners, so their destinations changed from port to port. They coasted in, unloaded their freight and sailed away like wraiths in the night.

Two miles from shore, a small boat slapped over the rolling sea, approached the ship and swung around on a parallel course. The pilot closed on the rust-streaked hull as a boarding ladder was thrown down from an open hatch.

The pilot, a man in his fifties with brown skin and thick gray hair, stared up at the ancient ship. Her black paint was faded and badly needed to be chipped away and repainted. Streams of rust flowed from every opening in the hull. The huge anchor, pulled tightly in its hawsehole, was completely covered by corrosion. The pilot read the letters, barely discernible on the upper bow. The weary old freighter was named *Oregon*.

Jesus Morales shook his head in amazement. It was a miracle the ship hadn't been scrapped twenty years ago, he mused. She looked more like a derelict than a cargo carrier still in service. He wondered if the party bureaucrats in the Ministry of Transportation had any idea of the condition of the ship they had contracted to bring in a cargo of chemical fertilizer for the sugar and tobacco fields. He could not believe the ship had passed maritime insurance inspection.

As the ship slowed almost to a dead stop, Morales stood at the railing and the pilot boat's bumpers squeezed against the freighter's hull. Timing the crest of a wave as it lifted the boat, Morales leaped agilely from the wet deck onto the boarding ladder and climbed to the hatch. It was a function he performed as often as ten times a day. A pair of crewmen were waiting beside the hatch and helped him up on the deck. The two were both burly-looking individuals, and they did not bother to smile in greeting. One simply pointed toward the ladder leading to the bridge. Then they turned and left Morales standing alone on the deck. Watching them walk away, Morales hoped that he'd never have to meet them in a dark alley.

He paused before climbing the ladder and took a few moments to study the upper works of the ship.

From his long experience and knowledge of ships, he judged her length at 560 feet, with a 75-foot beam. Probably a gross tonnage around 11,000. Five derricks, two behind the funnel and superstructure and three on the forward deck, stood waiting to unload her cargo. He counted six holds with twelve hatches. In her prime, she would have been classed as an express cargo liner. He guessed that she had been built and launched in the early 1960s. The flag on her stern was Iranian. Not a registry Morales had seen very often.

If the *Oregon* looked shabby from the waterline, she looked downright squalid from her main deck. Rust covered every piece of deck machinery from winches to chains, but the hardware at least appeared to be in usable condition. By comparison, the derricks looked as if they hadn't been operated in years.

To add further insult, battered drums, tools and what could only be described as junked equipment were scattered around the decks. In all his years as a harbor pilot, Morales had never seen a ship in such filthy condition.

He climbed the ladder steps leading to the bridge, past bulkheads with flaking paint and portholes whose lenses were cracked and yellowed. Then he paused before finally swinging the door open. The interior of the vessel was as bad, if not worse. The wheelhouse was dirty, with the scars of cigarette burns on the counters and on what had once been a polished teak deck. Dead flies littered the windowsills, the smell assaulted his nose. And then there was the captain.

Morales was greeted by a great slob of a man with an immense stomach that sagged over his belt line. The face was scarred, and the nose so badly broken it slanted toward the left cheek. The thick black hair was plastered back with some kind of greasy cream and his beard was scruffy and stringy. The captain was a cacophony of colors. His eyes were red and his teeth yellow-brown, while his arms were covered with blue tattoos. A grimy yachtsman's cap sat perched on the back of his head and he wore dingy coveralls. The tropical heat and the humidity on the non-air-conditioned bridge made it obvious to Morales that the man had not bathed for at least a month. Any dog worth his salt would have tried to bury the man.

He extended a sweaty hand to Morales and spoke in English. "Glad to see you. I'm Captain Jed Smith."

"Jesus Morales. Pilot for the Harbor Office of Santiago." Morales felt uncomfortable. Smith spoke English with an American accent—not what he'd expected on a ship of Iranian registry.

Smith handed him a packet of papers. "Here's our registration and cargo manifest."

Morales merely cast a brief glance at the documents. Officials on the docks would study them more closely. His only concern was that the ship had permission to enter the port. He handed back the packet and said, "Shall we proceed?"

Smith waved a hand toward a wooden helm that somehow seemed terribly old-fashioned for a ship built in the sixties. "She's all yours, Señor Morales. What dock do you want us to moor at?"

"There are no docks available until Thursday. You will have to anchor in the middle of the harbor until then."

"That's four days from now. We have a schedule to meet. We can't sit around for four days waiting to unload our cargo."

Morales shrugged. "I have no control over the harbormaster. Besides, the docks are full with ships unloading new farm machinery and automobiles, now that the embargo has been lifted. These have priority over your cargo."

Smith threw up his hands. "All right. I guess it's not the first time we had to twiddle our thumbs waiting to unload." He gave a broad, rotten-toothed grin. "I guess me and my crew will just have to come ashore and make friends with your Cuban women."

The thought made Morales's skin crawl. Without further conversation, he stepped over to the helm as Smith called the engine room and ordered half speed. The pilot felt the engine's vibrations through the deck as the tired old ship began to make way again, and he aimed her bow toward the narrow entrance of Santiago Harbor, which was bordered by high bluffs that rose from the sea.

From offshore, the channel that led inside to the bellows-shaped harbor was invisible until a ship was nearly on top of it. Rising two hundred feet atop the cliffs on the right stood the old colonial fortress known as Morro Castle.

Morales noticed that Smith and the members of his mangy crew standing on the bridge seemed interested in the defenses that had been dug into the hillside when Fidel Castro had thought the United States was going to attack Cuba. They studied the gun and missile emplacements through expensive binoculars.

Morales smiled to himself. Let them look all they wanted—most of the defenses were deserted. Only two small fortresses maintained a small company of soldiers to man the missile emplacements in the unlikely event an unwelcome vessel tried to enter the harbor.

Morales threaded his way through the buoys and steered the *Oregon* deftly around the twists and turns of the channel, which soon opened into the broad, ball-shaped harbor surrounded by the city of Santiago. The wheel felt strange to him, though. The odd feeling was barely perceptible, but there nonetheless. Whenever he turned the wheel, there seemed to be a short lag before the rudder responded. He made a quick but very slight turn to starboard before bringing the wheel back to port. It was definitely there, almost like an echo, a two-second delay. He did not sense sluggishness from the steering machinery, but rather a pause. It had to come from another origin. Yet when the response came, it was quick and firm. But why the hesitation?

"Your helm has an off feel to it."

"Yeah," Smith grunted. "It's been that way for a few days. Next port we enter with a shipyard, I'll have the spindles on the rudder looked at."

It still made no sense to Morales, but the ship was entering the open part of the bay off the city now, and he pushed the mystery from his mind. He called the harbor officials over the ship's radio and kept them informed of his progress, and was given orders for the anchorage.

Morales pointed out the buoys to Smith that marked the mooring area and ordered the ship brought to slow speed. He then swung the stern around until the bow was facing the incoming tide before ordering all stop. The *Oregon* slowed to a halt in an open area between a Canadian container ship and a Libyan oil tanker.

"You may drop your anchor," he said to Smith, who acknowledged with a nod as he held a loudspeaker in front of his face.

"Let go anchor!" he shouted at his crew. The command was answered a few seconds later by the rattling clatter of the chain links against the hawsehole, followed by a great splash as the anchor plunged into the water. The bow of the ship became hazy from the cloud of dust and rust that burst from the chain locker.

Morales released his grip on the worn spokes of the wheel and turned to Smith. "You will, of course, pay the pilot's fee when you turn over your documents to the harbor officials."

"Why wait?" snorted Smith. He reached into a pocket of his coveralls and produced a wad of crinkled American hundred-dollar bills. He counted out fifteen bills, then hesitated, looked into Morales's shocked expression, and said, "Oh, what the heck, suppose we make it an even two thousand dollars."

Without the least indecision, Morales took the bills and slipped them into his wallet.

"You are most generous, Captain Smith. I will notify the officials that the pilot's fee was paid in full."

Smith signed the required affidavits and logged the mooring. He put a massive arm around the Cuban's shoulder. "Now about them girls. Where's a good place in Santiago to meet them?"

"The cabarets on the waterfront are where you'll find both cheap entertainment and drinks."

"I'll tell my crew."

"Good-bye, Captain." Morales did not extend his hand. He already felt unclean just by being on board the ship; he could not bring himself to grip the greasy hand of the obnoxious captain. Morales's easygoing Cuban warmth had been cooled by the surroundings and he didn't want to waste another second on board the *Oregon*. Leaving the wheelhouse, he dropped down the ladder to the deck and descended to the waiting pilot boat, still stunned at experiencing the filthiest ship he had ever piloted into the harbor. Which is just what the owners of the *Oregon* wanted him to think.

If Morales had examined the ship more closely, he might have realized it was all a façade. The *Oregon* rode low in the water because of specially fitted ballast tanks, which when filled with water lowered the hull to make it look as though it were loaded with cargo. Even the engine tremors were mechanically staged. The ship's engines were whisper-silent and vibrationless.

And the coating of rust throughout the ship? It was artistically applied paint.

S ATISFIED THAT THE pilot and his boat had pulled away from the *Oregon*, Captain Smith stepped over to a handrail mounted on the deck that did not seem to serve any particular purpose. He gripped it and pressed a button on the underside. The square section of the deck on which Smith was standing suddenly began descending until it stopped in a vast, brightly lit room filled with computers, automated controls and several large consoles containing communications and weapons-firing systems. The deck in the command center was richly carpeted, the walls were paneled in exotic woods and the furniture looked as if it had come straight from a designer's showroom. This room was the real heart of the *Oregon*.

The six people—four men and two women—neatly dressed in shorts, flowered shirts and white blouses were busy manning the various systems. One woman was scanning an array of TV monitors that covered every section of Santiago Bay, while a man zoomed a camera on the pilot boat as it turned and headed into the main channel. No one bothered to give the fat captain half a glance. Only a man dressed in khaki shorts and a green golf shirt approached him.

"All go well with the pilot?" asked Max Hanley, the ship's corporate president, who directed all operational systems, including the ship's engines.

"The pilot noticed the delay in the helm."

Hanley grinned. "If only he'd known he was steering a dead wheel. We'll have to make some adjustments, though. You speak to him in Spanish?"

Smith smiled. "My best Yankee English. Why let him know I speak his language? That way, I could tell if he played any tricks over the radio with the harbor officials as we anchored." Smith pulled back a sleeve of his grimy coveralls and checked a Timex watch with a badly scratched lens. "Thirty minutes until dark."

"The equipment in the moon pool is all ready."

"And the landing crew?"

"Standing by."

"I just have time to get rid of these smelly clothes and get decent," said Cabrillo, heading toward his cabin down a hallway hung with paintings by modern artists.

The crew cabins were concealed inside two of the cargo holds and were as plush as rooms in a five-star hotel. There was no separation between officers and crew on the *Oregon*. All were educated people, highly trained in their respective fields—elite men and women who had served in the armed forces. The ship was owned by its staff, who were stockholders. There were no ranks. Cabrillo was chairman; Hanley, president; the others held various other titles. They were all mercenaries, here to make a profit—though that did not necessarily rule out good works at the same time—hired by countries or large companies to perform clandestine services around the world, very often at great risk.

THE MAN WHO left the cabin twenty minutes later did not look like the man who'd entered. The greasy hairpiece, scruffy beard and grimy coveralls were gone, as was the foul smell. So was the Timex, now replaced with a stainless-steel Concord chronograph. In addition, the man had dropped at least a hundred pounds.

Juan Rodriguez Cabrillo had transformed himself from the grimy sea dog Smith to his true self again. A tall man in his forties, ruggedly handsome, he stared through pixie-blue eyes. His blond hair was trimmed in a crew cut and a western cowboy-style mustache sprouted from his upper lip.

He hurried down the corridor to a far door and entered a control room perched high inside a vast cavern in the hull amidships. The three-deck-high moon pool, as it was called, was where all the *Oregon*'s underwater equipment was stored—diving gear; submersibles, manned and unmanned; and an array of underwater electronic sensors. A pair of state-of-the-art contemporary underwater craft by U.S. Submarines—a sixty-five-foot Nomad 1000 and a thirty-two-foot Discovery 1000—hung in cradles. The doors on the bottom of the hull slid open and water flooded in until it was level with the outer waterline.

The remarkable ship was not what she appeared from her exterior. The outer decks and hull were disguised to make her look like a rust bucket. The wheelhouse and the unused officers' and crew's quarters below were also kept in a slovenly condition to avoid suspicion from visiting port officials or harbor pilots.

Cabrillo entered the underwater operations room and stood before a large table showing three-dimensional holographic images of every street in the city of Santiago. Linda Ross, the *Oregon*'s security and surveillance analyst, was standing at the table lecturing a group of people dressed in Cuban military fatigue uniforms. Linda had been a lieutenant commander in the navy when Cabrillo had sweet-talked her into resigning and joining the *Oregon*. In the navy she had been an intelligence officer on board an Aegis guided-missile cruiser before spending four years in Washington in the navy's intelligence department.

Linda glanced sideways at Cabrillo as he stood quietly without interrupting. She was an attractive woman, not a head turner, but most men still considered her pretty. She kept her five-foot-eight-inch, 130-

pound body in firm shape with exercise, but rarely spent extra time on makeup or hairstyle. She was one smart lady, soft-spoken and greatly admired by the entire *Oregon* crew.

The five men and one woman standing around the detailed 3-D image of the city listened intently as Linda ran through the last-minute instructions, using a small metal rod with a light on the end to point out their objective. "The fortress of Santa Ursula. It was built during the Spanish-American War, and after the turn of the twentieth century it was used as a warehouse until Castro and his revolutionaries took over the country. Then it was turned into a prison."

"What is the exact distance from our landing to the prison?" asked Eddie Seng, the *Oregon*'s master of subterfuge and director of shore operations.

"Two hundred yards less than a mile," answered Linda.

Seng folded his arms and looked thoughtful. "We'll be able to fool the locals with our uniforms going in, but if we have to fight our way back a mile to the docks while herding eighteen prisoners, I can't guarantee we'll make it."

"Certainly not in the condition those poor people are going to be in," said Julia Huxley, the *Oregon*'s medical officer. She was going along on the raid to care for the prisoners. A short woman, large bosomed with a body suited for wrestling, Julia was the congeniality lady of the ship. She'd served as a chief medical officer for four years at the San Diego Naval Base and was well respected by them all.

"Our agents in the city have arranged for a truck to be stolen twenty minutes before you leave the prison. It's used for hauling food supplies to the hotels. The truck and a driver will be parked one block from the workers' maintenance shack situated on the wharf above your landing dock. He'll drive you to the prison, wait, and return you to the dock. From there he'll ditch the truck and ride home on his bicycle."

"Does he have a name? Is there a password?"

Linda smiled slightly. "The password is *dos*."

Seng looked skeptical. "Two? That's it?"

"Yes, he'll reply with *uno*, one. It's that simple."

"Well, at least it's concise."

Linda paused to flick a series of switches on a small remote control. The images of the city dissolved into a 3-D interior diorama of Santa Ursula Prison without its roof, revealing the inner rooms and cells and their connecting passageways. "Our sources tell us there are only ten guards in the whole prison. Six on the day shift, two in the evening and two from midnight until six in the morning. You should have no problem overpowering the two on the station. They'll think you're a military unit come to transport the prisoners to another secure facility. You're scheduled to gain entry at ten o'clock. Subdue the two on-duty guards and release the prisoners, then return to the submarine and make the ship by eleven o'clock. Any later and you jeopardize our escape out of the harbor."

"How so?" asked one of Seng's team members.

"We're told the harbor defense systems are run through an operational test every night at twelve. We've got to be well on our way to sea before then."

"Why not wait and go in after midnight, when most of the town is asleep?" asked a member of the landing force. "At ten o'clock, the local citizens will still be stirring around."

"You'll cause less suspicion if you don't sneak around the streets before dawn," she replied. "Also, the other eight guards are usually out on the town in the local bars until early morning."

"You're sure about that?" asked Seng.

Linda nodded. "Their movements have been watched and clocked for two weeks by our agents in the city."

"Unless Murphy's Law rears its ugly head," said Cabrillo, "the release of the prisoners and the escape should go smoothly. The tough part comes when you're all on board and we have to sail out of the harbor. The minute Castro's harbor security forces see us pull up the anchor and turn down the channel for the open sea, they'll know something is wrong and all hell will break loose."

Linda looked at Cabrillo. "We have the weaponry to knock them out."

"True," Cabrillo acknowledged. "But we cannot fire the first shot. If they strike the *Oregon* first, however, we'll have no choice but to protect ourselves."

"None of us has been told," said Seng, "who exactly are we breaking out of jail. They must be important or we wouldn't have contracted for the job."

Cabrillo looked at him. "We wanted to keep it under wraps until we got here. They're Cuban doctors, journalists and businessmen who opposed Castro's government, all highly respected men and women. Castro knows they are dangerous if they are free. If they reach the Cuban community in Miami, they can use it as a base to instigate a revolutionary movement."

"Is it a good contract?"

"Ten million dollars if we deliver them to U.S. soil."

Seng and the others around the holographic display smiled. "That should add a tidy little amount to everyone's nest egg," he said.

"Doing good for profit," Cabrillo said with a wide grin. "That's our motto."

A T PRECISELY 8:30, Seng and his small force boarded the Nomad 1000 along with the two crewmen who would pilot the sub and guard it during the operation. The sub looked more like a luxury surface yacht than a submersible. Capable of running at high speeds on the surface with its diesel engines, it was battery powered beneath the waves. With a speed of twelve knots underwater, the Nomad could dive to a thousand feet. The interior was designed to hold twelve people comfortably, but Cabrillo had had her configured to carry three times that number tightly packed together, for missions such as this one.

The entry door was closed and sealed, and the craft, secured by a large sling, was lifted by a crane into the center of the moon pool. The operator looked into the control room and was given the descent signal by Cabrillo. Then, slowly, the large craft was lowered into the black water. As soon as she settled, divers removed the sling and were carried upward to the surrounding balcony by the crane.

"Radio check," said Seng. "Do you read me?"

"Like you're in the same room," Linda Ross assured him.

"Are we clear?"

"No ship movement and only three fishing boats are heading out to sea. At thirty feet, you should stay well below their keels and props."

"Keep the coffee on," said Seng.

"Bon voyage," quipped Cabrillo.

"That's easy for you to say," Seng came back.

A few moments later, the lights inside the Nomad blinked out and it vanished into the dark water of the harbor.

T HE PILOTS OF the sub relied on their Global Positioning System to set them on an exact course for the section of the city docks that was their destination. Detecting the pilings by their laser monitoring system, they were able to slip between the stern and bow of two container ships unloading cargo and maneuvered their way amid the giant pilings. Once under the wharves and out of sight from anyone above, they surfaced and closed the remaining gap using a laser night-penetrating camera that magnified the city lights filtering beneath the pilings.

"Floating maintenance dock dead ahead," announced the chief pilot.

There was no hard check of weapons or survival gear. Though they all carried concealed handguns, they wanted to look like a small security unit moving through town without any menacing designs on the citizens. Their only inspection was to make sure their uniforms looked neat and presentable. The combat members of the team had all been members of the Special Forces. They were under strict orders not to commit mayhem unless it was absolutely necessary in order to save lives. Seng himself had served on a marine recon team and had never lost a man.

No sooner had the Nomad gently bumped against the floating dock than Seng, followed closely by his team, exited the sub and headed up the stairs to a little house that sheltered the dock and maintenance workers' tools and small equipment. The door was easily unlocked from the inside, and Seng, with only a brief look to see if anyone was standing nearby, silently motioned everyone to follow him.

The lights of the cranes and the ships they were unloading lit up the dock like daylight, but luckily the exit door was opposite and the team formed in the shadows. Then, in a column of twos and marching in cadence, Seng led them to the end of the dock and around the warehouse.

His watch said 9:36. Exactly twenty-four minutes to arrive at the front gate of the prison. They found the truck nine minutes later, parked under a dim dock light beside the warehouse. Seng recognized it as a 1951 Ford delivery van that looked like it had passed the two-million-mile mark years ago. In the gloom he could make out lettering in a fancy red script on the side of the fourteen-foot cargo body. It read GONZALES FOOD PURVEYORS in Spanish. The driver was visible only by the glow of his cigarette.

Seng walked up to the open window, hand on his Ruger P97 .45 caliber automatic with suppressor, and said quietly. *"Dos."*

The driver of the truck exhaled a cloud of nonfiltered cigarette smoke into the cab and replied, *"Uno."*

"Pile in the back," Seng ordered his team. "I'll ride in front." He opened the passenger door and slid onto the seat. There was no conversation as the driver crunched the worn-out transmission into gear and drove off the dock into the city streets. Every other light on the boulevard running along the bay was dark, either because the bulbs had burned out and had never been replaced or to conserve energy. After a few blocks the driver turned onto a main street and headed up a slight grade toward San Juan Hill.

Cuba's second largest city, Santiago was in Oriente Province and had been the island's capital in the seventeenth century. Surrounded by hills with coffee and sugar-cane plantations, the city was a maze of narrow streets, with small plazas and buildings of Spanish colonial architecture bearing hanging balconies.

Seng remained silent, concentrating on scanning the side streets and studying the numbers on his portable GPS to make certain the driver was heading in the right direction. The streets were mostly empty of traffic, except for fifty-year-old cars parked along the curbs, and the sidewalks were filled with people simply out for an after-dinner stroll or sitting in bars that reverberated with loud strains of the Cuban beat. Many of the stores and apartments above had paint that was faded and chipped, while others were coated in vivid pastel colors. The gutters and sidewalks were clean, but the windows looked like they had rarely seen a cleaner and a squeegee. For the most part, the people looked happy. There was much laughter and occasional singing. No one gave the truck a second look as it passed slowly through the main downtown section of the city.

Seng spotted a few men in uniform, but they seemed more interested in talking with women than watching for a foreign intrusion. The driver lit up another foul-smelling cigarette. Seng had never smoked, and he leaned further against his door and turned his face through the open window, lifting his nose in disgust.

Ten minutes later the truck reached the front gate of the fortress prison. The driver pulled past and stopped fifty yards down the road. "I will wait here," he said, in almost perfect English. They were the first words he had spoken since the dock.

Seng read him like a book. "Educator or doctor?"

"I teach history at the university."

"Thank you."

"Don't be long. The truck will look suspicious if it sits here past midnight."

"We should be out before then," Seng assured him.

Seng climbed out of the truck cab and peered up and down the street cautiously. It was empty. He rapped softly on the cargo doors. They opened and his team dropped out and joined him on the brick-surfaced street. Together they marched as a unit up to the front gate and pulled the bell cord. A ringing could be heard in the guard's office behind the gate. In a few minutes, a guard came wandering out, rubbing his eyes and temples. He had obviously been asleep on duty. He was about to tell the intruders to go away when he recognized Seng's uniform and insignia as a colonel's and he feverishly opened the gate, stood back and saluted.

"Sir, what brings you to the fortress this time of night?"

"Colonel Antonio Yarayo. I was sent by the Ministry of State Security with this team to interrogate one of the prisoners. A new investigation has turned up a suspected United States spy operation. We believe they have information which could prove useful."

"Pardon me, sir, but I must ask you for the proper papers."

"As a good soldier, Sergeant," said Seng officiously, "well you should." He handed the guard an envelope. "Why aren't there more guards on duty?"

"There is one other who watches the prisoners' cells."

"Hmm. Well, I see no reason to stand out here all night. Take me to your office quarters."

The guard immediately ushered them into a barren office that contained only a desk and two chairs. A photo of Castro, taken when he was a young man, hung alone on one wall.

"Who is the officer in command here?" asked Seng.

"Captain Juan Lopez."

"Where is he?"

"He has a girlfriend with a house in the city. He will be back at nine o'clock tomorrow."

"How very convenient," Seng said as if bored. "What is your name?"

"Lieutenant Gabriel Sanchez, sir."

"And the name of the other guard on duty in the cells?"

"Sergeant Ignez Macco."

"Please check the documents so we can get on with it."

The guard sat down at the desk and pulled some paper out of the envelope. Seng moved behind and removed a small gun from his pocket as Sanchez stared blankly at a pair of comic books. He looked up. "Colonel, I don't under—"

That was as far as he got before Seng shot a tiny dart filled with a tranquilizer into the nape of his neck. Sanchez looked at Seng oddly before slumping unconscious over the table.

Seng threw a roll of duct tape to one of his team. Every move was so well rehearsed that he did not have to give orders. Two men took the tape, bound the unconscious guard, searched his pockets—finding an unusual round key—and then stuffed him in a closet. Another man went to work carefully rendering the security alarms and communications equipment inoperable.

As they rushed through the passageways and tunnels and down stone steps to the cells below, Seng knew where he was within a foot, thanks to the holographic image of the fortress that he had committed to memory.

There was no desperate hurry, but they could not afford to throw away time. He could see now why only a few men guarded the entire facility. The walls were massively thick, and there was only one entrance in and out of the dungeon cells far below street level. The only way a prisoner could escape was the way the team from the *Oregon* had come—from the outside. A string of lightbulbs lit the passageway. The ceiling was very high, but the space between the walls was very narrow. The steps finally ended at an enormous steel door with the thickness of a bank vault. A TV camera stared ominously at Seng and his men. This was the tricky part, he thought, as he inserted the odd-looking key into the steel lock. Seng prayed that the key would do the job without a code being demanded.

His fear was confirmed when he turned the key and a buzzer could be heard from the other side of the door. A minute later a voice called through a nearby loudspeaker, "Who goes there?"

"Colonel Antonio Yarayo, State Security, with an interrogation team to question the traitors."

There was a pause. Seng didn't wait for a reply.

"Open up. I have the authority and necessary documents. Lieutenant Sanchez would have accompanied us, but he said he was not allowed to leave the front gate unguarded. Sergeant Ignez Macco, is it?" Seng held up the envelope. "If you have any questions, I have your service record in my hands."

"But sir," the voice of Macco pleaded, "if the door is opened before eight o'clock in the morning, alarms will go off in the state security office at Fort Canovar."

"I ordered Lieutenant Sanchez to turn off the dungeon alarm," Seng bluffed.

"But sir, he cannot do that. The door is on a separate system that is wired to the security commandant's office in the city. It cannot be opened until eight o'clock in the morning."

It was one more obstacle to overcome, but not totally unexpected. Seng was betting that the security officers would think the alarms were malfunctioning and call the fort to check it out before sending a squad of security police.

Macco fell for it. A few seconds later, the big steel lock clacked and the bolts that extended from the door into the framework could be heard withdrawing from their slots. Then the massive door swung open silently and smoothly. Sergeant Macco stood at attention and snapped a salute.

Seng wasted no more time on niceties. He aimed the tranquilizer gun at Macco's throat and squeezed the tiny trigger. The guard's eyes rolled back in his head and he dropped to the stone floor like a sack of sand.

The dungeon was not a state-of-the-art prison. The rusting iron cell doors had been hung in the late nineteenth century and still required the large antique key chained to Macco's belt. Seng ripped the key and its ring from the guard's belt and began opening the first doors. As soon as the door was swung ajar, Julia Huxley rushed into the cell to check the condition of its inhabitant. Seng's team helped by assisting the shocked prisoners, who feared the worst, into the dungeon's passageway.

"Five are in no condition to walk up the stairs and onto the street," said Julia. "They'll have to be carried out on stretchers."

"Then we'll haul them on our backs," replied Seng. "We don't have enough bodies to carry five stretchers."

"These poor devils think we're going to execute them," said a tall, ruggedly built team member with red hair in a buzz cut.

"We haven't got time to explain!" snapped Seng. He knew that the security officials downtown were wondering why the dungeon alarm in Santa Ursula had been triggered at this time of night. They were certain to call and find the phones down. How soon they would send a squad of men to check was anybody's guess. "Julia, you round up those who can move on their own two feet. The rest of you men carry the ones too weak to walk."

They moved off, almost having to drag the poor, suffering Cubans out of the dungeon and up the stairs, every team member with a Cuban over one shoulder, their free arms braced around other prisoners who could barely manage the steps. Julia brought up the rear, supporting two women and whispering encouraging words whose meanings could only come through in her soothing tone—she knew only enough Spanish to order a margarita.

Climbing the winding stone steps was a torturous exertion for the weakened prisoners, but there could be no turning back. Any capture now meant certain execution. They struggled up the steps, chests rising and falling, lungs gasping for air, hearts pounding. Men and women who had long ago given up hope now saw an opportunity to live normal lives again, thanks to these crazy people who were risking death to rescue them.

Seng could not afford the time to sympathize with their plight, or look into their gaunt faces. Any thoughts of compassion were fleeting. Sympathy could come once they reached the safety of the *Oregon*.

He concentrated on pushing them all toward the main gate, keeping his mind cold and logical.

At last the front of the column reached the guard's office at the gate. Seng stepped cautiously out onto the brick street. There was no whisper of sound or any sign of vehicles or people. The truck was right where they'd left it.

The team carrying those too weak to walk were huffing and puffing now and soaked in sweat from the tropical humidity. Warily, Seng studied the darkened street and buildings through his laser night binoculars. The area was clear. Satisfied, he hustled everyone through the gate and shoved them roughly in the direction of the truck.

He rushed back into the office and checked the guard. He was still unconscious. He also spotted a red light on a console beside the desk. The alarm had indeed been activated when they'd opened the dungeon door. The phone began to ring, and he picked it up and snapped in Spanish, *"Uno momento!"*

Then he set the receiver down and dashed out the door.

The rescue team and the freed prisoners were crammed into the cargo bed of the truck like Japanese workers during rush hour. The driver shifted the weary old transmission into gear with a brief metallic grind, and the truck leaped forward. The streets were as before, the auto traffic thin, while Cubans were enjoying a balmy evening outside on their balconies, sitting at chairs and tables on the sidewalks or drinking in the cantinas, dancing and singing.

Seng cocked his ear out the window and listened for any sound of alarms or sirens. There came only the strains of music in the night air. The harshest sound came from the truck's muffler, which seemed to be coming loose from the engine header pipe. The rattle of the exhaust soon drowned out the city noise. He saw Cubans glance at the truck and then turn away. Loose exhaust pipes and rusted-out mufflers were common on the old cars that traveled the streets of Santiago. The city's inhabitants had more entertaining thoughts on their minds.

The truck driver drove maddeningly slow, but Seng knew better than to push him. A truck casually taking its time through town would arouse no suspicion. After what seemed an hour, but was only fifteen minutes, the driver pulled up alongside a warehouse dock and stopped. A quick look up and down the deserted dock and Seng began goading everyone toward the maintenance shed. The five-minute journey to the shed was uneventful.

Their luck still held. The only activity was centered on the two cargo ships unloading their big containers. Though still apprehensive, Seng finally began to relax. He motioned them through the door of the main-tenance shed and down the wooden stairs. In the darkness he saw the vague shape of the Nomad sub's pilot, standing on the floating dock and helping the Cubans on board. The other pilot was down below, packing them tightly inside the narrow confines of the Nomad's main cabin.

When Seng and Julia Huxley, the last to board, climbed onto the sub's upper deck, the pilot quickly cast off the mooring lines, looked up briefly and said, "You made good time."

"Get to the ship as fast as this craft can take us," Seng replied. "We couldn't help setting off an alarm. I'm surprised Cuban security forces aren't already breathing down our neck."

"If they haven't tracked you here," said the pilot confidently as he closed and sealed the hatch, "they'll never guess where you came from."

"At least not until the *Oregon*'s found missing from her assigned anchorage."

In seconds the sub was dropping beneath the surface of the dark water. Fifteen minutes later it surfaced inside the moon pool of the *Oregon*. Divers attached the hook and cable of the big overhead crane, and the Nomad was lifted delicately until it was even with the second deck and moored to the balcony. Huxley's medical team was waiting along with several members of the ship's crew to help the Cubans to the *Oregon*'s well-equipped hospital.

The time was three minutes past eleven.

A thin man, his hair white before his time, recognized Cabrillo as an officer and walked unsteadily up to him. "Sir, my name is Juan Tural. Can you tell me who you people are and why you rescued my friends and me from Santa Ursula?"

"We are a corporation, and we were contracted to do this job."

"Who hired you?"

"Friends of yours in the United States," answered Cabrillo. "That's all that I can say."

"Then you had no idealistic purpose, no political cause?"

Cabrillo smiled slightly. "We always have a purpose."

Tural sighed. "I had hoped that salvation, when it came, would come from another quarter."

"Your people did not have the means to do it. It's that simple. That is why they came to us."

"It's a great pity your only motivation was money."

"It wasn't. Money is simply the vehicle," said Cabrillo. "It allows our corporation to pick its fights and to fund our charity projects. It's a liberty none of us had when we were employed by our respective governments." He glanced at his chronograph. "Now if you'll excuse me, we're not out of the woods just yet."

Then he turned and left Tural staring after him as he walked away.

E LEVEN SEVENTEEN. IF they were going to make a run for it, now was the time, thought Cabrillo. The alarm had long been answered at the prison, and by now patrols were certainly roaming the city and the countryside in search of the escaped prisoners and their rescuers. Their only link was the truck driver, but he could not provide any information to the Cuban security forces, even if he was captured and tortured. His original contact had made no mention of the *Oregon*. As far as the driver knew, the rescue team had come from a landing party on another part of the island.

Cabrillo lifted a phone and called down to the Corporation's president in the engine room. "Max?"

Hanley answered almost immediately. "Juan."

"Have the ballast tanks been pumped dry?"

"Tanks are dry and the hull is raised for speed."

"The tide is about to turn and will swing us around. We'd better leave while our bow is still aimed toward the main channel. As soon as the anchor comes free, I'll set the engines very slow. No sense in alerting any observers on the shore to a sudden departure. At the first alarm or when we reach the main channel, whichever comes first, I'll enter the program for full speed. We'll need every ounce of power your engines can give."

"You think you can get us through a narrow channel in the dead of night at full speed without a pilot?"

"The ship's computer system read every inch of the channel and the buoy markers on the way in. Our escape course is plotted and programmed into the automatic pilot. We'll leave it to Otis to take us out." Otis was the crew's name for the ship's automated control systems. It could steer the *Oregon* within inches of the intended route.

"Computerized automated controls or not, it won't be an easy matter to race through a tight channel at sixty knots."

"We can do it." Cabrillo punched off and hit another code. "Mark, give me a status on our defense systems."

Mark Murphy, the *Oregon*'s weapons specialist, replied in his west Texas drawl, "If any of them Cuban missile launchers so much as hiccups, we'll take them out."

"You can expect aircraft once we're in the open sea."

"Nuthin' we cain't handle."

He turned to Linda Ross. "Linda?"

"All systems are online," she replied calmly.

Cabrillo set the phone in its cradle and relaxed, lighting up a thin

Cuban cigar. He looked around at the ship's crew, standing in the control center. They were all staring at him, waiting expectantly.

"Well," he said slowly, before taking a deep breath, "I guess we might as well go."

He gave a voice command to the computer, the winch was set in motion, and the anchor slowly, quietly—through Teflon sleeves the team had inserted inside the hawsehole, which deadened the clank of the chain—rose from the bottom of the harbor. Another command and the *Oregon* began to inch slowly ahead.

Down in the engine room, Max Hanley studied the gauges and instruments on the huge console. His four big magnetohydrodynamics engines were a revolutionary design for maritime transport. They intensified and compounded the electricity found in saline seawater before running it through a magnetic core tube kept at absolute zero by liquid helium. The electrical current that was produced created an extremely high energy force that pumped the water through thrusters in the stern for propulsion.

Not only were the *Oregon*'s engines capable of pushing the big cargo ship at incredible speeds, but it required no fuel except the seawater that passed through its magnetic core. The source of the propulsion was inexhaustible. Another advantage was that the ship did not require huge fuel tanks, which enabled the space to be utilized for other purposes.

There were only four other ships in the world with magnetohydrodynamics engines—three cruise ships and one oil tanker. Those who had installed the engines in the *Oregon* had been sworn to secrecy.

Hanley took proprietary care of the high-tech engines. They were reliable and rarely caused problems. He labored over them as if they were an extension of his own soul. He kept them finely tuned and in a constant state of readiness for extreme and extended operation. He watched now as they automatically engaged and began pushing the ship into the channel that led to the sea.

Above in the command center, armored panels slid noiselessly apart, revealing a large window on the forward bulkhead. The murmur among the men and women gazing intently at the lights of the city was quiet, as though the men manning the Cuban defense systems could hear their words.

Cabrillo spotted another ship leaving the harbor ahead of them. "What ship is that?" he asked.

One of the team pulled up the list of ship arrivals and departures on his computer monitor. "She's a Chinese-registered cargo vessel carrying sugar to Hangchou," he reported. "She's leaving port nearly an hour ahead of her scheduled departure time."

"Name?" asked Cabrillo.

"In English, the *Red Dawn*. The shipping line is owned by the Chinese army."

"Turn out all the outer lights, and increase speed until we are close astern of the vessel ahead," he commanded the computer. "We'll use her as a decoy to lead us out." The outer deck and navigation lights blinked out, leaving the ship in darkness as she narrowed the gap between the two vessels. The lights inside the command center dimmed to a blue-green glow.

By the time the *Red Dawn* entered the ship's channel and passed the first of the string of marker buoys, the darkened *Oregon* was trailing only fifty yards off her stern. Cabrillo kept his ship just far enough back so that the Chinese vessel's deck lights would not cast their beams on his bow. It was a long shot, but he was betting the silhouette of his ship would be mistaken for the shadow of the *Red Dawn*.

Cabrillo glanced at a large twenty-four-hour clock on the wall above the window just as the long minute hand clicked onto 11:39. Only twenty-one minutes to go before the Cubans' defense systems test.

"Following the *Red Dawn* is slowing us down," said Linda. "We're losing precious time."

Cabrillo nodded. "You're right, we can't wait any longer. She's served her purpose." He leaned over and spoke into the computer's voice receiver.

"Go to full speed and pass the ship ahead!"

Like a small powerboat with big engines and a heavy hand on the throttles, the *Oregon* dug her stern into the forbidding water and lifted her bows clear of the waves as her thrusters erupted in a cloud of froth, creating a vast crater in her wake. She leaped down the channel and swept past the Chinese cargo ship less than twenty feet away, as if she were stopped dead in the water. The Chinese sailors could be seen staring in stunned disbelief. Faster and faster with each passing second she raced through the night. Speed was the *Oregon*'s crowning achievement, the thoroughbred heart of the vessel. Forty knots, then fifty. By the time she passed Morro Castle at the entrance to Santiago, she was making nearly sixty-two knots. No ship in the world that size could match her speed.

The beacon lights mounted high on the bluffs were soon little more than blinking specks on a black horizon.

THE ALARM SPREAD quickly onshore that a ship was making an unauthorized departure—but the radar and fire control operators did not unleash their shore-to-surface missiles. Their officers could not believe that such a large ship was moving at such an incredible rate of speed. They assumed their radar systems were malfunctioning, and they were reluctant to unleash missiles that they did not think could lock on to such an inconceivable target.

Not until the *Oregon* was twenty miles out to sea did a general in Cuban security put two and two together and deduce that the sudden departure of the ship and the escape of the Santa Ursula prisoners were somehow tied together. He ordered missiles fired at the fleeing ship, but by the time the word filtered down through the sluggish command, the *Oregon* was out of acceptable range.

He then ordered jets from the Cuban air force to intercept and sink the mystery ship before it reached the protection of a United States Coast Guard cutter. It could not possibly escape, he thought, as he sat back, lit a cigar and contentedly puffed a cloud of blue smoke toward the ceiling. Seventy miles away, two geriatric MiGs were sent aloft and set a course toward the *Oregon* as directed by Cuban radar.

C ABRILLO DIDN'T NEED to study a chart to see that sailing around the tip of Cuba from Santiago through the Windward Passage and then northwest to Miami was little more than a suicide run. For nearly six hundred miles, the *Oregon* would be less than fifty miles from the Cuban coast, a voyage in a shooting gallery. His safest option was to set a course southwest around the southern tip of Haiti and then almost due west to Puerto Rico, which was a territory under the U.S. flag. There he could unload his passengers, where they would be safe and cared for at proper medical facilities before being flown to Florida.

"Two unidentified aircraft closing," announced Linda.

"I have them," Murphy announced, hunched over a console with enhanced radar screens and an array of knobs and switches.

"Can you identify?" asked Linda.

"Computer reads them as a pair of MiG-27s."

"How far out?" Cabrillo probed.

"Sixty miles and closing," Murphy answered. "Poor beggars don't know what they're in for."

Cabrillo turned to his communications expert, Hali Kasim. "Try and raise them in Spanish. Warn them we have surface-to-air missiles on board and will knock them out of the sky if they show any sign of hostility."

Kasim didn't have to speak Spanish to deliver the warning. He merely ordered the computer to translate his message over his radio, which was tuned to twenty different frequencies.

After a couple of minutes he shook his head. "They are receiving, but not responding."

"They think we're bluffing," said Linda.

"Keep trying." Then to Murphy: "What's the range of their missiles?"

"According to specs, they're carrying short-range rockets with a range of ten miles."

Cabrillo looked solemn. "If they don't break off within thirty miles, take them out. Better yet, launch one of ours. Then manually guide it for a close flyby."

Murphy made the necessary calculations and pressed a red button. "Missile on its way."

An audible swoosh swept the command center as a rocket lifted from an opening in the foredeck and swept into the sky. They all watched on the monitors as it raced to the northwest and soon disappeared.

"Four minutes to flyby," said Murphy.

Every eye turned to the big clock above the window. No one spoke, all waiting in anticipation. Time dragged as the second hand on the clock seemed to take forever to make a sweep. Finally, Murphy spoke mechanically. "Missile passed two hundred yards over and between the hostiles."

"Did they get the message?" asked Cabrillo, a slight tone of apprehension in his voice.

There was a long pause, and then, "They're turning for home," Murphy reported happily. "Two Cubans who are very lucky men indeed."

"Also smart enough to recognize a no-win situation."

"Indeed," Linda said with a broad smile.

"No blood on our hands this day," Cabrillo said with an obvious sigh of relief. He leaned over in his chair and spoke to the computer. "Slow to cruise speed."

The clandestine operation was almost complete, the contract fulfilled. The *Oregon* and her crew of executives did not consider themselves lucky. Their achievement had come from a combination of special skills, expertise, intelligence and precise planning. Now, except for a technician to watch over the command center and the navigation systems, everyone could relax; some headed for their staterooms for well-deserved sleep, while others congregated in the ship's dining room to snack and wind down.

Cabrillo retired to his teak-paneled cabin and removed a packet from a safe under the carpet mounted in the deck. It was their next contract. He pulled out the contents, studied them for nearly an hour, and then began planning the initial levels of tactics and strategy.

Two and a half days later, the *Oregon* sailed into the port of San Juan, Puerto Rico, and discharged the Cuban exiles. Before the sun set, the remarkable ship and its strange crew of corporate officials were once again at sea on a course toward their next assignment. Before it was through, they would steal a priceless artifact, return a divine leader to power and free a nation. But when the *Oregon* left port, Cabrillo was not on board. He was winging his way east against a rising sun.

2

THE BURGUNDY FALCON 2000EX left Heathrow at just after six in the morning, arriving in Geneva around half past nine Swiss time. The jet aircraft cruised at Mach .80 with a 4,650-mile range; it cost $24 million. Winston Spenser was its sole occupant.

After arriving at Geneva International Airport in Cointrin, Spenser was met by a chauffeured Rolls-Royce that delivered him to the hotel. There, he was immediately taken to a suite without having to register. Once in his room, Spenser took a few minutes to freshen up. Standing in front of the beveled-edge mirror, he stared at his image. Spenser's nose was long and patrician, his eyes pale blue and distant and his skin in need of a tan. Neither his cheeks nor his chin were very defined. Truth be told, his image always appeared to be slightly out of focus, as if lacking character. His was not the face of a man others would follow. It was the face of a high-priced minion.

When he finished his examination, he placed his expensive cologne back in a Burberry toiletry bag, then left the room to get a mid-morning meal. The art auction he was in Geneva for was due to start soon.

"WILL MR. SPENSER require anything else?" the waiter asked. Spenser stared for a moment at the remains of his meal and said, "No, I think that will be all."

The waiter nodded, removed the plates, then took a brush from his apron and whisked up the few crumbs on the table. Then he silently retreated. No bill was presented, no money changed hands. The cost of the breakfast and the gratuity would appear on the room charge, which Spenser would never see.

In the far corner of the dining room, Michael Talbot stared toward Spenser. Talbot, an art dealer from San Francisco, had crossed paths with Spenser before. Three times in the last year, the stodgy Britisher had outbid Talbot's clients, for Spenser's own clients seemed to have unlimited resources.

Talbot could only hope today would be different.

Spenser was dressed in a gray suit over a sweater vest, a blue polka-dot bow tie around his neck. His black lace-up leather shoes were highly polished, as were his fingernails, and his neatly styled short hair was flecked with gray, as befitted his age, which Talbot estimated at close to sixty years.

Once, when Talbot had been in London on business, he'd tried to visit Spenser's shop. There was no telephone number available, the small stone building had had no name outside, and aside from an unobtrusive video camera above the buzzer, it could have been suspended in time from a hundred years before. Talbot had pushed the buzzer twice, but no one had answered.

Spenser sensed Talbot staring his way but only glanced at him out of the corner of his eye. Of the other seven men Spenser had determined had an interest in the artifact he'd come to purchase, the American would probably bid the highest. Talbot's buyer was a Silicon Valley software billionaire with a penchant for Asian art and argumentation. The billionaire's belligerency could only help Spenser. The man's ego might take him beyond his set price, but as the competition stiffened, he traditionally became angry and dropped out. The new rich are so predictable, Spenser thought. He rose to return to his room. The auction was not until 1 P.M.

"LOT THIRTY-SEVEN," THE auctioneer said with reverence, "the Golden Buddha."

A large mahogany crate was wheeled onto the podium and the auctioneer reached for the clasp holding the door closed.

The audience of bidders was small. This was a highly secret auction and the invitations had only gone out to the select few who could afford to pay for art masterworks with somewhat shady histories.

Spenser had yet to bid on anything. Lot twenty-one, a Degas bronze that he knew had been stolen out of a museum twelve years ago, had appealed to him, but the bidding had gone higher than his South American client had authorized him to pay. More and more, Spenser was weaning himself away from clients on a budget, even if the stop price ran into the millions. The auction today was the first step in his plan for retirement. The auctioneer opened the door to the crate at the same time that Spenser pushed a button on the miniaturized satellite telephone in his vest pocket. He spoke into the tiny microphone clasped to his lapel.

"Please tell your employer they have the object on display," he said to an aide thousands of miles away.

"He asks if it is everything you'd hoped," the aide asked.

Spenser stared at the massive gold statue as a hush fell over the crowd.

"Everything and more," Spenser said quietly.

A few seconds passed as the aide relayed the information. He said, *"At all costs."*

"It will be an honor," Spenser said as he thought back on the history.

T HE GOLDEN BUDDHA dated from 1288, when the rulers of what would later become Vietnam commissioned the work to celebrate their victory over the forces of Kublai Khan. Five hundred and ninety-six pounds of solid gold mined in Laos had been formed into a six-foot likeness of the Enlightened One. Chunks of jade from Siam had formed the eyes, while a ring of Burmese rubies wound around the neck. Buddha's potbelly had been outlined in sapphires from Thailand and his belly button was a large rounded opal that glowed iridescently. The icon had been given as a gift to the first Dalai Lama in the year 1372.

For 587 years, the Golden Buddha had remained in a monastery in Tibet and then accompanied the Dalai Lama into exile. While being transported with the Dalai Lama on a trip to the United States for display, however, it had disappeared from the airport in Manila.

President Ferdinand Marcos had always been the prime suspect. Since then, the ownership had always remained cloudy, until suddenly it had mysteriously reappeared for the auction. The seller's identity would remain an enigma.

While it was almost impossible to place a value on such a rare artifact, that was exactly what was about to happen. The preauction estimates had conservatively placed the value at between $100 million and $120 million.

"W E WILL START the bidding at fifty million U.S. dollars," the auctioneer said.

A low starting point, Spenser thought. The gold alone was worth twice that. It was the history, not the beauty, that made it a priceless piece of art. Must be the weak world economic climate, Spenser concluded.

"We have fifty million," the auctioneer said, "now sixty."

Talbot raised his paddle as the bid hit eighty.

"Eighty, now ninety," the auctioneer said in a monotone.

Spenser glanced across the room at Talbot. Typical American, ear on a satellite telephone, paddle in his hand, as if he were worried the auctioneer would miss his signal.

"Ninety, now a hundred," the auctioneer droned.

The hundred bid was from a South African dealer Spenser knew. The dealer's patron had made his fortune in diamonds. Spenser admired the woman—they'd shared a glass of sherry more than once—but he also knew her patron's habits. When the value exceeded what he felt he could sell it for later, he'd drop out. The man loved art, but he only bought at his price and if he could someday make a profit.

One hundred ten million came from the rear of the room. Spenser turned to stare at the bidder. The man's age was hard to determine, but if Spenser had to hazard a guess, he'd pick the low side of sixty, based primarily on the bidder's flowing gray hair and beard. Two things were odd, though. Spenser knew practically everyone in the room at least by sight or reputation, but this man was an unknown. And he seemed totally unconcerned, as if he were bidding on a weekend trip to a spa at a local charity auction instead of tendering a bid in the amount of a small country's yearly budget. The man was obviously qualified—the auction company would have made sure of that—but who was he?

One hundred twenty from a German pharmaceutical magnate.

"One twenty, now one thirty."

Talbot again, waving his paddle like a landing semaphore.

The bidding began to stall at $140 million, bid again by the gray-haired man. Spenser turned again and felt a touch of apprehension. The man was staring directly into his eyes. Then the man winked. A chill ran down Spenser's spine.

He turned to the side, where he could see Talbot talking animatedly into his telephone. He could sense then that the Silicon Valley billionaire was flagging.

"Tell him," Spenser whispered in his phone, "it's slowed at one fifty, with maybe one more bid still forthcoming."

"He wants to know if you've bid yet."

"No," Spenser said, "but they know I'm here."

Spenser had bought from the auctioneer many times; the man had been watching him like a hawk. Any smile, flinch or gesture of his would be taken as a bid.

"He asks that you bid two hundred," the aide relayed, "and blow them out."

"Acknowledged," Spenser said.

Then in almost slow motion, he placed two spread-apart fingers to his lips.

"The bid is two hundred million," the auctioneer said emotionlessly.

A raise of fifty million when the auctioneer was begging for ten.

"I have two hundred million in the room," the auctioneer said quietly, "anyone in for two hundred ten?"

The room was as silent as a tomb. Spenser turned to the rear of the room. The gray-haired man had vanished.

"Two hundred going once," the auctioneer said. "Going twice, fair warning." He paused again. "Sold! Two hundred million, plus buyer's premium, a stunning buy it is."

The room, which had been silent, now rippled with contained applause.

Spenser stayed another half hour to arrange the crating and security to the airport, and by five that night he was flying east for delivery. For security purposes, Spenser had chartered a plane that could not be traced to the Macau billionaire who was his client. The company was full service—it would both transport him to Asia as well as facilitate the delivery of the artifact to its new home by armored car. He was almost home free.

3

SIX DAYS AFTER depositing the Cubans in San Juan, the *Oregon* had rounded the Cape of Good Hope. Inside the control room, the seas beyond the bow were projected on a high-definition four-by-eight-foot screen. There was little to see. The sun was dipping in the west, and the *Oregon* was in an empty part of the Indian Ocean where few cargo ships steamed. Twenty minutes ago, Hali Kasim had caught the glimpse of a blue whale. Triggering the underwater sensors, Kasim made a record of the mass of the beast, then began to scan his data banks for a match.

"She's a new one," Kasim said.

Franklin Lincoln, the huge pitch-black man who was sharing duties in the control room, stared up from his game of computer solitaire. "You need to find a different hobby."

"It passes the time," Kasim noted.

"So does this," Lincoln said, "and it barely uses any computer power."

A buzzer sounded, then the ship slowed and went dead in the water.

From the north, a black amphibious plane approached, made a pass over the *Oregon* to check the direction of the wind by the flag on the flagstaff, then gracefully dropped into the water and taxied alongside.

"The chairman has arrived," Kasim noted.

ONCE SAFELY ABOARD the *Oregon*, Juan Rodriguez Cabrillo made his way to his stateroom. Walking inside, he shut the door, tossed the bag containing his gray wig and fake beard on the bed, then kicked off his shoes and started unbuttoning his shirt as he made his way to the head.

Unlike most ships, where the bathroom facilities are almost an afterthought, his was large and opulent. A sunken copper tub with jets sat against the side of the hull, with a brass-lined rectangular porthole giving a view of the water outside. Angled next to the tub was a separate shower decorated with Mexican tile. Along the bulkhead toward the bow was a cabinet containing a copper sink, with drawers beneath.

The floor was dark hardwood with thick cotton throw rugs. A recessed toilet was set back in the bulkhead across from the sink and a Philippine carved mahogany sitting bench graced one wall.

Cabrillo stared at his image in the mirror above the sink.

His blond crew-cut hair was in need of a trim and he made a mental note to schedule an appointment with the ship's barber, who also doubled as a masseuse. His skin had a light pallor, the result of stress, he knew, and his eyes showed red from the strain. He was tired and his joints felt stiff.

Sitting on the mahogany bench, he slid off his trousers and stared down at his prosthetic leg. The leg was the third he had owned since he had lost it in a naval battle with the Chinese destroyer *Chengdo*, when the Corporation had been covering a NUMA operation in Hong Kong. But it was a good one—it worked almost as well as the one he had lost.

Rising, he walked over and began to draw a bath in the copper tub.

While the bath filled, he shaved at the sink and brushed his teeth, then removed the prosthetic limb and climbed into the water. As he soaked, his thoughts drifted back. . . .

C ABRILLO CAME FROM a family that had descended from the first explorer to discover California, but despite his Spanish surname, he looked more like a Malibu surf rat than a conquistador. He'd been raised in Orange County by an upper-middle-class family. California in the 1970s had seen wild times, filled with sex and drugs, but Cabrillo had never drifted that way. By his nature, he'd been both conservative and patriotic, almost a throwback. When everyone he knew was growing long hair, he'd kept his short and well groomed. When clothing tastes had run toward torn denim and T-shirts, his wardrobe had remained neat and presentable. But this had not been his own form of protest against the time, it was just who he was.

And even today he was still a bit of a clotheshorse.

In college he'd majored in political science, and had been an active member of his university's ROTC program. So it was not a surprise when the CIA had offered him a job at graduation. Juan Cabrillo was just what they were seeking in new agents. He was bright without being bookish, stable without being boring, and flexible without being outlandish.

Trained in Spanish, Russian, and Arabic, he'd proved a master at disguise and stealth. Inserted into a country, he could read the pulse of the people instinctively. Fearless but controlled, within a few short years he'd become a valuable asset.

Then came Nicaragua.

Teamed with another agent, he and his partner had been ordered to stem the growth of the pro-communist Sandinistas, and at first Cabrillo had made inroads. But within a year the situation had spun out of control. It was the oldest story in the world—too many chiefs and not enough Indians. Chiefs in Washington calling the shots, native Indians in Nicaragua paying the price. And when bombs had burst, the fallout had blown back in their faces.

Cabrillo had been one of the fall guys, and he'd taken the hit for his partner.

Now the partner, high up the ladder at the CIA, was repaying the favor. The man had been funneling jobs to the Corporation almost since their inception, but he'd yet to offer one with a potential payday this large.

And all Cabrillo and his team needed to do was to accomplish the impossible.

WHILE CABRILLO FINISHED his bath and got dressed, Kasim and Lincoln continued their watch. By the time they were relieved at midnight, Kasim would log one more whale, Lincoln would have played thirty-two games of Klondike, and both men would have read three of the magazines that had been loaded aboard in San Juan. Lincoln tended to aviation periodicals, Kasim automobile digests.

Quite frankly, there was little work for the two men—the *Oregon* ran herself.

THIRTY MINUTES LATER—clean and dressed in tan slacks, a starched white shirt and a Bill Blass blazer—Juan Rodriguez Cabrillo was sitting at the large mahogany conference table in the corporate meeting room. Linda Ross was across the table, sipping a Diet Coke. Eddie Seng sat next to Ross, flipping through a stack of papers. Mark Murphy was farther down the table, stroking a throwing knife against a leather strap. Murphy found the action relaxing and he tested the edge against a piece of paper.

"How did the auction go?" Max Hanley asked.

"The target brought two hundred million," Cabrillo said easily.

"Wow," Ross said, "that's a hefty price."

At the end of the table, in front of a bank of floor-to-ceiling monitors that were currently blank, Michael Halpert turned on a laser pointer, then pressed the remote for the monitors. He waited for Cabrillo, who nodded for him to start.

"The job came from Washington to our lawyer in Vaduz, Liechtenstein: a standard performance contract, half now, half on delivery. Five million of the ten-million-dollar fee has already been received. It was washed through our bank in Vanuatu, then transferred to South Africa and used to purchase gold bullion, as we all agreed."

"It seems," Murphy said, shaving off a sliver of paper with the knife, "that after all those machinations, we should just steal the Golden Buddha for ourselves. It would save us a hell of a lot of time and effort. Either way, we end up with the gold."

"Where's your corporate pride?" Cabrillo said, smiling, knowing Murphy was joking, but making the point anyway. "We have our reputation to consider. The first time we screw a client, the word would get out. Then what? I haven't seen any want ads for mercenary sailors lately."

"You haven't been looking in the right newspapers," Seng said, grinning. "Try the *Manila Times* or the *Bulgarian Bugle.*"

"That's the problem with stealing objects out of history books," Ross noted. "They're tough to resell."

"I know a guy in Greece," Murphy said, "who would buy the *Mona Lisa.*"

Cabrillo waved his hands. "All right, back to business."

A map of the world filled the main monitor, and Halpert pointed to their destination.

"As a crow flies, it's over ten thousand miles from Puerto Rico to this location," he noted. "By sea, it's a lot farther."

"We're going to run up the costs just getting there," Cabrillo said. "Do we have any other jobs lined up in that part of the world after we finish with this?"

"Nothing yet," Halpert admitted, "but I'm working on it. I did, however, require the lawyer to include a bonus if we deliver the object by a certain date."

"How much and when?" Cabrillo asked.

"The bonus is another million," Halpert said. "The date is March thirty-first."

"Why March thirty-first?" Cabrillo asked.

"Because that's when they plan to have the leader return to his people."

"Ah. Good. All right, so we have a total of seven days, three of which will be spent traveling. That gives us four days to break into a secure building, steal a gold artifact that weighs six hundred pounds, then transport it nearly twenty-five hundred miles to a mountain country that most people have only heard about in school."

Halpert nodded.

"Sounds like fun," Cabrillo said.

4

CHUCK "TINY" GUNDERSON was dining on sausage and slabs of cheddar cheese as he steered the Citation X and watched the mountains that lay below. Gunderson carried nearly 280 pounds on his six-feet-four frame and had played tackle at the University of Wisconsin before graduating and getting recruited by the Defense Intelligence Agency. Gunderson's experience with the DIA had enhanced his love of flying, which he'd transferred into his job later in the private sector. Right now, however, Gunderson was wishing he could have a bottle of beer with his lunch. Instead, he finished a warm bottle of Blenheim's ginger ale to wash it all down. Checking the gauges every few minutes, he found them all in the green.

"Mr. Citation is happy," he said as he patted the automatic control switch and checked his course.

Spenser made his way forward to the cockpit, knocked on the door and opened it. "Has your company made arrangements with the armored car to meet us at the airport in Macau?"

"Don't worry," Gunderson said. "They've taken care of everything."

T HE PORT OF Aomen was bustling. Sampans and trading barges shared the sea-lanes with modern cargo ships and a few high-performance pleasure crafts. The wind was blowing from land to sea, and the smell of wood cooking fires on mainland China mixed with the scent of spices being off-loaded. Twelve miles out in the South China Sea, and only minutes from landing, Gunderson received clearance for final approach.

Spenser stared at the Golden Buddha strapped down on the floor across the aisle.

A T THE SAME instant, Juan Cabrillo was enjoying an espresso after a meal of chateaubriand, mixed vegetables, a cheese plate and baked Alaska for dessert. He held a napkin to his mouth as he talked from the head table in the ship's dining salon.

"We have a man on the ground in Macau," he said. "He'll arrange transportation once we have acquired the Buddha."

"What's his plan?" Hanley asked.

"He's not sure yet," Cabrillo admitted, "but he always comes up with something."

Seng was next to speak.

"I've retrieved detailed maps of the port, streets and entire city," Seng said. "Both the port and the airport are less than a mile from where we believe the Golden Buddha will be taken."

"That's a good twist of luck," Linda Ross said.

"The entire country's only seven square miles," Seng said.

"Are we planning to anchor offshore?" Mark Murphy asked.

Cabrillo simply nodded.

"Then I need GPS numbers for the entire country," Murphy noted, "just in case."

Another hour would pass as the corporate officers hashed out details.

"OM," THE MAN said quietly, "om."

The man who would benefit the most from the return of the Golden Buddha had no idea of the maelstrom of activity surrounding him. He was meditating in a tranquil rock garden outside a home in Beverly Hills, California. Now nearing seventy years old, he seemed not to age as did ordinary men. Instead, the passage of time had simply molded him into a more complete human being.

In 1959, the Chinese forced him to flee his own country for India. In 1989, he'd received the Nobel Peace Prize for his continued work toward the nonviolent freeing of his homeland. In a world where a hundred-year-old house was considered historic, this man was believed to be the fourteenth incarnation of an ancient spiritual leader.

At this instant, the Dalai Lama was traveling on the winds of his mind back to home.

WINSTON SPENSER WAS tired and irritable. He had not had any rest since leaving London, and the dreariness of travel and his age were catching up to him. Once the Citation X had rolled to a stop on the far end of the field, he waited while the pilot made his way to the door and extended the stairs. Then he climbed out. The armored car was only feet away, with the rear doors open. To each side of the vehicle was a guard in black uniform with a holstered weapon. They looked about as friendly as a lynch mob. One of the men approached.

"Where's the object?" he asked directly.

"In a crate inside the main cabin," Spenser said.

The man motioned to his partner, who walked over.

At just that instant, Gunderson climbed down the stairs.

"Who are you?" one of the guards asked.

"I'm the pilot."

"Back in the cockpit until we're finished."

"Hey," Gunderson started to say as the larger of the two men grabbed his arm and shoved him into the cockpit and slammed the door. Then the two men eased the crate onto a roller ramp to the ground. They pushed the crate on the ramp right into the truck. Two men couldn't lift it. Once it was inside, the truck was pulled forward so they could shut the doors. One of the guards was locking the doors when Gunderson reappeared.

"You can be sure this will be reported," he said to the guard.

But the guard just smiled slightly and walked forward to climb into the passenger seat.

"A-Ma Temple?" the driver said out the window.

"Yes," Spenser said.

The guard pointed to a dark green Mercedes-Benz limousine parked nearby.

"You're supposed to follow us in that."

Rolling up the window, the driver placed the armored car in gear and started driving.

Spenser climbed into the limousine and set off in pursuit.

T HE ARMORED CAR and the limousine carrying Spenser crossed the Macau-Taipa Bridge, went around the cloverleaf, passed the Hotel Lisboa and headed up Infante D. Henrique until the name changed and the road became San Mo La, or the New Road. On the west end of the island, they reached the intersection of Rua das Lorchas and headed south along the waterfront.

The waterfront was like a scene from an adventure movie. Junks and sampans floated on the water, while the street along the water was crammed with shops displaying everything from plucked chickens to silver opium pipes. Tourists stood snapping pictures while buyers and sellers negotiated prices in the singsong staccato of Cantonese.

At the fork with Rua do Almirante Sergio, the caravan veered slightly left, drove past the bus terminal, then entered the grounds of the A-Ma Temple. The temple was the oldest in Macau, dating from the fourteenth century, and it sat on a densely wooded hill with a view of the water. The complex held a total of five shrines linked by winding pebbled paths. The smell of incense was in the air as Spenser climbed from the limousine and walked to the armored car. At just that instant, someone lit a coil firecracker to chase away the evil spirits. He instinctively ducked, staring up at the driver's open window.

"You okay, sir?" the driver asked.

"Yes," Spenser said sheepishly, rising again to his full height. "I need to step inside for a moment. If you will just wait here."

The driver nodded and Spenser walked up the path.

Entering the A-Ma Temple, Spenser walked to a rear room he knew the leader of the monks used as an office, and knocked on the door. The door opened, and a shaven-headed man dressed in a yellow robe stood smiling.

"Mr. Spenser," he said, "you've come for your crate."

"Yes," Spenser said.

The monk rang a bell and two more monks appeared from another room.

"Mr. Spenser is here for the crate I spoke about," the head monk told them. "He'll explain what to do."

A large donation to the temple had ensured that his decoy would remain here until needed. A well-placed lie would solve the rest.

"I have a gilded Buddha outside I'd like to display for a time," Spenser said, smiling at the monk. "Do you have a space to put it?"

"Certainly," the monk said. "Bring it inside."

Twenty minutes later the switch had taken place. The Golden Buddha was now hiding in plain sight. Thirty minutes and less than a mile away, the armored car made its final delivery of the day. After the guards were dispatched, Spenser stood with the Macau billionaire, staring at the object.

"It's more than I could have hoped for," the billionaire said.

But less than you think, Spenser thought. "I'm glad you like it."

"Now we celebrate," the billionaire said, smiling.

Silver platters of delicacies littered the long cherrywood table in the palatial dining room of the man's estate. Spenser had passed on the monkey meat, as well as the sea urchin, and settled on poultry in a peanut sauce. Still, the spicy side dishes were wreaking havoc with his travel-weary stomach, and he just wished the night would end.

Spenser sat at the far end of the table, the owner at the head. A total of six concubines were seated, three to a side, in the middle. After a dessert of wild berry mousse, cigars and cognac, the man rose from his seat.

"Shall we take a soak, Winston?" he said, "and allow the ladies to do their job?"

The man had no idea he would possess the faux Golden Buddha for less than a week.

And Winston Spenser had no way to know he had less than a fortnight to live.

5

LANGSTON OVERHOLT IV sat in his office in Langley, Virginia. His hips rested in a tall leather chair sideways to the desk. In his hand was a black racquetball paddle, its handle wrapped with white cloth tape stained by sweat. Slowly and methodically, he hit a black rubber ball two feet in the air and then back down to the racquet. Every fourth hit, he flipped the racquet over to change sides. The rhythmic action helped him think.

Overholt was thin without being scrawny, more lean and sinewy than bony. One hundred and sixty-five pounds graced his six-foot-one-inch frame, with skin stretched tight over muscles that were long and squared rather than rounded and plump. His face was handsome in a rugged way, rectangular in shape, with hard edges abounding. His hair was blond, with just a touch of gray starting to appear at the temples, and he had it trimmed every two weeks at the CIA barbershop inside the compound.

Overholt was a runner.

He'd started the practice as a senior in high school, when the craze had swept the country, fueled by the Jim Fixx book *The Complete Runner*. Throughout college and graduate school he'd kept up the practice. Marriage, joining the CIA, divorce and remarriage had not slowed down his obsession. Running was one of the few things that relieved the stress of his job.

Stress was Overholt's other constant.

Since joining the CIA in 1981 fresh out of graduate school, he'd served under six different directors. Now, for the first time in decades, Langston Overholt IV had a chance to make his father's promise to the Dalai Lama a reality, while at the same time repaying his old friend Juan Cabrillo. He was wasting no time in moving his plans forward. Just then, his telephone buzzed.

"Sir," his assistant said, "it's the DDO, he'd like to meet with you as soon as possible."

Overholt reached for the phone.

T HE WEATHER IN Washington, D.C., was as hot as Texas asphalt and as steamy as a bowl of green chili. Inside the White House, the air conditioners were set as high as they would go, but they just couldn't drop the temperature below seventy-five degrees. The president's home was aging, and there was just so much adaptation you could make to an old building and still retain the historical structure.

"Has there ever been an official photograph of the president sitting in the Oval Office in a T-shirt?" the president joked.

"I'll check, sir," said the aide who had just led the CIA director inside.

"Thank you, John," the president said, dispatching the man.

The president reached across the desk and shook the director's hand as the aide closed the door to leave the men alone. The president motioned for him to be seated.

"These aides I have are sharp as tacks," the president noted as he sat down, "but short on a sense of humor. The kid's probably checking with the White House historian as we speak."

"If it was anyone," the director said, smiling, "I'd guess LBJ."

When you're seventeen years old and you know the director of the Central Intelligence Agency, the spy game seems pretty cool. When you later become president, you really have a chance to see what happens. Time had not diminished his enthusiasm—the president still found the intelligence game fascinating.

"What have you got for me?" the president asked.

"Tibet," the director said without preamble.

The president nodded, then adjusted a fan on his desk so that the breeze swept evenly across both men. "Explain."

The CIA director reached into his briefcase and removed some documents.

Then he laid out the plan.

I N BEIJING, PRESIDENT Hu Jintao was studying documents that showed the true state of the Chinese economy. The picture was grim. The race to modernization had required more and more petroleum, and the Chinese had yet to locate any significant new reserves inside their borders. The situation had not been such a problem a few years earlier, when the price of oil had been at twenty-year lows, but with the recent price spike upward, the higher costs were wreaking havoc. Adding to the problem were the Japanese, whose thirst for oil had led to a price competition the Chinese could not hope to win.

Jintao stared out the window. The air was clearer than usual to-day—a light wind was blowing the smoke from the factories away from central Beijing—but the wind was not so strong as to blow away the soot that had landed on the windowsill. Jintao watched as a sparrow landed on the sill. The bird's tiny feet made tracks in the powder. The bird fluttered around for a few seconds, then stopped and peered in the window and looked directly toward Jintao.

"How would you cut costs?" Jintao said to the bird, "and where do we find oil?"

6

THE *OREGON* SWEPT past the Paracel Islands under a pitch-black night sky. The air was liquid with rain that fell in sheets. The wind was blowing in gusts without firm direction or purpose. For several minutes it would rake the *Oregon* amidships, then quickly change to blow bow on or stern first. The soggy flags on the stern were pivoting on their staffs as fast as a determined Boy Scout trying to light a fire with a stick.

Inside the control room, Franklin Lincoln stared at the radar screen. The edge of the storm began petering out just before the ship passed the twenty-degree latitude line. Walking over to a computer terminal in the control room, he entered commands and waited while the satellite images of the Chinese coastline loaded.

A haze of smog could be seen over Hong Kong and Macau.

He glanced over at Hali Kasim, who was sharing the night shift.

Kasim was sound asleep, his feet up on the control panel. His mouth was partially opened.

Kasim could sleep through a hurricane, Lincoln thought, or in this part of the ocean, a cyclone.

A T THE SAME time the *Oregon* was steaming east, Winston Spenser awoke, startled. Earlier in the evening he had visited the Golden Buddha at A-Ma. The icon was still in the mahogany crate, sitting upright, door opened, in the room where it had been taken. Spenser had gone alone; simple common sense dictated that as few people as possible know the actual location, but he'd found the experience unnerving.

Spenser knew the icon was nothing more than a mass of precious metal and stones, but for some strange reason the object seemed to have a life force. The chunk of gold appeared to glow in the dim room, as if illuminated by a light from within. The large jade eyes seemed to follow his every move. And while its visage might appear benign to some— only that of a potbellied, smiling prophet—to Spenser the image seemed to be mocking him.

As if he had not known it before, earlier in the evening Spenser had become certain that what he had done was not a stroke of genius. The Golden Buddha was not some canvas, dabbed with paint—it was the embodiment of reverence, crafted with love and respect.

And Spenser had swiped it like a candy in a drugstore.

T HE DALAI LAMA listened to the slow flow of water over the smooth stones while he meditated. On the far reaches of his mind was static, and he willed the disturbance to clear. He could see the ball of light in the center of his skull, but the edges were rough and pulsating. Slowly he smoothed the signals, and the ball began to collapse in on itself until only a pinpoint of white light remained. Then he began to scan his physical shell.

There was a disturbance, and it was growing.

Eighteen minutes later, he came back into his shell and rose to his feet.

Eight yards away, sitting under a green canvas awning alongside the kidney-shaped pool on the estate in Beverly Hills, was his Chikyah Kenpo. The Dalai Lama walked over. The Hollywood actor who was his host smiled and rose to his feet.

"It is time for me to go home," the Dalai Lama said.

There was no pleading or disagreement from the actor.

"Your Holiness," he said, "let me call for my jet."

IN THE NORTH of Tibet, on the border between U-Tsang and Amdo province, the Basatongwula Shan mountains towered over the plains. The peak was a snowcapped sentinel watching over an area where few men trod. To the untrained eye, the lands around Basatong-wula Shan looked barren and desolate, a wasteland best left alone and deserted. On the surface, this may have been true.

But underneath, hidden for centuries, was a secret known only by a few.

A yak walked slowly along a rocky path. On his back was a black mynah bird that remained silent as he hitched a ride. Slowly at first, but growing in intensity, a light tremor rippled across the land. The yak began to shake in fear, causing the bird to take to the air. Digging his cloven hooves into the soil, he stood firm as the land trembled. Then slowly the disruption passed and the earth stilled. The yak resumed his journey.

Within minutes, the fur on his legs and lower body was covered with a haze from a mineral that over countless generations had made some men rich and others go mad.

* * *

VICE PRESIDENT OF Operations Richard Truitt was still awake. His body clock had yet to adjust and his night was still Macau's day. Logging on to his computer, he checked for messages. One had been sent by Cabrillo a few hours before. Like every e-mail he received from the chairman, this one was short.

Confirmation received from the home of George. All systems go. ETA 33 hours.

The CIA was still in and the *Oregon* would arrive in less than two days' time. Truitt had a lot of work to complete in a short span. Calling down to the hotel's twenty-four-hour room service, he ordered a meal of bacon and eggs. Then he walked into the bathroom to shave, shower and pick his disguise.

7

JUAN CABRILLO FINISHED the last bite of an omelet filled with apple-smoked bacon and Gorgonzola cheese, then pushed the plate away.

"It's a wonder we all don't weigh three hundred pounds," he said.

"The jalapeño cheese grits alone were worth waking up for," Hanley noted. "I just wish the chef would have consulted with my ex-wife. I might still be married."

"How's the divorce going?" Cabrillo asked.

"Pretty good," Hanley admitted, "considering my reported income last year was only thirty thousand dollars."

"Just be fair," Cabrillo cautioned. "I don't want any lawyers snooping around."

"You know I will," Hanley said as he refilled their coffee cups from a silver thermal carafe on the table. "I'm just waiting for Jeanie to calm down."

Cabrillo lifted his cup of coffee and then stood up. "We're less than twenty-four hours from port. How are things going in the Magic Shop?"

"Most of the props are constructed and I'm starting on the disguises."

"Excellent," Cabrillo said.

"Do you have any preferences for your look?" Hanley asked.

"Try to keep the facial hair to a minimum," Cabrillo said. "It can be muggy in Macau."

Hanley rose from the table. "Sahib, your wish is my command."

WHEN THE *OREGON* had been refitted by the Corporation in the shipyard in Odessa, two decks had been installed inside the hull, giving the interior a total of three levels, not including the raised pilothouse. The lowest level housed the engines and physical plants, along with the moon pool, machine shops, armory and storage rooms. One level above, reached by metal stairs or the single heavy-lift elevator amidships, was the deck containing communications, weapon systems, a variety of shops and offices, a large library, a computer room and a map room. The third level housed the dining room, recreation rooms, a full gym, plus crew cabins and meeting and boardrooms. Level three was surrounded by a two-lane running track for exercise. The *Oregon* was a city unto itself.

Hanley walked from the dining room and across the running track, then eschewed the elevators for the stairs. Opening the door, he started down. The stairway was paneled with mahogany and lit by sconces. At the bottom Hanley stepped onto a thick carpet in a room with insets in the walls that held plaques and medals awarded by grateful customers and nations to the men and women of the *Oregon*.

He made his way forward toward the bow until the walls in the hallway turned to glass on the port side. Behind the glass was what could have passed for a Hollywood costume and set shop. Kevin Nixon raised his head and waved.

Hanley opened the door to the shop and entered. It was cool inside and the air was scented with the smells of grease, vinyl and wax. A Willie Nelson CD was seeping from hidden speakers.

"How long have you been here?" Hanley asked.

Nixon was sitting on a three-legged stool in front of a metal-framed, wood-topped workbench that had a ring of hand tools around the perimeter. In his hands he held an ornamental headdress with silken gold fabric that flowed down his right side to the floor.

"Two hours," he said. "I woke up early, checked my e-mail and got the preliminary specs."

"Did you eat breakfast?" Hanley asked.

"I just grabbed some fruit," Nixon said. "I need to drop ten pounds or so."

Nixon was a big man, but he carried his weight well. If you saw him on the street, you would think him stocky but not fat. But he was in a constant battle, his weight running from 240 pounds to 210, depending on his vigilance. Last summer, when he'd taken a few weeks off and hiked the Appalachian Trail, he'd gotten down to 200, but his sedentary life aboard ship and the charms of the chef's cooking had caught up to him.

Hanley walked over to the bench and stared at Nixon's work. "That's religious garb?"

"For a Macanese in a Good Friday parade, it is."

"We'll need a total of six sets," Hanley said.

Nixon nodded. "I figured two shaman and four penitents."

Hanley walked over to the wall, where several more benches were abutting the bulkhead. "I'm going to start on the masks."

Nixon nodded and reached for a remote control for the CD player. He punched a button and Willie stopped. Johnny Rivers's "Secret Agent Man" began to play.

"Kevin," Hanley said easily, "you just love to do that, don't you?"

"There's a man who lives a life of danger," Nixon sang in a baritone.

* * *

"TRUITT SENT A map showing the parade route for Good Friday," Cabrillo said. "We lucked out—traffic in the downtown area will be at a standstill."

Eddie Seng reached across the table for one of the folders. "It's surprising that the Chinese would have such a large celebration for something that concerns Christianity."

"Macau was a Portuguese possession from 1537 until 1999," Linda Ross noted. "Roughly thirty thousand of the population is Catholic."

"Plus the Chinese love festivals," Mark Murphy said. "They'll form a parade at the drop of a hat."

"Truitt said they are going to do the same as last year and put on a massive fireworks display over the city," Cabrillo said, "fired from a series of barges in the bay."

"So the cover of night and a waning moon no longer apply," Franklin Lincoln noted.

Lincoln's friend Hali Kasim couldn't resist. "A real shame, Frankie—you blend in so well when the sky is dark."

Lincoln turned toward Kasim and brushed his nose with his middle finger. "That's okay, Kaz, the fireworks also make it harder for you lily-white Hugh Grant types."

"There's still the question of weight," Cabrillo said, ignoring the exchange. "The Golden Buddha weighs six hundred pounds."

"Four men on each side could lift that weight without too much strain on their backs," Julia Huxley said.

"I think I'll have Hanley and Nixon fabricate something," Cabrillo said. "Any suggestions?"

The crew continued planning the operation—Macau was just about a day's sail away.

* * *

THE CHAIRMAN OF the Tibet Autonomous Region, Legchog Raidi Zhuren, was reading a report on the fighting just across the border in Nepal. Last night, government forces had killed nearly three hundred Maoist insurgents. The ferocity of the attacks on the communist rebels had been increasing since spring 2002. After several years of growing rebel activity, the Nepalese government had begun to feel threatened and finally started to take firm action. The United States had sent army Green Beret advisors to the area to coordinate strikes, and almost immediately the body count had begun to grow.

To prevent the fighting from spilling over across the border into Tibet, Zhuren had needed to call Beijing for additional troops to station them on the high mountain passes that led from Nepal to Tibet. President Jintao had not been happy about the development. In the first place, the cost to secure Tibet was increasing at a time the president wanted to cut costs. In the second place, the Special Forces advisors added a dimension of danger to the mission. If a single American soldier was wounded or killed by Chinese forces protecting the Tibet border, Jintao was worried the situation might spiral out of control and China would be embroiled in another Korea.

What Legchog Zhuren did not know was that Jintao was starting to consider Tibet more of a liability than an asset. The timing was critical—if the Tibetan people launched a popular uprising right now, China might have another Tiananmen Square on its hands, and the world mood was not the same as in 1989. With the fall of communism in the Soviet Union and their increasingly close relations with the United States, any heavy-handed action against the Tibetan population might be met with force from two fronts.

American forces could be launched from carriers in the Bay of Bengal and from bases in occupied Afghanistan, while Russian ground forces could sweep in from the republics of Kyrgyzstan and Kazakhstan, as well as the area of far eastern Russia where it bordered northern Tibet. Then there would be a free-for-all.

And for what? A small, poor mountain country China had illegally occupied?

The reward didn't equal the risk. Jintao needed to find face—and he needed it fast.

8

WINSTON SPENSER TOOK his pen to paper to tally his ill-gotten gains. The 3 percent commission on the original $200 million sale of the Golden Buddha was $6 million. This was hardly a small sum. In fact, it was just over five times Spenser's income last year—but it was a drop in the bucket compared to the money he was about to collect for selling it again.

In the first place, against the $6 million commission check, he had the cost of the decoy. The fabricators in Thailand had charged nearly a million for that. In the second place, the company he'd had hired in Geneva to transport the Golden Buddha to Macau and provide armored-car service to A-Ma had charged too much, a flat fee of $1 million for their services, while Spenser had quoted the billionaire a cost of one-tenth of that so as not to arouse suspicion. Bribes now, and in the next few days, when Spenser was planning to transport the original out of

Macau and into the United States, would run him another million or so. As a result, right at this instant, for all practical purposes, Spenser was broke.

The art dealer had tapped all his available savings and business lines of credit to fund his nefarious operation—if he didn't have the commission check lying before him on the table, he'd be in trouble. If Spenser had not been completely certain he had a buyer for the Golden Buddha, he might be worried. Tearing the slip of paper from the pad, he tore the note into tiny pieces, tossed the pieces in the toilet and flushed. Then he poured himself half a glass of Scotch to calm his trembling hands. It had taken Spenser a lifetime to build his reputation—and if his crime was known, it would be gone in seconds.

Money and gold can make men do strange things.

THREE-QUARTERS OF THE way across the globe and sixteen time zones distant, it was almost midnight, and the Silicon Valley software billionaire was passing his time making changes to his newest yacht. The blueprints for the massive 350-foot-long vessel had been created on a computer, designed on a computer and refined on a computer. Each individual piece could be highlighted and changed, all the way down to the screws that attached the thirty toilets to the deck. Right now, the billionaire was playing around with the furnishings and upholstery, and his ego was running rampant.

The computer would generate a full-bodied hologram of him to welcome guests to the main deck salon, and that had been a cool touch, but at this instant he was deciding what font would be best for his initials, which were to be sewn into the fabric on all the couches and chairs. A few years ago, he'd bought himself a minor British title that had come complete with a coat of arms, so he inserted the script he'd selected into the emblem, then overlaid that onto the fabric. *A cameo of my face might look better,* he thought, as he stared at the royal crest.

Then people could sit on my face. The idea brought a smile; he was still smiling when his Philippine houseboy entered the room.

"Master," he said slowly, "I'm sorry to bother you, but you have a long-distance telephone call from overseas."

"Did they say their name?" he asked.

"He said he was a friend of the fat golden one," the man said.

"Put him through," the billionaire said, smiling, "at once."

T HE TIME WAS just before four in the afternoon in Macau, and while he waited for the software billionaire to come online, Spenser was fiddling with a voice-alteration device that he had placed over his satellite telephone. He had placed a new battery in the device and the tiny light was blinking green, but still he questioned if the scrambler would work as advertised.

"Yo," the billionaire said as he came on the line. "What have you got for me?"

"Are you still interested in owning the Golden Buddha?" a mechanical-sounding voice asked.

"Sure," the billionaire said. At the same time, he input commands into the computer hooked to his telephone to counter the effects of the scrambler. "But not at two hundred million."

"I was thinking"—the man's voice was scrambled, but then the computer did its magic and the voice cleared—"a price of one hundred million."

A British accent, the software billionaire thought. Talbot had told him a British dealer had made the successful bid for the Buddha, and maybe he had acquired it for a British collector—but that made no sense. No one would buy something for $200 million, only to offer it a few days later for half that. The dealer must have pulled the old switcheroo—or he was offering a fake.

"How do I know what you are offering is real?" the software billionaire asked.

"Do you have someone who can date gold?" Spenser asked.

"I can find someone," the billionaire said.

"Then I'll send you a sliver of metal along with a videotape of me removing it from the bottom of the artifact. The gold used in the Buddha was mined in—"

"I know the history," the billionaire said, cutting him off. "How are you going to send the sample?"

"I'll FedEx it this evening," Spenser said.

The billionaire reeled off an address, then asked, "If it checks out, in what form will you want payment?"

"I'll accept a wire transfer of American dollars to an account I'll specify at the time of the transfer," Spenser said.

"Sounds reasonable," the billionaire said. "I'll set it up tonight. One more thing, though," the billionaire added. "I just hope you're better at stealing than you are at picking electronics. Your choice in voice-alteration equipment is second-rate—your accent is as British as beans on toast, and that gives me a pretty good idea of who you are."

Spenser stared at the flashing green light in disgust, but said nothing.

"So just remember," the billionaire finished, "if you try and screw *me*—I can be real unpleasant."

"FULL STOP," HANLEY ordered.

The *Oregon* had crossed the outer edge of the harbor just after 11 A.M. and picked up the pilot. Several containerized ships leaving port had slowed their progress, and the trip to a mooring buoy in the water just off the main portion of the port had required most of the next hour. The time was just before noon when the vessel was finally secured.

Cabrillo stood next to Hanley at the helm and stared at the city, which encircled the harbor. The pilot had just left, and he watched the stern of the boat retreating.

"You don't think he noticed anything unusual?" Cabrillo asked.

"I think we're okay," Hanley answered.

The Corporation's previous ship, the *Oregon I*, had been involved in a sea battle off Hong Kong a few years before, which had resulted in them sinking the Chinese navy vessel *Chengdu*. If the Chinese officials figured out this was the same crew that had sunk their multimillion-dollar destroyer, they'd all be hung as spies.

"Truitt arranged for us to receive our cover cargo the day after tomorrow," Cabrillo said, scanning the sheet of paper on a clipboard that listed the operational plans. "You're going to love this—it's a load of fireworks bound for Cabo San Lucas."

"The *Oregon* delivering fireworks," Hanley said quietly. "It seems so fitting."

THE EXECUTIVE JET terminal in Honolulu was plush without being ostentatious. It was cool inside, the air conditioning maintaining an even seventy degrees. The smoked-glass windows gave the lobby a clear view of the runways, and Langston Overholt IV passed the time watching a series of private jets appear in the night sky and then touch down and taxi over to the refueling area near private hangars. Overholt never saw the passengers of the jets; they were either met by limousines or large black SUV's on the tarmac then transferred to their locations, or they stayed aboard while the jets were refueled and continued on their journies. Pilots or copilots came and went—stopping for weather briefings, to use the restrooms, to grab a cup of coffee or a pastry from a pantry to the side of the lobby—but for the most part it was quiet in a mid-evening lull. Overholt rose from the couch, walked over to the pantry and poured a cup of coffee, then was removing a banana from a fruit basket on the table when his telephone vibrated.

"Overholt," he said quietly.

"Sir," a voice a few thousand miles away said steadily, "tracking reports the target on final approach."

"Thank you," Overholt said as he disconnected.

Then he peeled the banana, ate it and walked over to the flight desk.

Taking a leather badge cover from the breast pocket of his suit, he flipped it open and handed it to the clerk. The man quickly scanned the golden eagle, then perused the ID card showing Overholt's picture and title.

"Yes, sir," the clerk said.

"I need to talk to the party on the Falcon you have inbound for landing."

The man nodded and reached for a portable radio on his belt. "I'll notify the ramp and call for a golf cart. Is there anything else you need?"

Overholt turned and stared out the window. The light mist was turning to rain.

"Do you have an umbrella I can borrow?"

The clerk was on the radio calling out to the ramp attendants and nodded at Overholt's request. "You can use mine," the clerk said, reaching under the counter and handing it across the desk.

Overholt slipped his hand in his trouser pocket and removed a money clip, then peeled off a fifty. "The CIA would like to buy you dinner tonight," he said, smiling.

"Is this when you say you were never here?" the clerk said, smiling in turn.

"Something like that." Overholt nodded.

The man pointed to the doors. "Your golf cart is here."

Outside the window, the landing lights on the Falcon jet reflected off the light rain and the wet surface as it lowered onto the runway with a chirp from the tires. A truck with a flashing light bar mounted on the roof raced down an access road in hot pursuit. The truck would lead the jet to the spot for refueling.

Then Overholt could board and ask the Dalai Lama if he was ready for the journey.

9

MACAU IS A tiny country consisting of three small islands connected by causeways. The farthest north is Macau, which houses the government buildings; the middle island, Taipa, has a man-made extension for the airport and runways, and is connected to the main body of the island with a pair of roads; and the farthest south island is Coloane. To the north and east of the country is the Chinese mainland, and to the west, across the body of water known as Zhujiang Kou, is Hong Kong.

Formerly a Portuguese colony, the country had reverted to China in 1999 and was administered as a special region similar to Hong Kong. The landmass of Macau is a mere 9.1 square miles, or just under a sixth of the size of Washington, D.C. The population is estimated at around 430,000 people.

The *Oregon* was moored off Coloane, and nearest to international waters.

"Dick," Cabrillo said as he reached the top of the ladder leading from the shore boat to the pier, "how goes it?"

"Mr. Chairman," Truitt said, "I think all is in order."

Bob Meadows and Pete Jones, former Navy SEALs and operational specialists, along with security and surveillance expert Linda Ross, followed. Once they were all on the pier, Truitt motioned to the van.

"Let me show you the layout," Truitt said quietly as they all entered the van.

Truitt steered the van onto the 1.3-mile-long bridge that would take them to Taipa. It was quiet inside the van, the only sound coming from the tires as they periodically crossed over the expansion joints.

"This is Taipa," Truitt said as the van reached the island. "Two bridges lead to Macau. We'll take the shorter, which is about a mile and a half long."

As Truitt steered the van onto the second bridge, Cabrillo stared to the west across the water toward the other bridge and Hong Kong. The road was crowded with trucks carrying cargo from the seaports and air terminal, but the traffic was moving fast.

"Can the authorities seal off the bridges?" he asked.

"There are no gates per se," Truitt said, "but they could easily station large trucks on the approaches and we'd be in trouble."

The high-rises on Macau were becoming more visible through the windshield.

"We're not going to luck out and have the building located along the waterfront?" Linda Ross asked.

"Sorry, Linda," Truitt said, glancing in the rearview mirror, "his home is on the hillside."

Cabrillo was staring ahead at the mass of humanity and buildings as the van covered the final hundred yards over the bridge. "So if we're caught making a run for it . . ." His voice trailed off.

Truitt slowed the van and turned onto a crowded side street. "That's the score, boss," he said quietly.

"How come we never steal things that are hidden in the middle of nowhere?" Meadows asked.

"Because the stuff we're paid to do never happens in an isolated area," Jones said, smiling.

L ANGSTON OVERHOLT HAD needed more time with the Dalai Lama to explain his proposal, so he'd made a quick call to Washington, then boarded the Falcon. Flying against the sun had made the night last a long time—it was still dark when they stopped in Manila to refuel. Lifting from the tarmac at Manila International Airport, the pilot set a course skirting Vietnam then over the southernmost strip of Thailand above Hat Yai. Once he passed over Thailand, he'd make a sweeping turn north over the Andaman Sea, stop at Rangoon for more fuel, and then he could make it to Punjab, where the Dalai Lama would take a small plane the rest of the way to Little Lhasa, his exile home in northern India.

Once the jet reached cruising altitude, Overholt continued the conversation.

"Your father was a friend of mine," the Dalai Lama said quietly, "so I've listened carefully to your proposal. But you have yet to explain how we make the Chinese simply hand back my country. You know I cannot agree to this if there will be bloodshed."

"The president feels if we enlist the Russians' help, the threat of war might make the Chinese back down. Their economy is in a pinch right now—the cost to occupy your country is starting to mount."

"So you believe the financial motive is sufficient?" the Dalai Lama asked.

"It might help if you offered them the Golden Buddha," Overholt said, saving his silver bullet for the last.

The Dalai Lama smiled. "Like your father, you are a fine man, Langston, but in this case your information is faulty. The Golden Buddha was stolen when I went into exile. The government-in-exile no longer has it to offer."

The sun was finally appearing over the horizon and it illuminated the wings on the Falcon jet in a golden glow. To the rear of the plane a steward was preparing a light breakfast of juice and muffins. The time had come for Overholt to show his hand.

"The United States has a plan to liberate the Golden Buddha," he said. "We should have it in a few days."

The Dalai Lama's smile became a grin. "I must say that is very unexpected news. Now I can see why you have flown halfway around the world with me."

Overholt smiled and nodded. "So you think the Chinese will accept the icon as payment when combined with the threat of war?"

The Dalai Lama shook his head. "No, my CIA friend, I do not. The true secret of the Golden Buddha is inside . . . a secret the Chinese would pay dearly for."

10

EXITING THE BRIDGE, Truitt steered the van through the cloverleaf. The thousand-room Hotel Lisboa and casino was to the right as they drove west on Avenida Dr. Mario Soares. To the right, the Bank of China soared into the air, a pink granite-and-glass structure whose top levels allowed the occupants a view across the border into China.

"For anticapitalists, they build a nice bank," Meadows said quietly.

No one replied; they were enamored with the scenery. Central Macau was a strange mishmash of new and old, European and Asian, traditional and modern. Truitt reached Rua da Praia Grande and turned left.

"From what I'm told, this used to be a beautiful drive," Truitt said, "until construction started on the Nam Van Lakes Reclamation Project."

The road was clogged with construction trucks, cement mixers and piles of materials.

Driving farther, the road became Avenida da Republica and skirted Nam Van Lake.

"That's the governor's residence," Truitt said, pointing up the hill. "I'm taking us the long way around the tip of the peninsula so you can see the geography. The hill north of the governor's residence is named Penha. This one on the end is Barra Hill. Our target is between the two, on a street named Estrada da Penha."

Angling left on the road, they climbed a rise until the van reached Estrada de D. Joao Paulino. Turning a quick right, they drove a few yards and made another sharp right onto Estrada da Penha, which formed a wavy U shape around the top of the hill until it met back up with Joao Paulino.

The van passed the bottom of the U and was halfway up the side when Truitt slowed. "Thar she blows."

"She" was a mansion, an old elegant structure worthy of a landed family. A tall stone wall encircled the grounds, broken only by a wrought-iron gate and the creeping growth of ivy. Giant, perfectly placed trees, planted generations past, studded the expanse of emerald grass. As the van rolled past, a croquet field was visible off to the side. Farther to the right, down a cobblestone driveway, was a two-story garage building, where a handyman was soaping down a Mercedes-Benz limousine.

The mansion looked like a wealthy nineteenth-century shipowner could live there now; the only compromise for the times was the series of security cameras atop the stone wall fronting the street.

"There are six cameras strategically located around the grounds."

The van was approaching the junction with Joao Paulino, and Truitt slowed before commenting.

"That *would* complicate things," Truitt said, as he slowed for the stop sign, "except for one thing I failed to mention."

"What's that?" Cabrillo asked.

"Our target is throwing a huge party," Truitt said as he steered the van left, "and we're booked as the entertainment."

Truitt took the scenic way back, past the temple and along the waterfront.

"WELL?" THE SOFTWARE billionaire asked pointedly.

One thousand dollars to the Stanford scientist had procured his services; a call to the president of the university reminding him of past donations had opened up the full use of the laboratory.

"The date shows thirteenth century, but for me to give you a more accurate estimate of the area from which it was mined, I'll have to melt half of your sample."

"Well? What are you waiting for?"

"It's going to take me thirty or forty-five minutes," the scientist said, already growing weary of the billionaire's rude manner. "Why don't you head to the cafeteria and grab something to drink?"

"Do they have Chai tea?" the billionaire said.

"No," the scientist said wearily, "but there's a Starbucks on the commons that does."

After giving him directions to the Starbucks, he waited until the man walked out and closed the door to the laboratory.

"Idiot," the scientist said.

Then he walked over to a small kiln and slid the metal plate holding the shaving of gold inside. After it melted, he placed the sample inside a computer-powered sampler that would give a breakdown of the percentages of the other metals present. By comparing the ratios with known ores already mined, the scientist could determine the general area where the gold had been mined.

As he waited for the machine to perform its magic, the scientist read a skiing magazine. Twenty minutes later, the machine stopped.

THE PRESIDENT OF the United States was sitting in an Adirondack chair behind the main house at Camp David, Maryland. The president of Russia sat across from him, a wooden table separating the two.

Though not visible, $2 billion in foreign aid was on the table.

"How does it sound, Vlad?" the president asked.

"You know I've never been a big fan of the Chinese," the Russian president said, "but the foreign aid is only a bandage. My country's factories need orders for our economy to mend itself."

The president nodded. "The biggest-ticket items in my budget are always the military planes and ships. The Taiwanese have got a shopping list a mile long. What if I could steer some of that business your way?"

The Russian president smiled. "You are a crafty one," he said. "You've managed to give me what my country needs while at the same time pitting us against the Chinese, who as you well know make an enemy of anyone who befriends Taiwan."

The president rose from the chair and stretched. "Now, Vlad," he said, "isn't that the nucleus of negotiation—to give both sides what they want?"

"I think," the Russian president said, rising, "we may just have a deal."

"Good, then," the president said, motioning toward the dining hall. "What do you say we go see what kind of pie the chef has in the oven?"

"THE GOLD WAS mined somewhere in the area of Burma," the scientist said when the billionaire returned, clutching a paper cup of tea.

"Can you be more specific?"

"South of the twenty-degrees latitude line, which means southern Vietnam, Laos, Thailand or Burma. I can try to pin it down more, but it will take time."

The billionaire sipped the tea, then shook his head back and forth. "Don't bother, you said the magic word."

The billionaire started toward the door while at the same time removing a cellular telephone from his belt. "Bring the car around," he said to the driver. Then he disconnected and reached for the door.

"Do you want your gold back?" the scientist shouted across the laboratory.

"Keep it," the billionaire shouted. "I've got a lot more where that came from."

"You're most generous," the scientist muttered as he scraped the sample from the now-cool plate and slid it into the envelope with the other.

Carrying the envelope over to his desk, he tossed it into the top drawer. Then he walked to the door, shut off the lights, and locked the door to the laboratory behind him. A few minutes later, he was tooling across campus on his moped, still shaking his head at the strange encounter.

I NSIDE A STORAGE hold on the lower level of the *Oregon*, Hanley was standing with Kevin Nixon, staring at a collection of wheeled conveyances.

"For certain, we should have a couple of the motorcycles and at least one of the all-terrain vehicles prepared," Hanley said.

Nixon nodded, then walked over to one of the motorcycles. Since the last time it had been used, it had been cleaned and oiled. All the tools used by the Corporation were kept in a constant state of readiness—it was one of the easiest ways to ensure success.

"I'll go ahead and test run everything," Nixon said. "Want me to fabricate Macau license plates for each?"

"Sounds good," Hanley said. "Just standard tags, nothing diplomatic."

Nixon stared at the clipboard with the sheet of paper Cabrillo had prepared earlier. "Looks like Ross wants earpiece communications for the ground operators, with a secondary channel to reach the ship."

"Make sure the batteries are charged, and check everything out,"

Hanley said. "I'll break out a repeater we can place on Barra Hill so we're not using local channels."

"Better place a beacon up there, too," Nixon said, glancing at the clipboard. "Murphy wants a fixed targeting point if he needs to loose a missile."

"Murphy," Hanley said, shaking his head, "he'd drive a thumbtack with a sledgehammer."

Nixon turned on an exhaust vent, then slid his leg over the motorcycle and poked the kick starter. The machine roared to life and settled into an idle. Shutting it off, he moved toward the second motorcycle and repeated the process. The hours passed as the pair of men checked then double-checked the equipment.

A T THE SAME instant, closer to the stern, Mark Murphy was in the armory. The room had a bench containing reloading equipment and rows of drawers containing ammunition, charges, timers and fuses. Along the walls were a series of recessed cases that housed automatic weapons, rifles and handguns. The room smelled of gunpowder, metal and oil.

Parts of a U.S. Army M-16 sat atop a piece of cloth on the bench. Murphy pushed the button on a digital timer, then reached for the stock and began to assemble the weapon. A minute later, he pushed the timer again, then raised his hands in the air. One minute and four seconds—he was slow today. Walking over to an ammunition drawer, he began to remove banana clips and load them with different types of ordnance.

"God, I love my job," he said aloud.

T HE VAN WAS entering the bridge leading from Macau to Taipa. "The Minutemen," Cabrillo said. "Where did you come up with that name?"

"It *could* be construed as an homage to Paul Revere and the revolutionary way," Truitt said, laughing.

"Wouldn't that be Paul Revere and The Raiders?" Jones said.

"But in fact," Truitt continued, "it's the name of the band that was already hired."

"Won't it be crowded when two bands show up?" Ross asked.

"It would be, but the real Minutemen, a California cover band doing a tour of the Far East, was detained in Bangkok after a two-week stint in the Phuket bars. Apparently a customs official found a joint in the drummer's shaving kit."

"Planted?" Cabrillo asked.

"Had to," Truitt noted. "The Minutemen are probably the only band in these parts that are clean—they met one another in a twelve-step group."

"The boys sound all right," Meadows said. "You can't fault someone who's turned his life around—we shouldn't let them rot in a Thailand prison."

"Not to worry, the customs official is on our payroll," Truitt said. "There's no record of the stop. One of our people in California made contact with their management company and explained the situation, and we upgraded them to first class for the flight home since the Macau gig was the last one on the tour. Right now, the Minutemen are convinced they were critically helpful in the war on terrorism—as per our standard cover story."

The van rolled onto Taipa and started across the island.

"I just have one question," Cabrillo said. "Which one of us is the lead singer?"

11

THE DALAI LAMA walked down the steps of the jet in Jalandhar, in the Punjab province of India, into an unusually hot day. Despite his forty-five years in exile in India, he had never learned to adjust to the weather. His Holiness was a man from the mountains and he missed snow and cold temperatures. He sniffed the air for the slightest smell from the glaciers far to the north. Instead of snow and pine trees, his nose was assaulted by fumes from the trucks passing by the airport on the traffic-packed highway.

He smiled anyway and gave thanks.

"Looks like my transportation is here," he said to Overholt, who had joined him on the tarmac.

A large, single-engine Cessna Caravan was nearby, with a pilot doing a walk-around.

"Very good, Your Holiness," Overholt said.

"As soon as I return, I will meet with my advisors and the oracle," the Dalai Lama said, staring directly into Overholt's eyes. "If they agree and you can ensure me no bloodshed, then I will agree to the plan we have designed."

"Thank you, Your Holiness."

The Dalai Lama began to walk toward the Cessna, then stopped and turned around. "I will pray for your father and for you," he said quietly, "and pray this all works out."

Overholt simply smiled as the Dalai Lama turned and walked over to the steps, then climbed into the Cessna for the rest of his journey. As soon as he was seated, the Dalai Lama turned to one of his assistants.

"As soon as we arrive in Little Lhasa, I will need the trunk containing the Golden Buddha documents brought to my office."

The assistant scribbled notes on a small pad.

"Then I will need to see my doctor," he said quietly. "There is something wrong with my physical shell."

"As ordered, Your Holiness," the aide said, "I shall do."

The pilot started the engine on the Cessna and ran through his checks. Four minutes later he was rolling toward a runway, and a few minutes after that he was airborne. Overholt stood on the tarmac and watched as the Cessna lifted off the ground and made a climbing turn to the right. The Caravan was just a speck against the backdrop of the white cloud cover before he turned to the pilot of the Falcon.

"Mind if I catch a ride back to Santa Monica with you?" he asked.

"We're going that way anyway, sir," the pilot said. "Might as well tag along."

O VERHOLT HAD A quality that was often overlooked in successful spies. He could sleep anywhere. By the time the jet stopped for fuel in Taiwan, the several hours of sleep had renewed his vigor. As the plane was being fueled, he walked a distance away and unfolded his portable telephone, then dialed a number from memory.

Bouncing off a satellite, the signal arrived in the Marshall Islands in the Pacific, then was redirected toward the ultimate destination. The signal was scrambled and untraceable and there was no way to determine where the receiving party was actually located. The voice answered with an extension number.

"2524."

"Juan," he said quietly, "this is Langston."

"*Qué pasa, amigo,*" Cabrillo said.

"Everything still looks good," Overholt said. "How is your crew coming?"

"We're ten by ten," Cabrillo said.

"Good," Overholt said.

"Looks like there's a little side deal here for us to grab," Cabrillo said. "I trust there's no problem with that?"

"As long as there's no blowback," Overholt said. "Your company's dealings are none of my concern."

"Excellent," Cabrillo said. "If it works out as planned, there will be no need to bill you for travel expenses."

"Money's not a problem, old friend; this is coming from the top," Overholt said, "but time is—make this happen for me before Easter."

"That's why we get the big money, Lang"—Cabrillo laughed—"because we're so damn prompt. You'll have what you need, you have my word."

"That's what I love about you," Overholt said, "your complete lack of ego."

"I'll call you when it's done," Cabrillo said.

"Just don't let me read about it."

Overholt disconnected, slid the telephone into his pocket, then did a series of stretching exercises before climbing back aboard the jet. Twenty-four hours later, he boarded a military transport plane from Southern California to Andrews Air Force Base in Maryland. There he was met by the CIA car service and transported to headquarters.

*   *   *

A T THE MANSION on Estrada da Penha, preparations for the party were moving at a blistering pace. One truck after another rolled through the gates, then parked and unloaded their contents. Three large yellow-and-white-striped canvas tents were quickly erected on the grounds, with portable air-conditioning units to make the tents more comfortable. They were followed by a pair of large portable fountains with spotlights that would shoot colored streams of water twenty feet into the air; red carpets for the guests to walk across; sound equipment; a baby grand piano for the musician who would play during the cocktail hour; parrots, doves and peacocks; and tables, chairs and linens.

The party planner was a middle-aged Portuguese woman named Iselda, whose black hair was kept in a tight bun on the back of her head. She was chain-smoking thin brown cigarettes with blue satin tips while she screamed orders to the staff.

"These are not the goblets I ordered," she said as a worker carried a case into the tent and began to unpack them. "I ordered the ones with the gold lip—take these back."

"Sorry, Miss Iselda," the Chinese worker said, scanning a sheet. "These are what are on the list."

"Take them back, take them back," she said as she furiously puffed away.

A peacock wandered into the tent and made a mess on the floor. Iselda grabbed a straw broom and chased it out onto the grounds.

"Where are the laser lights?" she shouted to no one in particular.

A T EXACTLY THAT same instant, Stanley Ho, host of the party, was standing in one of his three home offices, this one on the top floor of his house. This was his private sanctuary. None of the staff or assistants were allowed to enter this most private of spaces. The attic room was decorated to Ho's tastes, which ran to early eclectic. His desk was from an early sailing ship, his television a brand-new plasma screen.

Bookcases lined one wall, but they were not filled with the classy tomes Ho displayed in areas where guests visited; these shelves were filled with pulp spy novels, soft porn featuring damsels in distress, and cheap paperback westerns.

A giant wool rug with a stick-shaped phoenix design that had been woven by a Navajo in Arizona graced the wood floor, while the walls were dotted with framed posters from past and current popular movies. The top of the captain's desk was a study in disorderliness. Stacks of papers, a metal car model, a cup from Disney World holding pens, and a dusty brass lamp shared the crowded space.

Ho walked over to a small refrigerator shaped like a bank vault and removed a bottle of water. Twisting off the cap, he took a sip, then stared at the Golden Buddha sitting upright on the floor, the door of its case open.

Ho was trying to decide if he should display his latest prize at the party.

Right then, his private telephone rang. It was the insurance under-writer, who wanted to schedule an appointment. Ho set a time, then went back to staring at his treasure.

"A S LONG AS we don't lose power," Kevin Nixon said, "no one should be the wiser."

"Did you receive their song list?" Cabrillo asked.

"We got it," Hanley said, handing him the list, "and programmed the songs into the computer."

"Heavy on the sixties and seventies," Cabrillo noted, "with a fair amount of guitar riffs."

"Unfortunately, we can't change the playlist without arousing sus-picion," Hanley said.

"I'm just worried—if any of the guests happen to be guitar players, they'll know we're faking it," Cabrillo said.

"I rigged the guitar with tiny LED lights that are only visible with special glasses," Nixon said, smiling. "They're color-coded for the player's fingers. All he has to do is place his fingers where the light shows and he should be okay."

Nixon handed Cabrillo the guitar and a pair of black-framed sunglasses. He slid the strap over his neck and Nixon plugged the guitar into the power source.

"It goes thumb purple, index finger red, then down the fingers, yellow, blue and green," Nixon said. "Same on the frets. Hold a second and I'll start the computer."

Cabrillo slipped on the glasses and waited. Once the lights lit up, he pushed his fingers on the illuminated strings. A crude rendition of the "Star Spangled Banner" filled the Magic Shop.

"We won't win any Grammys," Cabrillo said when the lights went dark, "but it should get us past any casual scrutiny."

Hanley walked over to a bench and removed a clear glass bottle containing a pale blue liquid. "There's one other thing to consider," he said, smiling. "This stuff came straight from the labs at Fort Dietrich, Maryland. Once we slip some of this into the punch bowl, this party will be kicking."

"There's no long-term effects, right?" Cabrillo asked.

"No," Hanley said, "only short-term. It seems that after a few drops of this elixir, you'll have the time of your life."

12

"THE SAMPLE CHECKS out," the software billionaire said over the telephone.

Spenser had dispensed with the voice-alteration equipment, but his words were tinged with a fear that made his upper-crust accent less polished than perplexed.

"Then you are interested?" he said.

"Sure," the software billionaire said, "but I've decided that I want to make the transfer myself. I have the feeling you're about as trust-worthy as a hooker with a crack habit."

Spenser frowned. His plan of thievery and deceit was unraveling. The costs he had already incurred made a quick sale his only salvation—there was no time to line up another buyer. He was in the worst possible place. He was a seller who needed to sell—with a buyer who was calling the shots.

"Then you need to come here and take delivery," Spenser said.

"Where's here?"

"Macau," Spenser said.

The software billionaire stared at a calendar on his desk. "I'll be there the evening of Good Friday."

"I'll want cash or bearer bonds then," Spenser said. "No more bank transfer."

"Fair enough, but don't try anything, I'm bringing reinforcements."

"You bring the money," Spenser said, "and you get the Buddha."

The billionaire disconnected and Spenser sat quietly for a moment. He didn't have long to go.

"MONICA'S A GUEST," Cabrillo said as he glanced at the sheet of notes. "For this operation, she's a minor member of the Danish royal family."

"It's all so common," Crabtree said with a Scandinavian accent.

"You'll need to fake a speech impediment with that accent," Hanley said. "Stop by the Magic Shop and we'll make you a mouth guard that will add a lisp."

"Great," Crabtree said, "I get to play a lisping lady-in-waiting."

"It could be worse," Cabrillo said. "Linda's replacing the chain-smoking Portuguese party planner, Iselda."

"Excellent," Linda Ross said, laughing. "I finally quit smoking a few years ago and now the Corporation is going to get me hooked again."

"By the way," Hanley said, "we think Iselda also practices an alternative lifestyle."

"So I'm a chain-smoking Portuguese lesbian party planner," Ross said. "At least it's not as bad as when I was a German transsexual dominatrix."

"I remember that," Murphy said. "You looked like Madeline Kahn in that Mel Brooks film."

"I remember you being kind of turned on," Ross said.

"We were going to use Julia, but we couldn't, for the obvious reason," Cabrillo noted.

Julia Huxley, the *Oregon*'s medical officer, grinned. "I always knew growing up that these big boobs would pay off."

"You'd just better perfect your Pamela Anderson-Lee-whoever look," Hanley said.

"I get to play a slut?" Huxley said happily.

"Girlfriend of one of the band members," Cabrillo noted.

"Same thing," Huxley said eagerly. "Can Max do me some fake tattoos?"

"Be glad to," Hanley said. "We might even fake some piercings, if you like."

"And now to the band," Cabrillo said. "I'm playing keyboards—a lot of songs don't feature keyboards, so that will give me time to sneak away. Murphy's lead guitar, Kasim is our drummer, and the soul man Franklin is on bass."

"Oh, yeah," Lincoln said. "The pulsing beat runs through me."

"And the singer?" Huxley asked.

"That would be Mr. Halpert," Cabrillo said.

The entire conference table turned and stared at Michael Halpert. As the head of finance and accounting, he didn't exactly seem to fit the job. Easily the most conservative of the crew, the rumor was that he ironed his handkerchiefs. The idea of him posing as a rock musician seemed as ludicrous as casting Courtney Love as the Virgin Mary.

"Unfortunately, the lead singer of the Minutemen is tall, thin and slim, and the owner has seen a videotape of the band performing. If no one can think of anyone else, Mike's got to be our man."

"I can do it," Halpert said quickly.

"Are you sure?" Hanley asked. "There is only so much the Magic Shop can do."

"For your information, I was raised on a commune in Colorado," Halpert said. "I've forgotten more about the rock lifestyle than most of you ever knew."

Cabrillo was the only one who already knew that—he was the sole officer of the Corporation who had access to all employment files.

"Man," Murphy said, "I thought your baby clothes were a three-piece suit."

"Now you know," Halpert said. "My family got around. Jerry Jeff Walker was my godfather, and Commander Cody taught me how to ride a bicycle."

"Man," Hali Kasim said, "just when you think you know someone."

"Let's get back to the project," Cabrillo said. He knew Halpert's upbringing made him uncomfortable—the day Halpert had enlisted in the marines, his father had quit speaking to him. Ten years had passed before they'd talked again, and even now the relationship was strained.

Halpert waited for Cabrillo to continue.

"Right now we have two of our people posing as a landscaping crew. They will install parabolic microphones in the trees they're trimming. The microphones record the vibrations on the glass of the house and we should be able to hear everything that is happening inside."

"We're having trouble monitoring the telephone lines, however," Linda Ross noted, "Normally, we can tap into the mainframe, but since the Chinese took over the telephone system, they moved the major systems across the water into Hong Kong. We'll try and install something at the junction box leading into the house, but we're not sure how well it will receive."

"So there's a chance we will only be able to hear one side of the telephone calls?" Hanley asked.

"Right," Ross said. "Anyone talking inside will cause vibrations on the glass we can read."

"I'm not so concerned about that," Cabrillo said, "but we do need to be able to cut the lines leading into the house—the burglar alarms work through the telephone lines."

"That we can do," Ross said, "but people will still be able to use cell phones."

The hours passed as the planning continued. The party was less than thirty hours away.

L IKE A WHIRLING dervish, the oracle began to shake and parade about.

The Palace of Exile in India was much smaller than Potala, but it served the same purpose. Home to the Dalai Lama and his advisors, it featured a temple, sleeping rooms and a large stone-floored meeting room, where the Dalai Lama was sitting on a throne chair now, watching.

The oracle was dressed in his ceremonial robes, topped by one of golden silk, its interwoven designs of yellow, green, blue and red encircling a mirror on the chest surrounded by amethyst and turquoise stones. A harness held small flags and banners, and the entire outfit weighed nearly eighty pounds. As soon as the oracle had been dressed and entered a trance, his assistants had placed a heavy metal-and-leather helmet upon his head and cinched it tight.

Had the aging oracle not been possessed by a spirit outside his own, the weight of the helmet and robes would have been too much for him to bear. Instead, once the oracle reached his deep state, the weight seemed to be lifted and he hopped about like an astronaut walking on the surface of the moon. He exploded in motion. Arms akimbo, he danced like a praying mantis from one side of the room to the other. Strange guttural sounds radiated from somewhere deep inside his body, while his left hand flashed a heavy silver-plated sword in a figure-eight pattern.

Then he stopped in front of the throne chair and shook his entire body like a dog after a swim.

Once the oracle became motionless, the Dalai Lama spoke.

"Is it time to go home?" he asked.

The oracle spoke in a voice unlike his own. "The Dalai Lama returns, but to a smaller Tibet."

"The oracle explains," the Dalai Lama said.

A backflip, a flapping of arms, a stillness again.

"The north holds the key," the oracle said loudly. "We give the aggressors the land that once held Mongols, then they will go."

"Can we trust the Westerners?" the Dalai Lama asked.

The oracle bent his knees and strutted around in a circle. When facing the Dalai Lama again, he spoke. "We will soon have something they want; our gift of this will help strengthen the friendship. Our power is returning—our home is near."

Then all at once, as if a gust of wind had blown the skeleton from his body, the oracle collapsed on the ground in a heap. His assistants ran over and untied the helmet, then began to remove the sweat-soaked robes. They began to bathe the oracle with cool water, but it was almost an hour before he opened his eyes again.

13

"ONLINE," THE CORPORATION technician whispered.

On board the *Oregon*, a radio operator adjusted his receiver. The sound of a maid came through his headset. He flipped a switch to a recorder, then keyed his microphone.

"Okay," he said, "we're recording."

Climbing down from the tree, the technician gathered up the limbs he had trimmed, then spent the next few hours working on the bushes. When he had finished the job and loaded the rented truck with the debris, it was just past lunchtime. Walking around to the service entrance, he handed a bill to the manager of the mansion. Then he walked back to the truck and drove away.

Back on the *Oregon*, the radio operator monitored the conversation in the mansion and made notes on a yellow pad. Nothing much was happening, but that might change at any moment.

*   *   *

BELOWDECKS IN THE Magic Shop, the band was rehearsing. Kevin Nixon motioned for them to stop, then adjusted the control panel. "All right," he said, "from the top again."

Murphy started strumming his guitar, and the opening bars of the Creedence Clearwater Revival song "Fortunate Son" filled the shop. The rest of the band added their parts. Halpert's voice was surprisingly good. After being washed through the computer, it was hard to tell his rendition from the original. His moves were good as well—unlike those of most of the band.

Cabrillo on the keyboards came off as Liberace on methamphetamines. Kasim moved like Buddy Rich in a neck brace. Lincoln was slightly better—he kept his eyes closed and strummed the bass guitar and managed to tap his foot in time; the problem was that his hands were so large it looked like he was not moving his fingers. Nixon waited until the song was finished.

"It's not bad," he admitted, "but I have some videotapes of live bands and I suggest you men watch them so you can work on your choreography."

Three hours later, the band was as ready as they would ever be.

THIS WAS THE part of her job Iselda loved best—the last-minute nagging details.

She reached in her handbag and found a pack of thin brown cheroots. Unlike most smokers who stuck to a single brand, Iselda stocked her bag with three or four different kinds. She selected her poison depending on many factors. The aching in her lungs, the rawness of her throat, the amount of nicotine needed for the job. Menthols for that minty fresh buzz; thin cigars when she needed a boost; long, thin, brightly tipped tools when she needed to punctuate a conversation by using the burning sticks like a maestro's baton. She fired up the cheroot and took a drag.

"I specifically requested glacier ice for the cocktails," she screamed at the caterer, "not the round highball cubes."

"You asked for both," the caterer said, "but the glacier ice has yet to arrive."

"You'll have it here?" she asked.

"It's in the warehouse, Iselda," the man said patiently. "We didn't want it to melt."

Iselda stared across the tent to where a worker was adjusting the devices that made clouds of smoke from dry ice.

"We need more smoke than that," she shouted, then quickly walked across to the row of machines and began to berate the worker.

After a few minutes of adjustment, the man flipped the machine on again. Clouds of dense, cold gas billowed from the machine, then began to settle on the floor.

"Good, good," Iselda said. "Now make sure we have plenty of dry ice."

A technician was adjusting the light display and she raced in that direction.

O N BOARD THE *Oregon*, the technician monitoring conversations in the mansion made a note on the yellow pad, then reached for the shipboard communication microphone.

"Chairman Cabrillo," he said, "I think you need to come up here."

T HE LIMOUSINE SLOWED outside the gate leading to the runway at the San Jose, California, airport. A guard with a holstered weapon stood blocking the way. The driver rolled down his window.

"New security regulations," he said. "There's no more driving onto the tarmac."

The software billionaire had rolled down his window as well. This was an unwelcome inconvenience. Intolerable, in fact.

"Wait a minute, now," he shouted from the rear. "We've driven out to my plane for years."

"Not anymore," the guard noted.

"Do you know who I am?" the billionaire said pompously.

"No idea," the guard admitted, "but I do know who I am—I'm the guy that's ordering you to turn away from the gate now."

With nothing else to say, the limousine driver backed up and steered toward the terminal, then parked in front and waited for his employer to climb out. The encounter put his boss in a foul mood and he could hear him muttering as he carried the bags a safe distance behind.

"Good God," the billionaire said, "for what I pay for hangar space, you'd think I'd get some service."

As they approached the door leading out to the taxiway, a smattering of expensive jets sat awaiting their owners. There were a trio of Gulfstreams, a Citation or two, a half dozen King Airs, and a single burgundy behemoth that looked like it belonged to a regional airline.

The software billionaire was big on appearances.

If the rich had private jets—he wanted a large one. An airplane that screamed success and excess like a dog collar made from diamonds. The billionaire's choice was a Boeing 737. The aircraft was fitted with a single-lane bowling alley, a hot tub and a bedroom bigger than many homes. It was fitted with a large-screen television, advance communications equipment, and a chef trained at the Cordon Bleu. The pair of dancers he had ordered from the service were already aboard. The entertainment for his flight was a California blonde and a redhead who bore a striking resemblance to a young Ann-Margret.

The billionaire wanted some way to pass the time on the long flight.

He burst through the door leading outside without waiting for his driver with the luggage, then made his way over to the 737. Then he walked up the ramp and inside.

"Ladies," he shouted, "front and center."

Thirteen minutes later, they were airborne.

I NSIDE THE *OREGON*, the technician was entering commands in the computer when Cabrillo opened the door and walked inside.

"What have you got?" he said without preamble.

"Ho just had a telephone conversation with an insurance adjuster who is coming out to the mansion to inspect the Buddha."

"Damn," Cabrillo said, reaching for the microphone. "Max, you better get up to communications, we've got a problem."

While the technician continued to trace the source of the call, Cabrillo paced the control room.

Hanley arrived a few minutes later. "What is it, Juan?"

"Ho has an insurance adjuster coming out to inspect the Golden Buddha."

"When?" Hanley asked.

"Four p.m."

The technician hit a button and a printer spit out a sheet.

"Here's the location of the call, boss," he said. "I have it overlaid on a map of Macau."

"We need to come up with a plan," Cabrillo said, "posthaste."

W INSTON SPENSER WAS juggling chain saws.

Only his long stint as a customer of the bank had earned him an increase on his business line of credit, but the manager had made it clear he wanted the balance paid down in no less than seventy-two hours. His credit cards were at their limits, and calls had already come into his office in London, inquiring about the situation. For all intents and purposes, Spenser was, at this instant, in dire financial straits. As soon as the deal with the billionaire went down, he would be as flush as he had ever dreamed—right now, however, he could not afford an airplane ticket home.

All he had to do tomorrow was remove the Buddha, transfer it to the airport and receive his ill-gotten gain. Then he'd charter a jet and fly off into the sunset with his fortune. By the time his customer in Macau realized he'd been duped, he'd be long gone.

14

JUAN CABRILLO SAT at the table in his stateroom and studied the folder for the third time.

In nine minutes, the hands of the clock would pass twelve and it would officially be Good Friday. Game day. There was always a fair amount of luck combined with flexibility when the Corporation launched an operation. The key was to minimize surprises through rigorous planning, and always have a backup plan in place.

At this, the Corporation excelled.

The only problem was the object itself. The Golden Buddha was not a microchip that could be slipped into a pocket or sewn into clothing. It was a heavy object the size of a man that required effort to move and stealth to conceal. Any way you cut the cake, the movement of the icon would require men and machines to transport it to a safe place.

The mere size and weight of the Golden Buddha made that a condition.

Then there were the players themselves. The art dealer, Ho; the people at the party; the Chinese authorities; and now the insurance appraiser. Any one of them could throw a wrench into the works, and the stakes and timing were such that retreating and regrouping was not an option.

Cabrillo hated operations where a clear path of retreat was not available.

People could be captured, injured or killed when the plan was to execute the operation at all costs. The last time the Corporation had sustained losses was the operation in Hong Kong, where Cabrillo had lost his leg and others had been killed. Since then, he had consciously avoided ultra-high-risk assignments. The Golden Buddha assignment had started out fitting the lower-risk profile, but it was becoming more and more dangerous as time passed.

Just pregame jitters, Cabrillo thought as he closed the folder. Sometime tonight, they would have the Buddha and begin the process of transferring it back to the Dalai Lama. A few more days and the Corporation would be cashiered, out of the loop and sailing away to another part of the globe.

WINSTON SPENSER GULPED Glenmorangie whiskey like it was ginger ale.

Spenser's brilliant plan of deceit had hit a speed bump that had ripped off the oil pan, and now it was leaking its fluid onto the ground. Ho had called earlier in the evening and his words had been an ice pick to the brain.

"Please come to the party early," Ho had said. "I'd like you to be here when the insurance man examines the Buddha."

One day more and Spenser would have been long gone.

Uruguay, Paraguay, one of the South Pacific islands, anywhere but here. The fake Buddha was good—he'd paid a princely ransom to ensure it could withstand scrutiny—but if the insurance inspector was top-notch, he'd see through the ruse. The gold itself would probably pass muster. The problem was the precious stones. If the inspector was any sort of gemologist, he'd realize the stones were just too perfect. Massive rocks of the size that adorned the Golden Buddha were extremely rare. The existing stones that large almost always had flaws.

Only stones produced in a laboratory were lacking inclusions.

He drained the scotch and walked over to the bed and lay down.

But the bed was spinning and sleep was hard to come by.

S INCE HIS EXILE from Tibet, it would be easy to imagine that the Dalai Lama had lived in a vacuum concerning events inside his country. Nothing could be further from the truth. Almost from the time he'd stepped across the border, an ad hoc system of local intelligence had begun filtering south to his headquarters in Little Lhasa.

Messages were passed from mouth to mouth by a series of runners who breached the mountain passes far from Chinese scrutiny, then delivered their messages either in person or through intermediaries. With hundreds of thousands of Tibetans loyal to the Dalai Lama, the tentacles of the operation reached into every part of the country. Chinese troop movements were reported, intercepted cables sent south, overheard telephone conversations disclosed.

Snow tables and water flow from the rivers and other environmental concerns were memorized and transmitted. Tourists were monitored and casually engaged in conversation to glean more facts about the Chinese and their attitudes. Merchants that sold to the Chinese soldiers reported on sales and the troops' general demeanor. Times of alert were noted and sent south, as were times when controls over the population were loosened. Briefings were held for the Dalai Lama and his advisors, and most of the time the exiles in India had a better picture of the conditions in Tibet than the hated Chinese overlords.

"The troops seem to be buying more trinkets?" the Dalai Lama asked.

"Yes," one of his advisors noted, "things that are uniquely Tibetan."

"When has this ever happened before?" the Dalai Lama asked.

"Never," the advisor admitted.

"And we have reports that the fuel stocks at the bases are low?"

"That's what the Tibetan workers at the bases report," the advisor said. "Excursions by trucks into the countryside are being curtailed, and we have not had a report of a tank on exercises in nearly a month. It's as if the occupation is moving into a stagnant time."

The Dalai Lama opened an unmarked folder and scanned the contents. "This coincides with the reports from the Virginia consulting group we have under contract. Their latest report shows the Chinese economy in dire straits. The Chinese have the largest increase of any country in oil imports, while at the same time the value of their investments overseas are decreasing. If President Jintao doesn't make some much-needed adjustments, his country could be plunged into a full-scale depression."

"We can only hope," one of the advisors noted.

"That brings me to our main topic of discussion," the Dalai Lama said quietly. "If we could take a moment to meditate to clear our minds, I will explain."

THE BURGUNDY 737 was a flying sybaritic palace in the sky.

The software billionaire was dosing himself with a carefully calculated mixture of Ecstasy and male impotence pills to pass the time. The Ecstasy made him loving, but the impotence pills offset that by fueling his sexual appetite, which was a little aggressive.

At this instant, in a forward part of the jet, a flight attendant was making notes on the pad of a personal digital assistant. Once he was finished, he plugged it into the air phone and hit send. Now all he had to do was wait for a reply.

The other flight attendant seemed more concerned. This was her first flight on the billionaire's 737, and she found the debauchery unnerving.

Turning her head away from the rear section of the plane, she addressed the blond-haired man.

"You ever worked this gig before?"

"First time," the man admitted.

"If I didn't need the money," the brunette said, "I'd make this trip one-way."

The blond-haired man nodded. "Tell me about yourself," he said.

Thirty minutes later, the blond-haired man smiled. She'd fudged what he knew as the truth—but not by much.

"There's an opportunity you might be interested in," he said easily.

Just then, the buzzer from the rear rang and a voice was heard.

"Bring us another two magnums of champagne," the billionaire ordered.

"You keep that thought," the brunette said. "I'll go water the horses."

I N MACAU THE streets were filled with late-night revelers. Two men drove slowly along Avenue Conselheiro Ferriera de Almeida through the throngs. The man in the passenger seat stared at a portable GPS mapping unit and gave directions. Turning at Avenida do Coronel Mesquita, they headed northwest along the road until they were at a side street that led to a residential area within a half mile of mainland China.

"Find a place to park," the navigator ordered.

Pulling to the side of the road under a tree, the driver placed the van in park, then shut off the engine. The navigator pointed to a house set back from the road up the street.

"That's the house."

"Shall we?" the driver asked.

The navigator climbed out of the van and walked around to the front and waited while the driver reached under the seat, removed a leather bag, then met him in front of the van.

"You notice almost no one here has a dog?" the driver said.

"Sometimes," the navigator said, "you just get lucky."

Both men were dressed in dark clothing that blended into the night. Their shoes were rubber soled and their hands covered by dark vinyl surgical gloves. They moved with the certain sense of unhurried purpose that comes with competence, not arrogance. Slipping unseen to the front wall surrounding the home, they paused for a second at the gate. The driver reached into his pocket, removed a pick, and a second later sprung the lock. He opened the gate, allowed the navigator to pass inside, then closed the gate behind them.

There was little need to talk. Both men had memorized the plan.

Walking around to the rear of the house, where it was dark, they disabled the security system, jimmied the lock, and then crept silently into the house. Pausing at the foot of the stairs, the driver flipped open a small black plastic box and slipped an earpiece into place. Pointing the device at the floor above, he listened for a moment.

Then he smiled and nodded at his partner.

Placing his hands together, he tilted his head and placed his hands alongside his cheek, using the universal hand signal for sleep. With one finger, he pointed to the far end of the floor in the left corner. With the other, he pointed a distance away to where another bedroom was located on the second floor. Then he pointed a fist toward the spot on the left side. Primary target there, secondary target there.

Doing a kind of curtsy, he spread his hands apart.

Then he unsnapped a pouch clipped to his belt and handed an eight-inch leather case to the navigator and smiled. Taking the case the navigator slowly began to climb the stairs. Several minutes passed as the driver stood silently on the landing.

Then he heard the voice of his partner.

"I don't know about you," the navigator said as he began to walk down the steps, "but I'm hungry."

The driver removed his earpiece, stuffed the cord inside, then folded the case back together.

"Then let's eat," the driver said.

The navigator reached the landing and flicked on a tiny flashlight. "We can't ask our hosts what's good," he said. "They're in sleepyville."

"And by the time they wake up," the driver said, "we'll be long gone."

The two men made their way to the kitchen, but nothing looked good. So they walked back to the van, drove through town to the casino and ordered a meal of ham and eggs.

15

S UNRISE ON GOOD Friday, March 25, 2005, was at 6:11 A.M.
On the decks of the sampans in the inner harbor, the Chinese
traders began to stir. Along Avenida da Amizade in front of the Hotel
Lisboa, a dozen women dressed in cotton shifts with conical hats lashed
around their necks began washing the sidewalk with soapy water
splashed from tin buckets. Dipping straw brooms into the buckets, they
erased the debris from both the winners and the losers from the night
before. A few diehards stumbled from inside and squinted at the light
from a sun just beginning her day.

A few small three-wheeled motorized rickshaws plied the avenue,
their drivers stopping for strong black coffee served in small cups, then
continuing on to deliver packages or people to their destinations. At a
small restaurant two hundred yards northwest of the casino, the owner
finished a cigarette then walked inside. On the stove in the rear was a
pot of *caldo verde*, the Portuguese stew of potatoes, sausage and locally

grown greens. He stirred the mixture, then set the long wooden spoon onto a counter and started to prepare chickens marinated in coconut milk, garlic, peppercorns and chilies by rubbing them with rock salt. Later, the poultry would be slid onto skewers and slow-cooked on a rotisserie.

Across the water, Hong Kong was hidden by a haze of humidity and smog, but the sound of the first high-speed ferry leaving port could be heard. The first few jets of the day, mainly cargo planes, streaked across the blue sky and made ready for landing at the airport. A Chinese naval vessel left its moorage below A-Ma Temple and started out for a patrol, while a large luxury yacht with a helicopter perched on her fantail called on the radio for the location of her slip.

A lone cargo ship, decades past her prime, started into port to deliver a cargo of bicycles from Taiwan. On another cargo ship, this one appearing old and decrepit, a man with a blond crew cut was sitting at the table in his stateroom reading.

Juan Cabrillo had been awake for hours.

He was running every possible scenario through his head.

A light knock came at the door, and Cabrillo stood up and walked over and opened the hatch.

"Somehow I knew you'd be awake," Hanley said.

Hanley held a tray of plates covered by metal lids, steam escaping from under them.

"Breakfast," he said as he walked inside.

Cabrillo cleared a space on the table and Hanley off-loaded the contents. Next he pulled the lid off a dinner-sized plate and smiled.

Cabrillo nodded and pointed to a seat.

Hanley slid into the seat and poured two cups of coffee from a thermal carafe, then removed the lid from another plate.

"Anything unusual happen overnight?" Cabrillo asked.

"No," Hanley said easily, "everything is still according to plan."

Cabrillo sipped his coffee.

"There's a lot here that could go wrong," he said.

"There always is."

"That's why we get the big money."

"That's why we get the big money," Hanley agreed.

"So, DO YOU know when I lost my virginity?" the brunette flight attendant asked. "You seem to know everything else."

"That's too personal." The blond-haired man laughed.

"But my failed relationships and credit card bills aren't?" The attendant grinned.

"Sorry about the intrusion into your privacy. The group I work with has a thing for detail."

"Sounds like you're a spy," the attendant noted.

"Oh, heck no," the blond-haired man said, "we just work for them."

"Tax-free income enough so I can retire?"

"Everyone's dream," the blond-haired man admitted.

The brunette attendant glanced around the forward cabin. She was really nothing more than a glorified waitress on a restaurant in the sky.

"How can I say no?" she said finally.

"Good," the blond-haired man said, rising.

"Where are you going?" she asked.

"I have to go kill the pilot," the blond-haired man said lightly.

The look on the brunette flight attendant's face was priceless.

"Just kidding," the blond-haired man said. "I have to pee. I'm qualified in 737s, but I think Mr. Fabulous would think it odd if I disappeared."

"Who *are* you people?" the attendant muttered as the blond-haired man slipped into the lavatory.

"ARE YOU SURE this beast will make it to the border and back?" Carl Gannon asked.

Gannon was staring at a decrepit old two-and-a-half-ton truck parked under a tree alongside a stone building on a side street in Thimbu, Bhutan. Sometime in the past the truck had been painted an olive drab color, but most of the paint was gone and now it showed mostly a light dusting of hairy rust. The two-part windshield was cracked on the passenger side, and all six of the tires were worn past any margin of safety. The hood, which had a strip down the center so the sides could be flipped open to work on the engine, was bent and had been welded more than once. The running boards were wooden slats. The exhaust pipe hung down from the undercarriage and was held in place with rusted wire.

Gannon walked to the rear and stared into the bed. Some of the planks that formed the floor were cracked and some were missing, and the canvas flaps that covered the sides were in roughly the same condition as a World War II pup tent.

"Oh, yes, sir," the Bhutanese owner said easily. "She has a strong heart."

Gannon continued his walk around. Climbing onto the passenger running board, he peeked into the cockpit. The long bench seat was worn, with portions of the springs underneath visible, but the few gauges on the dash were not cracked and appeared functional. He climbed down, then walked over to the hood and lifted the passenger side, which he folded up and over. The engine was surprisingly clean. It smelled strongly of thick grease and fresh oil. The belts and hoses, while not new, were serviceable, and the electrical wires and battery looked good. Gannon climbed down.

"Can you start her up?"

The man walked around, opened the door and climbed into the driver's seat.

After pulling out the choke, he pumped the gas pedal, then twisted the key. After turning over a few times, the engine roared to life. Smoke drifted out of a rusted hole in the exhaust pipe, but the engine settled into an idle. Gannon listened carefully. There was no tapping from the valves, but he placed his hand over the covers just to be sure. Nothing was amiss.

"Rev her up," he shouted.

The owner depressed the gas pedal, then left off. He did this four times.

"Okay," Gannon said, "you can shut her off."

The owner turned off the engine, pocketed the key, and then climbed from the cockpit. He was small, a shade over five feet tall, with tanned skin and slightly almond-shaped eyes. Smiling at Gannon, he awaited the verdict.

"Do you have spare belts and hoses?"

"I can find some," the man told him.

Gannon reached into his pocket and removed a wad of bills wrapped with a thick rubber band. Removing the rubber band, he fanned out the bills.

"How much to take me and a cargo to the border with Tibet?" he asked. "With amnesia included."

"Amnesia?" the man said, not understanding.

"After this is over," Gannon said, "I want you to forget we ever met."

The man nodded. "One thousand dollars," he said easily, "and one DVD player."

"Sounds reasonable," Gannon said. "Now, do you know where I can buy an ox?"

16

THE *OREGON* WAS a buzz of activity. Belowdecks in the Magic Shop, the players in the band were checking their instruments and arranging their costumes. Juan Cabrillo flipped open his cell phone and answered a call.

"Situation is stabilized here," Linda Ross said. "I'm headed to the site now."

"We've got three men inside and one watching from outside the wall," Cabrillo said. "If anyone catches on, you sound the alarm and help will come running."

"Piece of cake," Ross said.

The telephone went dead and Cabrillo turned to Max Hanley.

"Iselda is making her entrance."

"So far so good," Hanley said.

Mark Murphy finished with Kasim and patted his back. "There you go," he said.

Michael Halpert was playing with a microphone. Murphy turned to him and motioned.

"Come on, kid," he said, "let me get you strapped."

Halpert walked over and turned his back to Murphy, who raised Halpert's shirt.

"This is a featherlight thirty-eight, Mike," Murphy recited as he taped a holster containing the weapon on Halpert's lower back. "Now I want you to reach back and yank the smoke wagon."

It was a line Murphy had heard from the movie *Tombstone*—ever since then, he'd used it unmercifully. Halpert reached back and pulled the pistol.

"Hang on," Murphy said. "It's too high, you're cocking your elbow."

He readjusted the holster and waited until Halpert tried it again.

"That's better," he said. "Let me see your boot."

Halpert turned and raised his pant leg. Murphy strapped on a knife inside a hard plastic case.

"Be careful with this, Mike," Murphy told him, "the blade has been dipped in a paralytic poison. If things turn to shit, you just have to nick someone and they'll go down. The problem is, the same thing happens to you if your target takes it from you. Be sure he's close and make sure you are in control of the situation."

"Okay, Mark," Halpert said quietly.

The knife was in place and Murphy climbed from his knees. "You worried?" he asked quietly.

"A little," Halpert said. "I'm usually not on the operational end."

Murphy nodded and smiled. "Don't worry, buddy, I'm going to be right next to you. If trouble breaks out, they have to get through me first."

Halpert nodded, then walked over to pick his microphone up again.

"Boss," he said to Cabrillo, "you're last."

Cabrillo smiled and walked over to Murphy. He was dressed in a costume that would make Elton John blush. Murphy raised one of the sequined pockets on the vest and slid two hypodermic needles in covers inside. In the other pocket, he slid an arced carbon-fiber blade that had holes for fingers.

"Your blade is dipped in paralytic agent, too," he said, spinning Cabrillo around and strapping a small automatic weapon to his lower back. "The bullets are wad cutters. There's not as much horsepower in the rounds as I like, so be close before you pull the trigger."

"Let's hope it doesn't come to that," Cabrillo said.

Lincoln had already been outfitted, and he stood to one side, playing with his bass guitar.

Cabrillo smiled, then spoke.

"Okay, everybody, we'll be going in soon," he said. "Remember the order of operations and make sure you've memorized the out. If at any time I give the signal to pull out, make your way to the extraction point. Keep in mind this portion today is only one part of the bigger picture—if this goes haywire, we still have ways of salvaging the operation. There are no bold heroes—only old heroes. The weapons are to be used only if everything goes to hell and one of our people is in danger of losing life or limb. What we want, as always, is an orderly operation where we do our job and return here safe and sound. Any questions?"

The Magic Shop was silent.

"Okay, people," Cabrillo said, "then give your letters to Julia."

Medical Officer Julia Huxley hated this part of her job. The letters gave instructions for the lengths of medical care each man wanted if critically injured. They also gave detailed instructions as to the dispersal of the operatives' funds and other bequests. Whatever was in the letters, Huxley was bound to see it through. She walked around the room collecting the sealed envelopes. When she was done, the room was quiet.

"That always puts a pall over the proceedings," Murphy said, laughing. "We're not going in to disable a nuclear warhead. We're just stealing some gold."

The sour mood dissipated and they resumed talking.

"We have some time before we need to leave," Hanley said, "so if you need to eat or whatever, the time is now."

Everyone filtered out of the room, leaving only Cabrillo and Hanley.

"Meadows and Jones ready?" Cabrillo asked.

"Right on schedule," Hanley said.

"And the flyboy?"

"Jetting his way here," Hanley said, "as we speak."

"Then the fun is about ready to happen."

A PAIR OF men on motorcycles with sidecars sat on the side of Rua de Lourenco and watched employees from the Macau Public Works Department erecting barricades along the route of the Good Friday parade. The side streets would all be blocked off, but the barricades were wooden sawhorses and would yield to the bumper of a car or the front tire of a motorcycle.

"Let's ride over to the staging area," one of the men said.

The other man nodded and pushed his starter button, then placed the cycle in gear and drove up the street. A few blocks away, he slid over to the side of the road and shut off the engine. The street leading out of the staging area was festooned with banners and crepe-paper streamers. Paper lanterns holding candles were placed along the route, waiting to be lit at dusk. Various vendors were setting up shop in hand-carts to offer food and drink to those watching the parade, while a street sweeper made a last-minute pass to make sure the street at least started out clean.

"They sure are big on dragons," said one of the men, pointing to a large line of floats.

There were at least seventy different floats. Ships, stages where musicians would play, sword swallowers and juggling acts. And dragons. Red crepe-paper monstrosities, a blue-and-yellow dragon with a long tail posed in the air.

The floats were built on motorized platforms, then outlined in thick wire and covered with cloth, paper or, in one case, what looked like hammered copper. A single driver perched inside each steered down the route by staring through a small slit in the front of the float. The exhaust from the small internal-combustion engines was vented out the side.

It was quiet now, but by the amount of speakers on the various floats, it was obvious that once the parade got under way there would be a medley of sights and sounds.

"I'm going to go take a look," one of the men said as he climbed off the motorcycle and walked over to a nearby float. Lifting the side curtain, he stared at the framework before a policeman walked over and shooed him away.

"Lot of room under there," he said to his partner as he returned and climbed back into his seat.

Several members of a marching band trudged past, followed by an elephant with a handler sitting atop in a basket chair.

"Hell of a deal," the second man said quietly, "hell of a deal."

R ICHARD TRUITT STARED in the mirror in his hotel room on Avenida de Almeida Ribeiro, then adjusted his tie. Reaching into his shaving kit, he removed a round container and opened it up. Touching his fingertip to the colored contact lens, he placed it over an eye and blinked it into place. After placing the second lens, he stood back and examined the result.

Truitt was pleased and he smiled.

Then he reached into another bag and removed a dental appliance and slid it over his top row of teeth. Now he had a slightly bucktoothed look. Removing a pair of tortoiseshell glasses from the bag, he placed them over his ears and adjusted them on the bridge of his nose. If it was geek he was seeking, he'd hit the mother lode. All that remained was to grease down his hair and sprinkle a little false dandruff on the collar of his tweed jacket. Perfect.

Walking into the living room of the suite, he removed a document from the out tray in his printer and gave it an examination. It was ornate and pompous in true British fashion. By royal appointment to the queen, said one line. Since 1834, said another. Truitt folded the document and slipped it into the inside pocket of his jacket. Then he turned off the computer and printer and packed it into its case. His bags were already packed and sitting by the door. He returned to the bathroom to gather up his things there, then walked back into the living room and slid them into a side pocket of one of the bags. Then he walked over to the telephone and dialed a number.

"On my way," he said quietly.

"Good luck," Cabrillo replied.

Now he just needed to make his way out of the room without being seen.

FOR THE MOST part, Linda Ross was a good-natured and positive person.

That's what made playing Iselda so much fun. Most people have a bitchy side—they just keep it suppressed. Since the report on Iselda claimed she suppressed the best and not the worst, Ross was playing the opportunity to the hilt. Riding down the elevator to the parking garage, she stepped over to the attendant's window and frowned. The man raced from the enclosure to bring her car. As Ross waited, she tried to decide what Iselda would tip and decided it was probably nothing.

The attendant pulled up in a dirty Peugeot and opened the door. Ross slid into the driver's seat and muttered "I'll get you next time" to the attendant and slammed the door. The inside of the car smelled like a Wisconsin roadhouse at closing time. The carpet was littered with ashes and the ashtray was overflowing. The inside of the windows were covered with a film of nicotine.

"Here we go," she whispered as she reached into the glove box and removed a pack of cigarettes and lit one up. Then she placed the Peugeot into drive and rolled out to the street. Ten minutes later she pulled in front of the mansion and passed her first test.

"Open the gate," she shouted at the guard, who stared inside and, seeing it was her, pushed a button. "I'm late."

Parking over to one side of the driveway, she climbed from the car and lit another cigarette.

"Dump my ashtray when you get a chance," she said to a gardener who walked past.

The man ignored her and continued on. Walking to the front door, she rang the bell, then waited until the butler opened the door.

"Out of my way," she said as she swept past and headed for where she remembered the kitchen to be from the blueprints she'd memorized. Bursting into the kitchen, she stared at the stove, then turned to one of the chefs Iselda had hired.

"Is that the bisque?" she asked.

"Yes, ma'am," the Chinese chef answered.

Strutting over to the stove, she removed the lid and smelled. "Spoon, please."

The chef handed her a spoon and she tasted the soup.

"Seems light on the lobster," she said.

"I'll add more," the chef said.

"Good, good," Ross said. "If Mr. Ho needs me, I'll be out back. Let me know when you bake the first shrimp puffs—I want to sample them."

"Very good," the chef said as Ross headed through the rear door leading to the grounds.

As soon as she was spotted leaving the house, the caterer in charge of the libations walked toward her. He paused and stared.

"You look particularly lovely today, Miss Iselda," he said.

"Flattery will get you zilch," Ross said. "Do you have everything ready?"

"Except for that one thing we spoke about yesterday," the caterer said.

Damn, Ross thought.

"What thing?" Ross said. "I can't be expected to remember every-thing."

"The glacier ice," the caterer said. "It will be here in another hour or so."

"Good, good," Ross said. "Now make sure all the glassware is pol-ished."

She hurried away to where a chef with an electric chain saw was cutting an ice sculpture.

The caterer shook his head at the exchange. Her demeanor was the same, but the caterer could swear that the mole on Iselda's cheek was a few inches lower. He banished the thought and went to check the glasses.

Ross crushed her cigarette out under her high heel. Her head was spinning from all the smoking, and she paused and took a few deep breaths. "More detail on the wings," she said to the chef, who nodded and continued working. A tall man walked past carrying several stacked chairs. He smiled and winked.

High in a hickory tree on the property, a Corporation employee dressed in a ghillie suit that blended into the leaves keyed a microphone and spoke.

"Linda's in and working," he said quietly.

S TANLEY HO WAS standing in his top-floor office staring down at the party preparations. He had seen Iselda walk onto the yard, but the last thing he wanted to do was talk to her. The butch Portuguese woman annoyed Ho—she was good at what she did, but she took her-self much too seriously. This was a party, after all, not a Broadway musical. From past experience, Ho realized that a few hours from now most of the guests he had invited would be so inebriated that if he served rat as an entrée, most wouldn't even notice.

Ho was more concerned by the insurance adjuster who was due to arrive.

That and the fact that on the history of the Golden Buddha he had commissioned, the historian had noted that the icon supposedly had a secret storage compartment Ho had yet to find. It was a minor detail, but it bugged him nonetheless. The insurance adjuster was apparently an expert in ancient Asian art. Ho figured he'd question him when he arrived and see if he could supply the answer.

If not, Spenser would be here soon and Ho could ask him about it.

R ICHARD TRUITT DROVE the rental car carefully up Praia Grande to the gate of the mansion, then stopped. Rolling down the window, he handed the guard his invitation.

"Let me call the house," the guard said.

Dialing Ho's extension, the guard waited.

"Mr. Ho," the guard said, "there's a Mr. Samuelson from the insurance company here."

That wasn't who he'd been dealing with, Ho thought.

"Go ahead and let him in," Ho said, "and have him wait downstairs."

Then he hung up and dialed another number.

"Go on in," the guard said. "Park by the garage and wait downstairs."

Ho tapped his finger on the desk while the telephone rang.

"Lassiter residence," a voice with a Cantonese accent answered.

"This is Stanley Ho. Is Mr. Lassiter available?"

"Mr. Lassiter sick," the voice said. "Doctor coming soon."

"Did he leave any message if I called?" Ho asked.

"Hold on," the voice said.

Ho waited a few minutes, then a croaking voice came on the line.

"Sorry, old bean," the voice sputtered, "I've taken ill. A Mr.

Samuelson from our main office was in town. He'll keep the appointment as scheduled."

Lassiter didn't sound anything like himself, Ho thought. Whatever he'd caught sounded serious. "He's here now," Ho said.

"Don't worry, Mr. Ho," the voice said, hacking, "he's very knowledgeable, an expert on ancient Asian art."

"I hope you feel better soon," Ho said.

The sound of a phlegmy coughing fit erupted that lasted for almost a minute.

"Me, too," the voice said, "and I hope I can view the Golden Buddha very soon."

Ho hung up the telephone and rose to walk downstairs.

On the *Oregon*, the operator disconnected the line and turned to the man who had portrayed Lassiter.

"For a chef," he said quietly, "you make a hell of a spy."

17

WINSTON SPENSER WAS not wired for a life of crime and deceit. At this instant, he was vomiting into the toilet in his hotel room. Someone might argue it was all the booze from the night before, but in fact it was the tension that was ripping his guts apart. The tension that comes from living a lie, from being wrapped in deceit, from doing what one knows is wrong. By now there was nothing but bile rising—any food he had ingested was long gone, any liquor left was in his pores.

Spenser reached up, grabbed a hand towel, then wiped the corners of his mouth.

Rising from the floor, he stared at his image in the mirror. His eyes were red and bloodshot and his skin pallor a ghastly gray. The tension he was feeling was revealed by the muscles in his face. They twitched and popped like a kernel of popcorn in a sizzling pan. He reached up to dab a tear from the corner of his left eye, but his hand was shaking.

He supported one hand with the other and finished the task. Then he climbed into the shower to try and sweat out the fear.

RICHARD TRUITT STOOD in the living room, waiting. He stared around the room and tried to form a picture of his target. If Truitt was to guess, he figured the man who resided here was self-made and had only recently become affluent. He based this judgment on the furnishings and general décor. The pieces in the room were expensive enough, they just had no soul. And they were arranged in a fashion favoring flash over comfort. The possessions of old money always contained a story—the story Truitt was seeing was of objects bought in bulk to fill a space and give a picture of the occupant that was neither real nor imaginative.

There was a stuffed lion, but Truitt doubted the owner had stalked and shot the animal himself. A few paintings from contemporary artists like Picasso, but the paintings were far from the artists' best works. Truitt imagined they had been bought for image value. Guests without foundation or substance would be rightly impressed. An ancient coat of armor that to Truitt's eye appeared to be a reproduction . . . a French Louis XVI–style couch that looked about as comfortable to sit on as a bed of nails.

"Mr. Samuelson," a voice said from the staircase.

Truitt turned to see who was speaking.

The man was small. Five and a half feet tall and slight of build. His hair was jet black and styled like a 1970s California hustler. The mouth was small, with teeth that held a certain feral rage. Although Truitt imagined the man was smiling to be friendly, the effect from his grin made Truitt want to reach for his wallet to see if it was safe.

"I'm Stanley Ho," the man said, reaching the bottom of the stairs and extending his hand.

The stage was set and Truitt became the actor.

"Paul Samuelson," he said, extending a slightly limp wrist for a handshake. "The home office asked me to take over for Mr. Lassiter, who has unfortunately been stricken with a bug."

Truitt's version of Samuelson was coming across as a light-in-the-loafers Michael Caine.

"I trust you're familiar with this type of sculpture?"

"Oh, yes," Truitt gushed. "I did graduate studies in Asian art. It's one of my favorite forms."

Ho motioned to the stairs, then led the way up. "The object is known as the Golden Buddha. Are you in any way familiar with the piece?"

They rounded the first leg of the stairs and crossed the landing to the second flight.

"I'm afraid not," Truitt said breathlessly. "Has it ever been displayed?"

"No," Ho said quickly. "It has been part of a private collection for decades."

"Then I shall examine it with an eye for comparison to the other pieces I am familiar with."

They had exited the second flight and were winding their way around to the last set of stairs.

"You have a beautiful home," Truitt lied. "The staircases are mahogany, are they not?"

"Yes," Ho said, pausing at the door to his office to scan a card that unlocked the door. "From Brazil and hand fitted without nails or screws."

Ho opened the door and stepped aside.

"How lovely," Truitt said. He stared across the office to where the Golden Buddha sat. "But nowhere near as lovely as this."

Truitt walked over to the Buddha, followed by Ho.

"Magnificent," Truitt said easily. "May I touch it?"

"Please," Ho said.

The insurance adjuster was acting just as Ho had hoped. Equal parts respect and sublimation. There was a good chance the appraisal would be in his favor. If it was not to his liking, Ho was sure he could bully the agent into capitulation.

Truitt rubbed his hand over the face of Buddha, then stared into the jeweled eyes. "Might I ask some about the history?"

"He's from the thirteenth century and from Indochina," Ho said.

Truitt opened a small leather clutch he had been holding and removed a jeweler's eyepiece. He placed it over one eye and examined the stones. "Exquisite."

Ho watched as the adjuster examined the Buddha from head to toe. The man seemed competent, so he decided to ask him about the secret storage compartment. "I had a historian dig into it a little and he mentioned that some of these pieces contained an inner chamber."

"The part of Buddha where there is no ego," Truitt said quickly, "the void."

"Then you are familiar with the idea?" Ho said.

"Oh, yes," Truitt said. He was glad the Corporation had seen fit to provide him with a report on ancient Asian art. The "void" had been part of the study.

"I can't seem to find one on this piece."

"Let's look closer," Truitt said.

The two men spent the next twenty minutes carefully examining the object, but no secret compartment was found. Truitt decided to use the revelation to his favor.

"Shall we sit for a bit?" he asked Ho.

The men took seats around Ho's desk.

"What value do you have in mind," Truitt said, "that you would like our company to underwrite?"

"I was thinking in the neighborhood of two hundred million," Ho said.

"That's an expensive neighborhood," Truitt said, smiling.

Leaning forward, he spilled the contents of his leather clutch on the floor. Scooping down to pick up the contents, he attached a small bug to the bottom of Ho's desk.

"Silly me," he said after the bug was attached and the bag placed back on his lap.

"What do you think is the value?" Ho asked.

"The absence of the secret compartment actually adds to the rarity of the piece," Truitt lied. "It places the age at least a few decades before what I had estimated. The voids date from the twelfth century and later. You may have something here that defies accurate pricing."

Ho smiled his feral smile. He loved it when he bested someone in a deal, and he was beginning to think he'd outsmarted some of the wisest art collectors in the world. At first, the $200 million he'd paid had seemed like a king's ransom—now it was looking like he'd bought cheap.

"What are you saying?" he asked.

"I could easily insure it for twice what you are seeking," Truitt said, "but of course the premiums would reflect the increased value."

This was going better than Truitt could have hoped—greed had removed Ho's doubt in his identity. He had come a stranger, but now he was a friend bearing gifts. Cons only work when the mark wants to believe. Ho wanted to believe.

"But . . . ," Ho said slowly, "if I insured it for more, banks would loan on the increased value."

"Yes," Truitt said, "banks tend to follow our lead."

Ho nodded slowly. "Why don't you figure the premiums on four hundred million."

"I would, of course, need to contact our main office for the quotes," Truitt said, "but I can easily attest to the value."

Ho sat back in his chair. The realization that he owned a truly priceless work of art was sinking into his soul. Now his ego needed stroking. A stroking that only other rich people could give him.

"I'm having a party today," he said.

"I saw the preparations," Truitt said, smiling.

"You, of course, are invited," Ho said, "but I was thinking of displaying the artifact to my guests. I would feel more comfortable if I had a rider covering the piece until I receive the actual quote. Just something to cover today."

"You are, of course, thinking of displaying it downstairs," Truitt said.

Ho wasn't, but he was now.

"Yes," Ho said. "Perhaps out on the grounds?"

Truitt nodded. "Let me make a quick call."

Ho pointed to his telephone, but Truitt whipped out a cell phone and hit the speed dial.

"Samuelson here."

"Richard, you're a magnificent bastard," the voice said. "We have been listening for the last few minutes over the bug. Nice work."

"I need a quote on a one-day rider to Mr. Ho's policy to cover a piece of art valued at four hundred million until we can come up with an accurate figure for long-term coverage."

"La de dah, de dah. All right then," the operator on the *Oregon* said, "let me make up a number for you. How about twenty thousand dollars? Or whatever you decide. But I'd take the fee in cash if I was you. Then we can have a party after this is over."

"I see," Truitt said, nodding, "so we will require increased security. Hold on a minute."

Truitt placed his hand over the telephone.

Back on the *Oregon*, the operator turned to Hanley.

"Truitt's red-hot today," he said. "I had not even thought of that angle."

Ho was waiting for the adjuster to speak.

"The fee for the rider for the day will be eighteen thousand five hundred U.S. But my company is insisting on increased security. Luckily, we have a local firm we use—my office will contact them and have some men out here within the hour, if that's okay with you."

"Does the fee include the security detail?" Ho asked.

Truitt thought for a second, but decided not to push.

"The fee includes three security guards, but we will want the fee in cash," Truitt said seriously.

Ho stood up and walked over to his safe. "Sounds reasonable," he said.

Truitt smiled—the offer was anything but reasonable, but Ho had no way to know that.

"I'll tell them," Truitt said.

Ho began spinning the dial to his safe.

"We have an agreement," he said to the operator on the *Oregon*, "but we'll need the security people here as soon as possible."

"Damn, you're good," the operator said.

"Yes, I am," Truitt said quietly, then disconnected.

Ho returned with two wrapped stacks of dollars. Each strip read $10,000. Removing fifteen of the hundred-dollar bills from one of the stacks, he handed Truitt the rest. Sliding the stacks of money into his leather clutch, he smiled at Ho.

"Do you have a sheet of paper?"

"What for?" Ho asked.

"I need to write you a receipt," Truitt said.

HANLEY REACHED FOR the telephone and dialed Cabrillo. "Dick Truitt just got us three more men inside the compound, acting as security guards."

"Excellent," Cabrillo said, "and there was no problem with the appraisal?"

"He handled it like the pro he is," Hanley said.

"Have we got security guard uniforms in the Magic Shop?"

"Absolutely," Hanley said. "I'll just call Nixon and have him blast off a jazzy patch on the embroidery machine."

"Get on it," Cabrillo said quickly, "so we can extract Truitt."

"Truitt's been invited to the party," Hanley said, "unless you want me to order him out."

"Have him wait until the fake security team arrives," Cabrillo said. "That way he can verify their identity to Ho. Then have him stick around—I have another job for him."

"Done," Hanley said.

Cabrillo disconnected and Hanley dialed the Magic Shop.

"Kevin," he said, "I need three security guard uniforms with the appropriate badges."

"Name?"

Hanley thought for a moment before answering.

"Make them Redman Security Services."

"As in Redford and Newman?"

"You got it," Hanley said, *The Sting.*

"It will take me twenty minutes or so to make the badges," Nixon said, "but send the three operatives down right away. I can fit the uniforms while the patches are forming."

"They will be there shortly," Hanley said in closing.

Hanley glanced at a clipboard in the control room. Most of the Corporation stockholders were already assigned to functions of operations, extraction or backup. His remaining choices were an assistant chef, Rick Barrett; a propulsion engineer named Sam Pryor; and a middle-aged man who worked in the armory, Gunther Reinholt. None had ever worked on the operations end. But beggars can't be choosers.

"Get me Reinholt, Pryor and Barrett," Hanley said to one of the communications operators, "and have them meet me in the Magic Shop."

The operator began paging the men.

"DON'T WORRY," MURPHY said to Halpert, "it just smells like marijuana."

Murphy was waving what looked like an incense stick near the members of the band when Cabrillo walked into the conference room.

"Smells like a Grateful Dead concert in here," he said.

Murphy walked closer and let the smoke waft over the chairman.

"It's the little things," he said with a grin, "that makes the Corporation successful."

"The real band was sober," Cabrillo noted.

"But Ho doesn't know that."

Cabrillo nodded. "Listen up. Dick Truitt has managed to get three more operatives inside. The men will be dressed as security guards. I'll have the company name shortly. Be careful, because there might be other guards Ho already hired. Don't slip up and mistake ours for them."

Just then, Cabrillo's telephone rang. He listened then disconnected.

"Redman Security is the name on our guys' uniforms," he said to the group.

A moment later Julia Huxley walked into the room.

"Wow," Kasim said.

Huxley was dressed in a pair of form-fitting leather pants that laced up the side and showed two panels of leg from foot to hip. Her top was a metal-studded vest that barely covered her ample bosom. Around her neck was a strap of leather with a D-shaped hook, and one of her arms was decorated with a flowing tattoo of barbed wire and flower vines. Her hair was teased and coated with hair spray in a wild fashion and her makeup was bold and thickly applied. Five-inch pumps and a dusting of glitter on her exposed skin completed the picture.

"Slutty enough for you boys?" she asked.

"I didn't know the Magic Shop had such costumes in stock," Halpert said.

Huxley walked over to Halpert and rubbed herself along his side. As the lead singer, he, of course, was the one who got the girl.

"What do you mean?" she asked. "This is from my own collection."

Huxley was lying, of course—but then this entire operation was a façade.

"Now, who would argue," Kasim said, "that America's not the greatest country in the world?"

18

ROSS WAS CHECKING the smoke machines when Ho walked out onto the lawn.

"Miss Iselda," he said as he walked over, "I have a new piece of artwork I've decided I want to display out here on the lawn."

Ross watched Ho carefully. The man was gesturing toward one side of the tent. He looked back at her expectantly. There was no hint he found anything amiss.

"Is it a painting?" Ross asked.

"No, it's a statue," Ho said.

Two workers were waiting alongside the colored lights near the smoke machine.

"Take a break for a few moments," Ross said.

The men walked into the shade of the tent.

"Describe it to me," Ross asked.

"Six foot tall and made of gold," Ho said.

Ross quickly thought. "Perhaps we could place the object there"—
she pointed a few feet away—"at the end of the red carpet leading into
the tent. As sort of a sentinel."

Ho and Ross walked over to the spot.

"I could light it with blue and red spotlights," she said.

"What else?" Ho asked.

Ross racked her brain. What could help the Corporation with the
theft?

"What do you think about some billowing clouds of smoke," she
said slowly, "so the object seems to appear and disappear like a mirage?"

"Excellent," Ho said eagerly.

Ross smiled. Out of the corner of her eye she caught a glimpse of a
trio of men from the *Oregon*; they were dressed in security guards'
uniforms. Somehow her team had sent help. Barrett, acting as the leader
of the guards, walked over to where she and Ho were standing.

"Are you Mr. Ho?" he said.

"I'm Ho."

"The insurance company sent us."

Barrett placed a finger to his eye and winked at Ross when Ho was
not looking.

"Good," Ho said, "I'm glad you arrived so quickly. This is Iselda;
she's in charge of planning. We were just now figuring out the best place
to place the object you will be guarding."

Barrett nodded.

"We're thinking there," Ho said, pointing, "near the entrance to the
tent."

Barrett scanned the grounds as if to determine the security of the
spot. He turned back to Ho and spoke.

"My company mentioned it was a statue."

"Right," Ho said, "a six-foot-tall Buddha."

Barrett nodded as if he were weighing his options.

"Is it heavy?" he asked.

"It weighs about six hundred pounds," Ho said. "Why do you ask?"

"Well, sir," Barrett said, "I thought you might want it to be more of a part of the festivities—you know, have it moved from place to place as the party proceeds. Six hundred pounds is too heavy for my men to move, however."

Ross was catching on.

"You mean to have the statue become one of the guests," she said eagerly.

"Something like that," the guard admitted. "The object would actually be safer the more people that are around."

"Interesting," Ho said.

"The party's almost ready to start," Ross said, "but I could see if I could scrounge up some other Buddha statues and do an entire theme in that direction."

"What do you mean?" Ho asked.

"Maybe I could find some plaster Buddha statues and have them placed around the grounds," Ross said.

"That would help with security," Barrett admitted, "by confusing the real and the fakes."

"Do you think you can?" Ho asked.

"Don't worry, Mr. Ho," Ross said, "my company can work miracles."

T HE BAND WAS assembled in the conference room on the *Oregon*. Hanley and Cabrillo were walking them through their last-minute instructions.

"As you know, we have three more men inside," Cabrillo said, "posing as security, so we don't need to worry about getting it down to ground level. It should already be there."

"That's a plus," Franklin noted.

"So the actual removal from the site has become easier," Hanley said, "but we have the added problem of more witnesses."

"That means we almost certainly need to drug the guests," Kasim noted.

"It's beginning to look that way," Cabrillo admitted.

"The playlist features three sets," Hanley continued. "That gives us two breaks between sets when you, as members of the band, can move freely about. Watch the chairman for the lead and be flexible—this entire caper is still unfolding."

"Do we have the plane waiting to receive the icon after the theft?" Halpert asked.

"Arranged," Cabrillo said. "A plane is inbound as we speak."

"When's the extraction scheduled?" Monica asked.

"Ten minutes before midnight, tonight," Hanley said.

"The *Oregon* sails away from here sometime tomorrow," Cabrillo said, "no matter what the outcome. So let's just do our jobs and take our leave."

"A little richer for the effort," Murphy said, smiling.

"That's the idea," Cabrillo agreed.

THIN TENDRILS OF richly scented incense smoke wafted toward the ceiling in the A-Ma Temple.

A scattering of tourists filed through the public areas and left offerings at the foot of various Buddhas. They walked on the pebbled paths, sat on the carved wooden benches on the grounds and stared at the sea in reflection. It was a place of tranquillity; a port of serenity in a storm of confusion and haste.

Winston Spenser was not feeling calm.

Fear gripped him. The Golden Buddha was laughing at him—of that he was sure. The calm gaze and unmoving solidness made him uneasy. Spenser dreamed of when he would be rid of the curse and collect his money. He could see it in his mind. The armored-car company picking up the icon again and delivering it to the software billionaire's plane. The crates of money he would receive.

He rose from the bench in the main temple, then walked out the door and down the hillside to his waiting limousine. The parking lot was half empty. Most of the people in Macau were preparing for the parade and tonight's parties. A pair of motorcycles sat off to one side under a tree. Spenser didn't notice them—he was wrapped up in his own certain failure. Climbing in the rear of the limousine, he gave the driver directions. A few moments later the limousine rolled out of the lot.

"I've seen what I need to see," one of the motorcyclists said.

"I agree," said the other.

S IX CHINESE VALETS awaited the first of the guests. After showing their invitations to the guard, they pulled through the gate, drove up the circular drive, then climbed from their cars near the front door of the mansion.

The sun was slowly dipping in the west and the view from the mansion was an expanse of sea lit with the golden hues of a waning sun. Spenser climbed from the rear of his limousine and stared at the scene. He was dressed in a black tuxedo that hid the pools of sweat under his arms. Squaring his shoulders, he walked into the foyer.

Juan Cabrillo rolled down the window of the van and handed the guard a slip of paper.

"Park over by the garages," the guard said, "then unload your equipment and wheel it around back."

Cabrillo nodded. When the gate opened, he drove around to the garages, then backed the van up near the edge of the lawn.

"Showtime," he said.

And the band climbed from the van and began shuttling equipment to the rear of the house.

Cabrillo walked around to the rear of the house, seeking Ross. He saw her in the distance talking on a cell phone. Several people were standing nearby.

"We're The Minutemen," he said when she had disconnected.

"Good," Ross said. "The bandstand is over there."

"We have some large speakers," Cabrillo said, "that we'll need some help moving."

"Let me summon some help."

"We like to take care of our equipment ourselves," Cabrillo said. "We just need some carts."

Ross nodded and turned to one of the caterers.

"This is the leader of the band," she said. "He needs to borrow a few of the carts you use to move the tables."

The man nodded and motioned to Cabrillo. "Right this way."

Mark Murphy stood on the bandstand and surveyed the surroundings. Three large tents were erected, forming a Y with the band at the far end. The bandstand was slightly elevated from the ground, and to the rear the back of the tent had slits that opened to provide access. Electrical cables to power their speakers and lights stretched out under the tent. He sat his guitar down and poked through the slit in the back. Forty feet behind the rear of the tent was part of the wall that formed the boundary of the house. To the right side of the Y portion of the tent, some thirty yards away, was the rear wall of the mansion and the doors leading to the kitchens and inside. He began to walk the perimeter of the tent.

At the front, or top, of the Y were the entrances for the guests. In the opening between the legs of the Y there was a portable fountain and a small wooden platform that was currently empty. Murphy continued around the other side, examining the way the tents were fastened to the ground. There were large metal stakes on the edges with guy wires running farther out onto the lawn, where they were staked into the earth. He stared up. Long metal poles, two per each section of the three separate tents, poked through the tops. He found a slit in the tent and walked over to one of the poles. The bases sat on plastic holders.

Murphy figured it wouldn't take much to bring it all down.

Ho was making his way back to the mansion when he stopped in his tracks.

Several longhaired men were approaching the tent, but that didn't concern him. What did concern him was the lady that was following. Ho pivoted on his heel and walked over.

"I'm Stanley Ho," he said, smiling. "I'm your host."

"I'm Candace," Julia Huxley said.

Ho's eyes were riveted on Huxley's ample assets. "I find this hard to believe," Ho said, "but I don't remember meeting you before."

"I'm with the band," Candace said, smiling wickedly. "At least I came with them."

"Performer?" Ho asked.

"In many ways," Candace said, smiling.

Ho was beginning to get the feeling that if he played his cards right, he might get lucky.

"I need to go inside and greet my guests," Ho said quickly as he saw Iselda approaching from the corner of his eye. "Perhaps we could talk later."

He turned and moved toward the back door of the mansion.

"Mr. Ho," Ross shouted after him, "I think we have the placement figured out."

"Just take care of it," Ho said over his shoulder.

Ross passed by Huxley. "Slut," she whispered.

"Lesbian," Huxley replied.

MAX HANLEY WAS sitting in a leather chair in the command center of the *Oregon*.

"Okay, people," he said to the trio of operators that remained, "we're a go. Display from the tree," Hanley ordered.

The image from the tiny camera in the tree filled one of the screens in the control room. Hanley could see Cabrillo rolling a cart containing several long speaker boxes across the lawn. Ross had just passed Huxley and was now turning to go back toward the tent. Murphy popped out from the side of one of the tents. As if on cue, he turned to the tree and smiled.

"Larry," Hanley said, "all okay."

Larry King was the Corporation member hiding in the tree. He adjusted his sniper rifle and then pushed the tiny microphone over his voice box and answered.

"How's the picture, boss?"

"Looks good," Hanley said. "You holding up?"

King had been forced to take his position above the party sometime just after 3 A.M. He'd been in his perch over twelve hours already. There was a good chance he'd need to remain there almost that long again.

"I did six days once in Indonesia," King said. "This is a piece of cake."

"Have you dialed in your fields of fire?" Hanley asked, already knowing the answer.

"About a thousand times, boss," King said, swatting away a fly on his arm.

King was a U.S. Army–trained sniper. If Hanley gave the order, he could lob a dozen shots onto the grounds in about as long as it took to sneeze. Hanley hoped it wouldn't come down to that—but if one of the crew was in trouble and there was no other choice, King was the great equalizer.

"Stand by, Larry," Hanley said. "We'll call you if we need you."

"Affirmative," King said as he continued to scan the grounds through his scope.

"Try the inside of the tent," Hanley ordered.

An image filled the screen from a camera that was inserted in the body of Cabrillo's electric keyboard. The image was slightly off.

"Juan," Hanley said.

Cabrillo was pushing the cart around the side of the tent, but he could hear through his tiny earpiece.

"You'll need to adjust your keyboard slightly to the right. We're missing a little of the left side of the tent."

Cabrillo made a slight nod to confirm.

"Go to the van," Hanley ordered.

Another picture flicked onto a separate screen that was split in half. The cameras had been attached to the van's folding mirrors. They were showing a pretty good view of most of the front of the house. Lincoln was removing a box from the back of the van.

"Frankie," Hanley said.

Franklin Lincoln moved out of the back of the van and stared into one of the rearview mirrors as if he were fixing his hair.

"Try to leave the van where it is," Hanley said. "You guys got lucky and placed it where we have a good field of view."

Lincoln made an okay sign at the mirror.

"Okay, men," Hanley said to the operators, "we're the eyes and ears, so be alert."

19

WINSTON SPENSER WALKED into the mansion, snagged a glass of champagne from a passing waiter, and slurped down half of the flute before approaching the receiving line. Stanley Ho was beaming and shaking hands with each guest that passed. Ahead of Spenser were an Australian couple who were just being greeted, and directly in front of him was the local Portuguese consular agent. Spenser waited patiently, finishing the first glass of champagne and summoning the waiter for another, then took his place in front of Ho.

"Winston," Ho said, smiling, "it's good to see you, but you're a little late—the insurance adjuster was already here."

"Sorry," Spenser said, "I was running late."

Spenser tried to keep moving along, but Ho reached out and took him by the arm.

"That's all right," Ho said. "It seems your timing is perfect."

Ho pointed to the staircase.

Spenser's stomach did a backflip. The Golden Buddha, strapped to a dolly like a patient in a mental ward, was descending the stairs, being helped down by the guards from Redman Security.

"I've decided to display my newest treasure," Ho said, "so all the guests can share in the glory. Don't worry, I'll let everyone who asks know who helped me handle the acquisition."

A thousand thoughts raced through Spenser's mind. None of them were good.

"Sir . . . ," Spenser began to say. But the line was moving along and Ho was already preparing to greet the next guest. "I don't think . . ."

"I'll talk to you when we are outside," Ho said quietly as he turned to shake a couple's hands.

"A T THE REAR door," Hanley said, pointing to a screen. He flipped a switch on the communication console, then spoke into a microphone.

"Juan, the Buddha is being wheeled outside."

On one of the screens, Cabrillo could be seen inside the tent checking the connection to his keyboard. He raised his head and made a signal that he understood. Ross walked over to the front of the tents as the Buddha was wheeled up, then supervised the placement near the fountain.

The target of all the planning and preparation was now in plain sight.

C HIEF INSPECTOR OF the Macau Constabulary Sung Rhee watched the statue from his place on the lawn near the rear door of the mansion. Rhee had known Stanley Ho since before he'd become wealthy. He was an acquaintance, not a friend. The first ship Ho had owned, the start of his shipping fortune, had been a constant thorn in Rhee's side.

The chief inspector had been a mere detective at that time, assigned to vice and smuggling, and he had become convinced Ho was moving drugs with the ship. Rhee had just never been able to catch him in the act. Ho's fortune had grown fast, and the chief inspector knew what that usually denoted—the problem was that as the shipowner's fortune had swelled, so had his power. Twice in the past decade Rhee had been ordered away from Ho's activities when he was close to amassing enough evidence to bring charges. Now Rhee was beginning to understand that as Ho legitimized his holdings, he probably never would pay the price for his past shady dealings.

Rhee had been invited to the party in an unofficial capacity—window dressing for the guests.

Like the mayor, the ambassadors of various countries, and the minor royalty who were present, Rhee was here today to add to the theme of legitimacy Ho so desperately craved.

He was a prop—but that didn't make the police officer inside him take leave. He stared at the chunk of gold and tried to decide how, if it was up to him, he would steal it. Rhee stared around the grounds, trying to imagine an escape route. The wall surrounding the grounds almost insisted on a departure through the main gate. The fact that the object was being placed out in the open actually helped the security. It would almost certainly always be in view of someone. He glanced around again, then shook his head slightly.

Rhee concluded theft was not a problem and went inside for some shrimp puffs.

A DARK GREEN Mercedes-Benz limousine pulled up to the gate and the driver was waved through. Tom Reyes, the driver, swung around on the circular driveway and positioned the passenger door near the front door of the mansion. He then climbed out and opened the door to the rear compartment and helped the occupant out.

Once Crabtree was standing alongside the limousine, Reyes raced to the front door and said to the butler, "This is Princess Aalborg of Denmark."

The butler stood aside as she swept into the foyer in a rustle of satin and lace, then walked toward Ho, who was now standing alone.

"Princess Aalborg," Reyes announced from two steps behind.

Ho bent over and lightly kissed the proffered hand, then raised his head and smiled. "I'm honored to have you visit my humble home."

"Charmed," Monica Crabtree said in a bizarre accent.

Ho snapped his fingers and a waiter instantly appeared. "May I offer you a libation?"

"Champagne with a strawberry would be nice," Crabtree said.

Ho motioned to the waiter, who scurried off.

"Jeeves," Crabtree said to the driver, "I'll be fine now—you may take your leave."

Reyes backed away a distance, then turned and walked toward the front door. Moving the limousine away from the front of the mansion, Reyes parked in a spot near the garage and climbed out. Then he walked around to the front of the limousine, tilted back his cap and lit a cigarette.

"Monica is safely inside," Hanley reported to Cabrillo.

TWILIGHT FELL OVER the grounds with a light breeze that brought the smell of the sea. A few miles away, at the staging area for the parade, the engines of the lead floats came to life. The marching band that was the first group to walk the route began to assemble in orderly rows, awaiting the signal to begin. Macau began to settle in for the night, and in the high-rises in the city center and along the waterfront, lights began to flicker on. Out to sea, the navigation lights of the ships approaching port began to be visible, and the scattering of airplanes both inbound and outbound appeared as light specks in the distant sky.

All of the guests had arrived and the front lawn of the mansion looked like a luxury car dealership. There were Jaguars and BMWs, a single Lamborghini, a pair of Ferraris. Twelve limousines, a lone armored Humvee and an old Rolls-Royce crowded the lawn. On the wall along the road, the security cameras swept back and forth, but no more cars approached and the guard tired of watching the monitor.

So no one noticed when a pair of motorcycles drove slowly past.

If someone had, and they were knowledgeable, they might have noticed that one of the motorcycle's sidecars had been enlarged and reinforced. The modifications were barely perceptible, but if you looked closely, you could see that there was a heavy-duty training wheel underneath, and that the passenger seat had been removed and made into a cargo compartment. The motorcycles continued north to the stop sign, then turned left and headed in the direction of the Inner Port. The bikers had an appointment to keep in a place not too far distant.

T HE BAND WAS performing a sound check. The wall of speakers behind the bandstand lent an air of full-on rock concert, but the actual sound coming out of them was less than one would have thought. Unless someone was standing directly in front of the speaker wall, he'd have no way to tell that many of the speakers were not functioning. Some were hollow shells, others held items that would be needed for the operation.

Ross walked over and spoke to Cabrillo.

"The first set starts at seven," she said. "Are you ready?"

Cabrillo stared at the players, then at the crowd that was still milling about the tent, some seated, more still flitting from table to table. "I'll put the background music on in a second. That should signal we're about to begin."

He walked over to the main console and adjusted a switch. At the sound of the music, the crowd began to make their way to their assigned seats. Stanley Ho was standing just inside one of the tents on the left side of the Y. He was attempting to regale Huxley with stories of his vast wealth and power.

"I love the Buddha," Huxley said, smiling. "Perhaps you have some other artwork you could show me later."

"I'd be glad to," Ho said. "In fact, there are many pieces in my upper office that might interest you. Maybe we could slip away later and take a look."

"I'd like that," Huxley said.

Ho nodded greedily. He was already imagining the possibilities the suicide blonde might offer his libido—if he needed to ignore his guests for the opportunity, so be it.

"I need to go to the front and make my introductions now," Ho said, "but we can meet later."

Huxley smiled and slinked away. Ho walked through the crowd, stopping at various tables to glad-hand his guests. A few minutes later, he was standing in front of the bandstand.

"I'm Stanley Ho," he said to Halpert. "Might I use your microphone to make an introduction?"

Halpert handed his microphone to Ho, who tapped the top to be sure it was working.

"Ladies and gentlemen," he said.

The crowd quieted down.

"I'd like to welcome you to my Good Friday party."

The crowd clapped.

"I hope that you are finding the food and drink to your liking."

Another round of applause.

"I hope each of you has a chance to view my latest acquisition, a good-luck charm. I have displayed the piece at the entrance to the tent. Like another we honor tonight, he signifies enlightenment and spirituality and that is the theme of this evening's festivities. Now, if we could take a second to remember those that have sacrificed themselves for our freedoms."

The crowd was silent.

"Thank you," Ho said a few moments later. "We will have fireworks and light displays tonight, as well as an excellent band straight from California in the United States. Please join me in welcoming the Minutemen."

He handed the microphone back to Halpert. At the same time, the lights in the tent began to dim until a single spotlight illuminated Halpert's back, which was turned from the crowd. The band keyed their instruments and the opening notes of the Eagles song "Already Gone" began pulsing through the crowd.

Halpert swung around and began to belt out the lyrics.

M ORE THAN ANY one thing, the key to a successful robbery is stealth. The pair of men on the motorcycles knew this and they moved quietly through the A-Ma Temple toward their target. The tourists had gone home for the night and most of the monks were in the dining hall partaking of their simple evening meal. The side room where their target stood was dimly lit, and the men, who were dressed in black clothes and face masks, blended into the air like whispery goblins.

"There he is," one man whispered.

The man was pushing a heavy-duty dolly stolen from a rental store the previous night. He wheeled it over, examined the artifact, then waited while his partner closed the door on the wooden crate and tilted it so the other man could slide the dolly underneath. After securing it with straps, they began to make their way toward the door.

W INSTON SPENSER WAS past wine and into cognac. He was pleasantly buzzed and beginning to feel that he might just accomplish his goal. He glanced at his watch. He had some time before he needed to slip away and meet the armored-car company at the temple. Then he would make his way to the airport and consummate the sale with the software billionaire.

By first light, he'd be on his way away from here, then he'd take a break from all the drinking.

Finishing the snifter, he motioned to a passing waiter for a refill. Then he turned to one of the guests seated next to him.

"Excellent band."

"They truly are," Crabtree replied.

T WO HUNDRED AND twenty-seven miles from Macau, in the South China Sea, the burgundy jet was passing over Tungsha Island, inbound for landing. The software billionaire walked forward, fastening a sash around his black silk kimono.

"The ladies are tired," he said with a barely hidden trace of pride. "Could you prepare pitchers of coffee, orange juice and some pastries and take them to the rear?"

"Immediately," the blond-haired man said, leaping to his feet.

Continuing forward, the billionaire knocked on the cockpit door.

The copilot opened the door. "Sir?" he asked.

"How far out are we?"

"Less than half an hour," the copilot said, glancing at his navigational chart.

"Have you arranged for refueling?"

"All taken care of, sir," the pilot said, turning his head toward the cockpit door.

Passing through the galley, the billionaire could smell the coffee brewing. "About a half hour and we'll be on the ground," he said as he passed.

The blond-haired man waited until he was gone, then removed a digital pager from his belt and pushed a few buttons. Then he winked at the other flight attendant and resumed his preparations.

T HE TRIO OF Redman Security officers glanced up as the band was finishing the last song in the first set. Then Sam Pryor turned toward a camera and touched his nose.

Back on the *Oregon*, Max Hanley reached for a microphone.

"Julia," he said, "you can start now."

Huxley slipped from behind the speaker wall and motioned to Halpert. Cabrillo, Lincoln and Murphy began to remove a few speakers from the bank behind them. Ho walked over.

"You have two more sets," he said.

"We have some electrical glitches," Cabrillo told him. "Three of the tower speakers aren't working. Don't worry—they haven't worked yet and we sound all right."

"Do you want me to take them back to the truck?" Huxley asked.

"That's part of your job," Halpert said.

Ho stared at Huxley. The thought of his suicide blonde becoming sweaty disturbed him.

"I'll have one of the guards give you a hand," Ho said. "Miss Candace asked earlier if she might have a tour of my home."

"Okay, Mr. Ho," Cabrillo said. "We'll move them around to the front of the tent, then have one of the guards help us put them in the van."

"Whatever," Ho said. "Now, Candy—may I show you my home?"

R OSS MOTIONED TO the caterer. "Before the second set, Mr. Ho wants to make a special toast."

"The passion fruit punch?" the caterer said.

"Correct," Ross said.

"Just before the main meal is served?"

"That's the plan."

"I'll go ahead and ice down the punch then," the caterer said.

"You look busy here," Ross said, "I'll take care of the punch."

When the chef had his back turned, Ross removed the flask of liquid and broke the seal. The viscous fluid was a strange blue green with flecks of what looked like powdered silver. She swirled it around then poured it into the vat. Taking a wooden spoon, she stirred the mixture and added a block of ice.

The caterer was on the far end of the kitchen, talking to the chef. Ross called across the room.

"Have the punch transferred to the crystal pitchers and taken into the tent," she said. "Then order the waiters to begin serving."

The caterer waved a hand in reply and Ross walked back outside.

"SIGNAL FROM ROSS," Larry King said. On board the *Oregon*, Hanley was watching the monitors. "We saw it too, Larry."

Hanley zoomed in on the Buddha; Reinholt, Pryor and Barrett were standing in a delta formation around the object, while to the left three large speaker stacks sat on carts awaiting removal.

"As soon as Ho makes his toast and the band resumes, we can begin the extraction," Hanley said. "Did anyone see where Ho went?"

"He headed inside with Huxley," King noted.

"I've got him on audio in the upper office," one of the operators on the *Oregon* said.

"Put him on speaker," Hanley ordered.

"It's a Manet," Ho was saying.

"I always get Monet and Manet confused," Huxley said. "But then, art is not my strong suit."

"What exactly *is* your strong suit?" Ho asked.

Just then, Hanley keyed the tiny earpiece in Huxley's ear. "Julia," he whispered, "you need to have Ho get back to the tent and make the toast now."

"It's something I need to show you, not tell you," Candace purred, "but it takes some time. Once the band starts the next set and my boyfriend is busy, I'd feel a lot safer."

"Safer is good," Ho said.

Huxley walked over to Ho and rubbed her ample assets against his side.

"I'll quickly go make the toast," he said with a growing need.

"I need to make an appearance, too," Huxley said, "then we'll have plenty of time."

Ho motioned to the door and the pair started out of the office.

INSIDE THE TENT, the waiters were clearing away the appetizers. Then they began to pour the punch from crystal pitchers into small glass cups at each setting. Most of the guests had returned to their seats by the time Ho walked through the center of the tent toward the stage. Snagging a cup of punch from a passing waiter, he continued toward the stage.

Mark Murphy was setting the last of the charges around the perimeter of the grounds and tent. He pocketed a small remote trigger, then walked around to the rear of the stage. Juan Cabrillo was standing off to one side of the stage, staring at the crowd. Crabtree had her large purse on the floor next to her and she moved her foot to make sure it was at her feet. Kasim, Lincoln and Halpert stood off to one side, awaiting their cues. At the front of the tent, the trio from Redman Security paced nervously.

Ho walked over to Cabrillo. "Is the P.A. system on?"

"Just a second," Cabrillo said as he flicked a switch. "Okay, sir."

Ho tapped the microphone to see that it was working.

THE MONK WALKED out from the dining room, then stopped in his tracks. There was a banner with Arabic writing stretched across the alcove where the Golden Buddha had been placed—but the massive golden icon was nowhere to be seen. He raced back to the dining room to alert the others. A dozen monks in yellow robes entered the main temple. After appraising the situation, the head of the monks walked into the office and lifted up the telephone.

"Why don't they make dollies with brakes?" one of the motorcyclists said as he dug in his heels to slow the descent down the hill outside the temple.

The other man was in front of the dolly, trying to slow Buddha down, but the loose soil was not allowing him much purchase and he was sliding downhill fast.

"Drop it down and dig in the rear," he whispered.

With more of a slide than a controlled descent, they reached the bottom of the hill. Once they had regained control of the dolly, they quickly wheeled it over to the motorcycle sidecar and cut the straps. The man at the front lowered the door on the sidecar.

"Let's get him in," he said.

At just that instant, a gong on the grounds of the temple started sounding.

"Damn," the first man said as the two wrestled the chunk of metal into the sidecar, "I figured we'd at least be out of the parking lot before someone caught on."

"I'll strap him down," the second man said. "You start your engine."

The man climbed aboard the motorcycle and pushed the starter. The engine roared to life. The second man finished with securing the Buddha and walked over to his motorcycle and started the engine. Looking up the hill, he caught a glimpse of several monks starting down, and he beeped his horn. The first man turned his head and, upon seeing the monks stumbling down the hill, reached for the clutch, then toed the motorcycle into gear. He twisted the throttle and began driving out of the parking lot.

"AGAIN," HO SAID, "thank you all for coming. Before I make a toast, let's give a round of applause to the Minutemen."

The crowd clapped.

"Now," Ho said, "if you will all raise your glasses."

He paused.

"To peace and prosperity on this holy day," he said. "Let us all remember the sacrifices the few have made so that the many may find peace."

Ho tipped the glass cup to his lips and took a drink. The crowd followed suit.

"The dinner will be served now," Ho said, "and in a second the band will begin again."

"T HE POTION IS in," Hanley said to everyone listening, "we move in five minutes."

Sometimes, if you know where to look, a person can realize that life is a well-orchestrated ballet. If one is in tune, seemingly unrelated events begin to reveal themselves. If there were someone high above the party, what he would see right now would be two distinctly different groups. The people from the Corporation began to move like pieces on a chessboard, while those who were part of the party seemed to act as a single unit.

Sung Rhee tried to focus his eyes, but the view of the inside of the tent was ebbing and flowing. Specks of blue dotted the far edges of his peripheral vision. Then he saw what he thought was a yellow-and-red weasel out of the corner of his eye, but when he moved his head, it was gone. At just that instant, his cellular telephone rang.

"Rhee."

"I can barely hear you, sir," one of his detectives said.

Rhee stared at the tiny telephone. He was holding it a foot from his mouth, as if unable to gauge distances. He tried to move it to the proper place, but he slammed it into his temple.

"How's that?" he asked.

"Better. Sir, we just received a call from the head abbot at the

A-Ma Temple. They report that a pair of men has just stolen a large golden Buddha they had on display."

Rhee thought for a second. The Buddha was right outside the tent.

"That's all right," Rhee said, "I saw our friend earlier."

"What are you talking about, sir?"

Rhee stared at the floral arrangement in the center of the table. The head of a tiny horse appeared and spoke in a British accent. *Take me for a ride*, it said.

"Listen, you," Rhee said, "my horse is here."

"Sir," the detective said, "I'm coming over there right away."

Rhee dropped the telephone and turned to the person next to him. "See my horse?"

The person was a troll and he was speaking in a language Rhee could not understand.

O VER THE ROAR of the motorcycle engine, a siren came from just over the hill. The two men shut off the engines and listened. The sound neither grew louder nor diminished.

"Good," the first man said, "they're stuck in traffic, just like we planned."

"Let's do it," the second man said.

They started their engines and roared away.

D ETECTIVE LING PO was screaming into the radio as he raced toward the mansion. He was a half mile away when the traffic ground to a stop.

"Can anyone reach the temple?" he shouted.

The units reported in one at a time. Only the car along the Inner Port Road was making any progress.

"We have a pair of men on motorcycles that have stolen a large gold Buddha," he said as he beeped his horn. "Has anyone seen them pass?"

The reports were negative.

Po steered his squad car onto the sidewalk and, blaring his horn, continued on.

THE BAND WAS performing the Thin Lizzie song "The Boys Are Back in Town."

On the *Oregon*, Hanley was watching the monitors in alarm. They had expected some unusual behavior once the potion was administered, but what he was seeing was chaos. A crowd of guests in tuxedos and evening dresses had suddenly filled the dance floor, and several of the ladies were shedding their clothes.

Stanley Ho was walking through the tent in a daze. He was feeling strange, but he had no idea why. Spotting Candace across the tent, he began to make his way toward her.

"Okay, everyone, we go in sixty seconds," Hanley ordered.

"I hear sirens," King reported, "and they are growing closer."

"Monica," Hanley said, "are you hearing?"

Crabtree turned to where she knew the camera was in the keyboard and winked.

"Now," Hanley said.

Crabtree bit down on a packet she had taken from her purse and slipped it inside her mouth. Ho was a few feet away and she stumbled toward him with foam seeping from the edges of her mouth. She grabbed him around his neck and held tight.

"Go ahead, Murph," Hanley ordered.

Murphy slipped his hand inside his pocket and hit the trigger. Almost instantly there was a series of explosions like fireworks. The outside lights and those inside the tent went dark.

"We're a go for switch," Hanley said.

At exactly that instant, Barrett and Pryor slid one of the speaker boxes off the cart and opened a back door. A gold-painted plaster Buddha replica slipped onto the ground. At the same time, Reinholt flipped the edge of the tent over the Buddha on display. Several potted plants placed in the Y inside the tent shielded the guards from anyone who might be watching.

"All dark on the western front," King said as he scanned the ground through the pale green light of a night scope.

"Anyone moving?" Hanley asked.

King swept across the grounds, then down the hillside.

"There's an unmarked police car with a portable light on the roof proceeding along Avenida Republica. He's three hundred and fifty yards distant."

"Can you hit at that distance?" Hanley asked.

"Oh ye of little faith," King said. "It's a car, not a bug. I doubt I can hit the driver's nose, but you never know."

"Just a tire, Larry," Hanley said.

"Hold on," King said.

Supporting the rifle on a branch, he regulated his breathing, then waited until the police car was in his field of fire. He was in an almost Zen state of concentration. When the target appeared, it was as if it were in slow motion. King squeezed the trigger, then willed the bullet to run true. Inside the rifle, the firing pin hit the shell primer and sparked, the gunpowder burned and propelled the shell out of the cartridge and sent it spinning through the rifling inside the barrel. Leaving the end of the barrel and passing through the noise suppressor, the slug started down the hill in a straight line toward the target.

"Shit," Po said as his front tire shredded. He slowed down and climbed out of the squad car, leaving the door open. Looking back onto the sidewalk, he tried to see what he had hit. There was nothing visible, but that didn't mean anything. He stared up the hill to his intended destination, then decided the hill was too steep to climb. Po slid back into the driver's seat and reached for the radio.

"Target has stopped and he's calling for help," King said.

"Good job," Hanley said.

Hanley was watching the monitors, but without lights there was little to see. He stared at his watch, then glanced at the schedule of actions. Thirty seconds passed. King continued to scan the grounds. A few of the kitchen workers had popped out from inside and were clustered around the rear door. He swiveled his scope to the front of the house and noticed that the front gate to the driveway had opened automatically when the power was cut. Ten seconds.

"Have you sighted the charge on the fireworks display?" Hanley asked.

"Got it," King said.

"Protect your eyes after the shot," Hanley said.

"I'll switch back to regular sights," King agreed.

"We go in five, four, three, two, one."

King squeezed the trigger and hit the explosive packet Murphy had laid in place hours earlier. The fireworks exploded with a roar. Roman candles streaked skyward and the large mortarlike devices began to spew forth in belches. There was shrieking and thumping sounds as the fireworks began to discharge. King rubbed his eyes and stared at the now-lit-up scene.

Three flickers from a flashlight at the front of the tent caught his attention.

"I have a signal the switch has been made," King noted.

"Signal the helicopter," Hanley said to one of the operators.

"She's having a seizure," Ho shouted.

Monica Crabtree hung on to Ho's neck and rolled her eyes back in her head. A doctor Ho knew was dancing on one of the tables nearby, but he didn't respond to Ho's request to come over. At just that instant, Barrett walked over.

"This woman is sick," Ho said.

The guard grabbed Crabtree and slid her to the ground. The inside of the tent was chaos, the music was blaring, but in the dim light no one noticed the band had left the stage. Ho's head was spinning and he was having trouble concentrating. The guard placed his lips over Crabtree's.

"No tongue, please," Crabtree whispered.

Faking CPR, the guard turned to Ho. "This woman is dying."

"Call for help," Ho said.

The guard reached for the radio on his belt and called for an ambulance.

"Juan," Hanley said, "the bird is inbound."

"Time to pull out," Cabrillo said to his team. "Round everyone up."

Reinholt and Pryor were rolling the cart containing the false-bottomed speakers over the lawn to the far side of the heliport. Once the cart was positioned, they removed green light bars from their pockets and bent them in half. The chemical reaction made the tubes glow and they spread them in a crude circle so the helicopter pilot would know where to land.

The scene inside the tent was absolutely chaotic. People were singing, howling, dancing and prancing. Sung Rhee was groping a woman at his table, the mayor of Macau was drinking the water out of the table arrangement.

Only Winston Spenser seemed composed. When his stomach was upset, he was sensitive to fruit juice. He had faked the toast and was beginning to see something was terribly wrong. Right then, he felt a prick on his neck. A second later, his head slumped over on the table.

T HE TRAFFIC OPENED up for a second and the police car racing along the Inner Port Road managed to make some headway. In the distance, the officer managed to glimpse the motorcycles making a turn onto Calcada da Barra. Pushing the gas pedal to the floor, he raced after the retreating pair of motorcycles.

"I have them in sight," he shouted over the radio. "They're northwest on Calcada."

The man aboard the motorcycle carrying the Buddha glanced in his rearview mirror and saw the police car approaching. He waved his hand in the air and the second motorcyclist turned his head. Dropping back a little, he waited until the police car was right behind him. Then he reached over and tripped a lever on his sidecar.

20

S TANLEY HO'S METICULOUSLY planned party had deteriorated into a bacchanalia.

Juan Cabrillo walked over to where Ho was standing next to the prone Crabtree. Ho was in a daze. There were so many things happening, his drug-addled brain could not comprehend them all. A few moments ago, the lesbian party planner had come to him and said that she could not figure out how to restore the lights inside the tent and offered to have some workers raise some of the side panels to allow the scant natural moonlight to filter inside. It was now a little brighter inside the tent, but many of the guests had started wandering outside onto the lawn.

"Sir," the security guard said, "the roads are choked with traffic and the ambulances can't get through. They recommended an air evacuation."

Ho stared down. A minor member of a royal family expiring at his party would definitely put a crimp in his social aspirations.

"Do it," Ho said through the fog in his brain.

"I already did," the guard admitted, "but we have another problem."

That was all Ho needed.

"What is it?"

"There's another guest slumped over," the guard said, pointing toward Spenser.

"Have him taken out, too," Ho said.

Juan Cabrillo spoke. "Mr. Ho. Some of my band is feeling queasy. We indulged in some of the appetizers and I think something was bad. I'd recommend we end this party and have the guests seek medical attention immediately."

The entire affair was collapsing before Ho's eyes.

"The band wants to leave," Cabrillo said. "We're going to pull our van around to the rear and load up our equipment."

"I need the P.A. system to make an announcement," Ho said.

"We already broke it down," Cabrillo told him, "but we have a portable megaphone we can let you use. I'll go get it from the van."

Ho turned to the security guard. "Who is watching the Buddha?"

"The other two guards," he said. "I'd recommend we place it back inside."

"Take it to my office," Ho ordered.

The sound of an approaching helicopter grew louder.

The guard reached for his walkie-talkie and ordered the Buddha to be moved upstairs. Then he reached down and lifted Crabtree and cradled her in his arms. He started walking out of the tent toward the landing zone. Cabrillo raced across the grounds to the van. Once inside, he adjusted the outside mirror and stared into the camera.

"We're collecting the props," he said as he twisted the key and started the engine.

﹡   ﹡   ﹡

ON THE *OREGON*, Max Hanley was watching the unfolding scene with amazement.

The two distinct groups were obvious. The Corporation members were moving about in a blur of motion and action, while the rest of the party seemed caught in a haze of indecision and disbelief. The element of chaos in the surroundings was complete. It was almost time to stoke the fires of escape.

"Murph, Lincoln, Halpert," Hanley said, "Juan's coming around with the van. Load up fast and make your way to the front of the mansion."

He saw the waves of acknowledgment.

"Ross, dispose of the punch and the doctored appetizers left on the tables."

"Larry," Hanley asked, "what do you see?"

"The policeman is leaning against the front of his car, waiting for help. I think we can count him out for now. One of the guards has just left the tent, carrying Monica. He's making his way to extraction point one." King scanned the grounds with the scope. "Two of the guards are wheeling the faux Buddha toward the rear door as I speak."

"Good," Hanley said, "everything is in play. You can make your egress anytime you deem fit. If you make your way along the wall and wait by the street, I'll have Juan slow the van down as he passes."

"Understand," King said.

He began to break down the rifle and fit it into its case. Once that was done, he climbed down to the edge of the wall and began to make his way west.

"Who haven't we used?" Hanley asked one of the operators, who stared quickly at the list of participants.

"Truitt," the operator replied.

"Where's Julia?"

"Last we saw her, she was going back inside the tent," the operator said. "But since the chairman broke down the keyboard set, we've lost the camera inside."

"Dick," Hanley said, "if you can hear me, signal someone in our team."

Cabrillo pulled the van to the rear of the tent. It had been slow going with all the people wandering the grounds. He slid the van into Park and opened the door. Truitt appeared at the rear of the tent and motioned to the camera in the van's mirror.

"Dick, I need you to find Julia," Hanley said. "She immobilized the art dealer. Carry him to the landing zone, then I want the two of you to exit via Crabtree's limousine."

Truitt gave the camera a thumbs-up and raced away.

The members of the team were tossing the remaining speakers and electronics into the rear of the van. Out over Nam Van Lakes, the landing lights of the helicopter were visible and growing brighter. The thumping of the rotor blades increased as the helicopter drew near.

Inside the tent it was pandemonium. Truitt found Huxley talking to Ho, who seemed unable to move from where he stood. Too much was happening, his brain could not put it all into place.

"The megaphone," he said in a daze. "I have to warn the guests."

"Who has it?" Truitt asked Ho.

"The band," Ho said. "The band said they had one."

"I just saw them at the rear of the tent," Truitt said. "You should go there."

Ho raced off.

Truitt reached over and whispered in Huxley's ear, "Where's the art dealer?"

Huxley led him over, and she and Truitt carried Spenser out onto the grounds.

The helicopter pilot slowed his forward speed and initiated a hover. The Eurocopter EC-350 that the Corporation had leased was a sweet machine—it hung in the air with little input from the controls. Reaching to the radio on the control panel, the pilot changed the radio frequency.

"I'm waiting," he said to the *Oregon.*

"What do you see?" Hanley asked.

The pilot flicked on his landing lights.

"I have two people carrying a body to the zone," the pilot said. "Everything else is in place."

"As soon as they reach the zone, touch down," Hanley said, "but watch for another party who will be arriving. We'll need four to get the object aboard."

"Tom?" Hanley said.

Crabtree's limousine driver was behind the wheel of the car. He flashed his lights.

"I have a car flashing their lights," the pilot said.

"Drive onto the lawn and park near the landing zone. Then load the helicopter."

The lights flashed again and the limousine began moving.

"He heard you," the pilot said.

Hanley was pacing back and forth. There were several carefully timed actions occurring. As long as everyone followed the plan, the team would be out in a few more minutes. This was what the Corporation called Critical Time. The time when it could all go to hell in seconds.

"Juan's waving," one of the operators said, pointing to a monitor.

Just then, Ho wandered over.

"What are you doing?" he asked.

Cabrillo turned and smoothed his hair back. "Just checking my hair."

Ho nodded. "You said you had a megaphone I could use?"

Cabrillo nodded and reached between the seats, removed the megaphone and handed it to Ho.

"It's battery operated," he said. "Just flick that switch."

Ho flicked it on. "Testing."

It worked. He stared into the van, where the rest of the band members were sprawled across the seats and atop the cases of equipment.

"Where's Candace?" Ho asked. His head was starting to clear. That was dangerous.

"We are going to meet her around front," Cabrillo said as he climbed into the driver's seat. "Now I need to get my people to the hospital."

"Tell her she can stay if she wants," Ho said.

"I'll mention it," Cabrillo said as he twisted the key, then placed the van in gear and slowly began to steer through the crowd.

Ho wandered back into the tent. He was thinking clearer now. The megaphone was not that powerful, but if he could find a spot above the crowd they would probably be able to hear his warning. His office—his office was on the top floor.

The helicopter pilot touched down and Truitt opened the rear door.

Then Truitt, Barrett, Reyes and Huxley struggled to slide the crate inside the cargo area. Once the Golden Buddha was safely stowed, they laid Spenser on the floor and helped Crabtree inside. Truitt slid the door closed, then slapped it twice to signal the pilot to lift off. Then they bent over and protected their faces from the rotor wash as the Euro-copter lifted back into the air.

Once the helicopter was safely away, Reyes stood up.

"I'm supposed to give you guys a ride," he said easily.

At that instant, Reinholt and Pryor had just reached the bottom stair. They opened the front door and walked out onto the driveway. The door had only been shut a few seconds before Ho raced to the first step and headed up to his office.

"What's the playlist?" Hanley asked an operator.

"The helicopter has Crabtree; the limo contains Reyes, Barrett, Truitt, and Huxley, with Reyes driving. Cabrillo has the band inside the van." The operator pointed to the screen. "They are just past the end of the tent and will be on the driveway momentarily."

"Where's Ross?"

"There, on the grounds," the operator said, pointing.

The van containing the band was passing and she came into view.

A few minutes before, Ross had ordered the waiters to dump all the cups of punch, then she wheeled the cart containing the pitchers outside and tipped it over.

"Linda," Hanley ordered, "go to your car now! I want you out of there."

Ross began walking quickly to the front.

"Who else?" Hanley asked.

"King is on the wall awaiting extraction, the other two guards should be in front now and that's it," the operator noted.

"Is the van full?" Hanley said to Cabrillo.

Cabrillo mouthed yes in the mirror.

The van rolled onto the drive, with the Mercedes-Benz limousine directly to the rear. Ross followed the retreating motorcade. She reached the Peugeot and started the engine.

"Slow at the front door and tell the guards they will be catching a ride with Ross," Hanley said to Cabrillo, who acknowledged the instruction.

A second later, he slowed the van and explained, then continued down the driveway toward the gate. The first team was almost off the property.

Stanley Ho opened the door to his office. He started toward the window to warn the guests, then stopped dead in his tracks.

Cabrillo made it out the gate and turned right.

"Slow along the corner of the wall," Hanley ordered. "The King is coming."

The limousine was not far behind the van; it slowed at the gate to turn at the same instant Ross pulled up at the front door, and Reinholt and Pryor climbed inside the Peugeot. She steered toward the gate.

"Close the gate," Ho screamed.

"The electricity's out," the guard said. "The gates are locked open."

"You need to stop anyone from leaving," Ho shouted.

Ross was twenty feet from the gate when the guard burst from the guard shack, fumbling with his holster. Ross never hesitated, never faltered. She steered toward the guard and hit the gas. At the same second the guard was making a life-and-death choice, Cabrillo heard a thump as Larry King jumped from the wall and landed on the roof of the van. Sliding off the roof, still holding the case containing his sniper rifle, he opened the passenger door, tossed the case between the seats, and climbed into Halpert's lap. The limousine passed the stopped van, and then blew through the stop sign at the end of the street.

The front gate guard could not get his weapon out of the holster. As the Peugeot accelerated toward him, he could only jump out of the way. Ross blew through the gate at nearly fifty miles an hour, then stomped on the brakes and twisted the wheel to the stops.

The Peugeot slid around in a hard right turn. Ross hit the gas. Cabrillo's van was moving again. He raced through the stop sign and turned right, following the limousine, just as the guard made it to the middle of the street in front of the mansion and removed his sidearm. Sighting down the barrel, he began to squeeze off rounds.

The first hit the left rear taillight, the second and third went wide. The fourth entered the rear window and shattered the rearview mirror at the same instant Ross passed the stop sign and did a left-hand turn toward the water.

21

ONCE THE LEVER was pulled back, the cargo inside the sidecar of the motorcycle began sliding down a chute and spilling onto the road. The small metal orbs were about the size of marbles but were shaped like children's jacks. The difference with these jacks was that the dozen points sticking out were razor-sharp. They bounced off the asphalt and spread across the road.

The motorcycle accelerated away as the police car hit the patch of metal shards.

The two front tires exploded, followed a second later by the rears. The police car careened out of control as the officer fought with the wheel, while at the same time stomping on the brakes. The police car slid hard to the left, slammed into a newspaper rack, then into a telephone pole just beyond the rack. A microsecond later, the air bag deployed and slammed the policeman back against the seat. By the time the cloud of powder from the airbag inflating cleared, the motorcycles were two blocks away.

After pushing the bag away from his face, the officer reached for the radio. "I've crashed and lost them," he said.

D ETECTIVE LING PO was monitoring the radio inside his unmarked squad car as the tow truck pulled alongside. Headquarters had just reported the robbery at the mansion and Po knew his immediate superior, Sung Rhee, had been scheduled to attend. Po had no idea why Rhee was not already coordinating the efforts to capture the thieves. A few minutes before, he'd heard the report from the officer chasing the motorcyclists who had robbed the A-Ma Temple, and he was beginning to think the two were related. He jumped out of the car and ran over to the tow truck.

"Hook this up fast," he said, "then tow me up to Estrada da Penha."

"Right away," the driver said.

Po reached into his car and removed a portable radio. He continued listening as the driver hooked his car to the rear. A few moments later they were on their way around the hill, then up to the mansion. Eight minutes later, the tow truck stopped on the street outside the wall around the mansion, and Po raced toward the gate. A guard stood in the dark near his shack and Po flashed his badge.

"Detective Ling Po," he said quickly. "Macau Police."

"I'm glad you're here," the guard said. "Mr. Ho is going crazy."

"Tell me what happened," Po said.

The guard related what had occurred. "I got off a few shots," he said, "but they kept going."

Po made notes on the vehicles' descriptions and radioed them in to headquarters. "I want a countrywide bulletin issued. If anyone sees the vehicles, he is to follow them but not make a stop unless he has backup."

After headquarters had confirmed his request, Po turned to the guard. "Have you seen any other officers here tonight?" he asked. "My boss, a Mr. Rhee, was scheduled to attend."

"I saw him when he came," the guard noted. "He hasn't left."

Po nodded and raced up the driveway. Cutting across the lawn, he made his way to the front door and flung it open. Stanley Ho was sitting in the front living room on the couch, a portable telephone at his ear. Chief Inspector Rhee was in a chair nearby.

"What happened, sir?" Po asked Rhee.

Rhee rubbed his face before answering. "I think I was drugged—my head is starting to clear, but I'm still having trouble concentrating."

Po nodded, then listened to Ho on the telephone.

"What do you mean?" he shouted. "We called the emergency number."

"We have no record of any call," the operator said.

"We'll get back to you," Ho said, disconnecting.

"Who are you?" he asked Po.

"This is Detective Ling Po," Rhee answered, "one of my best men."

"Here's the situation," Ho said. "A priceless piece of artwork I owned was stolen tonight."

"What exactly, sir?" Po asked.

"A six-foot-tall solid-gold Buddha figure," Ho said.

"A similar icon was heisted from the A-Ma Temple earlier tonight," Po said. "I doubt that is a coincidence."

"That makes me feel better," Ho said sarcastically.

"The telephone call you just completed?" Po asked. "What was that about?"

"A guest became ill and we called a helicopter ambulance to take her to the hospital," Ho said. "Only the hospital has no record of our request."

"Did you call for the helicopter?"

"No, it was a security guard," Ho said, "but I was standing right there."

"I'll question the guard," Po said.

"That's the problem," Rhee interjected. "The guards are gone."

"Did you hire them yourself?" Po asked.

"The insurance company supplied them," Ho admitted.

"Which company?" Po asked.

Ho retrieved a card from his tuxedo and Po dialed the number. After explaining who he was, he grilled the company operator, left his cell phone number, and then hung up.

"She's calling her boss, Mr. Ho," Po said, "but she has no record of any contact with you in the last month."

"That's nonsense," Ho said. "They had an underwriter come out here and everything."

"Was he your usual agent?" the detective asked.

Suddenly it all became very clear to Ho. He'd been set up from the start.

"Those bastards," Ho screamed. Sweeping his arm across a side table, he spilled the knickknacks on the floor then threw a chair against the wall.

"Calm down, Mr. Ho," Detective Po said quietly, "and tell me what has happened from the start."

HANLEY WATCHED THE blips on the GPS screen showing the progress of the van, limousine and Peugeot. All were progressing according to plan, so he flipped over the page in the playbook.

"Time to report the kidnappings," he said to an operator.

The man dialed the Macau police and gave them Lassiter's address. Then he did the same with Iselda. Two minutes later, police cars were racing to the separate scenes. It was one more element of confusion and discord in an already confusing situation.

Below A-Ma Temple near the Maritime Museum, Linda Ross slid

the Peugeot to a stop and climbed out. Reinholt, who was sitting in the passenger seat, had been hit by the bullet that had shattered the rearview mirror and was bleeding from his right ear.

"Help him to the boat," she said to Pryor.

Then she raced over to the dock, where a thirty-foot-long high-performance Scarab sat waiting. Climbing aboard, she raced to the helm and started the motors. Once the engines had settled into an idle, she climbed off again and walked toward the Peugeot.

"Get him aboard and keep his head elevated," she said as Pryor scurried past.

Then she took the keys to the Peugeot, opened the trunk and stared inside. Twisting a timer, she waited to make sure that it was counting down, then raced back to the boat.

"Can you drive this?" she asked Pryor.

"Damn straight," he said as he engaged the drives.

Ross started to administer first aid to Reinholt as the Scarab pulled away from the dock. The boat was one hundred yards from the dock and just climbing up on plane when the Peugeot erupted in a fireball that lit the night sky.

"WE HAVE AN explosion near the Maritime Museum," the dispatcher reported to Po.

"Summon fire and rescue," Po said. "What's the status on the kidnapping calls?"

"Units are just now arriving at the first scene," the dispatcher said. "It's a home in the northern section. A second group should be at the high-rise location in a few moments."

"Keep me posted," Po said, walking to the window and staring at the column of smoke in the distance.

*   *   *

O N THE FRONT seat of the limousine next to Reyes, Barrett started removing his Redman Security uniform. He was wearing a pair of lightweight slacks and a black T-shirt underneath.

"So, Rick, do you like the engine room or operations better?" Huxley asked.

Huxley was in the rear compartment with Richard Truitt. She had pulled a sleeveless blue sweater over her leather top and was now fumbling around inside the sweater, unfastening her vest. Once she got it off and slid it out from under the sweater, she rolled down the window and tossed it out. Barrett had been watching the entire affair through the rearview mirror.

"I can't say the engine room is quite this exciting," he admitted.

Truitt flicked on a light in the center console of the limousine's rear compartment, then removed a fake mustache from a small clutch and slapped it on his face. Once it was straight, he removed a set of false teeth from the same bag and slapped them over his own. He stared at the results in the mirror. He was rubbing gray liquid from a small bottle in the bag as he spoke.

"By now they're on the lookout for this vehicle," he said.

Reyes reached to his chest and pulled on his limo driver's uniform shirt. It ripped cleanly away, revealing another shirt underneath. Tearing at the tabs on his pants, he unleashed the pleats. "Sunglasses," he said to Truitt, who handed them over the seat. He placed them over his eyes. At the same time, Huxley ripped the Velcro-attached legs off her leather pants and reached into a compartment in the rear of the limousine and removed a conservative skirt, which she slipped under herself and zipped up. Peeling off her false eyelashes, she took a plastic bag from Truitt and removed a wet cloth and scrubbed her face clean of the garish makeup.

"Looks like we're good to go," Truitt said.

Reyes pulled to the side of the road and the four climbed out. Walking through an alley, they made their way toward the Main Market and split into groups of two. Back on the street, the limousine sat running with the door open. A police officer would find it there in less than ten minutes. But the vehicle had been cleaned of clues and there would not be much to report.

C ABRILLO TOUCHED THE garage door opener halfway down the block and the door began to rise.

Once the van was inside and the door had shut again, everyone piled out. "They have descriptions of everyone by now," he said quickly as he popped the top off a fifty-five-gallon drum containing their change of clothes and disguises, "so change fast and make an exit."

Removing a folder from the top of the clothes, he set it aside and quickly dressed. Once he was changed, and the others were doing the same, he opened the packet and began to remove documents.

"A couple of you are staying in town tonight," he said, removing passports and hotel reservation forms. "We don't want too much traffic heading back to the *Oregon*. As always, the rule is no boozing, and stay where we can reach you so if there's a change we can alert you."

He handed out the various assignments, then stared at the group.

"So far so good," he said, just as a siren approached.

Cabrillo ran over to a window, but the car continued past the building. "Fire truck," he said. "Ross must be safely away."

He walked back to the group. "Okay, men," he said, "make like an egg and scramble."

Filing out through a side door, the men went their separate ways.

P RYOR STEERED THE Scarab around the end of the Southern Peninsula, then set a course for where the *Oregon* was anchored. Ross stepped into the opening between the seats next to the helm.

"How's he doing?" Pryor asked over the noise of the racing boat.

"Not too good," Ross said. "He's lost some blood and the top of his ear as well."

"Is he in pain?"

"Damn right, it hurts," Reinholt said.

"We should contact the *Oregon*," Pryor said, "so they can have the clinic ready."

"We're on radio silence," Ross said. "The authorities might hear."

Pryor turned and looked back at his fallen friend. Reinholt smiled gamely. "The *Oregon*'s monitoring all the frequencies, right?" he asked.

"Ground, sea and air," Ross agreed.

"And we need to maintain silence on the marine bands."

"Right."

"But the helicopter can talk, because if it goes silent, air traffic control will know something's up, right?"

"Yeah," Ross said, suddenly understanding.

Pryor reached for the walkie-talkie on his belt. "These can sometimes transmit on the aviation bands."

Ross grabbed for it and hit Scan. A few seconds later, a burgundy 737 passed overhead and Ross could hear the pilot receiving final clearance. Pressing Talk, she gave the call sign for the helicopter. A few moments before, he had landed and transferred Spenser and Crabtree to a waiting car. He had just returned to remove his headset when the call came in. Another two minutes and he would have been gone.

"Helicopter four-two, X-ray, Alpha," he said, "go ahead."

"Six-three, report one Indio," Ross said over the roar of the boat's engines.

Sixty three was Ross's employee number; Indio was the code for injured party.

On the *Oregon*, Hanley reached for the microphone. "Helicopter four-two, X-ray, Alpha, I've got it, continue to point agreed. Six-three, report Indio."

"Eight-four."

"Get me the file on eighty-four," Hanley shouted to an operator, who pulled up Reinholt's records on the computer screen. His blood type was at the top of the chart.

"Six-three, understand," Hanley said, "Bravo affirm."

"Six-three, ETA in five."

"Terminate communications," Hanley ordered.

Ross clicked the button three times. "Hit the gas," she shouted.

"Go down to the clinic and check the blood supply," Hanley said, staring at the computer, "we need AB positive standing ready."

"You," he said to another operator, "go on deck and watch for Linda's approach through the night scope. As soon as you see the boat approaching, flash the deck lights, then help her off-load the injured party."

"Got it," the man said, racing away.

At that exact same instant, the helicopter pilot was pulling a white Chevrolet SUV out of a gate at the far end of the runway. Driving down the road, he stopped at a stop sign then merged with the traffic leaving the airport. He was just touching thirty miles an hour when two police cars with flashing lights passed and then slowed to turn down the road where he had come from. Punching the accelerator to pass a bus, he turned to Crabtree.

"That was close," he said.

Crabtree was checking Spenser's pulse by placing her hand on his jugular.

"True, but we're free and clear," she said.

THE BOAT SLID alongside the *Oregon* and Pryor grabbed a line tossed through the air. Tying the Scarab into the sling that would lift it back onto the deck, he waited until Ross and the operator from the control room had carried off Reinholt. Then he loosened the lines and positioned the Scarab in the slings that were already in the water. Shutting off the engines, he climbed off the boat and walked over to a switch on a nearby bulkhead. Slowly the Scarab rose from the water. Once it was clear of the upper deck, he pushed another button that rotated the davits around so the Scarab was over the deck. The entire operation required only a few minutes and that was good. In the distance, across the water, he could see the sweep of the searchlight from a police patrol boat.

As soon as the davit stopped in its arc, he pushed another switch. Four of what looked like rusty metal plates rose from the deck of the ship and surrounded the Scarab. Then he pushed another button and a retractable roof slid closed over the vessel. By the time the patrol boat passed alongside in the channel, the man was already inside and making his way to the clinic.

22

I N HIS DISGUISE, Juan Cabrillo looked like an aging academic or a
retired bureaucrat, not the leader of a group of specialized operatives. Walking through downtown Macau, he fiddled with his personal
communicator, then waited for Hanley to answer.

At this instant, his team was about one-quarter of the way through
the assignment and there was still a host of variables. The first part of
the operation had gone well—the team had loaded the Buddha onto the
helicopter as planned and made a smooth exit, but he had no way to
know the progress of team two. That information would come from the
control room on the *Oregon*.

Cabrillo had just passed a goldsmith's shop when his communicator
vibrated.

An address was displayed and he made his way toward the location.

*   *   *

"Y ES, SIR," THE Macau police officer said into a cellular telephone, "both he and his wife were bound and left in bed."

"Were they harmed?" Po asked.

"No, sir," the policeman said. "In fact, whoever did this left music playing on the stereo to entertain them, and a note of apology."

"How were they restrained?" Po asked. "Do they have a description of the assailants?"

"No," the policeman admitted, "they witnessed nothing. Both of them have small punctures on their upper arms, like they were given shots from a hypodermic needle, and they were bound with plastic ties. They only awoke when we arrived."

Whoever this crew was, they were good—Po had to give them that.

"Take the note to the lab," he said, "and make sure the technicians carefully search the house for clues."

"They're doing that now, sir," the policeman said.

"Good," Po said, "I'll be in touch."

He disconnected and turned to Rhee.

"They drugged the insurance man and his wife," he said quietly, "and left a note of apology."

Stanley Ho was becoming increasingly agitated. Not only had he been made a fool of—he had been made a fool of in an open and obvious manner. It was that son-of-a-bitch British art dealer.

"So I was set up from the start," Ho said loudly. "The countess was fake, her illness a ploy and the air evacuation a ruse."

Po raised his hand to be quiet as his telephone rang again.

"Po."

"Sir," the officer said, "we entered the apartment in the high-rise and found a woman named Iselda tied up in her closet."

"Was she harmed?"

"Other than severe nicotine deprivation, no," the officer said. "She's smoked half a pack of cigarettes since we untied her."

"Did she see her assailants?"

"She said it was like staring into a mirror," the policeman relayed.

"A woman disguised to look like her popped out of the closet and held a rag soaked with something to her mouth. That's all she remembers."

Po held his hand over the cell phone and spoke to Rhee. "They switched the party planner."

Ho raised his hands in the air and began cursing.

"Carefully search the apartment for clues," Po ordered. "Then have the kidnapped woman fill out a report at the station house."

"Got it, boss," the officer said as Po hung up.

Rhee's mind was almost back to normal. He paced the living room as he spoke.

"This was a high-budget, carefully orchestrated operation," he said. "So let's take a minute and look at what happened from the start."

"The insurance man was a plant," Ho said. "They replaced my party coordinator and band with others, then put fake guests inside as well."

"It appears they even provided their own security," Rhee noted. "The alleged protectors were the thieves."

Just then, the tow truck driver who had brought Po to the mansion walked into the living room.

"What do you need?" Po asked.

"Your tires have been changed," the driver said, "but I found a hole inside the inner fender well."

"What do you mean?"

"I think someone shot out your tire," the tow truck man said. "There's probably a slug somewhere inside the engine compartment."

"We'll look into it," Po said. "If the car's ready, you can take off. Just bill my department."

The tow truck driver walked from the room.

"This is not some haphazard group of thieves," Rhee noted. "They have snipers capable of long-range shooting, helicopter pilots and masters of disguise."

"They sure as hell aren't locals," Po said quietly.

"Oh, that makes me feel so much better," Ho said loudly. "At least I was robbed by professionals. How about you two work on recovering my Buddha first, then you can play all the mind games you want about their modus operandi."

At this second, there were seventeen Macau police officers and two other detectives searching the grounds and mansion. In addition, a trio of teams had been dispatched to the airport and the two kidnapping sites. The entire force had been mobilized and Ho was complaining.

"We are doing everything in our power, Mr. Ho," the detective said. "We're going to catch them."

Ho shook his head with disgust and walked out of the room.

T HE PARADE CAME down the hill just as the fireworks barge in the inner harbor launched the first several rounds of the evening's display. The Macau police had moved quickly and surrounded the edges of the route as soon as the pair of motorcyclists had been spotted. There was no chance of escape except a shoot-out. It was just a matter of time until the police captured the men. The man driving the motorcycle containing the Buddha steered down a side street, then honked his horn for the crowd to part. His partner followed close behind with the sound of sirens growing closer.

A tall float of a dragon was just ahead. At regular intervals, his mouth spewed fire.

O N THE *OREGON,* Max Hanley stared at the screen, then moved the joystick a little to the left. The dragon moved to the center of the road. On another screen, a camera was showing a view from the side. Hanley caught sight of the motorcycles. Another screen displayed a GPS map of Macau, with pulsing dots that showed the location of the police cars. The net was closing in on the motorcyclists. He adjusted the movement of the float again, and then stared at the blueprints stolen from the Macau Public Works Department.

*   *   *

CLIFF HORNSBY WAS tired and sweaty. Staring at his watch, he arose from the crate he was sitting on in the storm drain, then inflated a lift bag at the base of a metal ladder. Once that was in place, he climbed the rungs of the ladder. On the way up, he tested the wooden ramp to ensure it was solid. Finding it fine, he touched his hand to the bottom of the manhole cover he had already removed once, earlier in the night, to make sure that it was free.

Now he just had to wait for the signal.

Hanley stared at the control box. Gas jets for the fire from the dragon's mouth, aluminum powder charges for the maelstrom, joystick for control. Just then, a voice came over the radio.

"They have blockaded the route at Avenida Infante D. Henrique," Halpert said.

"Got it," Hanley said. "You're done, Michael, get out of there."

Halpert began walking in the direction of his hotel for the night.

"Go now," Hanley said to the motorcyclists.

Steering the float with the dragon over the top of the manhole cover, Hanley stopped it in its tracks. From the side camera, he could see the motorcycles approaching from the side street.

"Pop the top, Hornsby," he said over the radio.

Hornsby pushed against the manhole cover and lifted it in the air. Then he slid it to the side and stared up into the bowels of the beast that had stopped over his lair. Unclipping a flashlight from his belt, he scanned the inside. There was a metal frame constructed of welded tubes with a fabric outer layer. A round gas canister with tubing was attached to one side, another tube with a small explosive charge on the other. The explosive charge was flashing with a tiny green light. At just that instant, Hornsby heard the sound of motorcycles approaching and he ducked down.

The first motorcycle drove under the fabric side wall and slid to a stop inside. It was as if he were inside a tent. The interior of the dragon float was fifteen feet long and more than eight feet wide, and the peaked top reached nearly seven feet above. The motorcyclist felt like a kid in a secret fort as he climbed off the seat. The second motorcycle steered under the fabric side curtain and stopped. Hornsby climbed from the hole.

Bob Meadows was unfastening his helmet; he got it off and tossed it to the side.

"I could see the cops," he said quickly. "They're right at the end of the street."

Pete Jones tossed his helmet aside. "So be it," he said to Meadows.

"Hey, Horny," Meadows said as he began to unfasten the Golden Buddha from the sidecar.

Jones walked over and dropped the hinged metal sides of the sidecar. "This is heavy, Cliff."

"I've got a ramp," Hornsby said. "If we walk it to the ground and over to the ramp, we can just let go—it'll slide down to a lift bag at the bottom."

"Slick," Meadows said as he started to wrestle with the Buddha.

Hanley stared at the image from the forward camera. The Macau police had organized, and with weapons drawn, they were walking carefully through the parted crowd. He hit the button for flames and the dragon's mouth roared.

The Golden Buddha was lined up above the ramp, then released. It plunged down the wooden ramp onto the lift bag, then tumbled over on its side. Hornsby wrestled the ramp over to one side, then motioned to Meadows and Jones.

"You two first," he said. "Pull the ramp aside when you hit bottom. I'll close the cover."

Meadows and Jones started climbing down the ladder. Hornsby walked over to the charge on the metal tube and armed the device. The light flicked red. He was walking back to the hole when Hanley came over the radio.

"The police are less than a hundred feet away," he said quickly. "Where are you at?"

Hornsby climbed down the ladder a few feet, then reached up and slid the manhole cover back in place. He flicked a tiny switch on the lapel of his thin jacket and spoke.

"We're armed and the door closed," he said. "Give me ten seconds to reach the bottom."

"Got it," Hanley said.

Hornsby reached the bottom of the ladder and stared at the crate containing the Golden Buddha. "So what have you guys been up to?" he asked.

Hanley pushed a button and increased the flow of gas to the dragon's mouth. A flame shot forty feet forward and the crowd backed away. Then he pushed the button to ignite the charge. A small explosion ripped into the side of the metal tank containing the aluminum powder. It began to burn with a hot white light. Almost instantly the fabric covering of the float ignited and began to burn. In a few seconds, the float was a maelstrom, with flames reaching twenty feet into the air.

"We need fire and rescue," one of the officers said, giving the address.

Then he stared at the firestorm, waiting for a pair of men to run screaming forth.

But no one emerged from the glowing pile.

THE WHITE CHEVROLET SUV pulled to the side of the road and Cabrillo climbed into the front seat. The helicopter pilot, George Adams, pulled away from the curb.

"Gorgeous George," he said, "any problems?"

Adams looked like a poster child for the American way. He had a chiseled jaw, short brown hair parted to one side, and a smile that could sell toothpaste. Strangely enough, in spite of his looks, he was almost without ego. Married to his high school sweetheart, he had been an army warrant officer before joining the Corporation.

"No, sir," he said.

"Monica?" Cabrillo said, turning to the rear seat.

"No, boss," she said. "Our guest is still out of it, however."

Cabrillo stared at Spenser slumped against the window. Then back to the rear compartment, where the speaker frame holding the fake Buddha was sitting.

"Did the folding ramp work?" he asked Adams.

"Like a dream," Adams said. "We just adjusted the legs to the same height as the helicopter floor, then pushed the package across on the wheels."

"Good. We've rented part of a small hangar at the airport," he said to Adams. "We need to go there now."

Adams nodded and steered the Chevrolet back toward the bridge.

23

A LIGHT RAIN began falling over Macau. Sung Rhee and Ling Po were standing on the front porch of the mansion staring toward the city. Po disconnected his cellular telephone and turned to Rhee. Down the hill, near the Maritime Museum, the lights from the fire trucks that had extinguished the burning Peugeot were still visible. To the right, along the parade route, a column of smoke lit by the city lights was visible from the burning float.

"Whoever's stealing Buddhas tonight, they're well trained and well funded," Po said to Rhee.

Rhee's mind was back to normal. And he was as mad as a Doberman. It was bad enough that some team of thieves was using his city as a playground—it was worse that he had been made part of the heist.

"Whatever happens," he said, "they still have to spirit the icons out of the country."

"I have men at the airport and patrolling the waters," Po said, "and the border into China has been alerted to be on the lookout. They won't be able to leave Macau, that's for sure."

"All of the suspects except the British art dealer are American," Rhee said. "Did you pull up the list of tourist visas?"

"The tourism authority is closed for the night," Po admitted, "but I'll have someone there first thing in the morning."

"These guys are professionals," Rhee said quietly. "They won't hang around. By the time we get the list and begin to question all the Americans, they will be long gone."

Po's telephone rang and he unfolded it and pushed the button.

"Po."

"The fire reached part of one of the buildings," an officer at the parade reported, "but the fire department has got that under control. They are hosing down the float as we speak, but the framework is still hot and it melted in onto itself. There is a pile of twisted metal that is still too hot for inspection."

"Can you see the motorcycles inside the wreckage?"

"It seems they are inside the frame," the officer said, "but it's hard to be certain."

"I'm coming down there," Po said. "Keep the crowd back and order the rest of the floats to the end of the route. The parade has officially ended."

"Excellent, sir," the officer said. "See you shortly."

Po disconnected and turned to Rhee. "I'm going down to the parade. Would you like to come along, sir?"

Rhee considered this for a moment. "I don't think so, Ling," he said. "We're going to get some flack over this—I think it's best if I go to headquarters and coordinate efforts there."

"I understand, sir," Po said as he started to walk down the driveway.

"You find these men," Rhee said, "and recover the objects."

"I'll do my best, sir," Po said.

Then Rhee opened the door to the mansion and went inside to report to the mayor of Macau.

*   *   *

I NSIDE THE CHEVROLET SUV, Juan Cabrillo adjusted his radio and
called the *Oregon.*

"Where are we at, Max?"

There was a slight lag as the scrambled signal was rearranged and
delivered.

"The Ross team took a casualty," Hanley said. "He's being worked
on in the clinic."

"Report to me as soon as you know more," Cabrillo said. "What
else?"

"The temple team has made it to the catacombs, as planned."

"I saw the smoke," Cabrillo said. "No injuries?"

"None," Hanley said. "So far so good. They are initiating the extraction."

"What about the others?"

"Most everyone staying in town has reported in," Hanley said.
"King made it back to the boat and is going to direct offensive actions
until Murphy returns."

"Target three?"

"The 737 landed a few moments ago," Hanley reported. "They
should be going through customs as we speak."

"Our man is still with them?"

"Awaiting instructions."

"What else?"

"The second leg of the journey is almost ready to activate," Hanley
said. "The way it looks so far, we can deliver the package on time."

"Good," Cabrillo said. "We're almost at the airport."

Hanley stared at the flashing blip on one of the monitors. "I've got
you made, Juan."

"Now all I have to do is collect on our side deal," Cabrillo said,
"and we can be on our way."

"Good luck, Mr. Chairman," Hanley said.

"Cabrillo out."

M EADOWS, JONES AND Hornsby looked like three tourists on an Arizona mine tour.

They were wearing silver hard hats made from pressed metal, with small battery-operated lamps that spewed beams of light from the front. Hornsby was holding a blueprint that showed the underground drainage systems. The map looked like the tentacles of an octopus. Jones stared overhead as the first drops of water from the rain above filtered down through an aged tile drainpipe in the wall.

"Did the operations plans factor in possible rain?" he asked.

"As long as there isn't a prolonged shower," Hornsby noted, "we should be okay."

"What if there is?" Jones asked.

"That's not good," Hornsby admitted.

"So we should get moving," Meadows said.

"Exactly," Hornsby said. "But let's not worry too much—the plan states we can have six hours or so of continuous rain before the drains reach chest-high level."

"We can be out of here by then," Jones said.

"That's the plan," Hornsby agreed.

The Golden Buddha was resting on the wooden ramp. When Hornsby had entered the storm drain through a side tunnel earlier that evening, he had brought along a bag that contained four rubber-tired wheels that attached to the ramp. It was a crude arrangement, but it would allow the three men to wheel the heavy object along the tunnels. A pair of olive drab ditty bags was atop the crate containing the Golden Buddha; these contained emergency supplies and weapons. The entire affair stood at nearly chest height.

"Here's where I came in," Hornsby said. "It's a shame we can't leave the same way—it's only about two hundred yards to the grate.

The problem is, when we emerge, we're right in the middle of town and the police should be everywhere by now."

Meadows looked to where Hornsby's finger was pointing. "So which way did the control room route us?"

Hornsby traced the route with his finger.

"That's a long way," Jones noted.

"A couple of miles," Hornsby agreed. "But we come out in a se-cluded spot alongside the Inner Port, where we can be extracted."

Meadows wiped the edge of his hard hat to dispel a few drops of water, then walked around behind the Golden Buddha. "You've got the map, Horn Dog," he said. "Why don't you pull the front strap and navigate. Me and Jonesy will push from the rear."

Slowly, the three men began trudging along the storm sewer. Out-side, the rain grew in intensity. Within the hour, it was a full-fledged monsoon.

L INDA ROSS WALKED into the *Oregon*'s control room. Max Hanley was pouring a cup of coffee from a pot on a side table. His face was lined with tension and Ross could see he was stressed.

"Reinholt's rebounding," she said quietly. "It looked worse than it was. If we keep any infections at bay, he should pull through."

"Will there be any lasting damage?" Hanley asked as he motioned to the coffee and Ross walked over and poured a cup.

"The top of his ear is gone," Ross said. "He'll need plastic surgery to make that right."

"How's his attitude?"

"He came out of the stupor once and asked where he was," Ross said. "When I told him he was on the *Oregon*, he seemed happy."

"Propulsion engineers always seem more comfortable on board ship," Hanley said.

"How's the rest of the operation going?" Ross asked.

"The actual Golden Buddha is currently in an underground storm sewer," Hanley said, pointing to a monitor. "That team is making its way to the waterfront."

"I thought the Buddha was lifted out by helicopter," Ross said.

"That was the fake," Hanley said.

"But . . . ," Ross started to say.

"It was on a need-to-know basis," Hanley said. "Remember when the chairman arrived by seaplane?"

"Sure," Ross said. "When we were under way at sea."

"He had just returned from the art auction where the icon was sold. The Corporation jumped in then—we arranged the shipment to Macau. Gunderson was the pilot. Then a couple of our men met the plane with an armored car—we thought we'd just grab it then. The art dealer had other plans, however. He was planning to screw the owner with a fake, so we just went along with his plan, knowing all the while where the true artifact was hiding."

"So all the efforts at the party were a façade?"

"It was designed to throw off the authorities and confuse the picture," Hanley said. "Meanwhile, if all goes well, Cabrillo will complete the art dealer's sale and the Corporation will pocket the proceeds."

"So Reinholt was shot for no reason," Ross said.

"There were a hundred million reasons Reinholt was wounded," Hanley said. "A hundred million and one, if you count the fact that we confused the Macau police and made the art dealer the prime suspect."

"So the art dealer is the patsy," Ross said.

"He's our Oswald," Hanley agreed.

"Diabolical," said Ross.

"It's not over yet," Hanley said quietly. "We still need the payoff. And to get out of here."

I N BEIJING, THE foreign secretary, the head of the Chinese army and President Hu Jintao were staring at satellite photographs.

"As of yesterday," the foreign secretary said, "Novosibirsk in Siberia is the busiest airport in the world. The Russians are ferrying in military supplies at an alarming rate. Cargo planes are landing at the rate of one every few minutes."

Hu Jintao was examining a photograph with a magnifying glass. "Tanks, personnel carriers, attack helicopters are already on the ground."

The head of the Chinese army handed Jintao a photograph. "The amount of supplies already on the ground can support nearly forty thousand ground troops, and more is arriving every minute."

"I've already contacted Legchog Zhuren in Tibet," Jintao said. "He's mobilized his forces and they are starting toward the northern border."

"How many men are under his control?" the foreign secretary asked.

"He has twenty thousand combat and support troops in Tibet," the head of the Chinese army answered.

"Then it's already two to one," the foreign secretary noted.

Jintao pushed the photographs aside. "To maintain control inside Tibet, we have sponsored mass immigration from the other regions of China over the years. Zhuren has mobilized the Chinese citizens in Tibet and drafted them into the army. That gives us nearly twenty thousand more that are of the right age to serve. Some have already left Lhasa for the march north—we are trying to train them as they travel."

"The Russians have crack troops," the head of the Chinese army said. "Our recently recruited farmers and shopkeepers will be wiped out."

"That's if the Russians cross the border," the foreign secretary noted. "They are still claiming through diplomatic channels that this is just an exercise."

"That's a damn big exercise," Jintao said quietly.

He sat back in his chair to think. The last thing he wanted was to face off with the Russians—but he could not back down from the threat, either.

24

THE BOEING 737 was still undergoing customs inspection when Cabrillo and the others arrived at their rented hangar. Spenser had started to come out of his stupor a few minutes before. Adams opened the rear door of the white SUV, then waved smelling salts under his nose. Spenser shook his head several times, then cracked open his eyes. Adams helped him to his feet just outside the door of the Chevrolet. Spenser stood on the floor of the hangar on wobbly legs and tried to remember what had happened.

"Come here," Adams said, leading him over to a chair alongside a workbench and seating him.

With the help of Kevin Nixon, Cabrillo was erecting the folding ramp to unload the fake speaker case holding the faux Buddha. Nixon had arrived at the hangar several hours earlier and had been busy ever since.

"Is everything ready?" Cabrillo asked.

"Yes, sir," Nixon said as he grabbed one side of the speaker case.

The two men rolled the case onto the wheeled metal conveyor. When it reached the end, they tilted the case upright, folded the legs of the ramp under, then bent it in half on the hinges and slid it back into the SUV.

"We have the clothes?" Cabrillo inquired.

"I stopped at his hotel room on the way over. His bags were already packed," Nixon said.

"The best-laid plans," Cabrillo said, "of mice and men."

Cabrillo, followed by Nixon, walked over to where Spenser was sitting.

The art dealer stared up at Cabrillo. "You look familiar," he said slowly.

"We've never met," Cabrillo said coldly, "but I know a lot about you."

"Who are you people?" Spenser said, shaking his head to clear the fog, "and what do you want from me?"

Adams was standing a few feet from Spenser. While his rugged good looks did not make him appear menacing, Spenser was sure that if he tried to stand, he wouldn't get far. Cabrillo walked right in front of the art dealer and invaded his space. He stared into Spenser's eyes and spoke quietly.

"Right about now," Cabrillo said, "you're not in a good position, so shut up and listen. A few miles from here, you have one infuriated Asian billionaire who is convinced you bilked him out of a couple of hundred million dollars. And contrary to what you might think, he is not a nice man—he launched his fortune by running drugs for an Asian triad, and though he's legitimized his actions, he's still connected. I would guess he's already made a call, and the entire criminal element of this country is searching for you as we speak."

"What are you—" Spenser began to say.

"You're not listening," Cabrillo said acidly. "We know you switched Buddhas and were just about to resell the icon. If you cooperate, we will give you a chance to run. Otherwise, we'll do the switch anyway, then phone Ho and tell him where you can be found. As they say, you are out of options."

Spenser thought wildly for a moment. Without the sale of the Buddha, he was financially ruined. But as soon as word got around about what he had tried here in Macau, his life as an art dealer was finished. His only hope was to change his identity and disappear. Escape to some faraway place and start his life anew. He truly was out of options.

"I can't run without papers," he said. "Can you help me there?"

Cabrillo had him and he knew it—now he just needed to reel him into the boat.

"Kevin," Cabrillo said, "are you linked to the ship?"

"Yes, sir," Nixon answered.

"Good," Cabrillo said. "Then shoot Mr. Spenser for me."

"My pleasure," Nixon said.

T HE LAST FERRY from Hong Kong slowed near the dock and the captain began manipulating the thrusters to line the ship up with the dock. On the bow, a man wearing highly polished Cole Haan loafers, a pair of lightweight wool pleated slacks and a silk-and-cotton-blend shirt waited to depart. His hair was longer than usual and wavy, and tucked into his shirt was a cravat of fine silk. If you knew what to look for, the signs of a face-lift were barely visible. But one would need to look close, as it had been an expensive and painstaking operation. Save for the fact that the man was exhausted from the flight from Indonesia to Hong Kong, and the long day he had already faced, you might not have noticed anything odd about him at all.

The man was forty-five but appeared a decade younger.

He watched the deckhands secure the lines. The men were young and fit and he liked that. He liked the ethnic look and enjoyed young men's passions. In the country where he resided, he tended to seek out companions of Latin descent; there were many where he was from, and luckily they seemed attracted to him as well. Quite honestly, he wished he was home right now, cruising the hilly streets of his city in a quest for love or lust. But he was not. He was thousands of miles from home and he had a job to do. He smiled at one of the deckhands as he walked past, but the man did not return the greeting. Slowly, the ramp on the front of the ferry lowered.

Along with the few other passengers at this late hour, he made his way up the slight rise, then into a door marked Visitor. Handing over his passport, he waited as his entry into Macau was approved. Ten minutes later, he walked from the building and hailed a cab. Then he flipped open a satellite telephone and checked his e-mail.

B ACK ON THE *Oregon*, Max Hanley was catching a catnap. His feet were propped up on a desk in the control room and his head slumped to one side in his chair. One of the operators touched his shoulder and he was instantly awake.

"Sir," the operator said, "I think we have a problem."

Hanley rubbed his face, then rose and walked over to the coffeepot and poured a cup. "Go ahead," he said.

"Someone flagged just passed through Macau immigration."

The Corporation maintained a large database on their computers. Over the years, the names of many people had been entered. Whenever any of them cropped up on any of the numerous systems the Corporation hacked into, the information was examined and analyzed. Hanley took a sip of coffee and then read the sheet of paper the operator handed to him.

"We considered that possibility," Hanley said quietly, "and now he's here."

N IXON WALKED OVER to Spenser, aimed at his head and pushed the button.

Then he stared at the image in the digital camera.

"Can you grow facial hair?" Cabrillo asked.

"It's sparse," Spenser admitted.

"What have we got," Cabrillo asked Nixon, "to make him look different?"

Nixon walked over to the bench and rustled through a box of disguises. "We've got hair, makeup and prosthetic mouthpieces. How far do you want to go?"

"It's the new you," Cabrillo said. "Where are you planning to hide?"

Spenser considered the question. On the one hand, he was not interested in having anyone know his ultimate destination—on the other hand, from what he had seen so far, these people would probably find out anyway.

"I was thinking South America," Spenser said.

Cabrillo nodded. "Go with a light tan, medium matching mustache, nothing big, and slightly longer hair," he said to Nixon, who nodded and began removing items from the box.

"I know from your file you don't speak Spanish or Portuguese, so if I were you I'd try Uruguay or Paraguay, where your British accent won't stand out as much."

Crabtree walked over. "Why don't you have Kevin make him a Canadian?"

Cabrillo nodded. "Here's the deal," he said. "You do the switch for us and we will build you a new identity. You become a Canadian who immigrated to Paraguay a few years ago and hold citizenship. We'll give you a flat one million U.S. dollars to start over and a plane ticket from Hong Kong to Asuncion. What you do then is up to you and luck."

"The authorities will stop me if I try to leave Hong Kong with a million cash," Spenser said, feeling hope.

"We'll take care of that," Cabrillo said. "Now pick a name."

Nixon walked over and began to apply the disguise.

"Norman McDonald," Spenser said.

"Norm McDonald it is," Cabrillo agreed.

TINY GUNDERSON WAS watching the customs officials walk through the 737 when his digital communicator vibrated. He removed it from his pocket and stared at the readout. Memorizing the message, he erased it and slid the device back in his pocket. The customs agents walked to where Gunderson was standing, then signed a sheet of paper and handed it to the pilot.

"We'll move to the fuel ramp now," the pilot said to the officials, who nodded and walked out the door and down the ramp. The ramp was retracted and the operator drove it away.

"Close the door," the pilot said to Gunderson. Then he steered down the wet runway.

Thirty minutes later, the 737 was refueled and parked in a large hangar only yards from where Cabrillo and his team were waiting. The software billionaire dialed his satellite telephone.

HORNSBY, MEADOWS AND Jones stopped to catch their breath. All along the walls of the storm sewer, metal and tile pipes were funneling water into the main line. There was eight inches of water on the floor of the main sewer and it was dotted with cigarette butts, scraps of paper and the refuse from the world above their heads.

"We're gaining an inch every few minutes," Meadows said.

Hornsby was staring at the blueprint under the light of his miner's helmet. He traced the route and stared at his compass. "I don't think the water is rising that fast," he said, "but it is cause for concern."

Jones stared around the crowded space. He didn't like being in confined spaces and he wanted out as soon as possible. "Which way do we go, Horny?"

"We take the left passage," Hornsby said.

*   *   *

I NSIDE THE CONTROL room on the *Oregon*, Max Hanley was staring at a weather radar image. A cell of clouds, the center an angry
red color, was situated in the water between Hong Kong and Macau.
"Show the movement," he said to an operator.

The man entered commands into the computer and the image moved
in a slow, sweeping wave to the west. At the present speed, the storm
center would pass over Macau around four A.M. Sometime during
breakfast, the trailing edge would reach the Chinese mainland and the
weather would clear. Between now and then, there would be only rain.

"Eddie," Hanley said, "I'm going to need you to take a team into
the tunnel."

Eddie Seng was the Corporation go-to guy. He had served in marine
RECON, had spearheaded more than a few Corporation projects and
had an innate knack for making good out of bad. So far, Cabrillo and
Hanley had kept him on the sidelines in this operation. He was their
reserve man in case of unforeseen circumstances, and he was itching to
get in the game.

"I'll need a couple of Zodiac boats, and a method of locating the
men if the water keeps rising," Seng said.

"Murphy, Kasim and Huxley," Hanley said quickly. "I'll have the
boats prepped and the equipment arranged. You assemble the team and
meet me back here."

Seng walked quickly from the control room.

"N O COMMENT," SUNG Rhee said, slamming down the telephone.
The reporters for the local newspapers had gotten wind
something was happening—they just did not know what. The hospital
was filled with guests from Ho's party, but as the drug wore off they
were leaving one by one. Food poisoning was mentioned as the source
of the guests' discomfort, but the cover story was flimsy and someone

would soon pierce through that lie. The kidnappings were being investigated; reporters with police scanners had ensured that. The theft at the A-Ma Temple, the burning Peugeot, the fire at the parade—all were being investigated by reporters. Only Stanley Ho's house was sealed from them. Once he had cleared the house, he had locked the doors to outsiders. Once morning came, Rhee would be compelled to comment.

Just then his telephone rang again.

"The wreckage of the float is cooling, but we have yet to get close enough to inspect for remains," Detective Po said. "But my guess is they burned up in the conflagration."

"Was the float being observed the entire time?" Rhee asked.

"Yes, sir," Po said.

"Then find me some teeth," Rhee said, "and melted gold."

"Yes, sir."

Po stared at the firemen who were still spraying water over the twisted mess of metal. Within the hour, he should be able to inspect the wreckage. In the meantime, Ho's theft would take center stage. Somewhere in Macau was another Golden Buddha. And Po intended to find it.

"OUR DEAL WAS cash," Spenser said in answer to Cabrillo's question.

Monica Crabtree was on the secure line to the *Oregon*. She made notes on a sheet of paper, then disconnected. "Mr. Chairman," she said, "I think you should see this."

Nixon was doing layout on Spenser's new documents. Once he had the basic package together, he entered a command and they were sent through the lines to the *Oregon*, where there was a store of blank passports, immigration documents and blank credit cards. Someone on board would print up the material and deliver it to the hangar.

Cabrillo stared at the notes and handed them back to Crabtree. "Shred them."

*   *   *

TOM REYES WAS driving at breakneck speed, with Franklin Lincoln in the passenger seat. Lincoln stared at the cab dispatch records, then out the windshield once again. "There were three cabs dispatched to the ferry dock, numbers twelve, one twenty-one, and forty-two."

"I've been listening to the scanner," Reyes said. "Forty-two has already dropped its fare at the Hotel Lisboa, and number twelve is heading along the New Road. He must be on number one twenty-one. He called the dispatcher to report that he was inbound to the Hyatt Regency on Taipa, then he was supposed to wait for his fare and take him onward."

Reyes steered onto the bridge leading to Taipa. "Call Hanley and explain the situation."

Lincoln turned on his radio and reported to the control room.

"Give me a minute or so," Hanley said.

"Access the Hyatt computer and search for this name," he said, handing Eric Stone, an operator, the sheet of paper, "and get me a room."

Stone's hands danced over the keyboard; a second later he turned to Hanley.

"What timing," Stone said. "He's just now checking in."

Stone waited until the data filled the screen. "Room twenty-two fourteen," he said.

"Hyatt Regency, room twenty-two fourteen," Hanley said to Lincoln, "and grab him fast—if he asked the cab to wait, he's headed for the airport soon."

"Got it," Lincoln said. "Then what?"

"Bring him here."

Reyes steered up the driveway to the Hyatt Regency.

"Room number twenty-two fourteen," Lincoln said. "We grab him and bring him to the *Oregon*."

Reyes stopped the car and slid it into Park. "You got any money?"

"Sure, what for?" Lincoln asked.

"There's the cab," Reyes said, pointing. "Pay him off and tell him to leave. Then meet me on the twenty-second floor."

MICHAEL TALBOT PAID the bellman, then closed the door. He was due at the airport any minute, but he was grimy and decided on a quick shower. Undressing, he walked into the bathroom and adjusted the shower.

Tom Reyes reached into his wallet and removed a universal key card. Then he slid it through the slot and waited until the light went green. Then he slowly opened the door. At first, he thought no one was in the room, then he heard the shower running. Reyes started to close the door but heard the sound of footsteps approaching down the hall. He peered out and saw Lincoln. Reyes touched his finger to his lips, then motioned Lincoln inside.

"BARRETT," HANLEY SAID, "are you cross-trained in the Magic Shop?"

"I've worked it before," Barrett said.

"Go down there and warm up the latex machine."

"You've got it, boss," Barrett said, walking quickly out of the control room.

TALBOT WAS TOWELING himself off and trying to decide what he would wear. He stepped from the bathroom and into the bedroom. A large black man was sitting at his table, and the image so surprised him that his mind was unable to process the discovery for a second.

Then, from the side of the door, he felt a hand around his mouth. He was thrown facedown on the bed, his eyes pressed tight against the bedspread. Next, he was quickly gagged and blindfolded, with his arms and legs secured with plastic ties.

Earplugs were slipped into his ears. He could not hear Reyes tell Lincoln, "I'll go find a room service cart. You stay here."

Lincoln nodded and flipped on the television. Their prisoner was not going anywhere. He lay trussed like a Thanksgiving turkey, not moving a muscle. Eight minutes later, Lincoln and Reyes had snuck him out a back entrance of the hotel, then brought the car around and slid him onto the backseat.

"I'm hungry," Reyes said as he reached over to place the car in Drive.

"Man," Lincoln said, "you always say that."

25

AT THE SAME instant that Reyes and Lincoln were pulling alongside the *Oregon* and parking, Max Hanley was checking a device in the Magic Shop. In the background, on one of the numerous work-benches, the machine that heated liquid latex beeped to signal it was at operating temperature, then automatically went to standby.

Hanley turned and stared at the latex machine, then diverted his eyes back to the small box in his hand. "Okay," Hanley said to Barrett, "let's try it again."

"Testing, one, two, three," Barrett said. "The brown cow jumped over the red moon, four score and seven years ago our—"

"That's fine," Hanley said, cutting him off.

He stared at the small box, then placed it to his throat and repeated what Barrett had said. Staring at a computer screen displaying a series of bar graphs, he noted the discrepancy and adjusted a series of tiny stainless-steel screws on the rear of the box with an optometrist's screwdriver. "Go again."

"I did not have sex with that woman, Miss Lewinsky," Barrett said. "Read my lips, no new taxes. Out of respect for the family, I will not answer that question, la de dah."

"Hold on," Hanley said.

He repeated Barrett's ramblings while staring at the screen. Barrett watched and raised an eyebrow. His voice was coming from Hanley's mouth. It was both eerie and amazing.

"My mother couldn't tell the difference," he said.

"Modern technology," Hanley said, "still astounds me."

"How are you going to attach it?" Barrett asked.

Hanley showed him.

REYES GLANCED AROUND the port; no one was watching. With Lincoln's help, he removed Talbot from the rear seat, then dragged him up the gangplank onto the *Oregon*. Met at the inner door by Julia Huxley, the trio was directed down to the Magic Shop. Talbot, still blindfolded, stumbled down the passages, into the elevator, then along the last stretch of hallway until they reached the Magic Shop. Once Lincoln opened the door, Reyes directed Talbot to a chair, then sat him down and placed straps across his body. A light was moved to the front of Talbot's seat, then turned on. Talbot could feel the heat from the lamp. A few seconds later, his blindfold was removed and the blinding light met his eyes.

"You Michael Talbot?" Hanley asked.

"Yes," Talbot said, turning from the light.

"Eyes forward," Hanley said.

Talbot complied, but he had a hard time looking into the light. He could sense someone was behind him, but the straps were too tight to turn.

"Did you have sex with a teenage boy in Indonesia?"

"Who are you people?" Talbot said.

A second later, he felt a touch on his neck, then a surge of electricity hit his body.

"We ask the questions here," Hanley said. "Did you have sex with a teenage boy?"

"He told me he was eighteen," Talbot said through gritted teeth.

"We're tired of slime like you coming over to Asia to partake of your sick desires," Hanley said. "It's giving America a bad name."

"I'm here on busi—" Talbot started to say.

The sharp bite of electricity.

"Silence," Hanley snapped.

Talbot was afraid, the kind of deep-down fear of the unknown and unseen that creeps into a man's soul and plays with his nerves and internal organs. Talbot began sweating from his forehead and the need to urinate was overpowering.

"I have to pee," he said.

"When we say you can," Hanley said. "First we are going to make a mold of your head. Then we will produce a three-dimensional image of it, which we will transmit over our computer network. From here on out, the Asian police organizations will be on the lookout for you. Then you are going to read a confession aloud. If you cooperate and perform these tasks, you will be taken to Hong Kong so that you can catch the first flight to the United States. Screw with us in any way and you will be washing up on the beaches of mainland China a few days from now. What'll it be, lover boy?"

"Okay, okay," Talbot blurted. "But I'm about to pee my pants."

"Take him to the facilities," Hanley said.

Blindfolded once again, Talbot was led to a restroom and his hands untied.

Four minutes later, he was back in his seat and strapped in place. Fifteen minutes after that, the mask was formed and the voice print recorded. A few minutes later, Michael Talbot was placed facedown on the rear seat of the sedan again and was driven toward the ferry dock.

W INSTON SPENSER WAS trying to figure an angle. There was none. He had grabbed for the brass ring and come up short. His choice now was to live or to die, and the people that were controlling him had made a compelling argument. He'd walk out with a new identity and a million in funding. He decided this was a deal he would honor.

Spenser stared at his new passport and documents, then watched the lady in the group talking on the cellular telephone. She disconnected and turned to the leader.

"The president is on his way, Mr. Chairman," she said. "He's taken care of the problem."

Spenser had no idea of the identities or affiliation of the people who had taken him hostage. He only knew from what he had witnessed so far that they had a power that went far beyond anything he had ever seen. They seemed to exist in a world of their own creation, a world of control and illusion, and whatever Spenser may have planned, they had always been one step ahead. And then it hit him.

"You were at the auction in Geneva," he said to the leader.

Cabrillo stared at Spenser, as if trying to decide. "Yes, I was."

"How did you know I'd switched the Buddhas?"

"You paid our company to fly the icon here to Macau, then take it by armored car to the temple," Cabrillo said.

"So you staged the entire affair at the party as a ruse?"

"That, and we wanted to fulfill your deal with the man outside," Cabrillo said.

"Unreal," Spenser said. "And the one hundred million?"

"It will go to charity," Cabrillo said. "We were hired to bring the real Buddha back to its rightful owner—this side deal is just frosting on the cake."

Spenser thought for a moment. "What is your ideology, your group's motivation?"

"We are a corporation," Cabrillo said. "That is the only ideology we need."

"So you exist to make a profit?"

"We exist," Cabrillo said, "to make right from wrong. But along the way, we've learned how to make that a very lucrative enterprise."

"Amazing," Spenser said.

"Not as amazing as this," Cabrillo said as the door to the hangar opened and the car carrying Hanley drove inside. Once the door closed, Hanley climbed from the passenger side of the SUV. "Meet Michael Talbot," Cabrillo said to an astonished Winston Spenser.

THE SOFTWARE BILLIONAIRE took a key from a chain around his neck and opened the leather portfolio on the table. Then he removed a folder and flipped through the papers. The stack of papers was nearly an inch thick and was composed of bearer bonds in various amounts. The largest denomination was for an even $1 million. The smallest, $50,000. The banks that had issued the bonds were from a hodgepodge of European countries, from Great Britain to Germany to the most prevalent, Switzerland and Liechtenstein. The total was $100 million.

It was a king's ransom to purchase a princely prize.

But to the software billionaire, it was just money. He lived for the fulfillment of his own desires. It was not the art of the Golden Buddha that intrigued him, nor the history that surrounded the icon like a cloud; it was the fact that it had once been stolen and now it had been stolen again. It was the crime that turned him on, the inflation of his ego he would feel when he knew that he was the only man in the world to possess the rare and priceless artifact. Truth be told, he already owned a collection of stolen art that rivaled any museum in Europe. Monet,

Manet, Daumier, Delacroix. Da Vinci sketches, Donatello bronzes. Illuminated manuscripts, crown jewels, stolen historical documents.

Warehouses in California were filled with antique automobiles, historic motorcycles, and early airplanes. Stolen Civil War artifacts, Romanov icons heisted from a museum in St. Petersburg, scientist Nikola Tesla's writings lifted from a museum in Romania after the fall of communism, secret presidential letters, even a toilet from the White House.

The first computer, the first personal computer, the first massproduced consumer computer.

Those last were for nostalgia, since computers were where his fortune had come from. He still had a hard copy of the first program his company had sold—one he had stolen himself from an unsuspecting programmer who'd believed he was just helping another enthusiast. That had been his first and largest theft, and it had set the stage for all the others.

He stared at the bonds again, then reached for the satellite telephone.

E DDIE SENG WATCHED as a pair of olive-green Zodiac boats were raised from a lower deck on a utility elevator that exited amidships on the *Oregon*. As soon as the elevator stopped, Sam Pryor hooked a cable to the center hoisting ring of the first boat and swung it over the side, then into the water. Down at water level, Murphy took the bowline of the boat and tied it to the dock. While Pryor was hooking up the second boat, Murphy climbed aboard and checked the fuel and oil for the high-output four-stroke outboard motor. The oil was fresh and full, the tanks topped to the rim. Murphy turned the key and watched the lights on the dash; once he was sure everything was fine, he twisted the key and the engine started and settled into an almost silent idle.

Once the second boat touched the water, Kasim duplicated Murphy's efforts. The two boats sat idling in the night. Seng climbed aboard Murphy's vessel and checked the supplies that had been loaded aboard down in the inner workings of the *Oregon*. Finding all in order, he spoke to Huxley in a low voice.

"You got everything?"

Huxley stared at her list, then found the last item. "We're good."

Next, Seng reached across between the boats and handed Kasim a CD. "These are the coordinates for the onboard GPS—we are running an exact copy on this boat. Let's try to stay within ten feet or so of one another, that way the radar shielding should hide us both."

Kasim nodded. "You got it, Eddie."

"Okay, Mark," Seng said quietly as he threw off the line, "you can take us out."

Murphy slid the control lever down and the boat backed in reverse. A few minutes later, the two boats were skimming across the rain-splashed water at speeds of nearly thirty knots. For all intents and purposes, they were undetectable. Any radar that might try to paint them was being jammed; anyone listening for the engines would not be able to hear the noise over the storm. Help was coming.

T WO IN THE morning and the trio in the tunnel had between three and four hours until first light.

That was not as much of a problem as it might seem. Right now, the main threat was drowning. Hornsby stared ahead to where a large tile pipe was spilling its contents into the main sewer. What had begun as a trickle from the offshoot pipes had grown into angry torrents of water. The pipe ahead was raging with such force that the stream of water was slapping against the far wall of the main sewer like the torrent from a broken fire hydrant.

"From that point forward," Meadows said, "we lose the bottom half of the sewer to water."

Already the water was knee-deep, and the farther the men had gone, the more it had risen. Now they were at an impasse. From here to the end of the line, the water would be too deep to walk through. "Let's inflate the rafts," Jones said wearily.

Hornsby opened one of the duffle bags and removed a pair of folding rafts. Taking a high-pressure air supply from inside the bag, he attached it to a raft and turned the switch. The raft unfolded and quickly became rigid. Two minutes later, Hornsby turned off the inflator.

"We need to place the Buddha in one raft," Hornsby said, "and the three of us in the other."

"Weight problems?" Jones asked.

"Each raft can carry a maximum of seven hundred pounds," Hornsby said. "Since none of us weighs under a hundred pounds, he'll need to ride alone."

Meadows was unpacking the second raft. He laid it out and attached the inflator. As it was filling with air, he spoke. "What do you think?" he asked his partners. "Should we let the Buddha lead or follow?"

Hornsby thought for a moment. "If he's behind, the weight might push us into something."

"But if he leads," Jones said, "we can let go of the lead rope if we get into trouble."

Meadows stared at the rapidly filling pipe just ahead. "There will not be much steering required," he said, pointing to the rising water. "I think we'll all just go with the flow."

"Then he leads," Hornsby said as he grabbed one end of the Buddha to wrestle it onto the raft, "and we just go along for the ride."

"Hear, hear," Meadows said.

"Makes sense to me," Jones added.

26

"TALBOT?" SPENSER SAID. "You're part of this?"

Hanley walked over to Spenser and stood as the art dealer examined him. At least he seemed to be passing the visual test—Spenser was waiting for him to answer.

"Win . . . ston Spen . . . ser, you old . . . ," Hanley croaked.

He sounded like a cheap P.A. system in a run-down school. Hanley moved the small device from his voice box and spoke in his normal voice. "Kevin," he said, "come take a look at this—I thought I had it dialed in right."

Nixon walked over and flipped the device over. He took a pen from his shirt pocket and clicked a small toggle switch over two notches. "You had the delay used for telephone transmissions engaged, boss," Nixon said. "Try it now."

"Hi, Winston," Hanley said. "Long time no see."

Spenser stared at the man and shook his head. Had he not seen the device malfunction, he might have been all right—as it was, everything that had happened to him was rushing back in a flood. Now these people had created some kind of robot. Who knew what they might do next?

"Mr. Talbot," Spenser managed to say.

"I think you fixed it, Kevin," Hanley said.

Spenser stood mute.

"Okay, everyone, listen up," Cabrillo said, "it's almost time."

D ETECTIVE LING PO stared at the mass of melted metal. The support beams of the float had been twisted into grotesque shapes by the intense heat of the fire, and they were wrapped around the remains of the motorcycles like the blackened tentacles of an octopus. A handler with a dog was poking at one side of the wreckage.

"Sir," the handler said, "the dog is not signaling any human remains."

"Does that mean there are none?" Po asked.

"Usually, it would need to be an extremely hot fire to fully turn a corpse to ash. Anything less than that he'll smell."

Po glanced at the wreckage. It had melted the asphalt of the road, and parts of the metal support beams were imbedded into the roadway. There was no way to tell with any certainty what was underneath.

"Hook a chain to the end," Po said, "and drag it with one of the trucks. I want to see what's under there."

A fireman ran to remove a chain from the storage compartment on his truck. A few minutes later he had one end secured to the wreckage and the other end to the truck's bumper. Slowly, the fireman eased the truck forward and the wreckage was wrestled from down in the asphalt. After dragging it a few feet north, the fireman stopped his truck.

"It that far enough?" he shouted out the window to Po.

"Perfect," Po said, staring at the manhole cover.

Bending down, Po tried to lift the cover, but he had no luck. Another fireman removed a tool from the truck and slid it into the small opening on the manhole cover, then pried it open. He slid the cover a few feet away. Po removed a small flashlight from his pocket and shined it down into the hole.

"Bingo," he said.

Reaching for his cell phone, he dialed the number for headquarters.

"Sir," he said, "I think I know where the A-Ma Temple Buddha went."

THERE ARE A total of sixteen places in Macau where the storm runoff exits into the bay. Seng and his team were pulling up to the only one that mattered. After securing the Zodiacs to some rocks alongside the grate, Seng walked over and examined the metal shield. The square screen was made of tubular stock, with the openings measuring some two feet by two feet, or large enough to allow any trash to pass through. It was connected to the angled concrete slab that attached to the storm sewer by a series of large bolts. Seng walked back to the Zodiac and removed a toolbox. Finding the proper size socket, he attached it to a battery-operated wrench, then walked back over to the grate and began to remove the bolts. Once the bolts were all free, Seng, Huxley, Murphy and Kasim positioned themselves on all four corners of the grate and lifted it free. The water was racing out of the outflow, and on the far side Murphy and Kasim had some trouble pulling the grate onto the rocks. Once it was out of the way, everyone stared into the opening.

"It's becoming a river in there," Huxley said finally.

Seng threw a strip of bright yellow plastic in the stream and then timed the movement. He stared at the second hand of his watch intently. Once the piece of plastic was fifty yards out in the Inner Harbour, he calculated the speed.

"The water's flowing about ten miles an hour," he said, "but you know that's going to increase."

"Piece of cake for the Zodiacs," Murphy said.

Seng nodded.

"As long as we don't run out of headroom," Kasim said, "we should be able to collect our boys and be back on the *Oregon* in an hour or so."

Seng started walking back to the Zodiac. "Okay, you two," Seng said, "drive on in and collect the team. Julia and I will be providing security, just like we planned."

"Be back shortly," Kasim said as he climbed behind the wheel.

If only it'd be so easy.

27

CABRILLO TOOK AN erasable marker and drew on a board placed on one of the benches.

"I just checked again and the 737 is parked here," Cabrillo said, making an X on the board. "They won't be moving until they taxi out to leave. Adams will drive Spenser in the SUV to the ramp, then park."

Adams nodded in agreement.

"Once you've stopped, climb out and erect the portable awning over the rear of the truck," Cabrillo said. "Then you can open the crate displaying the Buddha."

"What if the buyer wants us to bring the Buddha aboard?" Spenser asked.

"Tell him no," Cabrillo said. "He needs to do his inspection on the ground and take ownership on Macau soil."

Spenser nodded, but he didn't look convinced.

"Max," Cabrillo continued, "you are going to leave in a few

minutes and make your way around to the front terminal, where a cab will bring you back to the 737."

"Got it," Hanley said.

Cabrillo paused and stared at the team. "This should go nice and easy," he said quietly. "Hanley will verify the authenticity, the payment will be made, and then the billionaire can haul the Buddha aboard. Any questions?"

No one spoke.

"All right then," Cabrillo said. "Good luck, Max."

Hanley nodded and walked toward a rear door to the hangar.

"George," Cabrillo said, "you and Spenser can climb in the SUV. We'll want to give Hanley a few minutes to make contact and some small talk, then we need to make the approach."

Adams nodded and motioned to Spenser to climb in the passenger seat of the Chevrolet.

THE SOFTWARE BILLIONAIRE was drinking tea with coconut milk and smoking a thin cheroot. The intrigue of the event had caught up to him and, a few minutes before, he had retired to the rear compartment of the 737 to change into all black clothing. His success in the software industry, a condition of luck and timing more than skill and ability, had over the years allowed his ego to swell into dangerous proportions. He was beginning to believe his own hype. At this instant, with the drugs and sex wearing off and the nicotine and caffeine increasing, he was beginning to think he was a secret agent. The heist, followed by the payoff, and then absconding with the goods. He was already thinking about the fun he would have relaying the story to his friends.

HANLEY WALKED OVER to the Macau taxi and climbed into the backseat. The taxi rolled around the edge of the main terminal, then back down toward the 737. Once it was close to the ramp, Hanley ordered the driver to slow, then sound the horn.

The billionaire heard the sound and glanced out a window of the jet. Seeing Talbot in the rear of the taxi, he walked forward toward the open cabin door, then stood at the top of the ramp. Hanley climbed from the rear of the taxi. The billionaire motioned for him to climb the ramp.

Hanley started up the steps.

At that exact instant, Juan Cabrillo picked up a portable radio and pushed Talk.

"Flyswatter," he said, "how you holding up?"

Larry King was perched inside the scooped intake of the hangar's air-conditioning system. The rain was occasionally blowing inside the shaft, but at least he had something over his head. "I stopped by the *Oregon* after the party," King said, "and picked up a thermos of tomato soup, a waterproof cover for the nightscope and some depleted uranium rounds. I'm in tall cotton."

Cabrillo was always appreciative of King's professionalism. The Corporation could parachute him into a barren wasteland with a few packaged meals and his rifle, and within hours he would have found a nest and lined up his shots. Then he would patiently wait until his special services were needed or not, without complaint. Since Cabrillo had access to the operatives' personal records, he knew that King was also the owner of a piano bar in Sedona, Arizona. It had been odd the single time Cabrillo had traveled through the area and caught King at work— not only had the sniper been dressed in a black tuxedo instead of camouflaged sniper clothes, but he'd sung mainly love songs and ballads in a sweet melodious voice.

"How's the reception, Larry?" Cabrillo asked.

"The parabolic is distorted some by the droplets on the glass," King admitted. "But I can make out some of what's being said."

"You know to call if something big happens."

"Yes, sir," King said, staring through the nightscope and touching the earpiece to the microphone. "Hanley just made his greetings."

Monica Crabtree was on the far end of the hangar, staring out a crack in the door. "Mr. Hanley just walked inside," she said across the space of the hangar.

"Come on in out of the rain, Michael," King heard the billionaire say.

Hanley passed Gunderson in the aisle as he followed the billionaire. He touched the middle finger of his left hand to his eyebrow, as if to wipe away a droplet. Gunderson brushed his chin in reply.

"Have a seat," the billionaire said as they reached a conference table in a compartment in the front section of the 737.

Hanley slid into a seat and stared at the man.

"I couldn't tell you what was happening over the telephone," the billionaire said. "But the Buddha that you bid on for me has come up for sale once again."

"That's quick," Hanley said.

The billionaire nodded but offered nothing more. "Your voice sounds rough. Can I offer you something?"

"The rain and the air on the commercial flights I've been taking," Hanley said. "I think I'm coming down with something."

The billionaire pushed a button and Gunderson appeared.

"Could you bring Mr. Talbot some tea with lemon and honey?"

"And for you, sir?"

"I'll have a snifter of warmed Ouzo, please."

"Right away, sir," Gunderson said.

On the roof of the hangar, King heard the exchange. "They are ordering drinks, sir."

"Open the door, Monica," Cabrillo ordered.

Crabtree hit a button and raised the hangar door far enough for the SUV to exit.

"Time to go, men," Cabrillo shouted to Adams and Spenser.

Adams placed the Chevrolet in gear and drove slowly to the door. Then he exited the hangar into the pouring rain.

Gunderson returned with the drinks to find the billionaire staring silently at Hanley. "The pilot asked me to tell you that a truck is approaching," said Gunderson.

The billionaire turned from Hanley and stared out the window. A white Chevrolet SUV pulled near the ramp, and a man he didn't recognize climbed from the driver's seat and walked to the rear. Once there, he removed a folded, portable, aluminum-legged awning from the rear and erected it. Then the billionaire watched as Spenser climbed from the passenger seat.

"Come on," the billionaire said to Hanley. "Our prize has arrived."

At the same time Hanley and the billionaire were walking toward the ramp, Adams pulled the crate containing the Buddha forward and opened the top. Then he walked back to the driver's seat and climbed inside out of the rain.

The billionaire appeared at the top of the stairs and Spenser, under the awning, motioned for him to descend. The two men walked down the ramp.

"Let's do this out of the rain," the billionaire said when he reached the tarmac. "Inside my plane."

Spenser shook his head in the negative. "I don't know you, and you don't know me," he said, "so until I receive payment and you take delivery, the Golden Buddha remains on the ground."

The billionaire turned to Hanley. "Is this the dealer that made the winning bid?"

"Yes," Hanley said.

"You're Mike Talbot," Spenser said.

"Michael," Hanley corrected.

"Did you bring cash like we agreed?" Spenser asked.

"Bearer bonds," the billionaire answered. "If everything checks out."

Hanley stood quietly, with the gusts of wind blowing sprinkles of rain onto his mask.

"Check it out," the billionaire said to Hanley.

Hanley walked over and examined the Buddha in detail, then reached down and shaved a small sample of gold from the foot. "Did you bring the other sample?" he asked the billionaire, who reached into his pocket and removed an envelope.

Hanley removed an eyepiece from his pocket and pretended to study the sample for a few minutes. "They match," he said at last.

"I'll retrieve the payment," the billionaire said.

At exactly the same time, Chuck Gunderson was placing the last strip of duct tape over the mouth of the copilot. Binding the men's wrists with plastic ties, he laid the pilot and copilot together on the floor of the cockpit.

"Target's heading up the stairs," King radioed Cabrillo.

"Make the call," Cabrillo said to Nixon.

Inside the 737, Gunderson turned to the brunette flight attendant. "Do me a favor," he said, "close that cabin door."

As the billionaire climbed the stairs in the rain, he could not hear the footsteps as Adams, Spenser and Hanley sprinted through the puddles to the rear of the hangar. His mind was on the Golden Buddha and retrieving the briefcase that held the key to owning the icon. He was halfway up the ramp when the door to his jet started to close. Just as he reached the top step, the hatch was locked in place. Banging on the door, the billionaire began screaming at the top of his lungs.

ACROSS TOWN, LING Po was just about to enter the manhole when his cell phone rang.

"Things have gotten too hot for us," an unknown voice said to Po. "You win, Detective. There is a white Chevrolet Tahoe on the runway at Macau airport. It has the Buddha that was stolen from the party. Good-bye."

The telephone went dead in Po's ear. For a moment, he stared at it in amazement—then he quickly dialed Sung Rhee.

"I just had a call from the thieves," Po said rapidly. "They claim the Buddha is in a white Chevrolet truck on the runway at Macau airport."

H ANLEY, SPENSER, AND Adams ran to the rear of the hangar to where a limousine was sitting with the engine running. Monica Crabtree was behind the wheel. Once the trio of men was safely in the rear compartment, she placed the limousine in gear and raced toward the gate.

"Okay, Kevin," Cabrillo said.

Using a remotely operated device he had installed a few hours earlier, Nixon began to back the ramp away from the 737. As soon as the ramp lurched backward, the billionaire knew he had been had—he swiveled around at the top of the ramp and glanced down. The truck was there, but no one was visible.

Larry King watched the 737 through the nightscope. Less than a minute later, he watched as Gunderson slid into the pilot seat, then motioned he was ready. King flashed a red laser on his rifle sight at the pilot's window of the 737, and, at the signal, Gunderson fired the engines on the jet. The ramp was retracting faster and faster, and Nixon steered it to the side. Once it was safely clear of the jet, he let his joystick go neutral and the ramp began to roll to a stop. Tossing the controller into a box, he did a final visual sweep of the hangar with Cabrillo. He and Crabtree had packed everything else into the trunk of the limousine in the half hour before Spenser had made his approach. All that remained was for Nixon and Cabrillo to hightail it off airport property.

Once the ramp was free of the 737 and a safe distance away, King signaled again with the laser and Gunderson began to advance the throttles.

Cabrillo and Nixon were walking quickly for the rear door when King radioed.

"Chuck's started his taxi," King said.

The ramp had finally slowed enough for the billionaire to leap off. He ran down the tarmac after his retreating 737. A few seconds of that and he knew the situation was hopeless, so he raced toward the Chevrolet. Once he reached the vehicle, he was surprised to find the Buddha still aboard. Pushing over the aluminum awning, he slammed the rear door closed, then climbed into the driver's seat. Another break, the keys were still in the ignition. His $100 million in bonds were lost—but the Buddha was worth twice that. Now his plan was to escape with the Golden Buddha and worry later about who had stolen his jet. He started the truck and placed it in gear.

On board the 737, the brunette flight attendant was guarding the cockpit door. No one had told her to do this, she had just thought it prudent. One of the bimbos walked forward and started for the cockpit door.

"Get back," the brunette said.

"I need to talk to the pilot," the blonde said.

She started for the door again, and the brunette threw a punch that never landed. The blonde deflected the blow, then struck the brunette in the breadbasket with a chop.

"Chucky," the blonde shouted over the noise of the engines, "will you tell this bitch you need me up there?"

The brunette was bent over, trying to catch her breath, when the cockpit door was flung open. Through the open door, the brunette could see the 737 taxiing faster toward the runway for takeoff. Gunderson was sitting in the pilot's seat. He turned and smiled.

"That's okay, honey," Gunderson said quickly. "She's my copilot."

The Macau taxi was sitting to the rear of the hangar, the purring engine making puffs of smoke in the rain-soaked air. Cabrillo and Nixon climbed into the rear just as King radioed again. "Okay, boss," he said easily, "he went for the truck."

"Come out of the nest," Cabrillo said, "and we'll meet you around front."

King began to extract himself from inside the air intake at the same time the billionaire had the Chevrolet up to speed on the road leading from the hangars to the main terminal.

I NSIDE THE BURGUNDY 737, Gunderson scanned the storm scope and answered a call from the control tower. Then he hit the switch to allow him to talk over the cabin speakers. "Ladies, if you could take a seat, I'd appreciate it—we'll be taking off in a second. Also, after we get in the air, if one of you could bring a pot of coffee and some sandwiches to the cockpit, you'd be our hero."

Then he turned to the blonde sitting next to him. "Hi, Judy, long time no see."

A LONG THE BRIDGE leading from Macau proper to the island where the airport was situated, twelve police cars with sirens screaming and lights flashing formed a rolling barricade as they raced to the main terminal.

"There they go," Crabtree said as she drove in the opposite direction.

She watched in the rearview mirror as several cars left the bridge, then crossed the median and sealed off both lanes of traffic. "Just made it," Adams noted.

The driver steered the cab slowly around the front of the building, then waited as King slid down the drainpipe and climbed into the front seat. Then he turned his head and stared at Cabrillo.

"Take us to the far south end of the airport across from Coloane," Cabrillo said. "We have a boat to catch."

* * *

O N BOARD THE 737, the final clearance was approved at the same time as the Chevrolet SUV passed in front of the main airport terminal. In the distance, the billionaire could see a line of police cars blocking the road. Turning his head, he could see through the rain the flashing lights on the wings and fuselage of his burgundy 737 as it lifted from the runway and headed out over the bay.

"Destination?" Judy asked.

"Singapore," Gunderson answered. "Now tell me—how was it for you and Tracy?"

"We took a couple for the team," Judy said. "Then he got tired."

28

THE FULL FURY of the storm descended on Macau only a few minutes after Gunderson and the 737 cut a wide arc out over the South China Sea to head south. Inside the storm sewer, the waters were rising faster now, and the rafts holding the Golden Buddha and his three liberators hurtled faster toward salvation or destruction.

Prior to reaching each junction, one of the men would climb off the raft and drag the rear rope to slow the raft with the Golden Buddha. Then he would push the side of the raft toward the proper channel and let the current do the rest. The randomly spaced overhead pipes that drained into the main sewer were running full now, and each time the rafts passed under the spray some of the water made it into the floors of the rafts. The men were using their hats to bail out the buildup, but as each mile passed the effort was becoming harder and harder.

Hornsby stared at the blueprint carefully. "We've passed the half-way point," he said, "but if we make the same rate of progress and the water continues to rise at the current pace, by the time we reach the exit to the Inner Harbor the water will be almost at the top of the pipe."

"The *Oregon* will have sent help by now," Jones said, "and they will have a copy of the blueprints."

Meadows wiped some water from his forehead before speaking. "That doesn't change the problems we face. It just places more people in harm's way."

Hornsby was standing in water up to his waist, pushing the raft with the Buddha to the left with his hip. Once the raft entered the other stream and started to move, he rolled back inside the following raft. "Not only that," he said, "if the pace continues when we *do* reach the Inner Harbor—*if* we do—it will be at first light and then we risk detection."

Hornsby turned his head. He could see Jones grinning in the dim light from his faltering hard-hat lamp. Then he spoke.

"We're the Corporation," Jones said quietly. "We're always one step ahead."

The trio of men nodded as the pair of rafts hurtled faster in the growing current toward a rendezvous with a rescuing force that was fighting problems of their own.

T HE FOUR-STROKE OUTBOARD on the Zodiac being driven by Mark Murphy was blasting water out of its jet drive. The current was running stronger every few feet, but the powerful engine was propelling the craft forward in spite of the strong stream running against the bow. To the middle of the inflatable, Hali Kasim was unscrewing the tubular metal top that supported a canvas sun awning and the electronics sensors to gain a few feet of needed clearance. Finishing the job, he stacked the last of the pipes inside the Zodiac and turned to Murphy.

"Maximum headroom," he said. "Now hit the gas. If we don't meet up with the other team and tow them out of here soon, we're all going to be swimming."

Murphy advanced the throttle and steered around a bend. For lights he used a handheld spotlight; for navigation, a portable GPS unit held between his knees. "Find the air horn," Murphy said to Kasim. "I have a feeling we'll need it soon."

S HEETS OF RAIN washed from east to west as Rick Barrett steered the Scarab close to the southernmost strip of man-made land that comprised the Macau airport. Barrett was wearing a bright yellow rain suit that should have made him stand out, but in the dark of night and the pouring rain, he and the Scarab were virtually invisible. He listened for a sound in his earpiece but heard only static.

Scanning the shoreline with a pair of night-vision binoculars, he began to fear the worst.

"W HAT DO YOU mean?" Po shouted in anger.
The head of the Macau Public Works Department was far from happy himself. He'd been awakened from a sound sleep and ordered to make his way to his office to locate the blueprints of the storm sewer system. Once there, he had been unable to find the documents.

"I mean that they are gone," the man told Po. "Deleted from the computers, and the hard copies removed from the office."

"Are you certain?" Po asked.

"I have had the entire night shift searching," the man said. "Nothing is left."

"So we have no way to know for certain where the water exits into the bay?" Po asked.

"We don't have a map of it," the man agreed, "but there is one way to tell."

"Well," Po said, "how?"

"Pour some dye into a drain," the man said. "Then see where it goes."

Po turned to one of the patrolmen nearby. "Find a hardware store," he said quickly, "and buy me a dozen gallons of paint."

Then he stared down the manhole. There was no use entering the maze; the rats would be flushed from the hole by the water, and, when they were, Po would be waiting. He smiled at the thought, but failed to notice a man standing some ten feet distant in the entryway of an all-night café. The man touched his ear to adjust his earpiece, then walked inside the restaurant.

T HE BILLIONAIRE SLID the Chevrolet into park. There was really no other choice. To his front, three police cars were blocking the road. The officers were standing behind their vehicles with pistols drawn. To the rear were more cars and an armored personnel carrier that was being used as a temporary command post. Inside the APC, Sung Rhee peered through a gun port at the stopped truck. Reaching for a microphone, he spoke over the P.A. system.

"You are surrounded," he said. "Step slowly from the vehicle with your hands above your head."

Then he turned to one of the officers driving the APC. "Light him with the spotlight."

The man flicked a switch and a four-million-candlelight-powered spotlight turned night into day. Rhee watched as the driver's door slowly opened. Then a man dressed entirely in black stepped onto the wet pavement and took a few steps away from the truck.

"Stop," Rhee ordered.

The man stopped dead in his tracks.

"Keep your hands in the air," Rhee ordered. "If you are the only occupant of the vehicle, wave your left arm slowly."

The man's left arm moved back and forth.

"Take six steps into the direction of the light."

The man complied.

"Now lay down knees-first, then belly-down, on the road."

The man eased himself down until his entire body was prone on the wet road.

"Two officers forward," Rhee said, "and restrain the suspect."

A pair of officers approached from behind the police cars to the front and slowly made their way over to the man. With one covering, the other man bent down and handcuffed the suspect's hands behind his back. Then he yanked him to his feet.

"I'm an American," the billionaire said, "and I demand to see the ambassador."

Rhee waited as the rear door of the APC was lowered, then he stepped out into the rain and walked over to the Chevrolet. After first flashing a light inside to verify the other seats were empty, he scanned the rear storage area and caught sight of the Buddha. Flipping open the rear gate, he glanced at the six-foot-tall chunk of gold. Then he reached for his cell phone.

T HE LIMOUSINE CARRYING Hanley was just pulling up in front of the *Oregon*. "Wipe it carefully and get rid of it," he said to Crabtree. "You come with me."

Spenser followed Hanley as he bounded up the gangplank. Once on the deck of the ship, he motioned for Spenser to follow him inside and started in the direction of the control room. Opening the door, he nodded at Eric Stone.

"Call for a guard for Spenser here."

Stone spoke over a microphone.

"Where's the chairman?" Hanley said next.

Stone pointed to a screen that showed a flashing light almost at the end of the airport island and a second separate light a few yards distant. "There," Stone said, pointing. "The other is Barrett doing extraction."

Hanley watched as the first light slowed, then stopped.

"Signal Barrett that they have arrived."

Spenser was staring at the operation in amazement. He was just about to ask Hanley a question when the door to the control room opened and Sam Pryor walked in. "Take this man to the brig," Hanley ordered, "and secure him."

"Level?" Pryor asked.

"Minimum," Hanley said, "but you stay with him—he's not to use any communications devices or talk to anyone. You can feed him and you may allow him to sleep or use the entertainment system for television or movies, but no computer."

"Yes, sir," Pryor said.

Hanley turned to Spenser. "You fulfilled your end of the bargain," he said. "Don't try anything stupid now and we'll do exactly what we promised."

Pryor started to lead Spenser away by his arm. "When will I be free to go?" the art dealer asked.

"We'll let you know," Hanley said, "but it will be soon."

Pryor led Spenser into the hall. Just before the door closed, he looked back to see Hanley begin to peel the latex mask from his face.

B ARRETT HEARD A beep in his earpiece and stared at the shoreline with his binoculars. A quick flash of headlights appeared like twin explosions in the green screen of his night-lit viewer, then the white dots faded to black.

Barrett flashed the docking lights on the Scarab, then steered closer to shore.

Tom Reyes finished wiping his fingerprints off the steering wheel and controls, then twisted the key to off. Turning around in the seat, he stared at Cabrillo and Nixon.

"We're clean and green, boss," Reyes said as he slid the keys into his pocket.

"Let's go get wet," Cabrillo said as he opened the rear door of the cab.

Nixon climbed from the cab, clutching the last box of props and tools, and followed Reyes and Cabrillo to the water. Staring to the east, he could just make out the sky beginning to lighten. To the west, the wind was diminishing. In a few hours it would be morning and the storm would have passed over Macau, but for now the sheets of rain continued to rake the islands.

Barrett angled as close to shore as he dared, then tilted the drive up to avoid rocks. Cabrillo waded into the water and grabbed the bow and held it in place. Reyes climbed into the Scarab, then took the box Nixon held in his arms. Placing it on the deck, he reached over again and helped Nixon over the gunwale. Once Nixon was on the deck, Cabrillo gave the Scarab a push backward and reached for Reyes's hand. As the boat drifted backward he climbed over the side and Barrett lowered the drive and slid the control into reverse.

Slowly, he backed away from the southernmost edge of the airport island.

Once free from obstructions, Barrett slid the control forward and steered toward the *Oregon*.

"WHAT DO YOU mean?" Hanley asked.

"The lead detective sent for buckets of paint," Michael Halpert said quietly. "They are planning to pour them down the storm sewer to trace the flow of the water."

"I understand," Hanley said. "Good job. You can return to the *Oregon* now."

Stone was studying the returns on the radar scope and he turned to Hanley. "Barrett is headed back across the water. He should reach us in a few minutes."

Hanley was watching the storm scope.

"Make sure there are a couple of deckhands standing by," Hanley ordered. "We need the Scarab back in the hangar and out of sight."

"Yes, sir," Stone said as he reached for the microphone.

*   *   *

S UNG RHEE WALKED over to the suspect, who had been moved
under the overhang just outside the departure terminal at the airport. In the bright lights spilling from inside the terminal, the man
looked vaguely familiar.

"One of your partners turned on you," Rhee said, "and phoned in
your location."

The man stared at Rhee with a look that contained equal parts pity
and contempt. "I've got no idea what you are talking about."

"There is no reason to try to be coy with us," Rhee said. "We caught
you red-handed."

"You caught nothing," the man said. "I was buying a piece of art,
and a team of thieves scammed me. They're the ones you should be
harassing, not me."

"When did you arrive in Macau?" Rhee asked.

"A couple of hours ago," the man replied.

"The last ferryboat was three hours ago," Rhee said, "and the next
does not leave for two more. In addition, there are no commercial airline
flights from the hours of one a.m. until five a.m. Your story is obvious
nonsense."

"I have my own jet," the man noted.

"Indeed. Where is it now?" Rhee asked.

"I have no idea," the man said. "The thieves stole it."

"How convenient," Rhee said. "You understand: If you refuse to
answer our questions, we can make this very uncomfortable."

The billionaire's ire was rising fast. Any dealings with bureaucrats
were usually limited to him telling them what he wanted to do. He was
tired, slightly hungover and missing his hundred million dollars.

He looked right into Rhee's eyes.

"Listen, you asshole," the man said. "My 737 was stolen from your
airport, and inside was a briefcase containing one hundred million dollars in bearer bonds. I don't know what the hell has been happening

tonight in this little pisspot of a country, but if you just unhook me from these handcuffs and let me use a telephone, I can clear this up in about ten minutes."

Had Rhee listened to the billionaire, the 737 might have been tracked. Instead, the man's belligerent attitude doomed him. Rhee motioned to one of the officers holding the man's arms. "Take him to headquarters," he said.

B ARRETT STEERED THE Scarab into the sling, then Barrett, Cabrillo, Reyes and Nixon climbed up the boarding ladder while the deckhands secured the boat.

"Doing some operation time tonight," Cabrillo said to Barrett. "Do you like it?"

"Not as easy as frosting a cake," Barrett admitted, "but a lot more exciting."

The four men walked through a hatch into the interior of the *Oregon*. Cabrillo motioned down the hallway. "You men go and clean up. I've still got some work to do."

The men started down the hallway to their cabins.

"Hey," Cabrillo said to the retreating men, "good job."

Then he walked down to the control room and opened the door. Stepping inside, he began to unbutton his wet shirt, then turned to Hanley.

"Where are we at, Max?"

F OUR FEET OF space remained between the surface of the rising water and the top of the storm sewer. The batteries on the hardhat lights were growing dim, the water was rising fast, and the men could no longer safely climb from the raft to steer the Golden Buddha along.

Meadows had lashed the rafts together, and he and Jones were on each side where the two rafts met, standing in a half crouch. As the rafts careened along, they attempted to alter their direction by pushing against the hard sides of the pipe with their legs.

"Junction coming up," Hornsby shouted. "We need the left channel."

At the V in the pipes just ahead, the fast-flowing water was being parted like the bow wake on a nuclear submarine. Chunks of debris littered the water, the roof of the pipe was dripping so hard they might as well have been outside, and the pair of rafts was accelerating almost beyond control.

Jones watched ahead and timed his action. As the rafts reached a spot twenty feet in advance of the V, he reached over with his leg and shoved against the wall. The rafts lumbered to the left side, and then were carried in the current past the junction.

"We made that one," Jones shouted, "but if we get much more water in this pipe, we're going to have trouble on the next one."

"If we don't get some help soon," Meadows said, "we're going to need to cut the Buddha loose and try to save our own skin."

29

"ONE AT A time," Detective Po said to the officer.

Using a screwdriver on his key chain, the officer opened the first can of paint and poured the contents through the open manhole into the racing water below. From the light of his flashlight, Po could see the purple paint mix with the water, then spread out. Placing the empty can to the side, the officer pried open a second and repeated the process. At just that instant, Po's cell phone rang and he stepped a few feet away and answered.

"Ling," Sung Rhee said. "I want you to come to headquarters. We've captured a suspect."

"Right, boss," Po said.

"THE AUTHORITIES HAVE decided to trace the flow of water in the storm sewers with paint," Hanley said to Cabrillo.

Cabrillo was wiping his wet face and hair with a hand towel. Once he was finished, he tossed it onto a table and ran a comb quickly through his hair.

"If they did realize our men had escaped through the sewers, I was hoping that removing all the blueprints would slow down the pursuit long enough for our men to be extracted," he said. "Looks like we need to implement one of the backup plans."

Hanley pointed to a computer screen. "As you know, the outflow pipe we picked for the exit into the bay is the only one on the southwest point of the Southern Peninsula. The outflow runs between the Nam Van Lakes and enters the water just north of the island of Taipa."

Cabrillo stared at the computer screen. The image of the storm sewers looked like a crooked tree with sagging limbs. The sewer his team would use to exit was the trunk at the roots.

"Have we been able to establish contact with them?" Cabrillo asked.

"No luck with Hornsby, Meadows and Jones," Hanley admitted. "The portable radios they carry just don't seem to have enough power to penetrate the layers of soil overhead."

"What about Murph and Kasim?"

"We've been trying," Hanley said, "but the voice transmission is spotty. Data seems to be passing through, however—we are in contact by alphanumeric signals."

"So we can type orders to the Zodiacs and they can respond?" Cabrillo asked.

"So far," Hanley said.

Eric Stone interrupted the conversation. "Sirs," he said, pointing to a screen, "the portable camera Halpert left near the manhole is showing something you might want to watch."

Cabrillo and Hanley watched as the officer poured paint into the hole.

"Give me a simulation of how long that paint will take to reach our men," Cabrillo said quickly.

Stone's hands danced over the keyboards, and a few seconds later the screen showing the sewer system began slowly to take on a red color. The men stood watching as the color advanced along the arteries of the sewer system. A counter in the corner of the screen timed the movement.

"Seventeen minutes until the paint reaches where we believe the men are now," Stone said slowly. "Twenty-two until it reaches the water above Taipa."

At just that instant, a printer off to the side whirled and a sheet was spit into the tray. Hanley walked over and picked it up. "The order just went through to the police boats and the two Chinese navy boats here in Macau. They are supposed to begin patrols immediately to scan for the colored water, then, when they find an outflow, remain there on station."

"Start a timer," Cabrillo ordered quickly. "We're in crunch time now. Make sure everyone is aboard and prepare the *Oregon* to sail. I want my team out of that storm sewer with the Golden Buddha and safely back aboard—then we need to vacate Macau by first light. With the Chinese navy on patrol, this ship is in jeopardy."

"Broken Arrow?" Hanley asked.

"Confirm, Broken Arrow," Cabrillo said.

"Put it out, Mr. Stone," Hanley said.

Stone sounded the alarm. In a few minutes, the *Oregon* was a blur of activity.

TINY GUNDERSON WAS eating a salami sandwich and sipping on a glass of iced tea as he flew over the South China Sea. The brunette flight attendant, Rhonda Rosselli, was sitting in the flight engineer's chair. The door to the cockpit was open, and the blonde copilot, Judy Michaels, walked inside and slid back into her seat. She was dressed in a khaki flight suit and her face was freshly scrubbed.

"Tracy is changing and checking the equipment," she said.

"Did I tell you, you did a great job?" Gunderson asked. "You both are most convincing ho's."

"A master's degree in political science from Georgetown and four years with the National Security Council, and I'm sleeping with the enemy," Michaels said.

Gunderson popped the last of the sandwich in his mouth, then brushed the crumbs off his hands. Washing the last bite down with a sip of iced tea, he spoke.

"I think you forget I seduced a Romanian countess a few years ago," Gunderson said. "We do what we have to, to accomplish the objective."

"I remember, Chuck," Michaels said. "In fact, I seem to remember you rather enjoyed the assignment."

Gunderson smiled. "So you didn't like yours?"

Michaels noted readings from the instrument panel on a clipboard. "The guy was a freak," she said. "Capital PH, phreak."

"Then it serves him right," Gunderson said as he unbuckled his seat belt and slid from the pilot's seat, "that we swiped his plane."

"On the controls," Michaels said.

"I have to use the restroom," Gunderson said to Rosselli. "Be right back."

I N THE DINING room on the *Oregon*, Winston Spenser was sipping tea and worrying. Off to one side, at a separate table, a guard sat on silent watch. Juan Cabrillo entered the dining room, walked over to Spenser, and handed him a slip of paper.

"That's the account number of the bank in Paraguay," Cabrillo said. "The transfer has taken place and the funds are available now. If the account is not accessed within one year of today, the funds will automatically bounce back to one of our banks. The second you make a deposit or withdrawal, however, within the next year the computer erases all traces of where the money came from or would go to."

"Why one year?" Spenser asked.

"Because," Cabrillo said, "in the financial shape you're in, if you don't touch the money in a year, it'll be because you're dead."

Spenser nodded.

Next, Cabrillo handed Spenser a folder with a plane ticket. "Hong Kong to Dubai, then on to Paraguay, first class. It's the first available flight tomorrow morning."

Spenser took the ticket.

"Here is ten thousand dollars in U.S. currency," Cabrillo said, handing Spenser an envelope. "Any more will arouse suspicions."

Spenser took the envelope.

"That concludes our agreement, Mr. Spenser," Cabrillo said. "We have called a cab to take you where you want to go. It will be pulling up at the side of the ship in a few minutes."

The guard stood up and waited for Spenser to rise. Cabrillo started for the door.

"Can I ask you a question?" Spenser said.

Cabrillo had just opened the door. He stopped, turned and nodded.

"This all seems a little too perfect," Spenser said. "What's the catch?"

"You still have to make it to Hong Kong," Cabrillo said as he walked through the door.

O N THE *OREGON'S* rear deck, George Adams waited as a landing pad on the fantail rose up to deck level. A hard rain was raking the deck and the winds were a steady twenty knots from east to west. He turned to Tom Reyes.

"Once the deckhand locks the lift in place, we need to rotate the whirlybird into the wind," he said. "Then I'm going to need to make a hot takeoff into the wind."

Reyes nodded and watched as another deckhand rolled a metal cart containing several boxes near the lift. The elevator operator signaled that the lift was locked, and Adams and Reyes walked over.

The Robinson R-44 helicopter was a medium-sized piston-engine craft with a top speed of just over 130 miles an hour. The weight was

1,420 pounds, the horsepower of the power plant 260, and the cost was about $300,000.

The two men attached ground-handling wheels, spun the ship around, then removed the wheels and handed them to the deckhand.

"We distributed the dye into plastic baggies like you ordered," the deckhand noted.

Adams nodded and turned to Reyes. "Keep the box at your feet, but away from the foot pedals. I'll take us down as low as we can safely go, but the ride will be touchy because of the wind."

"I understand," Reyes said.

Adams did a quick walk around the helicopter, checking fuel oil and general condition, then motioned to Reyes. "Hop in," he said, "and we'll get this show on the road."

Once both men were in the seats, Adams reached down and ran through the preflight checklist. Once he was done, he screamed "Clear" out the window and engaged the starter. Once the engine had fired and the clutch was engaged, the rotor blades started slowly spinning, then gathered speed until the helicopter was shaking and vibrating. Adams watched the gauges closely, and when the engine was warmed and everything had settled down, he spoke through the headset microphone to Reyes.

"Hold on, Tom," Adams said, "this will be like a giant jump."

Neutralizing the cyclic, Adams quickly lifted the collective and the tiny bird left the pad. A second later, Adams eased the cyclic forward and the helicopter nosed over into the wind, rising and moving forward at the same time.

Clear of the *Oregon*, Adams flew directly into the wind. Heading offshore a distance, he then started to angle back toward Macau. Around the knee of his flight suit was a strap with a metal clip, and in the clip was a folded slip of paper showing the locations of the storm sewer outflows.

"There we go," Adams said, spotting the dirty water where a pipe spilled into the bay.

Reyes reached down in the box, removed a baggie, slid the top open partway, and then tossed it out the small window opening in the passenger door. It tumbled through the ten feet from the helicopter to the water and began to spread out like blood from a rare steak.

In the distance, a police boat heard the noise from the helicopter but it could not make it out in the rain. Adams moved the helicopter up the line, salting the water on the east side of Macau. Then he steered around the end of the peninsula between Macau and Taipa to repeat the exercise.

D ETECTIVE PO PARKED in front of the headquarters of the Macau Police Department, then walked through the rain toward the front doors. In the east, the sky was lightening some, but the rain continued on unabated.

Entering the building, he rode the elevator up to Rhee's floor, then exited the elevator and walked down the hallway. Upon reaching the reception area, he instantly knew that there was trouble afoot. The U.S. consular agent, the mayor of Macau, a Chinese general and four reporters were clustered around a man dressed entirely in black.

"This isn't a case of shoplifting," the man in black said loudly. "They've stolen a Boeing 737, for God's sake."

It had been a case of blind luck for the software billionaire. Still refused a telephone call, he had been brought to headquarters to be questioned by Rhee in his office. As soon as they had entered the office, however, the billionaire had noticed a copy of *Fortune* magazine on Rhee's side table. His face was gracing the cover. Once he'd pointed that out to Rhee, things had begun happening fast.

The billionaire had turned from suspect to victim in seconds.

Po walked over and stood next to Rhee.

Po heard him whisper "Damn" as the elevator door opened again and Stanley Ho started down the hall.

"Have you found my Buddha?" Ho said as soon as he was within range.

"Who the hell is this?" the billionaire asked.

"I'm Stanley Ho," Ho said in aggravation. "Who the hell are you?"

"Marcus Friday," the billionaire said loudly. "You might have heard of me?"

"And you of me," Ho said, affronted. "I'm one of *Forbes*'s richest people."

"I know all the people ahead of me on the list—you aren't one of them," Friday retorted.

Detective Po smiled to himself. If all this was true, it was the greatest game of one-upmanship he had ever seen. Here was a pair of obscenely rich men vying for attention like children trying to be picked for kickball.

"Yeah," Ho began to say, "well, this is my town, and you can—"

"Mr. Ho," Detective Po said quickly, "why don't you come down to my office so we can sort this out?"

"I'm not going anywhere," Ho said loudly.

"Everyone calm down," Rhee said.

He motioned to a conference room, pointed for the reporters to remain in the foyer, and then led the rest inside. Once everyone was inside and seated, he picked up the telephone, ordered tea to be delivered, then spoke.

"Okay, everyone," he said slowly, "who wants to begin?"

Ho stared at the chief inspector. "A Buddha I purchased for two hundred million dollars in Switzerland was stolen tonight while you were at a party at my house. I demand to know if you have recovered it yet."

"I lost a hundred million dollars in bearer bonds and my 737 to a gang of criminals," the billionaire said, "and want to know what is going *on* in this godforsaken country."

· Po stood up and paced for a second. "Was your plane valued over a hundred million?" he asked Friday.

The billionaire shook his head.

"Then it looks like two hundred million is the highest bid here tonight," Po said.

30

THE STORM SEWER was fast becoming a watery grave.

Less than three feet separated the rising water from the arched dome of air overhead. The drainpipes on the top of the tube were gushing like a downpour. The water was littered with refuse washed from the streets above. Hornsby saw a rat swimming toward them in the current and slapped at the creature with a paddle. Just ahead was another junction.

"We need to make a decision," he shouted over the roar of the water. "Sink or swim."

Meadows looked forward. In the dimming light from the miner's hard hat he could just see the torrent ahead, a cascade of white water that would make the rafts uncontrollable.

"Ready with the paddles," he shouted. "The horse has to lead the cart."

Digging into the water on the left side of the raft, they swung the stern of their raft to the right. The nose of the lead raft, which was carrying the Golden Buddha, pulled hard left but made the turn into the proper channel. The turn was not as smooth for the raft carrying the trio of men. It slammed amidships into the junction, and the corner struck Jones hard in his right side. He hung there for a minute pressed against a concrete arch until the rope holding them to the lead raft went taut and yanked them down the channel.

"Jonesy's been hurt," Meadows shouted above the din.

Pete Jones was clutching the side of his chest and wheezing to catch his breath. Turning his head, in the dim light Hornsby could just make out his shredded shirt and anguished expression.

"My ribs," Jones managed to groan.

"We need to cut the raft loose," Hornsby shouted. "There's no way we'll make the next turn."

"Maybe we should slit the side and sink the Buddha," Meadows shouted. "Then we can return when the water recedes and pull it out of here."

Jones gritted his teeth and stared at his watch. "The *Oregon*," he said painfully, "is due to sail this morning. If we don't get this out now, we never will."

Hornsby thought for a second, then decided. The next junction would be coming up in a few minutes. Taking a pen from his shirt pocket, he stared at the GPS, then drew the rest of their intended course on the back of his hand.

"Bob," he said, "I'm going onto the lead raft. My weight will place it low in the water, but it should still remain afloat. As soon as I'm on top of the case holding the Buddha, cut me loose."

He handed Meadows the GPS.

"You sure, Horny?"

Hornsby threw his paddle onto the top of the Buddha, pulled the rope to bring the rear raft closer, then turned.

"Ready your knife," he said.

Unclipping a folding knife from his belt, Meadows opened the blade and nodded.

Hornsby crouched and hopped the short distance to the lead raft. As soon as he was clear, Meadows sliced through the tether, then dug his paddle into the side to slow down his raft. Hornsby squirted ahead. In the dim light, Meadows could see the Buddha was awash, and only a portion of Hornsby's head and torso were above the waterline.

"Going right," Hornsby shouted as he pulled ahead, "then left."

A S THE STORM sewer pipes came closer to the water, they increased in diameter so the storm water would not become pressurized and blow apart the tiles. At six places under Macau were large square pond-like storage facilities where the water could pool and lose some speed before spilling out into the last series of pipes and eventually the bay.

Murphy and Kasim were motoring around in circles in one of them.

"Five more minutes," Murphy shouted. "Then we go in and find them."

Kasim gave three more blasts on the air horn. "They should be here by now," he agreed.

At just that instant, Murphy's digital pager beeped and he pushed the button to light the screen. Scrolling through the message, he nodded his head.

"They poured paint into the sewers to follow the flow," he said as he steered the Zodiac into another tight circle. "If it makes it down our escape channel, we're screwed."

"What do you mean?" Kasim asked.

"The paint will bring the Chinese to the area, as well as marking the sides of the Zodiac," Murphy said. "Then they'll grab us and take us in for questioning."

"What's the *Oregon* recommend?"

Murphy was quiet for a moment before answering. "They want us to blow up the tunnel leading into here and seal off the tainted water."

"How long do we have?"

"Six minutes and forty-seven seconds," Murphy said, removing a satchel charge from one of the bags in the bottom of the boat.

"What about the others?" Kasim asked.

"If they aren't out by then," Murphy said, "the *Oregon* said to assume they took a wrong turn or drowned inside. Then we need to protect our own asses and make a safe retreat."

Murphy angled the Zodiac over to the pipe leading into the holding pool. Using the power of the outboard motor, he held the boat in place against the strong current until Kasim had attached the charges to the top of the storm sewer. Once the explosives were in place, Kasim activated the digital timer. Four, three, two, one, and the red light blinked.

"Give the signal again," Murphy said as he backed the Zodiac away.

I T WAS LIKE Hornsby was riding a log down a flume. He was almost awash and the distance over his head to the top of the pipe was narrowing as the water continued rising. The last turn had been made by gouging his paddle into the water and bringing the bow slightly to one side. He readied his leg to push against the wall for the next bend. Hornsby had lost sight of the others. The light on his hard hat was nearly out and he had no way to know if Meadows and Jones had taken the correct channel. Anyway, there was nothing he could do if they hadn't. He was more concerned for his own survival. He jammed his leg against the wall and the raft lumbered over into the correct channel.

And then, like the distant chirping of a mother bird calling her young, he heard the faint sound of a horn sounding three times. The raft, with Hornsby atop the Golden Buddha, raced on the current in the direction of the sound.

A S THE ZODIAC circled, Kasim attempted to keep a portable spotlight trained at the opening of the pipe. The timer on the satchel charge was ticking down and, quite honestly, he was beginning to lose faith this was all going to work out.

"Two minutes," he said over the sound of the motor.

Murphy listened intently. A sound was coming from the tunnel that sounded like the bellowing of a wounded animal. And then, riding on a scream and a prayer, Cliff Hornsby shot from the pipe and slid halfway across the pond. Murphy quickly angled the Zodiac alongside and Kasim grabbed the edge of the raft.

"Where are the others?" Murphy shouted.

Hornsby wiped the water from his eyes and glanced at the highbarreled ceiling just barely visible from the spotlight trained on the timer. "They were right behind me."

"Did you see any colored water?" Kasim asked.

"What do you mean?"

"They poured paint in the manhole to trace the flow of water," Murphy said. "Did you see anything in the water?"

"No," Hornsby said.

"One minute, thirty seconds," Kasim said.

"What's happening?" Hornsby asked.

"We've been ordered to seal off this exit," Murphy said, "so we have a chance at a clean escape. Sound the horn."

J ONES WAS LYING in the bottom of the raft, barely able to move. If they had to go in the water or needed to attempt an escape, Meadows figured he'd have to carry him. They had made the last turn, but just barely. Anything from here on out had a limited chance for success.

"How's it going, pal?" he asked.

Jones listened to the distant sound, then opened his eyes and grimaced. "Did you hear that?"

"What?" Meadows asked, thinking Jones was hallucinating.

"They came for us," Jones said.

Eighteen seconds later, their raft shot out of the pipe and into the holding pond.

"I don't have time to explain," Murphy yelled, "but take this line and hold tight."

"Just passed thirty," Kasim yelled.

Murphy finished tying the leads for the two rafts to the rear of the Zodiac, then slammed the throttle forward. The outboard prop dug into the water and the boat lurched forward across the holding pond, then into the exit tunnel.

"Heads down," Murphy shouted, staring at his stopwatch.

At just that instant, a roar filled the square holding area and reverberated out the escape tunnel. A second later, the inflow pipe collapsed down on itself and sealed off the holding pond. At the same time, a wave began to build that rolled across the pond and sought the only opening. The top of the wave was higher than the exit pipe and filled the outflow to overflowing. Kasim swung the spotlight around and noticed the approaching tsunami.

"Shock wave approaching," he shouted as the Zodiac with the rafts in tow entered the pipe leading to the bay.

31

ON BOARD THE *Oregon*, preparations for departure were moving at lightning speed.

Juan Cabrillo reached for the telephone and placed a call to the acting harbormaster.

"Don't worry," he said, after lying that his parent company had ordered him to leave immediately, "we have another ship lined up in Manila to take the load of fireworks to the United States. She'll be here day after tomorrow."

The harbormaster seemed to accept this as fact. Because it was late and little was happening, he was talkative.

"Singapore," Cabrillo said in answer to his question, "but they haven't told me the cargo, only that we need to be there seventy-two hours from now."

Singapore was fifteen hundred miles as a crow flies, and from what the harbormaster had heard, the *Oregon* would be hard-pressed to make twenty knots an hour. The man had no way to know that if the ship made it into open water by sunrise, it could be in Singapore by lunch the next day. Nor did he know the *Oregon* was not going to Singapore at all.

"Yes," Cabrillo said, "it's pushing for sure, but orders are orders. Is the pilot on his way here?"

The harbormaster answered in the affirmative, and Cabrillo hurried to get off the telephone.

"We'll keep an eye out for him," Cabrillo finished, "and thank you."

Hanging up the telephone, Cabrillo turned to Hanley. The time was 4:41 A.M.

"Sounds like he bought it," Cabrillo said. "Order the lookout to watch for the approaching pilot boat."

Hanley nodded. "The helicopter with Adams and Reyes is back, and I've ordered all the hatches battened down. Which means we need to retrieve the Zodiacs in open water."

"What do you hear from them?" Cabrillo asked.

"Seng and Huxley report they are still waiting outside," Hanley said, staring at his watch. "Murphy was ordered to blow up an inner cavern any time about now to seal off the flow of paint and at least allow the four rescuers to escape. As of the last communication a few minutes ago, Hornsby, Jones and Meadows had not shown up with the Golden Buddha."

"I don't like it," Cabrillo said.

"I had to make a decision when you were dealing with the art dealer," Hanley said quietly. "If the helicopter salting the water didn't throw off the Chinese, not only would we lose the men in the tunnel, but the rescue crew as well."

"I know, Max," Cabrillo said. "You're just following the book."

The two men stared at one another for a moment. Then Eric Stone spoke.

"Sirs," Stone said, pointing at a screen, "we just detected a shock wave from an explosion."

MURPHY HAD THE throttle on the Zodiac as far forward as she would go. The trio of boats was rocketing down the tunnel leading out to the bay. They were only ten feet ahead of the approaching wave from the explosion, but now that they were at full speed, the margin was remaining constant.

"Try to reach Seng on the radio," Murphy shouted over the noise, "and tell him what's happening."

Kasim nodded and reached for the microphone.

"Eddie," he shouted into the microphone, "we have the target with us. Clear away from the opening—we're coming out hot."

"Got it," Seng shouted from just outside the pipe.

A few minutes before, Seng and Huxley had heard the rumble from the explosion and had climbed aboard the second Zodiac. They were just backing away from shore when Kasim radioed. Seng turned the Zodiac and then accelerated away into the bay. Once they reached the edge of the fog and rain band, he turned toward land and pointed a spotlight at the outflow pipe.

"Call the *Oregon*," he said to Huxley, "and report team two is on their way out."

THE PILOT BOAT pulled alongside the *Oregon*. A single tugboat hovered nearby, awaiting instructions from the pilot. The pilot climbed off his boat at a boarding ladder, made his way on deck, and then stared around. The upper deck was a tangled mess of rusting equipment and cables. He stared above, where the smokestack was polluting the air around the slip with smoky, oily fumes. This was a ship begging to be put out of her misery at a scrapyard.

"What a pile of junk," the pilot muttered to himself.

A man stepped from behind a pillar. "I'm Captain Smith," he said. "Welcome aboard."

The captain was dressed in tattered yellow rain slickers spotted with grease and dirt. His face had a full beard, stained around the mouth by nicotine, and when Smith cracked a smile, he showed a forest of yellow stubs.

"I'm ready to guide you out," the pilot said, staying a safe distance away from the man's odor.

"This way," the captain said, turning.

The pilot followed the captain as he wove his way around the tangled mess on the decks to the rusted metal stair leading to the pilothouse. Halfway up the stair, the pilot gripped for a handrail and it came off in his hand.

"Captain," he said.

Smith turned, then walked a few steps to where the pilot was stopped. Then he took the length of rusted pipe in his hand and tossed it over his shoulder onto the cluttered deck.

"I'll make a note of that," he said, swiveling around again and climbing the last few steps to the pilothouse.

The pilot shook his head. The sooner he was off the ship, the happier he'd be.

Six minutes later, the *Oregon* was turned and partway out of the port. The pilot ordered the line from the tug removed and the *Oregon* headed away from land under her own power.

To the rear of the *Oregon*, now growing dimmer in the distance, the mountain peak on Macau began to recede in the rain and fog. Only a few lights from the airport remained in sight.

"How long until you can be picked up?" Cabrillo asked the pilot.

The pilot pointed to a channel marker thirty yards ahead. The high-powered light was penetrating the gloom. A few more minutes and he could be off this beast of a ship.

*   *   *

"LIGHT AT THE end of the tunnel," Murphy shouted.

The Zodiac was racing toward the bay just ahead of the shock wave that would fill the pipe to the top. Hornsby was holding tight to his raft and the top of the Golden Buddha, while Meadows gripped the side of the Zodiac and glanced down at Jones, who was clutching his side in the bottom of the raft.

"A few more seconds, Jonesy," he shouted, "and we'll be in the clear."

Jones nodded but did not speak.

The exit from the pipe was like riding over a waterfall on a class IV rapid. The water was spewing out of the pipe with tremendous force. The plume cascaded through the air twenty feet, then dropped seven feet down to the water of the bay. Murphy held to the wheel as the Zodiac was propelled through the air. As soon as he felt the boat leave the water, he pulled back on the throttle so he wouldn't over-rev the engine, then braced himself for the splashdown.

"Let go," he screamed to Hornsby and Meadows.

The lines on the two towed rafts were released and they separated a few feet from the Zodiac at the same instant the wall of water filled the pipe, then burst through the air with tremendous force.

"Wow," Seng shouted at the sight of the rafts squirting through the air.

"Hold on," Meadows shouted to Jones as the raft flew through the air, then slapped on the surface of the water before slowing almost to a stop.

"Are you okay?" Meadows said a few seconds later. "Do you need anything?"

Jones wiped the water from his face, then shifted his body to ease the pain of his cracked ribs as the raft stopped in the water and bobbed.

"I've been better," Jones said. "I think it would help if you would hum a few bars of 'Suwannee River.'"

*   *   *

P O WAS INSIDE the conference room with Rhee, Ho and Marcus Friday. A police sergeant entered and whispered in his ear.

"What the hell do you mean?" he asked.

"A few of our people heard what sounded like a helicopter," the sergeant said. "Now all the waters around Macau are a bright pink color."

"Those bastards," Po said. "They're covering their tracks."

"Who?" the sergeant asked.

"I don't know who," Po said, "but I intend to find out."

Po waved the sergeant away, then walked over to Rhee and motioned for him to move a few feet away so they could talk in private. Once he explained what the sergeant had told him, Rhee had only one thing to say.

"Seal the port," Rhee said. "No one in or out."

A S SOON AS Kasim helped Meadows and Jones aboard the Zodiac, Murphy slit the rubber raft with a knife. The raft drifted away and began to sink. At the same time, Seng and Huxley helped Hornsby aboard and the three of them wrestled the Golden Buddha aboard their Zodiac. Murphy idled his boat close just as they had finished stowing the golden icon amidships.

"I just spoke to Hanley," he said to Seng. "The *Oregon* is almost to the outer buoy. We are supposed to rendezvous with them in open water."

Kasim raised his hand for quiet as the radio barked. He listened intently over his earpiece.

"Got it," he said.

"That was the *Oregon* again," he said. "They just intercepted a transmission from the police to the port authorities. They have ordered the port sealed—no one in or out. The police and port authority boats have been given orders to fire on any craft that refuses to comply."

"Shh . . . ," Seng said.

The sound of a ship under power came across the water.

"They're coming," Seng said.

C APTAIN SMITH WALKED the pilot to the ladder leading down and bid him farewell. The pilot climbed down the ladder, then stepped across to the pilot boat, which quickly backed away from the *Oregon*. Smith watched the pilot boat accelerate away into the rain.

The pilot boat was still visible when it began to slow and turn.

Cabrillo reached for a tiny radio at his belt and flicked it on. "Max," he said quickly, "what's happening?"

"The authorities have ordered the port sealed," Hanley said. "The pilot's been ordered to bring us back to port."

Cabrillo sprinted across the deck as he spoke. "Full steam ahead," he shouted. "I'll be in the control room in a few minutes."

R HEE WAS IN his office. The port's night manager was on the other end of the phone line.

"They won't stop?" he asked.

"The pilot boat can't reach them," the port manager noted. "The pilot that guided them out mentioned that the vessel was in terrible shape—maybe their radios are faulty."

"Have the pilot boat outrun them and deliver the message in person."

"I already ordered that," the manager said in exasperation. "But the ship keeps gaining speed—the pilot boat can't seem to catch up with her."

"I thought you said the ship was a rust bucket," Rhee said.

"She's a fast rust bucket," the manager noted. "Our pilot boats can do over thirty knots."

"Damn," Rhee said. "How long until the ship reaches international waters?"

"Not long," the manager admitted.

"Get me the navy," Rhee shouted to Po, who reached for another telephone.

"What do you want us to do?" the port manager asked.

"Nothing," Rhee said. "You've already done enough."

He slammed down the telephone and took the one in Po's hand. The second in command of the Chinese navy detachment in Macau was on the line.

"This is the chief of the Macau police. We need you to stop a ship heading out into the South China Sea," he said quickly.

"We have a hydrofoil that can run at sixty-five knots," the Chinese navy officer told him, "but it isn't very heavily armed."

"This is an old cargo ship," Rhee said loudly. "I doubt she'll put up much of a fight."

Rhee had no way of knowing it, but he'd just made the biggest error of his life.

C ABRILLO BURST INTO the control room, shedding his grimy rain suit while at the same time removing the dental appliance that made his teeth appear as stubs. He tossed both to the side and tugged at his fake beard as he spoke. "Okay, what's the situation?"

"We just intercepted a communiqué from the Chinese navy to their high-speed hydrofoil. They've been ordered to intercept us—a naval frigate and a fast-attack corvette are following."

"Any other ships?"

"No," Hanley said. "That's the only Chinese navy firepower currently in Macau."

"Where's our team with the Golden Buddha?" Cabrillo asked as he tossed the beard aside, then spit out a sliver of latex left over from the false teeth mold.

"They are driving at full speed out of port," Stone said, pointing to a screen. "But it looks like they have picked up a tail."

"Get me Adams," Cabrillo said. "While he's making his way here, have the deckhands drop the walls on the helicopter pad and start raising the Robinson from the lower hangar."

"Got it," Stone said.

"Max," Cabrillo said, "get me Langston Overholt on a secure line."

Hanley started to assemble the satellite link.

Cabrillo stared at the screen showing the progress of the Zodiacs and the ship pursuing them. Then he glanced over at another screen that showed the *Oregon*'s location and the path of the Chinese navy vessels giving chase. The screens were filled with blinking lights and estimated paths.

"Adams will be here in a second," Stone said.

"Sound battle stations," Cabrillo said quietly.

Stone pushed a button and a loud whooping noise filled the *Oregon*.

Belowdecks in the sick bay, Gunther Reinholt heard the sound and sat up in bed. Swiveling to one side, he slid his feet into a pair of carpet slippers. Rising to his full height, he reached around and tightened his hospital gown around his body. Then with one hand on his IV drip, which was hanging from a stainless-steel rack with a wheeled base, he began to shuffle from the sick bay to the engine room.

Reinholt knew that if the *Oregon* went to war, they would need every hand on station.

32

THE CAPTAIN OF the Chinese navy hydrofoil *Gale Force*, Deng Ching, stared through the square floor-to-ceiling windows of the control room with a pair of high-powered binoculars. His craft had risen up to her full height of twelve feet above the water a few moments before. The hydrofoil was now reaching speeds of nearly fifty knots. Ching turned and glanced at the radar screen. The cargo ship was still a distance away, but the gap was closing.

"Are the sailors on the forward guns locked and loaded?" he asked his second in command.

"Yes, sir," the officer replied.

"Once we draw closer, I'll want to send a volley over their heads," Ching said.

"That should be enough," the second in command agreed.

*   *   *

L ANGSTON OVERHOLT SAT in his office in Langley, Virginia. On his left ear was the secure telephone connected to Cabrillo on the *Oregon*. His right ear was occupied by a telephone connected to the admiral in command of the Pacific theater.

"Presidential directive four twenty-one," he said to the admiral. "Now, what do you have nearby?"

"We're checking now," the admiral said. "I'll know in a few minutes."

"Can you bring some force to bear on the Chinese without it being tied to the U.S.?"

"Understood, Mr. Overholt," the admiral said. "Force from afar."

"That's it exactly, Admiral."

"Leave it to the navy," the admiral said. "We'll come up with something."

The telephone went dead. Overholt replaced the receiver and spoke to Cabrillo.

"Hold tight, Juan," he said quietly. "Help's a coming."

"Fair enough," Cabrillo said before disconnecting.

I N THE MOVIES, when a submarine goes to battle stations, it does so with much whooping from sirens and gongs. Men scurry down narrow passageways as they race to their stations and the tension that comes over the big screen is palpable and thick.

Reality is somewhat different.

Noise inside or outside a submarine is the enemy—it can lead to detection and death. On board the United States Navy Los Angeles–class attack submarine *Santa Fe*, the motions for battle were more like a roadie setting up a rock concert than the chaos of someone yelling "fire" in a crowded theater. A red light signaling action pulsed from numerous fixtures mounted in all the rooms and passageways. The crew moved with purpose, but not haste. The action they would take had been rehearsed a thousand times. They were as natural to the crew as shaving and showering. The commander of the *Santa Fe*, Captain Steven Farragut, stood on the command deck and received the condition reports from his crew with practiced ease.

"Electric check completed on packages one and two," an officer reported.

"Acknowledged," Farragut said.

"Boat rising to optimal firing depth," the driver reported.

"Excellent," Farragut said easily.

"Countermeasures and detection at one hundred percent," another officer reported.

"Perfect," Farragut said.

"Sensors report clear, sir," the chief of boat said. "We appear to be alone out here. We can commence operation inside of eight, repeat eight, minutes."

"Acknowledged," Farragut said.

The great beast was rising from the depths and preparing to bite if necessary.

ADAMS BURST INTO the control room of the *Oregon*. He was dressed in a tan flight suit that he was zipping up as he approached.

"Mr. Chairman," he said, smiling a blindingly white smile, "what can I do for you?"

Cabrillo pointed to one of the computer screens. "George, we have a situation. We have the two Zodiacs along with seven of our people trying to get out of Macau waters. We can't turn to pick them up because we're being pursued ourselves." Cabrillo pointed to another screen. "You can see they also have a tail. You need to provide support."

"I'll mount the experimental weapons pods Mr. Hanley designed for the Robinson. That gives me mini-rockets and a small chain gun, so I can cover their exit."

"What about the extraction system?" Cabrillo asked.

"I can't pull seven people aboard," Adams said, "I don't have the payload."

"That's not what I was thinking," Cabrillo said. "Let me explain."

C APTAIN CHING STARED at the radar screen. He had been told the ship he was supposed to intercept was an aging cargo ship named the *Oregon*. From the description given by the pilot, the vessel was little more than a bucket of rust. Somehow, Ching was beginning to doubt that—*Gale Force* was steaming at fifty knots, and if the radar on the computer screen was correct, the cargo ship was doing forty-five. At the current speeds, the *Oregon* would be safely in international waters in less than five minutes. Then there would be the risk of a major incident if the sailors on *Gale Force* attempted a boarding.

"Give me full speed," Ching ordered the engine room.

"T HE HYDROFOIL IS accelerating," Hanley noted. "At the increased speed, they will intercept us a minute or two before we reach the demarcation line."

Cabrillo glanced at the screen showing the water in front of the *Oregon*. The clouds were finally clearing and soon they would be free of the fog bank.

"Let's raise them on the radio," Cabrillo said, "and explain the situation."

Stone started tuning the radio while Cabrillo reached for a different microphone.

"Engine room," he said.

"Sir," a voice said, "this is Reinholt."

Cabrillo didn't bother to ask why the ailing engineer was not in sick bay as he had been ordered. The man had obviously felt well enough to help.

"Reinholt," Cabrillo said quickly, "is there any way to coax out a few more knots?"

"We're on it, sir," Reinholt answered.

D OWN BELOWDECKS, THE weapons pods had already been attached to both sides of the R-44. While the elevator lifted the helicopter up to launch height, Adams slid a pair of Nomex flight gloves over his hands, then slid a pair of yellow-tinted sunglasses over his eyes. He stepped from foot to foot in anticipation, and as soon as the elevator stopped and locked in place, he raced over, did a quick preflight and checked the underneath harness, then stepped to the pilot's door of the Robinson and cracked it open. He was sliding into the seat as a deckhand raced over.

"Do you want me to pull the pins?" the deckhand asked.

"Arm me," Adams said quickly, "then clear the deck. I'm out of here as soon as I have operating temps."

The man bent down, removed the pins from the missiles and checked the power to the mini-gun. Once he was finished, he popped his head inside the door again.

"Check your weapons console."

Adams stared at the small screen attached to the side of the dashboard. "I'm green."

The deckhand shut the door and raced away. Adams waited until he was clear, then engaged the starter. Four minutes and twenty-eight seconds later, using the surface wind from the accelerating *Oregon* as a crutch, Adams lifted from the deck, then pivoted the R-44 in midair, turned and headed back toward Macau.

T HE ZODIACS WERE skimming across the water at thirty knots. According to their crude radars, they were keeping ahead of the pursuing boats, but just barely. Seng's boat, with the added weight of the Golden Buddha, was straining to maintain speed. He had the throttle all the way to the stops, but there was no more speed to be coaxed from his engine. The fog and rain were still thick and they shielded the inflatable boats from the pursuers, but Seng could sense they were just out of visual and auditory range. If one thing went wrong—an engine miss or overheating, a leak in the inflatable pontoons that slowed them down—they would be toast.

At the same instant Seng was having his dark thoughts, Huxley heard the *Oregon* calling over the radio. She cupped her hand over her ear so she could hear. Because of the potential for interception, the message was brief and to the point.

"Help is on the way," Stone said.

"Understand," Huxley answered.

She turned to Seng and Hornsby. "The *Oregon*'s sending the cavalry," she said.

"Not a moment too soon," Seng said as he stared at the temperature gauge for his engine, now beginning to creep into the red.

Not too far distant, the Zodiac carrying Kasim, Murphy Meadows, and Jones heard the message as well. Kasim was steering, Meadows standing alongside, with Jones lying prone on the deck to the stern. Once Meadows heard the news, he turned, crouched down, then yelled the news over the sound of the wind and waves to Jones.

"I wish I'd have known," Jones quipped. "I would have asked them to bring some aspirin."

"You want another bottle of water?" Meadows asked.

"Not unless there's a bathroom on board," Jones said, grimacing.

"Hang in there, buddy," Meadows said. "We'll be home soon."

L IKE THE DISTANT view of a shoplifter across a crowded store, the outline of the *Oregon* started to form through Ching's binoculars as the fog began to clear. Concentrating on the hull, Ching could see the large white-capped wake being created by the racing cargo ship. The wake and the cargo ship's track were like nothing he had ever witnessed before. Most cargo ships, and Ching had tracked and intercepted more than a few, moved through the water like lumbering manatees—this Iranian-flagged vessel he was chasing moved like a thoroughbred in heat.

The water out the stern was not churning, as with most ships; instead, it seemed to be forming into concentric whirlpools that flattened the sea to the rear, as if a large container of glycerin had been poured overboard. Ching stared at the decks, but no crew was visible. There was only rusty metal and junk piled high.

Though the decks were deserted, the *Oregon* did not give the appearance of a ghost ship. No, Ching thought, beneath her metal skin, much was happening. At just that instant, a medium-sized helicopter flew over the *Gale Force* about a hundred yards to the port side, just above wave-top level.

"Where did that come from?" Ching asked his electronics officer.

"What, sir?" the officer said, staring up from a screen.

"A helicopter," Ching said, "heading from sea toward land."

"It didn't show up on the sensors," the officer said. "Are you sure you saw it through the fog?"

"Yes," Ching said loudly, "I saw it."

He walked over to the screen and stared at the radar returns.

"What's happening?" he asked a few seconds later.

The electronics officer was short and slim. He looked like a jockey in a fancy uniform. His hair was jet black and straight and his eyes brown-edged with bloodshot red from staring at the radar.

"Sir," he said finally, "I'm not sure. What you see has been happening intermittently since we began the chase. One second we seem to get a clear return, then it jumps to the other side of the screen like it's a video game playing hide-and-seek."

"The image is not even the correct size," Captain Ching noted.

"It grows, then diminishes to a pinprick," the officer said. "Then jumps across the screen."

Ching stared out the window again; they were drawing closer to the *Oregon*. "They're jamming us."

"I can detect that," the officer said.

"Then what is it?" Ching asked.

The officer thought for a minute. "I read in a translated science journal about an experimental system an American engineer was building. Instead of making objects disappear, as with stealth, or using extra signals, as on most jamming equipment, this system has a computer that takes in all the signals from our hull and reforms them into different shapes and strengths."

"So this system can make them appear or disappear as they decide?" Ching said incredulously.

"That's about it, sir," the officer said.

"Well," Ching said finally, "there's no way an old rust bucket has anything like that on board."

"Well, let's hope not, sir," the electronics officer said.

"Why's that?" Ching asked.

"Because the article also stated that by changing the object dimensions, they can increase the targeting potential."

"Which means?"

"That if the frigate to the rear or the fast-attack corvette coming up quick on our stern fires anything other than bullets, and they have a system like this, they could redirect the fire to us."

"Chinese missiles used to sink Chinese ships?"

"Exactly."

"RAMMING AND JAMMING," Eric Stone shouted.

Lincoln was on the far side of the control room at the primary fire control station. He was running a quick diagnostic check on the missile battery. He stared intently at the bar graphs as they filled the computer screen.

"Mr. Chairman, I'm good to go," he shouted toward Cabrillo a few seconds later.

Cabrillo turned to Hanley. "Here's the deal as I see it. The entire thrust of this operation was the retrieval of the Golden Buddha. We have it, but it's still inside the circle of Chinese influence. Our first priority must be to get our teams and the Golden Buddha safely back on the *Oregon*, while at the same time making our escape."

"I hate to say it, Juan," Hanley said, "but I wish the weather wasn't clearing."

"A wasted wish, but I agree," Cabrillo said.

"We don't know what the navy is sending," Hanley noted, "but we can safely assume there won't be surface ships involved—our sensors don't detect any other vessels for a hundred miles."

"They launched cruise missiles from the Persian Gulf into downtown Baghdad," Cabrillo said, "so we can assume either missile or aircraft support."

"The enemy has rockets on the fast-attack corvette, and some long guns that can fire high-explosive rounds, plus the frigate should have some Chinese-made cruise-type missiles."

"They any good?" Cabrillo asked.

"Not as accurate as ours," Hanley admitted, "but they can sink a ship."

"The hydrofoil?"

"Deck-mounted machine guns only," Hanley said.

"And the Zodiacs are being pursued by harbor patrol boats?"

"Correct," Hanley said. "A pair of forty-six-foot aluminum cruisers with diesel power. They each have a single bow-mounted machine gun."

"Radios?"

"Nothing special," Hanley said.

"So even if we took out the harbor boats," Cabrillo said, "the Zodiacs would still need to pass the trio of vessels on our tail."

"I'm afraid so," Hanley agreed.

Cabrillo started sketching on a yellow pad with a black Magic

Marker. When he finished, he handed the pad to Hanley. "Make sense to you?"

"Yep," Hanley said.

"Okay then," Cabrillo said forcefully, "hard a' starboard. We're going back toward land."

33

A DAMS EASED THE cyclic to the left and banked the R-44. A few
seconds earlier he had passed to port of the Chinese corvette and
had just picked up a glimpse of the vessel through the fog. It was a
wonder the Chinese vessel had not fired on him—surely they had detected the helicopter as it flew toward land. The frigate was fast approaching and Adams planned to give it a wide berth.

He was keeping the Robinson five to ten feet above the tops of the
waves—maybe that was shielding him from detection, but Adams
doubted it. To avoid radar detection, he needed to be closer to the wave
tops—two, three feet maximum. With the weapons pods hanging from
each side of his skids and seawater detrimental to their correct operation, Adams was taking no chances. If he had to trade avoiding fire
from the Chinese ships to arriving too high to help his team members,
he'd do it.

Adams eased forward on the cyclic and watched as the governor adjusted his rotor speed. He was doing 130 miles an hour, and according to his calculations he should be seeing the first Zodiac one minute forty-five seconds after he passed the frigate. He strained his eyes to catch sight of the Chinese vessel, while at the same time watching the dash-mounted storm scope, which was sending a radar signal into the weather.

H UXLEY POINTED TO the dash of the Zodiac but said nothing. Seng nodded, then bent down and shouted into her ear. "If I was to guess," he screamed, "I'd say we have something partially blocking the raw water intake holes on the drive. Might be something as simple as a piece of soaked paper or part of a plastic bag—the problem is, we need to stop and raise the outboard out of the water to check."

"It doesn't seem to be getting any worse," Julia Huxley said.

"No, it doesn't," Seng said. "We are in the low red and staying there. If the engine can run at those temperatures for a little longer, we might just make it out of here alive."

Huxley scanned the water through the fog as they raced along. She turned and caught a quick glimpse of the Zodiac being piloted by Kasim off the starboard stern. The pair of diesel cruisers had yet to get close enough to catch sight of either vessel, and if they maintained their speed they never would.

"Too bad we can't ask for a time out," Huxley said, "so I can clean the water intake."

Eddie Seng strained to hear Huxley's voice over the noise of his racing outboard motor. Something else was causing his ears to perk up—a slight thumping coming from the bow. Then, through the fog, he caught a glimpse of the R-44. And a voice came over the radio.

T HE COMMAND BRIDGE on the *Gale Force* was a buzz of shouted instructions. Messages were repeated more than once as the news that the *Oregon* was starting a turn back to land was relayed from radar operator to captain, captain to helmsman, then around to the other officers. The event was relayed to the captains of the corvette and the frigate, who immediately began to slow.

Captain Ching figured it would take the *Oregon* close to a nautical mile to complete the turn.

Once again, Ching would underestimate.

W ITH MAGNETOHYDRODYNAMICS ENGINES powering the *Oregon*, there was no need to slow down to change directions on the drives. There were no shafts to twist, no props to bend, no gears to strip. The water jets from the stern came out of a rectangular shaft with a scoop on the end that could be diverted like the thrust of a Harrier jet engine to the fore or to the rear. With the push of a few buttons, one of the propulsion engineers could divert the flow of one engine forward and one back and the *Oregon* would almost pivot on her keel, so long as the speeds were kept below thirty knots. Such an abrupt maneuver made for a rough ride—the ship would kneel over and the gunwales would dip almost into the water—but the Corporation had done it more than once. Other than a few broken dishes and other objects being tossed around, the *Oregon* had been none the worse for the wear.

The engineer plotted in a turn-radius profile on the computer that resembled a U-turn. Then he alerted the control room that they were ready. Once the ship commander gave the order, the engineer simply pushed a button and held on to a nearby table as the *Oregon* threaded herself across the surface of the water as if she were on rails. Down in the engine room, Sam Pryor glanced over at Gunther Reinholt, who had just disconnected his IV and was sipping from a cup of strong coffee after inputting the command for the turn.

"Elementary, Mr. Reinholt," Pryor said, smiling.

"Indubitably, Mr. Pryor," Reinholt said.

Both men stared at the lying-down U-shaped track on the computer screen for a second.

"Mr. Chairman," Reinholt said over the intercom, "we're ready when you are."

"WE'RE GOING TO do a fast turn and bunch up the three ships chasing us," Cabrillo said over a scrambled radio link. "You will need to take out the pair of cruisers fast so the Zodiacs can slow before they run up on the stern of the frigate."

"Understand," Adams said.

"We'll alert Seng and Kasim to slow as soon as the cruisers are disabled."

"I'll blow all the ordnance of the port pod on the lead cruiser," Adams said, "and the starboard on the following craft. That should stop them cold."

"Do your best to hit them in the sterns," Cabrillo said. "If possible, we want to keep casualties to a minimum."

AT ALMOST THE same instant that the lead harbor police patrol boat caught sight of Kasim's Zodiac in the lessening fog, the lookout also reported a helicopter approaching from out to sea. Adams had turned and looped the R-44 around to intercept the lead boat straight on her rear quarter. Placing the crosshairs on the firing screen on the rear third of the forty-six-foot aluminum ship, Adams flipped a switch so all the missiles were targeted to the same spot just above the waterline.

Then he took a deep breath and squeezed the trigger.

The lookout caught a quick glimpse of the bubble canopy of the helicopter a second before the port weapons pod erupted with a volley of four missiles. The missiles were small—only slightly thicker than a man's arm—but their noses were packed with high explosives. With a six-foot plume of fire belching from the rear, the missiles raced across the gap and slammed into the side of the lead cruiser and severed the bow from the stern as easily as a machete through a pineapple.

The captain just had time to sound the alarm to abandon ship before the bow started sinking.

"NOW, MR. REINHOLT," Cabrillo said as an alarm sounded throughout the ship.

Reinholt reached up to the console and pushed a red button, then took hold of the table next to him in a death grip. The *Oregon* keeled over and started to turn. It was as if the ship were on the track of a roller coaster. The g forces were severe. Everyone in the ship clutched the nearest immovable object and bent their knees like mogul skiers on a gnarly slope. A few moments later, the *Oregon* came out of the fallen U and rolled upright again.

Lincoln, sitting in a tall fire control chair with a seat belt across his lap, shouted, "Yeah, baby."

"We'll pass abreast of the hydrofoil in twenty seconds," Hanley said.

"Hit them in the pontoon, Mr. Lincoln," Cabrillo said.

"WHAT THE—" CHING started to say as he watched the massive cargo ship change directions. "Hard a' port," he ordered.

But before the order could be carried out, the *Oregon* was almost alongside them.

"*EVERYWHERE I GO, I'm just a gigolo . . . ,*" Lincoln sang as he lined up his target and fired.

The missile battery on the bow of the *Oregon* popped up and rotated toward the target. Now, at Lincoln's command, a pair of Harpoon missiles burst from their launchers and streaked across the distance. They slammed into the thin slab-sided pontoon that reached down into the water and blew it off as cleanly as a guillotine would a finger.

The *Gale Force* was still making fast forward speed when she was hit. Once the pontoon allowing her to ride up above the waterline disappeared, her main deck lurched to the side, then began to topple over. She didn't quite flip over on her back—it was more of a crippled disintegration into the water. The helmsman managed to place the engines in neutral before she flipped, and that saved lives if not the ship.

A minute after being hit, the *Gale Force* had her decks awash and she was rapidly sinking.

Captain Deng Ching was bleeding from his nose and mouth after slamming into the command console. He was in a daze from pain. The second in command gave the order to abandon ship.

"A HELICOPTER JUST attacked," the captain of the rapidly sinking harbor police boat shouted into a portable radio as he climbed into the emergency raft. "Our boat is sinking."

"Understood," the captain of the second harbor boat said. "We'll come pick you up."

"I'll shoot a flare."

"We'll watch for it."

Then the captain turned to a sailor nearby. "Man the deck gun," he said quickly, "and if any aircraft approaches, shoot it down."

The first time had worked so well, Adams decided to do it again. Once again approaching from the port side, he lined up the crosshairs on the second harbor boat and pushed the button. Nothing happened. Perhaps the starboard weapons pod had been splashed with more seawater than had the port. Maybe it was simply that the few extra minutes of time had allowed the fog and rain to seep into the circuitry. It could have been a glitch—this was the first time the weapons pod had been used—and rarely did a system work flawlessly the first time out.

Whatever the case, the missiles wouldn't fire from the tubes.

The R-44 passed over the harbor patrol boat just as the sailor yanked back the lever on the deck gun and flicked off the safety. He pivoted the gun to the correct height and started shooting at the rear of the retreating helicopter. Adams felt the cyclic get mushy as a single bullet nicked a control rod to the main rotor. He flew away into the fog to assess the situation.

"Control," he said over a secure channel on the radio. "I've eliminated one target, but now my horse is wounded and they broke my bow."

Hanley took the call in the control room of the *Oregon*.

He scanned the radar screen before answering. "Do you have control of the craft?"

"It's not too bad," Adams said calmly. "I think I can set her down okay."

"We're coming in your direction now," Hanley said. "Blow the pods and bring the ship home."

"What do you mean?" Adams asked.

"There's a toggle switch on the weapons control panel," Hanley said. "Flip up the cover and lower the switch and the racks will drop free. We'll deal with the second boat."

Adams started an arc toward the harbor boat. "Give me a second," he said. "I have an idea."

ACROSS THE ROOM, Juan Cabrillo was on the satellite telephone to Langston Overholt in Virginia.

"We had to sink the vessel closest to us," he said. "But there's a corvette and a frigate still to contend with."

Overholt was pacing in his office while talking on the speaker phone. In front of his desk, sitting in a chair and dressed in full uniform, was a United States Navy commander who was attached to the CIA. "I have a naval officer here in my office. My superiors are worried about fallout if you attack and sink the other two ships. How far away from you are they?"

"We are in no imminent danger for a few more minutes," Cabrillo stated.

"If we can stop them in their tracks," Overholt asked, "can you affect an escape?"

Cabrillo thought for a minute before answering. "We can retrieve our men and the object we came for and be back at full steam in five to ten minutes," he said. "As long as the Chinese don't launch any planes at us, I think we will be home free."

"As of this instant," Overholt said, "the only radio transmission that got through was about a helicopter attacking a harbor police boat. Right now, at least as far as the Chinese are concerned, you're just a cargo ship they can't reach on the radio. That could change, however, once the survivors of the ship you sank are collected."

"By then we should be far out to sea traveling south," Cabrillo said, "and back into the fog bank. With the electronics on board, we can hide from ship-to-sea radar. The fog will keep us hidden from above."

Overholt turned to the navy commander. "Will this new device affect our ship as well?"

"Not if they turn all the electronics off as it passes alongside."

"Juan," Overholt said, "did you hear that?"

"Yes," he said, "but I don't understand."

"It's a new toy the navy has," Overholt said, "called a FRITZY. It is designed to short out electrical circuits and we believe it will disable the remaining ships. What we'll need you to do is shut down all the systems on the *Oregon* when we give you the order."

Eric Stone was scanning the radar and said, "We're coming up on the Zodiacs now."

"Slow to stop," Cabrillo ordered. "Prepare to take our people aboard."

* . * *

ADAMS CLIMBED TO three thousand feet, then dove toward the harbor boat in the steepest angle the R-44 could handle. He could feel his body go light in the seat, and then tighten against the shoulder harness. Through the Plexiglas bubble windscreen, the harbor boat came into view, then grew in size as he streaked down from above.

The bow gunner tried firing on the helicopter, but his arc of fire was limited by the wheelhouse directly behind him. The gunner got off a few hundred rounds while the helicopter was still high in the air, but the rounds went wide and then he could fire no more.

Adams raced down in a steep dive. When he was only eighty feet above the stern, he pulled back on the cyclic and up on the collective. This slowed the dive, then began to raise the nose. Just as the R-44 hit the bottom of her arc, Adams flipped up the cover and down on the toggle switch. Both pods dropped from the sides of the helicopter and plunged straight down into the stern of the last harbor police boat. A static spark from the pods being cut loose fired one of the remaining missiles and it streaked down the last twenty feet, igniting the rear of the boat in a maelstrom of destruction.

With the weight and drag of the pods gone, Adams found he had better control. Turning the Robinson toward the direction of the *Oregon*, he began to scan the water for the outline of the ship.

"Scratch two," he said quietly. "I'm coming home."

WHEN A PERSON is far out in the ocean and the weather is bad, the sight of anything man-made brings comfort and solace. For the seven people and one Golden Buddha on the small boats being chased by the Chinese navy, the bow of the *Oregon* looming up through the fog was as welcome as the sight of four of a kind to a losing poker player.

"Steer over to the davits," Hanley said over the radio. "We need to get you aboard fast."

The two Zodiac pilots eased their boats into a pair of davits located off the port and starboard stern of the *Oregon*. The deckhands had the boats and the people hoisted through the air and back on the deck in less than two minutes. Murphy was climbing off the Zodiac when Franklin Lincoln walked over.

"I played with your toy," he said. "You can put another ship sticker on the console."

Murphy smiled. "Good shooting, Tex."

"Everyone okay?" Lincoln asked.

"All but Jones," Murphy said, pointing. "We need to carry him to sick bay."

Lincoln walked across the deck to the second Zodiac and stared inside. "Jones," he said, smiling, "you look pitiful."

"Don't make me laugh," Jones said. "My ribs are killing me."

"You do what you set out to do?" Lincoln asked.

"Always," Jones said, pointing to the case containing the Golden Buddha. "Now get me below to the sick bay and fill me up with pain-killers."

"Up you go," Lincoln said as he reached into the inflatable and carefully lifted Jones from the floor as easily as plucking a puppy from a litter.

"THREE MINUTES TO fire," a voice said over the intercom on board the *Santa Fe*.

Down in the launch bay, the pair of modified Tomahawk cruise missiles with the experimental FRITZY electronic destruction modules sat ready to launch. The FRITZY system used a burst of electronic waves to scramble the circuitry of any powered electronics. Captain Farragut was waiting anxiously for the launch. The anxiety did not stem from being worried about his crew's actions—they were highly trained and would perform the task flawlessly. It was caused by the unknown. Farragut was curious if FRITZY was all it was cracked up to be—and if he could soon claim the crown as the first commander to use it in battle. That fact might help at promotion time; at the very least it would be worth a few free drinks once the *Santa Fe* made port again.

"Doors open, sir," the chief of boat said, "and all is in order."

"WE SEE YOU," Hanley said to Adams, "but you need to land now."

Adams was making his approach behind the stern of the *Oregon* and lining up for his descent onto the landing pad.

"Two minutes or so," Adams said.

"In a minute thirty," Hanley said, staring at a timer, "your electronics will cease to function."

"Clear the decks," Adams said loudly. "I'll climb, then shut the engine off and initiate auto-rotation."

"Fire-foam the decks," Hanley said over the intercom. "We shut down all the electrical power in one minute."

Many people think that once a helicopter loses power it plunges from the sky. Actually, if power to the rotor is lost, the pilot can use the wind from his descent to spin the blades. The procedure, auto-rotation, is tricky, but the maneuver has saved more than a few lives over the years. Usually the pilot has a reasonably large field or clearing to land on. Doing a forced auto-rotation onto a pad just slightly bigger than the helicopter herself takes nerves of steel and fortitude. Adams used his minute to gain altitude. Then he lined up behind the landing pad. When his watch said it was time, he flicked off the governor and rolled back the throttle. The R-44's freewheeling unit engaged and the drive shaft to the main and tail rotor disconnected.

Adams reached up and turned off the key.

Suddenly, without the noise from the engine, it was strangely quiet, the only sounds the whooshing of the wind racing past the fuselage and the sound from Adams's lips as he whistled Bobby Darrin's "Mack the Knife." The R-44 was making a steeper descent than normal, but Adams was in complete control.

Only when all the lights on the *Oregon* went dark in the fog did he give it a second thought.

"ONE AWAY," THE chief of boat said quietly. "Now two."

The cruise missiles left the launch tubes and streaked skyward, then turned and dived down to wave level. Programmed to the target by a sophisticated computer, the missiles raced toward the Chinese corvette and the frigate at 450 kilometers an hour. Once the cruise missiles were close to the two ships, they sent out a concentrated burst of electronic friction similar to that emitted after an atomic bomb blast.

The electronic circuits throughout both ships shorted as cleanly as if a switch had been thrown. The engines ceased to function and the electronics in the wheelhouse and below went black. Both ships slowed in the water just as a burst of wind and rain raked across the sea.

"YEE-HA!" ADAMS SHOUTED as the wind hit the R-44.

He was eighty feet back of the stern and twenty feet in the air when he initiated his flare. Pulling up on the cyclic, he pitched the nose up using the drag on the powerless rotor to bleed off forward speed. He was four feet above the pad when the forward speed ceased and the Robinson dropped down on the deck with a thud. The foam reached halfway up the fuselage as Adams pulled on the rotor brake to stop the blades from spinning. Then he unlocked and pushed the door open. Next, he began to unsnap his harness.

Richard Truitt waded through the dissolving foam to the door as soon as the rotor stopped.

"You okay?" he asked.

"Shaken but not stirred." Adams smiled. "What's new?"

At just that instant the *Oregon* started moving again.

Truitt shrugged. "We're heading out."

"Open seas," Adams said, climbing from the cockpit, "here we come."

"Fill out a repair order," Truitt said, "then meet me in the cafeteria. We need to do a little planning."

The two men reached the edge of the foam just as a deckhand began to hose the foam over the side with a stream of seawater. They brushed flecks off their pants as they made their way to the door leading inside.

"Do I need to bring anything special?" Adams asked.

"High-altitude performance charts," Truitt answered.

34

THE *OREGON* STEAMED south just inside the edge of the storm. The time was 6 A.M. and the cafeteria aboard smelled of bacon, sausage, eggs and cinnamon rolls. Cabrillo was sitting at a table talking with Julia Huxley as Hanley walked toward them with a cup of steaming coffee in his hand. He smiled and nodded.

"Now that," he said to Cabrillo, "was exciting."

"Never a dull moment around here," Cabrillo agreed.

"How are Reinholt and Jones?" Hanley asked Huxley.

"Minor injuries," Huxley reported. "Jonesy has a couple of cracked ribs—I gave him pain medication and he's sleeping in sick bay. Reinholt claims he's better, but I have him resting in his cabin just to be sure."

"Did you check on repairs to the R-44?" Cabrillo asked.

"Yes, Mr. Chairman," Hanley said as an attendant walked over and set a plate containing a cinnamon roll in front of him. "A buckle that controls movement to the rotor head was bent. They are replacing it now and estimate it will be ready to fly in a couple of hours."

"Good," Cabrillo said. "Once the *Oregon* steams closer to the mainland, I'll need Adams to drop me off at the airport."

"Just like we planned," Hanley agreed.

"Now all we need to do is find the secret compartment inside the Golden Buddha," Cabrillo said, "and see if its contents are still intact."

S UNG RHEE CAUGHT sight through the window of the four men approaching his office. They did not look happy, and the aide did not bother to knock before swinging the door open. Rhee rose from his desk as the aide stood aside and allowed the admiral to enter.

"We managed to get air bags under the hydrofoil to keep her afloat until a salvage ship can tow her back," the admiral said without preamble, "but my men tell me repairs will require close to six months."

"Sir—" Rhee started to say.

"Enough," the admiral thundered. "I have one ship out of commission and our only frigate and fast-attack corvette disabled and dead in the water. You set me up—and you will pay."

"Sir," Rhee said quickly, "we had no idea . . . the ship to all appearances was merely a decrepit cargo vessel."

"The ship was far from that," the admiral said loudly. "She shot the side out from under the hydrofoil as if it was a routine exercise. We still don't know what happened to the other two ships."

Just outside the door, the admiral's aide was whispering into a satellite telephone. He poked his head into Rhee's office.

"Admiral," he said quietly, "Beijing's on the line."

C HUCK "TINY" GUNDERSON smiled at Rhonda Rosselli and held out one of the bearer bonds. "So," he said, "here's the deal.

Tracy, Judy and I need to make an unscheduled midair exit. Once we are safely out, you can untie the pilots."

"You're abandoning me?" Rosselli asked pointedly. "All that talk about me joining your team was a lie?"

Gunderson pulled a thick cigar from his flight-suit pocket and slid it under his nose. Then he bit off the end and lit it with a solid gold lighter. He puffed the stogie to life. "I never lie to a pretty girl," he said, smiling, "and I'm always right."

"Then what's the deal?"

Gunderson slipped the bearer bond into a plastic envelope and sealed it inside with the others. "The bond I showed you will be mailed to your home address once I reach land. That's your payment for a job well executed."

"What do I say when we land?" Rosselli asked.

"I'd tell them everything," Gunderson said, "except about the bond. That should remain our little secret."

"Just tell them?" Rosselli said incredulously.

"Why not?" Gunderson said. "I was careful not to relay any information that can incriminate my group. My team will make sure that the United States embassy is notified in whatever country the plane lands. Just spill your guts and they'll let you go in a few days. Once you get back to California, someone that works with me will make contact in due time."

"So I won't see you again?" she asked.

"You never know," Gunderson said as red-haired Tracy Pilston walked over.

"Our ride is only a few miles ahead," Pilston noted, "and we're both ready to fly the coop."

"Did you take her down?" Gunderson asked.

Pilston nodded. "We're to receive a signal, so we can time the jump."

Gunderson removed two parachutes from a storage compartment where a Corporation team member had hidden them when the 737 was in her hangar in California. He helped strap one on Pilston's back, then strapped on the other. Removing a sack containing goggles, he handed one over to Pilston.

"We'll alert Judy," he said quietly, "and exit from the rear."

"Go forward," Gunderson said to Rosselli. "Tell Judy it's time, then stay in the cockpit."

"Won't everything be sucked out the rear?" Rosselli asked.

"We're not pressurized," Gunderson said, "so it won't be that bad— I wouldn't try walking around, however. Just stay in the cockpit, and after the egg timer goes off, raise the rear door and untie the pilots."

"Okay," Rosselli said as she went forward, opened the cockpit door and reported the news to Michaels.

"Understood," Judy Michaels said.

Then she checked the speed once more, made sure the autopilot was operating, then pushed the lever to lower the rear door. The door began to lower slowly and the alarms on the dashboard began to beep. Twisting a cheap plastic egg timer, Michaels slid past Rosselli.

"Keep the door closed, and when that timer chimes, you know what to do."

Rosselli nodded.

"Nice meeting you," Michaels said as she slipped out the door.

Racing down the aisle, Michaels stopped for Gunderson to check her parachute. The farther the rear door lowered, the more wind raced through the fuselage of the 737. Magazines rustled, and any loose items inside fluttered in the wind. Gunderson watched as a silk kimono filled like a sail and shot out the rear. Then the trio made their way to the rear, where the steps were now pointing straight below the tail of the 737.

"What do you think they'll do to Rhonda?" Pilston asked.

"Not much they can do," Gunderson said as he adjusted his goggles and helped Michaels into position to jump.

"I think she's sweet on you," Pilston said as she moved into place next to Michaels.

"There's something about," Gunderson said, "an Aqua-Velva man."

At that instant, the signal was received from the satellite to his alphanumeric pager. The pager began to vibrate. Gunderson took one lady under each arm. Then he ran off the end of the ramp and, once he was clear, pushed them away.

P LODDING THROUGH THE South China Sea, the helmsman on the *Kalia Challenger* noticed the sky was finally clearing. He noticed it because the sky overhead was suddenly filled with a pair of Chinese antisubmarine aircraft as well as a single long-range heavy-lift helicopter. The *Kalia Challenger* had originally been built in 1962 for the United States Line as one of an eleven-ship class of express cargo cruisers. Later sold to a Greek shipping concern, she plied the seas on a regular schedule from Asia to the west coast of the United States.

At just over five hundred feet with a seventy-foot beam, the vessel featured derricks on the upper deck for loading and unloading of cargo. Her lower hull was a rusty red with a black band along the gunwales. She was a work ship who had served a long and useful life, and the wear and tear showed. Still functional, though dated, she was possessed of one major flaw.

From a distance, to an untrained eye, she resembled the *Oregon*.

She was far out in international waters when the antisubmarine aircraft dropped the first depth charge. It landed a hundred yards ahead of the bow and exploded with a cascade of water that reached eighty feet into the air.

"Heave to!" the captain shouted.

The alert reached the engine room, and the *Kalia Challenger* slowed, then stopped in the water.

It would be nearly an hour before a Chinese boarding party climbed across her decks.

The illegal stop was never explained.

*   *   *

D ELBERT CHIGLACK STARED up at the sky in amazement. He had
seen some incredible things in the fourteen years he had worked
on offshore oil rigs: strange sea creatures that defied explanation, unidentified flying objects, weird weather phenomena. But in all the years
he had drilled offshore, he had yet to see a trio of parachutists come
from nowhere and attempt to land on his rig. Gunderson, Michaels and
Pilston had leapt from the 737 at an altitude of fifteen thousand feet,
just above a cloud layer that hid the airplane from view. Sucking on
oxygen bottles as they made their descent, they had floated around near
the target before directing their parachutes in arcing corkscrews until
they lined up above the helicopter pad on the offshore rig.

The rig was twenty miles off the coast of Vietnam, eight hundred
miles from Macau, and owned by Zapata Petroleum of Houston, Texas.
George Herbert Walker Bush owned the company—and someone from
Virginia had asked him for a favor.

Tracy Pilston landed nearly dead center on the X in the center of
the pad, Judy Michaels only six feet away. It was Chuck Gunderson
who had the worst landing. He alit on the side of the elevated pad. The
breeze tugged at his parachute before he could cut it away, and had Del
Chiglack not grabbed him, he might have gone over the side.

Once his chute was free and Chiglack had yanked him back from
the edge, Gunderson smiled and spoke.

"My friends called," he said. "I believe we have a reservation for
three."

Chiglack spit some snuff juice into the wind. "Welcome aboard,"
he said. "Your ride will be here soon."

"Thanks," Gunderson said.

"Now," Chiglack said, "if you and the ladies will come inside, I'll
buy you a cup of coffee."

*   *   *

B ACK IN THE control room, Hanley turned to Cabrillo. "We just received word from Tiny," he said. "They arrived safe and sound with the bonds. They're awaiting a ride home."

Cabrillo nodded.

"You look beat," Hanley said. "Why don't you catch a few hours' sleep and let me hold down the fort."

Cabrillo was too tired to argue. He rose and started for the door. "Wake me if you need me."

"Don't I always?" Hanley said.

Once Cabrillo was walking down the hall to his stateroom, Hanley turned to Stone. "Truitt will be here in a few minutes to relieve you. Take four hours and get some sleep."

"Yes, sir," Stone said.

Then Hanley accessed the computer next to his seat and began to read the plan again.

L ANGSTON OVERHOLT SLEPT all the way to Paris. The Challenger jet he was riding inside was registered to a company named Strontium Holding PLC, which was allegedly based in Basel, Switzerland. In reality, the jet's tires had never touched Swiss soil.

The Challenger CL-604 had been purchased from a broker in London using CIA funds and outfitted with advanced electronics at a shop in Alexandria, Virginia, near Bolling Air Force Base. The large Canadian-made business jet seated ten people, had a cruise speed of 487 miles per hour and a range of 4,628 miles.

The distance from Virginia to Paris was just over 3,800 miles, where the jet was refueled and provisions were loaded aboard. The second leg of the trip, Paris to New Delhi, would cover 4,089 miles. The first leg of the journey required eight hours to complete; the second leg was made with a favorable tailwind and took just over seven hours. Within an hour of receiving word from Cabrillo at 6 A.M. Macau time that the Corporation was in possession of the Golden Buddha, Overholt had left

U.S. soil. Virginia time had been 6 P.M. Good Friday. By the time the Challenger touched down, the time changes and flight time made it 9 A.M. Saturday.

The trip by turboprop to Little Lhasa in northern India took just over two more hours, so it was almost exactly noon on Saturday when Overholt finally met with the Dalai Lama again. The revered leader of Tibet had made it clear that if there was to be a coup d'etat, it needed to take place on Easter Sunday, March 31, exactly forty-six years after his being forced into exile.

That gave Overholt and the Corporation twenty-four hours to make a miracle happen.

C ARL GANNON HAD been earning his keep the last several days. After procuring the truck in Thimbu, Bhutan, and plotting a route into Tibet, he had received a shopping list of tasks from the control room on the *Oregon*. As the Corporation's head scrounger, Gannon was used to accomplishing the impossible. To obtain what was required, Gannon would have to use the vast network of contacts he had carefully nurtured over the years.

The funding would come from the Corporation's bank on the island of Vanuatu in the South Pacific Ocean, and the *Oregon* had made it clear that time, not cost, was the object. Gannon loved it when he received directives like this. Using a laptop computer linked to a cell phone, he began typing in a stack of telephone numbers, codes and passwords from memory at seventy words a minute.

Eighty Stinger missiles were bought from a friendly Middle Eastern nation, with delivery arranged to Bhutan using a South African company that had never failed to comply. Eight Bell 212 helicopters with extra fuel pods from an Indonesian company that specialized in offshore oil work arrived to deliver the load of missiles and small arms. Eighteen mercenary pilots from throughout the Far East were recruited, sixteen to fly, two extras in case someone got sick. Fuel pods, food for all the participants, and a series of hangars manned by Philippine Special Forces guards were secretly arranged.

Gannon's last item was the strangest. The *Oregon* wanted to know if he could procure a large but slow-moving plane in Vietnam. That, and a winch with a hundred feet of thin but strong steel cable that could be mounted on the floor of the plane. It took Gannon a couple of telephone calls, but he found a 1985 Russian-built Antonov AN-2 Colt owned by a Laotian company that had a logging contract with the Vietnamese government. The big biplane, with a wingspan of fifty-eight feet, a cruise speed of only 120 miles an hour and a stall speed of 58, could best be described as a flying pickup truck. The large interior was mainly cargo space and she could carry nearly five thousand pounds of payload.

The winch he bought new from a dealer in Ho Chi Minh City on a company credit card.

After finishing the arrangements for the plane and winch, Gannon slurped the last drop from a bottle of Coca-Cola and dialed the *Oregon* on the satellite telephone. He waited as the number beeped and popped while the signal was scrambled.

"Go ahead, Carl," Hanley said a minute later.

"I've got the plane, Max," he said, "but you didn't ask for a pilot."

"One of our guys will be flying," Hanley said.

"It's a Russian Antonov," Gannon noted. "I doubt we have someone typed in this model."

"We'll download some manuals off the Internet," Hanley said. "That's about all we can do."

"She's fueled and waiting at the airport in old Saigon," Gannon said. "The mechanic should be finished bolting the winch in place in the next hour. I'm faxing a picture."

"We'll be seeing you soon," Hanley said. "Everything okay in the meantime?"

"Smooth as a baby's bottom," Gannon said easily.

* * *

O N THE ZAPATA Petroleum rig off Vietnam, Delbert Chiglack took the sheet that had just printed out of the fax machine, then called once more to the incoming helicopter. When finished, he returned to the lunchroom on the rig and handed the sheet to Gunderson.

"This just came for you."

"Thanks," Gunderson said quickly, staring at the picture of the biplane the *Oregon* had sent, then folding it and placing it in his flight-suit pocket.

Just then, a siren on the rig sounded twice.

"Your ride's here," Chiglack said.

Walking the trio out to just below the helicopter pad, Chiglack waited until the helicopter touched down, then shouted over the noise.

"Up the ladder, heads down, the door should be open," he said.

"Thanks for the hospitality," Michaels shouted.

"Watch your hair, ladies," Chiglack called as they started up the stairs.

Four minutes later the helicopter was airborne again, heading back toward land. Chiglack shook his head as the helicopter retreated in the distance. Then he walked back to his office to report his guests had left the rig.

G UNDERSON HANDED THE photo of the biplane to the copilot. "She's on the north side of the airport," he said as the copilot clipped the photo to a strap around his knee. "If you can land nearby, we'd sure appreciate it."

The copilot replaced his headset over his ears, then relayed the information to the pilot, who made an okay sign with his fingers. The copilot smiled at Gunderson, nodded yes, then motioned for him to sit back in his seat.

Twenty minutes later, the coast of southern Vietnam came into view. As they passed over shallow water, he caught sight of a wrecked ship below the surface of the water. In the bushes nearby was what looked like the remains of a bombed-out tank from the war some thirty years before.

Pilston tapped on Gunderson's arm as the helicopter approached the airport and located the Antonov from the air. Slowing his speed, the pilot neared the large biplane, then hovered in the air above the tarmac. After touching down smoothly some fifty feet away, the copilot unbuckled his belt, then slipped back and unlatched the door to the Bell.

"Later, alligators," he shouted.

Gunderson, Pilston and Michaels bowed their heads and sprinted away from the helicopter.

Once they were clear, the pilot throttled up, pulled up on the collective and moved the cyclic so the Bell rose in the air and made a sweeping turn. The helicopter disappeared into the haze as it flew off to the south.

The trio was ten feet from the biplane when Michaels spoke.

"What are we going to do with this beast?" she asked.

"The plan is," Gunderson said as he approached the open door and stared inside, "to fly out to the *Oregon*."

"What on earth for?" Pilston asked.

"Our chairman has a meeting to attend."

35

INSIDE THE *OREGON'S* Magic Shop, Kevin Nixon was loosening the top off a long wooden crate with a pry bar. The crate was stamped U.S. Air Force, Special Operations. The second line read: (1) ea. Fulton Aerial Recovery System, checked 02-11-90, and then the initials of the airman who had rendered the verdict that the system was operational. Setting the top aside, Nixon peered inside. Then he began to remove the contents.

First was a harness made out of nylon webbing similar to that on a parachute. On the front of the harness was a swivel hook. Next was a length of high-tension strength line. Last, a deflated balloon and the fittings to hook the system together. Nixon checked each piece carefully as he removed them from the box. Everything looked fine.

Just then, the door to the Magic Shop opened.

"How's it look?" Hanley inquired.

"Good," Nixon answered.

Hanley pointed to a strange forged-metal three-pronged hook on the ground. "What's that?"

Nixon nodded at the bottom of the crate's lid, where a set of directions had been stenciled on the surface. "That's the hook that grabs the line at the end of the balloon."

"Doesn't it have to be aboard the pickup plane?"

"Ideally," Nixon admitted.

"So?" Hanley asked.

Nixon pointed across the room. "Good thing we have rules around here," he said.

"Always have a backup," Hanley said, smiling, reading the sign.

"But of course," Nixon said.

"I'll notify the plane," Hanley said. "We have a few hours yet."

"Mr. Hanley," Nixon said, "you just tell me when."

T HE SINGLE ENGINE on the Antonov Colt droned with a monotonous sound as Gunderson, Michaels and Pilston headed out into the South China Sea. The skies were clear, the wall of the south-moving storm still hundreds of miles ahead. Gunderson just hoped that the *Oregon*, which was cruising at full speed, made it out of the leading edge of the storm before he reached the ship. He was a great pilot, but even in clear skies what they were about to attempt was akin to trying to hit a bull's-eye on a dartboard at ten paces while blindfolded.

Gunderson had the windows in the cockpit and the cargo area cracked open to vent the gasoline fumes as they cruised along. The Antonov normally carried 312 gallons of fuel, but since this plane was used for remote logging operations, two more tanks of 300 gallons each had been fitted along the center of the cargo bay. That was a good thing. Without the additional fuel capacity, there was no way they could make it out to the *Oregon* and back to Vietnam, a distance far beyond that of a helicopter. The problem was, the inside of the plane smelled like an Exxon station after a big spill. Gunderson stared at his portable GPS receiver.

"How's it look, Tiny?" Michaels asked.

"So far so good," Gunderson answered, "but this unit burns through batteries like a kid with a video game. Did they by chance load any spare batteries on board?"

Pilston, who was crouched between the pilot's and copilot's seat, rooted around in a pair of paper bags but came up empty. "Sorry, Chuck," she said, "no luck."

"What did we get?" he asked.

Pilston did a quick inventory. "Some MREs, two thermoses of what I assume is coffee, some Hershey bars and M&M's, bottled water, maps, and some mouthwash."

"What about towels and soap?"

Pilston dug around in the bottom of one of the bags. "Yep."

"Gannon's pretty good about that," Gunderson said, yawning.

Michaels stared at the speed indicator. "We have five more hours until we reach the *Oregon*," she said. "Tracy and I got some sleep last night. Why don't you clean up a little and try to get some rest. We'll wake you when we get close."

"Think you can fill the copilot's duties?" he asked Pilston.

"I received my private pilot's certificate last year," Pilston told him. "I don't have many hours, but I think I'm qualified to watch the needles quiver."

Gunderson nodded wearily. "Off the controls," he said.

As soon as he was sure Michaels had the plane, he stood up, slid out of his seat, and slid past Pilston, who quickly climbed into the pilot's station. The Antonov could be flown from either the left or right seat, so there was no reason for Michaels to move across the cockpit. Once Pilston was situated, she turned around to Gunderson.

"There's a cot that folds out of the wall," she said, "and a toilet that basically dumps out the side of the plane. You want anything to eat first?"

"No, ladies," Gunderson said. "Just wake me if you need me."

Then he walked back to the cot, removed his shirt and crumpled it up as a pillow, stretched out and was asleep within minutes. The Antonov droned north for the rendezvous.

O VER THE YEARS of its existence the Corporation had invested in a variety of legitimate businesses. The company was either owner or part owner of mining concerns, a coconut plantation, a specialty firearms manufacturer, hotels, resorts, a machine tool company, even a charter jet service with divisions in North America, South America, Europe and Asia.

None of the employees of these concerns had any idea of the source of the parent company's funding and true purpose. They only knew they were highly paid and treated well and never subject to cutbacks or layoffs. For the most part, the actual operations end of the Corporation— the specialized army and intelligence apparatus that formed the nucleus of the growing fortune—left these companies alone to operate on their own. Sometimes, however, they came in handy.

Right now was just such a time.

Max Hanley returned to the *Oregon*'s control room and slid into his chair.

"Pull up the flight operations center of Pegasus Air," he asked Stone.

Stone punched commands into the computer, and a few seconds later a worldwide map filled one of the large monitors. "What's the fastest way to fly the chairman to his meeting?"

Stone punched in commands and the route filled the screen. "It's a long flight," he said, "and I assume you want it nonstop?"

"Absolutely," Hanley said.

"That pretty much ensures that we'll need to use the G550, then."

"Where are they now?" Hanley asked.

Stone punched in commands and flight records overlaid the map.

"The Asian G550 is in route to Hawaii, so that's out," Stone noted.

"Paris on one—no, hold on—the South American G550 just landed in Dubai. She's due to leave again tomorrow."

"How long for her to reach Da Nang?"

"It's thirty-six hundred miles, so roughly six and a half hours."

Hanley took a pad of paper and a pencil and began writing numbers. "It'll be tight," he said finally. "We're bucking time zones, refueling and getting fast clearances to land, but it's doable."

"Want me to book the jet?" Stone asked.

Hanley handed him a sheet of paper. "This is the flight plan."

"What else?"

"Make sure our man in the Vietnamese air force is greased so we don't have any problems getting in and out of Da Nang for a quick refuel," Hanley said.

"What else?"

"Set up a secure link to Karamozov," Hanley said. "I need to confirm."

"Anything else?" Stone said as he made notes on a pad.

"When all that's done," Hanley said, "call Truitt to relieve you and go get some sleep."

"What about you, sir?" Stone asked.

"I'll catnap here," Hanley said, "right where I like to be."

T HE DALAI LAMA was praying in front of a statue of Buddha when Overholt walked into the room. He stood quietly until he rose.

"I sensed you come into the room," the Dalai Lama said, "and you seem happy."

Overholt asked, "Are you ready to return?"

"Yes," the Dalai Lama said, "very much so."

"Good," Overholt said, "it will be tomorrow."

"Did your people recover the Golden Buddha?"

"They did," Overholt said, nodding.

"And have they found the compartment yet?"

"They're still working on it, Your Holiness."

The Dalai Lama nodded and smiled. "They'll figure it out. And then they'll know what to do with what they find." He paused. "Hard to believe," the Dalai Lama said, "that something my people have owned all along shall be our salvation."

"We're not home free yet, Your Holiness," Overholt said.

The Dalai Lama smiled and considered this for a few moments. "No, Mr. Overholt, we're not—but we will be. Greed is what brought the Chinese to my country. And greed again will set us free."

Overholt nodded silently.

"Life is a circle," the Dalai Lama said, "and someday you will see that."

Overholt smiled as the Dalai Lama began to walk toward the door.

"Now," he said kindly, "let my people feed you. You must be hungry from your long journey."

The two men walked out of the room toward a destiny determined by an obscure ship manned by mercenaries.

A T 11 A.M. local time, the *Oregon* exited the fog bank. In front of the advancing storm, the weather was perfect, a calm before the storm. The sky was azure blue and the seas were as flat and reflective as a mirror. In the hours since leaving Macau, the *Oregon* had made good time. The ship was off Hainan Island in international waters. At the current rate of speed, the vessel would pass along Singapore tomorrow at noon local time. After turning and traveling through the Strait of Malacca and heading north, she was due to arrive high in the Bay of Bengal off Bangladesh sometime around 2 P.M. Sunday.

By then, if all went according to plan, the Dalai Lama would be in power again, and the Corporation would make its exit with no one ever the wiser.

Juan Cabrillo woke in his stateroom, then showered and dressed. Leaving his suite, he walked along the gangways toward the control

room, then stopped and opened the door. Max Hanley was asleep in
his chair, but he sat upright as soon as Cabrillo entered. Hanley rose
and walked over to the coffeepot and poured two cups.

Handing one to Cabrillo, he asked, "Feel better?"

"Amazing what a little rest will do," Cabrillo said, taking the cup.
"Richard?" Hanley asked.

Truitt turned from the screen he was studying. "I'm okay," he said.

"What's the score?" Cabrillo asked without further preamble.

Hanley walked back to his chair and motioned for Cabrillo to sit.
Then he pointed at a screen that showed a red line from Ho Chi Minh
City directly toward the *Oregon*. "That line is Gunderson and his team.
They will be arriving in about a half hour to pick you up."

"They aboard the amphibian?"

"Nope," Hanley said. "It was still too far south to get here in time."

"So we secured another seaplane?" Cabrillo asked.

"Gannon pulled out all the stops," Hanley told him, "but there were
none available."

Cabrillo sipped his coffee while Truitt swiveled his head and stared
back at him.

"You're *yanking* me off?" Cabrillo said.

"Sorry, Mr. Chairman," Hanley said. "It was the only way you
could make your flight out of Vietnam on time."

"And the Buddha?"

"He'll go first," Hanley noted.

"Why," Cabrillo said, "do I always end up in these situations?"

"The money?" Truitt said, smiling.

"Or the thrill of victory?" said Hanley.

ON BOARD THE Antonov, Gunderson was brushing his teeth and
washing his face. Spitting out the window, he rubbed the wash-
cloth across the stubble on his cheeks. Once he had finished, he walked
forward and motioned to Pilston. "Why don't you let me take over."

Pilston slid out of the pilot's seat and Gunderson climbed aboard. "How'd our rookie do?" he asked Michaels.

"She's not a bad pilot," Michaels noted. "I had her do most of the flying while I napped."

Gunderson smiled and turned back to stare at Pilston. "Be sure and log the hours," he told her. "When you have two hundred you can apply for a commercial license. Our last operative who certified got a five-thousand-dollar bonus from Cabrillo."

"This old beast is a smooth flying plane," Pilston said. "Slow as a slug but as stable as a table."

"How far out are we?" Gunderson asked Michaels.

Michaels stared at the GPS and examined her marks in the charts, then did a couple of calculations in the flight computer. "Twenty-four minutes, give or take."

"Have you maintained radio silence?"

"As we planned," Michaels replied.

Gunderson adjusted the mixture to the engine and watched the gauges a few seconds. Satisfied all was okay, he spoke again. "Tracy, can you pour me a cup of coffee? It's time to call the mother ship."

Pilston unscrewed the cup off the thermos, put a piece of folded duct tape on the bottom, then poured a cup and handed it to Gunderson. He sipped the hot liquid, then set the cup down on a flat surface, where it stuck. Then he reached for the radio, adjusted the frequency, and spoke.

"Tiny calling the chairman of the board, you out there?"

A few seconds passed before an answer came. "This is control, go ahead."

"The ladies and I," Tiny said, "will be there in a few minutes to hook you on board."

"We have you on the scope," Cabrillo said. "You should be seeing us shortly."

"What's the drill?" Gunderson asked.

"You'll have two yanks," Cabrillo said. "The first is the object—remember it's heavy."

"We have a cargo slide with a belt, but the door to this old bird is on the side," Gunderson said. "My plan was to winch whatever we were taking aboard close, then do some fancy flying to get the load aboard."

Back on the *Oregon*, Cabrillo shook his head in amazement. "Don't try that on the second load."

"Why's that, boss?"

"Because the second load is me."

Michaels was staring out the window. A speck that was the *Oregon* came into view.

"I have a visual," she said.

"We have you in sight," Gunderson said, "and we'll take it easy bringing you aboard, Mr. Chairman, don't you worry."

"I'm going topside to strap up," Cabrillo said. "Is there anything else you need?"

Gunderson looked at Pilston and Michaels, who shook their heads no.

"Maybe just some ham-and-cheese sandwiches," Gunderson said.

"I'll see what I can do," Cabrillo said.

"We're descending now," Gunderson said. "See you in a few."

CABRILLO OPENED THE door and walked into the Magic Shop. Nixon had the Golden Buddha on a small table and was waving a small electronic radar device across the belly. He stared at a monitor and shook his head.

"There's a space there, boss," Nixon said to Cabrillo, "but I'll be damned if I can figure out the access."

Cabrillo stood thinking for a moment, then turned to Nixon. "Hand me a heat gun," he said.

Nixon walked over to the tool bench and removed a heat gun from a peg, attached an extension cord, then dragged it over to the Golden Buddha. Cabrillo flicked the switch on and started to heat the Buddha's belly.

"What are you thinking, boss?" Nixon asked over the roar of the heat gun.

"People always want to rub Buddha's belly for good luck," Cabrillo said. "Rub something enough and you make heat."

Nixon reached over and touched the golden belly. It was becoming warm, like human skin.

Cabrillo stared at the icon, then turned to Nixon. "Get me a single-edge razor blade," he said.

Nixon walked to the workbench, found a box of razor blades, grabbed them, then walked back, peeling the paper off one of the blades.

"There," Cabrillo said. "There's a crack forming."

Nixon slid the blade into the tiny gap.

"Slide in another," Cabrillo said, "and begin to wedge off the belly plate."

Minutes passed as the gap widened. As it did, Cabrillo diverted the heat under the plate, which heated the glue applied centuries before. At last the crack was large enough that a hand could fit inside. Cabrillo handed Nixon the heat gun, slid his fingers inside the crack, then gently pried back the plate while Nixon continued heating the yak's-hoof glue.

Slowly the plate peeled back. Then, all at once, it came off in Cabrillo's hand.

He stared through the opening into an inner compartment. Inside lay ancient parchments rolled into a tube and secured with a decomposing strip of rawhide. Cabrillo reached in and carefully removed the bundle.

Nixon looked at Cabrillo and smiled. "What now, boss?"

"We copy them," Cabrillo said quietly, "and put them back."

*   *   *

S UNG RHEE WAS in the center of a maelstrom of angry people. The
admiral from the Chinese navy had called Beijing to report the damage to his ships, the two billionaires had both returned with teams of
attorneys, and his assistant had just called to report that the mayor of
Macau was downstairs and on his way up.

And then his telephone rang.

"I told you," he told his receptionist, "no interruptions."

"President Hu Jintao's office is calling."

"Put him through," Rhee said, motioning with his hand to clear his
office. "Put him through."

A few seconds later, a voice said, "President Jintao is on the line."

"Good morning, Mr. President," Rhee said.

"Good morning, Mr. Rhee," Jintao said quietly. "I understand you
had a bit of trouble last night."

Rhee began to sweat. "A . . . a minor theft," he stammered. "Nothing we can't handle, Mr. President."

"Mr. Rhee. We've received calls this morning from the United States
embassy, the head of the Chinese navy, and the vice president of Greece
wanting to know why one of his ships was illegally stopped and boarded
on your orders. That does not sound like a *minor theft* to me."

"There . . . has been some trouble here," Rhee admitted.

The telephone was silent for a few seconds. "Mr. Rhee," Jintao said
coldly, "I want you to tell me everything that happened. Right now,
from the start."

Slowly, Rhee began speaking.

G UNDERSON STARTED A long lumbering turn around the *Oregon*.
As he stared out the cockpit window, he could see a large balloon
do a fast inflate, then head up in the air, towing a line.

On the stern deck of the *Oregon*, Kevin Nixon checked the straps
around the crate containing the Golden Buddha again. The three-
pronged hook was duct-taped to the crate and would be used to yank

Cabrillo aboard if they were successful getting the icon aboard the Antonov. Hanley stood off to the side, checking the fit on the harness that wrapped around Cabrillo's chest and upper thighs. Satisfied it was properly attached, he snapped a smaller bag containing the sandwiches to one side of the harness.

"The old Fulton Recovery System," Cabrillo said. "You'd think with all our funds we'd have found a replacement by now."

"It's so rare we're this far offshore," Hanley said. "Past the point our amphibian or a helicopter can reach us."

"You ever ridden one of these?" Cabrillo asked.

"Never had the pleasure," Hanley said, smiling.

"It feels like a mule kicked you in the ass," Cabrillo said.

"That's the least of your worries, the way I see it."

"How do you figure?" Cabrillo asked.

"The only winch we could find was designed for light trucks," Hanley noted. "I just hope they can reel you in fast enough before you strike the rear stabilizer."

"You make it all sound so appealing," Cabrillo said wryly.

The sound of the Antonov was growing louder.

"Clear the decks," Nixon shouted, "for the first approach."

G UNDERSON WAS NOTED for never becoming flustered. No matter what the situation, he always maintained his cool. Lowering the flaps on the Antonov, he slowed the speed to just above stall, then lined up less than a hundred feet above the deck.

"Anybody got any gum?" he asked.

Michaels quickly peeled the foil off a piece and jammed it in his mouth.

"Head back to help Tracy," Gunderson said. "I'll hook the fatso on the first pass, then I'll shout back before I roll her over."

Inside the *Oregon*, the cameras on the deck relayed an image of the operation throughout the ship. Everyone watched as Gunderson steered closer.

In the cargo compartment, Pilston and Michaels were watching out the open door. The steel cable stretched backward, but the hook on the end was out of view. Gunderson was peering out the front window, then the side window, in a rapid ballet of visual Olympics. At the top of the cable leading to the Fulton Aerial Recovery System, just below the balloon, the cable spread into a Y shape. Gunderson chomped on the gum as he steered the Antonov closer.

"It's show time," he shouted.

The hook dangling back from the plane slid cleanly into the Y and snagged the cable. A split second later the crate containing the Golden Buddha was yanked from the deck as cleanly as ripping a bandage off a wound. Gunderson instantly felt the drag on the plane and shouted for Pilston to engage the winch.

She threw the lever forward and the package started to reel aboard, while at the same time Gunderson eased the biplane over on her side. Hanley watched from the deck in amazement.

"Tell me when the load's within ten feet," Gunderson shouted.

A minute or so later, Michaels shouted, "Okay, Chuck."

Gunderson did a quick sideways dive to the ocean, now only some eighty feet away, and the crate went temporarily weightless from the g forces. The crate floated in the air for a second.

"Rolling flat," Gunderson shouted.

Pilston and Michaels moved away from the door, and the cable tightened and reeled the Golden Buddha aboard as easily as a book sliding into a bookcase. The crate slammed against the far inner wall of the fuselage and stopped. The crate was cracked, but not much. Pilston turned the winch motor off.

Gunderson stared back, quite happy with the results. He reached for the radio.

"Mr. Hanley," he said. "I scratched your box a little, but the cargo is safe and sound."

Hanley pushed the button on his portable radio as Gunderson began to climb and bank around. "Hell of a job, Tiny. There's a different hook attached to the box. Attach that to the cable before you pull the chairman aboard."

"Roger that," Gunderson said.

Then he shouted back to Michaels to attach the other hook to the end of the line. By the time Gunderson had passed over the top of the *Oregon* again and was starting his turn to line up, the hook was attached and Pilston started to reel out the cable once again. Gunderson adjusted his flight controls, they set the speed of the Antonov to right at stall.

"Once I hook the boss man," Gunderson shouted, "you reel him in as fast as possible. When he's next to the door, reach out and pull him inside."

"Got it," Pilston shouted.

"Here I come, boss," Gunderson said into the radio, "ready or not."

Cabrillo had moved onto the rear deck and Nixon inflated the balloon. It shot in the air when the Antonov was only a hundred yards off the bow.

"Clear the decks," Nixon shouted as he sprinted away.

Juan Cabrillo stood quietly. There was really no way to prepare for what was about to happen. In a few seconds, he would be yanked from the safety of the *Oregon* and into the air over the ocean. From the known to the unknown in a split second. So Cabrillo simply cleared his mind and waited.

Gunderson chewed his gum, watched the line carefully, and then put the three-pronged hook directly into the center of the Y once again. Bam! One second Cabrillo's feet were on the deck, the next second he was yanked into the air. He moved his feet back and forth like he was trying to run. The wind crept past the goggles he was wearing and his eyes began to weep as the Antonov grew larger. Cabrillo could see hands reaching out of the door as he rose, closer to safety. He tilted his head back and looked. Every few seconds the cable was bumping against the rear stabilizer and he prepared to push himself off as he grew closer.

"He's going to hit the tail," Pilston shouted to Gunderson.

Cabrillo put his feet in the air to push against the stabilizer. He was only a few feet away when Gunderson pulled back on the controls and pitched the nose of the Antonov up. Cabrillo, hanging from the cable like a pendulum, dropped a few feet and slid past the tail. A few seconds later he was next to the door; Michaels and Pilston grabbed his arms and pulled him inside.

Gunderson started the Antonov climbing, then glanced back into the cargo area.

"Hey, boss," he yelled, "how was the ride?"

36

MICHAEL HALPERT FLICKED on the computer in the *Oregon*'s library. Working the party in Macau had been exciting—the element of danger involved in operations ensured that. Even so, Halpert's forte was the arcane accounting and banking network he had constructed for the Corporation's activities. In that, Halpert was a master. The twisted matrix of corporate law and structure was exciting to him—he loved to hide the Corporation's assets like a penny under a glacier, and shield its ownership in companies through complex structures that would take teams of accountants years to unravel.

Today he would need to use all his skills.

Halpert was building what he liked to call a skeleton. A skeleton was a series of corporations forming the bones to support the skull that held the nerve center of an operation. Each would need to be structured, funded and interlinked until the actual source of ownership and control was as cloudy as a London morning.

He scanned a database of available existing companies.

First would come the skull itself—the eventual owner of the assets that would soon be created. For that he chose a corporation based in the tiny country of Andorra. The company, Cataluna Esteme, had been founded in 1972 with the purpose of mining and trading of lead.

Andorra, all 181 square miles of territory, is perched in the Pyrenees Mountains, with Spain to the south and France to the north. The population of Andorra is some sixty-five thousand people, and the primary industry is tourism, with an emphasis on snow skiing. The country had been in existence since 1278 and was modern and progressive, plus Halpert had never used it before.

Cataluna Esteme itself had been active in the lead business until 1998, when the aging owner had been felled by heart trouble while on a visit to Paris. Over the next year or so, the assets of the corporation had been distributed to the owner's heirs, and the company itself had gone dormant. Cataluna Esteme existed in the desk drawer of a lawyer in Andorra's capital city of Andorra la Vella.

Halpert scanned the history and found it ideal. The company had perfect credit, a past history of large sums passing through the corporation coffers, as well as the shield of privacy offered by Andorran law. The remaining stock in the company was available for the equivalent of $50,000. This sum would give them complete control of a corporation that had existed for over thirty years, had a charter similar to the intended use, and was completely untraceable.

Halpert decided to buy Cataluna Esteme.

For the feet of the skeleton, he used two companies the Corporation already owned. The first was Gizo Properties, based in the Solomon Islands in the South Pacific. The second was Paisen Industries, based in San Marino, a country on the Adriatic coast completely surrounded by Italy. Accessing the companies' accounts over the computer, Halpert deposited $874,000 in Gizo Properties and $418,000 in Paisen Industries. In the blink of an eye, Halpert had moved $1.292 million into already existing accounts. The money would not remain there long.

Next, Gizo Properties and Paisen Industries, through a special share-holders' resolution that Halpert drafted and passed, each agreed to buy stock in two more companies. The first was Alcato, based in Lisbon, the second, Tellemedics of Asunción, Paraguay. Both of these companies were operating concerns—Alcato built specialized marine electronics, Tellemedics made telemetry equipment used in hospitals throughout South America. The Portuguese company had a book value of $3 million U.S.; the Paraguayan, nearly $10 million.

Both had been secretly owned by the Corporation for nearly a decade.

Halpert pulled up the corporate records of both and found sufficient cash reserves for his plan.

With the legs now in place, he looked for the torso.

He would need a recognizable and stable platform that would appeal to the Corporation's soon-to-be partners. For this he could only use Central Europe. Halpert needed a company based in a country with rock-solid political stability, iron-clad currency and worldwide recognition of financial wherewithal. He scanned his database and found he had three companies to choose from—the first was based in Basel, Switzerland; the second in Luxembourg; the third, which he favored, in Vaduz, Liechtenstein.

Liechtenstein it was.

Albertinian Investments S.A. was a currency-and-gold-trading concern that had proved widely successful since the recent upward move in precious metals prices. The company, secretly controlled by the Corporation, owned a beautiful six-story building in Vaduz, where it occupied the top two stories, had a cash balance in accounts amounting to over $18 million U.S., and frequently invested in other companies that showed promise.

Next, Alcato and Tellemedics passed corporate resolutions making loans of $1.25 million each to Albertinian Investments. These were composed of the monies transferred from Gizo Properties and Paisen Industries, plus some cash from the coffers of each. Albertinian Investments agreed to pay each company 7 percent interest for the loans, as well as an option to convert the loans to stock at a set price for the next five years. The trail of money was becoming cloudier by the minute.

There was now an extra $5 million of washed and clean funds in Albertinian Investments.

Halpert sipped from a glass of iced tea. Then he entered the commands into the computer and Albertinian Investments offered to buy Cataluna Esteme for the $50,000 asking price. The transaction would take several hours for the attorney in Andorra to complete.

Next, Halpert scanned a base of lawyers the Corporation had used in the past in Spain. Finding one in Madrid, he dialed the telephone and waited.

"Carlos the Second, please," he said in Spanish when the receptionist answered. "Mr. Halpert calling."

Exactly forty-two seconds later, the lawyer came on the line.

"Sorry for the wait, Mr. Halpert," the lawyer said. "What can I do for you?"

"I need you to fly to Andorra, immediately," Halpert said. "We are buying another company."

"Standard protocol?" the lawyer asked. "Open bank accounts, rent offices and such?"

"That's the idea," Halpert said, "and we need it done yesterday."

"I'll need to charter a plane, then," the lawyer said. "I doubt there are commercial flights available at this late hour."

"We will approve the costs," Halpert said.

"How big are you looking, sir?"

"The initial funding will be ten million," Halpert said. "Five will be a direct loan from one of our divisions in Liechtenstein, the second five will be in the form of a line of credit, available immediately."

"I understand, sir," the lawyer said. "I'll leave right away."

"One more thing," Halpert said. "Find us a public relations firm in Andorra—I have a feeling what we are planning will garner some press interest."

"Anything else?"

"If there is," Halpert said, "I'll contact you when you reach Andorra."

"Very good," the lawyer said as he hung up the telephone.

Then the lawyer sat back in his chair and smiled. He knew his rather excessive fees would be paid in cash—which he would fail to report to the tax authorities. Reaching for the telephone, he called a local company to charter a prop-jet for the trip north.

"L IKE BEING KICKED by a mule," Cabrillo said over the noise of the droning engine.

Pilston was closing the side door of the Antonov. She wrestled it in place and held it closed while Michaels locked it down. Cabrillo placed his hand on the Golden Buddha to stabilize himself, and then removed the package of papers and the satchel of food. He placed them on the floor, then unsnapped the harness and set it aside. He stared around the cargo bay of the Antonov before walking forward to the cockpit.

"How's she fly, Tiny?" he asked as he slid into the copilot's seat.

"She's as slow and steady as a diesel trawler," Gunderson answered.

"Did you get any sleep?"

"Yep," Gunderson said. "Tracy needed to rack up some flight time, so she and Judy flew us here from Vietnam."

Cabrillo nodded and turned his head back to the cargo area. "How'd it go with Mr. Silicon Valley?" he asked.

"We made it through," Michaels said.

"I want to apologize to both of you," Cabrillo said quietly. "If there was any other way . . ."

"We know, sir," Pilston said. "It was just a job—and we treated it as such."

"Still . . . ," Cabrillo said, "it was above and beyond what we should ask of you. I approved a special bonus for you both, and Hanley has scheduled you for a month off with pay as soon as we finish this mission."

"Thank you, sir," Michaels said. "And this helped soften the blow somewhat."

She held up the stack of bearer bonds.

"I trust," Gunderson said, "you mean that figuratively and not literally."

T HE U.S. AMBASSADOR to Russia sipped from a small glass of vodka, then smiled at President Putin. The men were seated in front of a roaring fire inside the presidential offices in Moscow. Outside, a spring storm was finally exhausting itself after dumping nearly a foot of wet snow on the capital city. Soon the first flowers would pop their heads from the soil. Then it would all turn green.

"How much are we talking about?" Putin asked.

"Billions," the ambassador said.

"And the structure?"

"As you know," the ambassador said, taking another sip, "this is not a United States government operation. For all intents and purposes, you will be making the agreements with a separate company that we subcontract with."

"But they work for you?" Putin asked.

"Not on paper," the ambassador said, "but we have used them in the past."

"Give me some details," Putin said as he rose to stoke the fire with a poker. "I'd like to know with whom I'm getting into bed."

"They call themselves the Corporation," the ambassador noted quietly. "They handle things of a sensitive nature for us and other countries. The company has specialized skills, huge amounts of funding and an unparalleled reputation for integrity."

"They can be trusted?" Putin asked.

"You may consider their word their bond," the ambassador confirmed.

"Who runs this Corporation?" Putin asked.

"A man named Juan Cabrillo," the ambassador answered.

"And when do I meet this Juan Cabrillo?" Putin said, turning from the fire, placing the poker back in the rack and sliding into the armchair.

"He will be in Moscow late this evening," the ambassador said.

"Good," Putin said. "I welcome the chance to hear him out."

The ambassador finished the small glass of vodka and waved away Putin's attempt to refill it. "Now," he said, "how much hassle are you getting from the Chinese?"

"Enough," the Russian president admitted, "but not more than we can handle."

"If you need to," the ambassador asked, "are you ready to go in?"

Putin pointed to a folder of papers on the table. "There is the plan. In less than twenty-four hours, we can cross the Tarim Basin in a lightning-fast raid and reach the border of Tibet."

"Let's hope it doesn't come to that," the ambassador said.

"If I have to order that approach," Putin said, "I want your president on paper supporting that move. There is no other way."

"We don't think you'll need to do that," the ambassador said. "It won't go that far."

"Just know," Putin said, "if we stand up—he does too."

"I'll let him know," the ambassador said.

"THEY APPEARED OUT of nowhere," the head of Chinese state security said.

Chinese president Hu Jintao stared at the man with barely concealed contempt.

"Five hundred Buddhist monks just materialized out of the mist in People's Park in downtown Beijing?" Jintao said. "That's some magic."

The man sat mute. There was nothing to say.

"And they are chanting and calling for Tibetan freedom?"

"Yes, sir," the man from state security said.

"When was the last time we were faced with a Tibetan protest?" Jintao asked.

"In Beijing?" the man said. "It's been over a decade—and then it was tiny and easily dispersed."

"And this one?"

"It's growing by the minute," the man admitted.

"I've got a massive Russian war exercise on the border with Mongolia, Tibetan separatists in downtown Beijing, and I'm not sure what's going on in Macau province. This spring is not coming up with fresh-smelling flowers."

"Do you want me to order troops to disperse the protesters?" the head of state security asked.

"Absolutely not," Jintao said. "Our world standing still has not been repaired from Tiananmen Square, and that was in 1989. We take action against peaceful Buddhist monks, the repercussions will reverberate for decades."

"Then do nothing?"

"For now," Jintao said, "until we figure out what is happening."

"WHERE ARE WE at on this thing?" the president of the United States asked.

"Off the record, sir?" the Director of Central Intelligence asked.

"I did not sneak you into the White House through the underground tunnel so that I could discuss it tonight on *Larry King*, Director. Yes, completely off the record."

"It's progressing perfectly," the DCI noted. "And we are shielded behind an armor of deniability that couldn't be penetrated with an antitank round."

"How soon before you need me to do my thing?" the president asked.

"Tomorrow," the DCI said, "if all goes according to plan."

"Then," the president said, rising, "you make sure it does."

"Yes, Mr. President," the DCI said as the president walked through the door and down the hall to a state dinner that was already in progress.

T HE *OREGON* WAS flying across the water. The schedule called for the ship to stop in Ho Chi Minh City. Once there, the operatives that would be needed in Tibet would be off-loaded and flown in a C-130 northwest to Bhutan. Then the *Oregon* would continue on, passing Singapore. Traversing the Strait of Malacca, the vessel would race north into the Bay of Bengal, arriving off Bangladesh on Easter Day.

That was the closest to Tibet that the *Oregon* would ever be.

No one in the Corporation enjoyed it when the *Oregon* and her battery of electronics and firepower were far from the operation. The ship was the lifeline to the crew, their home away from home, their anchor in the stormy sea of intrigue where they operated.

Ross and Kasim were doing their best to smooth the difficulty.

"I've tested the satellite uplink," Kasim said. "The *Oregon* will have command-and-control capability. Everyone will be reachable either by radio or secure telephone."

Ross glanced up from her computer screen. "I'm programming the drones. We have two. That's less than I would like, but they're just so damn expensive."

"Who will fly them?" Kasim asked.

"They will need to be operated from within three hundred miles," she noted. "Thimbu or inside Tibet itself."

Kasim nodded.

She scanned a sheet of paper that listed crew qualifications. "Four of us are trained in the operation. You, me, Lincoln and Jones."

"Lincoln would stand out in Tibet like a debutante at a tractor pull," Kasim noted. "If he operates the drone, at least he'll be hidden inside a tent. If I were you, I'd recommend to Hanley he get the job."

Ross nodded her head in agreement. "He's good," she said, "and the drones are critical—they will be our only eyes in the sky. If Lincoln can keep them over station above Lhasa Airport, the control room here can watch the action unfolding."

"What have the Chinese got in Tibet to shoot them down?" Kasim asked.

Ross glanced at the sheet listing Chinese defenses that had been recently smuggled out of Tibet by the underground freedom movement. "Some old antiaircraft guns and one ten-year-old missile defense battery. Around Gonggar Airport near Lhasa there's not much," she said. "Looks like a couple of cargo planes, some helicopters, and rifles carried by the troops."

"I'd make a note to Hanley to target the antiaircraft guns for early destruction," Kasim said, "then have Lincoln fly only one drone at a time."

"That's what I was thinking," Ross said. "If he flies high, he can scan the entire city, plus keep the bird out of sight of riflemen."

"Makes sense," Kasim said.

"What do you find for radio and television transmitters?"

"There is one television," Kasim said, "and a pair of radios. We need quickly to gain control of both so we can keep the Tibetan people alerted."

"What's the report say?" Ross said. "Will they rally against the Chinese when the time comes?"

"We think so," Kasim said, "and God help the Chinese when they do."

"The *Dungkar*?" Ross said.

"Tibetan for blackbirds with red beaks," Kasim said. "The fighting arm of the Tibetan underground."

Ross glanced at the sheet holding the assembled intelligence. "*When it is time, we will feed on the carcasses of the oppressors and the beaks will be red with blood and the day will be black with death."*

"Brings a chill to my spine," Kasim said.

"And I thought," Ross said, "we had the air conditioning too cold."

ONE FLOOR BELOW where Ross and Kasim were planning, Mark Murphy was in the armory. Munitions and crates were piled to one side, and Sam Pryor and Cliff Hornsby were slowly moving them toward the elevator to be taken to an upper storage area where they would be off-loaded in Da Nang. On each crate to be used, Murphy attached a red-taped sticker. Then the contents were labeled with a felt-tipped pen. He was singing a ditty while he worked.

"I'm a gonna blow some stuff up tomorrow," he said. "Gonna blow me up some stuff."

Pryor wiped his forehead with a handkerchief before bending down to lift another crate to carry to the elevator. "Shoot, Murph," he said, "you packing enough C-6?"

"You can't have too much," Murphy said, smiling, "at least in my opinion. Heck, it doesn't spoil and you never know what might come up."

"You got enough here to blow up an Egyptian pyramid," Hornsby said, walking into the room after placing his crate in the elevator, "and enough mines to register shock waves on a seismograph."

"Those are for the airport," Murphy said. "You don't want the Chinese to be able to land troops, do you?"

"Land?" Pryor said. "You use all these, there won't be an airport."

"I have other plans for some of them," Murphy said.

"I've got the feeling you're looking forward to this," Hornsby said.

Murphy started singing again as he walked over to crates of Stinger missiles and began to attach the red tags. Letting loose a long whistle, he finished with the sound of a blast.

Hornsby and Pryor carried crates out the door and headed for the elevator.

"I'd sure hate to have him mad at me," Pryor said.

37

THE ANTONOV WAS less than a hundred miles from Da Nang, heading due west. At its current speed, the plane would touch down in about forty minutes, or just around 4:30 P.M. local time. The biplane, although slow, had performed flawlessly. Gunderson balanced the yoke with his knees and reached into the air and stretched.

"This baby's a peach," he said to Cabrillo.

"After this mission is completed, you can check into buying one for the company, if you think we'll use it enough," Cabrillo said.

"Take the wings off and we could probably fit it into a forty-foot shipping container," Gunderson said. "If we had Murphy mount a fire cannon out the door, we'd have a hell of a gunship."

For the last hour Cabrillo had been checking arrangements with the *Oregon* over his secure telephone. The last call from Hanley had placed the Gulfstream G550 on final approach to Da Nang airfield. Cabrillo was nodding at Gunderson's comment when his telephone buzzed again.

"The Gulfstream's on the ground and refueled," Hanley told him. "The pilot is setting the course now. I contacted General Siphondon in Laos and received permission for you to cross through their airspace."

"How is the general?" Cabrillo asked.

"His usual self," Hanley said. "Dropping hints about a classic car he'd like."

"At least he's upfront about his wants," Cabrillo said. "And an old-car fetish I can understand. What is it he's after?"

"Hemi Roadrunner convertible," Hanley said. "Apparently some Air America pilot had one shipped over to use during the war. The general was only a kid then, but it stuck in his mind."

"Any around?"

"I've got Keith Lowden in Colorado checking out the market," Hanley said. "He'll get back to us when he knows what's available."

"Excellent," Cabrillo said. "Now what about Thailand and Myanmar?"

"All cleared," Hanley said, "so it'll be a straight shot to India."

"C-130?"

"She's due to leave Bhutan and touch down in Da Nang just after eight P.M."

"Do you have the team ready?" Cabrillo asked.

"They'll be ready by the time the *Oregon* reaches port," Hanley said.

"This is a tight timetable," Cabrillo said, "and we only have one shot at this."

"No do-overs," Hanley said quietly.

"No do-overs," Cabrillo agreed.

I N NORTHERN INDIA at Little Lhasa, the oracle was deep in a trance. The Dalai Lama sat to one side as the man spun and danced. From time to time the oracle would race over to a sheet of rice paper and scribble notes furiously, then return to his ritualistic motions. A

strange animal-like sound seeped from his vocal cords and drops of
sweat flew through the air.

At last he collapsed in a heap on the floor and his helpers removed
the headpiece and robes.

The Dalai Lama picked up a wooden bowl filled with water, damp-
ened a sheep's skin, then stepped over, bent down, and began to wash
the sweat from the aging man.

"You did well," he said in a soothing voice. "There is much information written on the sheets."

The oracle allowed the Dalai Lama to drip some water into his
mouth. He swished it around and spit it to the side. "I saw bloodshed
and fighting," he said quietly. "Much bloodshed."

"Let us pray not," the Dalai Lama said.

"But there was a second way," the oracle said. "I think that is what
I wrote."

"Bring some tea and tsampa," the Dalai Lama ordered an aide, who
rushed out of the room.

Twelve minutes later, the oracle and the Dalai Lama were sitting
around a table in the great room. The Tibetan tea, flavored with salt
and butter, as well as the tsampa, roasted barley flour usually mixed
with milk or yogurt, had brought the color back to the oracle's cheeks.
Where only moments before he had seemed aged and weak, he now
appeared animated and in control.

"Your Holiness," he said eagerly, "shall we see what I received?"

"Please," the Dalai Lama said.

The oracle stared at the sheets of rice paper. The letters were in an
ancient script only he and a few others could read. He read them
through twice, then smiled at the Dalai Lama.

"Is someone from the west coming to see you?" the oracle asked.

"Yes," the Dalai Lama said, "later this evening."

"Here is what you tell him," the oracle said.

Thirty minutes later, the Dalai Lama nodded and smiled at the oracle.

"I will have my aides prepare notes to buttress our argument," he said, "and thank you."

Rising from the chair, the oracle walked unsteadily from the room.

L ANGSTON OVERHOLT WAS using a borrowed office in a far corner of the compound at Little Lhasa. He was speaking on a secure line to the director of Central Intelligence in hushed tones.

"I didn't order that," he said. "I simply don't have the apparatus in China to pull it off."

"The estimates from our people on the ground place the number at five hundred and growing," the DCI noted.

"I'll ask the contractor," Overholt said, "but it may just be a lucky break."

"Whatever the case," the DCI said, "reports say the Chinese are paying close attention to the protests."

"What about the Mongolians?" Overholt asked.

"I had a secret meeting with their ambassador," the DCI said. "They'll play it either way."

"What did that cost?" Overholt asked.

"Don't ask," the DCI said, "but suffice it to say the United States' strategic reserves of tungsten and molybdenum won't need replenishing for some time."

"That gives us choices for the contractor to offer to the Russians," Overholt said.

"As soon as he meets with them, I need to know what they have decided," the DCI told him.

"No matter what the time," Overholt said.

"Day or night," the DCI said before disconnecting.

G UNDERSON COULD NOT believe the lift the pair of wings gave the Antonov. Though he and the others had been flying the plane for nearly eight hours, this was the first time he had needed to land. Lining up to land, he floated the Antonov down to the runway like a feather fluttering to the floor. Halfway down the length of the runway, Gunderson realized he'd need to force the plane to the ground. Moving the yoke forward, he felt the wheels finally touch.

"Sorry about that, boss," he said, pointing out the window at the Gulfstream on the far end of the runway. "She floats like a butterfly. I'll taxi us back over to the Gulfstream."

Cabrillo nodded and unsnapped the seat belt. Walking into the cargo area, he began to collect his things. Lifting the stack of bearer bonds, he placed them all in his bag, then thought better of that. He turned his head toward the cockpit.

"Do you have to take the plane back south again?" he asked Gunderson.

"No, sir," Gunderson said, slowing as he approached the Gulfstream. "Gannon worked it out—the company will pick it up here. The ladies are boarding the *Oregon*, and I'm flying north on the C-130 as soon as it arrives."

Cabrillo began to count the pile. When he finished, he spoke again.

"I'm leaving you a pile," he said to everyone. "Give them to Hanley when he arrives. Tell him I took the rest north—I may need them to grease some wheels."

Gunderson stopped the Antonov, then reached for the checklist for postflight. "Okay, boss," he said as he started through the steps to shut down the engine. Michaels was unlatching the door while Pilston stood off to the side.

"You have some time to kill until the *Oregon* arrives," Cabrillo said. "You'll have guards from the Vietnamese air force, but I'd stay close. Hanley will make payment to their general when he arrives, so you shouldn't have to deal with much."

"Will they take us to a bathroom?" Michaels asked.

"I'm sure they will," Cabrillo said as he walked for the door, "but one at a time, please. And whatever you do, don't let anyone know you have that stack of bonds."

"You got it, boss," Gunderson said.

Cabrillo stopped at the door for a second. "Ladies, Tiny," he said, smiling, "I'll see you soon."

Then he stepped off the Antonov and began walking to the Gulf-stream. The pilot and copilot were standing next to the open door. The pilot smiled at Cabrillo and motioned for the step.

"We're ready for you, sir," he said. "Welcome aboard."

"There's a box on the biplane," Cabrillo said. "Get some help and haul it aboard."

Cabrillo walked up the ramp, made his way to a seat, and then waited while the pilots got the crate loaded inside, shut the door, and started the engines. Two minutes later, they were airborne. The Gulf-stream was still climbing to cruising altitude when they crossed over the mountains of Laos.

I N NOVOSIBIRSK, RUSSIA, General Alexander Kernetsikov was star-ing at a large chalkboard inside a hangar at the airport. Troops and material continued to pour into the area at a rate of deployment seldom seen in times of peace. There were thousands of details to attend to, but there was one that bothered Kernetsikov the most.

"Have we received an answer yet?" he said to his aide. "If this is a go, I need to know which fork to take at Barnaul. We either violate Kazakhstan and enter China near Tacheng, or we need to move the troops into Mongolia, take the road toward Altaj and cross over the mountains there, then sweep quickly across the plains and pass Lop Nur."

The aide stared at the general. Lop Nur was the home of the Chinese nuclear test base and he imagined it would be heavily defended. The other route featured mountains that were still covered in snow. It was like choosing between a root canal and ripping off a toenail.

"There's been no communication, General," the aide said, "*including* whether this is not merely an exercise in fast deployment and war planning."

"It's just a feeling," the general said quietly, "but I think that before this is over, we'll be crossing the mountains like Hannibal."

The aide nodded. Every good officer under whom he had served had a strong sense of history. He just hoped the general was wrong—facing off with the Chinese, even with the firepower they had amassed, was not a welcome thought.

I N BEIJING, GENERAL Tudeng Quing was offering President Jintao a possible solution.

"If we pull all but two thousand troops out of Tibet, concentrating those left only in Lhasa, we could divert the rest to Ürümqi in the Xinjiang Province. They could be in place starting tomorrow."

"How many?" Jintao asked.

"Say a thousand by plane in the next few hours," Quing said. "The tanks and armored carriers have a nine-hundred-mile journey. Running them full out at forty miles an hour with refueling and such, they could be in place tomorrow this time."

"We don't have any troops closer?" Jintao asked.

"Airborne, we can bring them in from anywhere," Quing noted. "It's the armor we need—other than Tibet, the closest armored division we require is almost twice that distance away, and the trip is over rougher terrain. My aides have calculated three or four days minimum."

Jintao sat back in his chair and stared at the ceiling. Then he turned to Legchog Raidi Zhuren, the chairman of the Tibet Autonomous Region, who had so far remained quiet.

"Will two thousand troops give you a sufficient level of security until we can replace your armor in four or five days?" Jintao asked.

"Mr. President," Zhuren said. "Tibet has been quiet for years—I don't see that changing any time soon. Now, if I may be excused, I should be leaving for my return to Tibet."

Jintao turned to General Quing. "Order it done."

Next, Jintao turned to the Chinese ambassador to Russia.

"You," he said loudly, "figure out what the Russians have planned. If they are planning to annex Mongolia, let them know we won't stand for that. The Mongols conquered us once—I'm not going to give them a chance to try it again."

Within two hours of the meeting, the first Chinese transport planes began to land at Lhasa Airport and began ferrying troops north to Xinjiang Province. In the haste to counter the Russian threat, the organization of the Chinese army in Tibet would suffer. Junior officers would be placed in charge of partially staffed battalions. Weapons and ammunition would be depleted. The mission and purpose would be compromised.

C ABRILLO WAS NAPPING in the rear of the Gulfstream when his secure telephone buzzed.

"Go ahead," he said, instantly awake.

"It's me," Overholt said, "with good news. The NSA just called the DCI, who called me. The Russian bluff is working. Transport planes are leaving the airport in Lhasa and hauling troops north. In addition, a column of tanks has just left the city and they're traveling at breakneck speed. Everyone said it's looking up so far."

Cabrillo glanced at his watch. "I'll be there in about an hour or so. Are we all set up for the meeting?"

"It's all taken care of," Overholt said.

"Good," Cabrillo said. "If we reach an agreement there, I'll continue north."

"You really think you can sell everybody on this idea?" Overholt asked.

"This mission's like an onion," Cabrillo said. "Every time I peel back a layer, there's a layer underneath."

"That's not the half of it," Overholt said. "The Dalai Lama has a new plan."

"I can't wait," Cabrillo said.

"I think you're going to like it," Overholt told him.

38

THE *OREGON* DOCKED off Ho Chi Minh City. The team that would enter Tibet was transported by shore boat to land. Then they were driven in a Vietnamese air force truck to the airport, where the C-130 sat waiting. The total Corporation force would number a baker's dozen.

Six men—Seng, Murphy, Reyes, King, Meadows and Kasim—would be tasked with the offensive operations. They would link up with the *Dungkar* already inside the country and direct them in the proper targets to hit first. Crabtree and Gannon, who were already in Bhutan awaiting the team's arrival, would handle supply and logistics. Adams and Gunderson would fly, while Lincoln was in charge of setting up and operating the Predator drones. Huxley was tasked with setting up a medical facility to treat anyone wounded or injured.

The thirteenth member was Cabrillo. He would arrive after he finished his pair of meetings.

To the untrained, the mission looked like suicide: a dozen or so against a force that was close to two thousand. Odds of one hundred and fifty-plus to one. It looked like a bloodbath in the making. A trained observer, however, would be praying for the Chinese troops. First, one had to consider the *Dungkar*, the shadowy underground Chinese opposition thought to number in the thousands in Lhasa. When unleashed, the *Dungkar* would burn with a fever that only comes when fighting an enemy on home soil. Second was the element of surprise. The Chinese were not planning for a concentrated and expertly executed coup d'etat in the next twenty-four hours. The third was the most basic. It is almost a certainty that a well-planned offense will defeat an unplanned defense every single time.

That was where the Corporation excelled.

Already, most of the Chinese forces inside Tibet were heading north in a helter-skelter deployment that had left little time for planning and even less for preparation. The troops left around Lhasa were not the cream of the crop; they were the leftovers—the administration clerks, mechanics and painters, plodders and planners. The officers were not combat trained, would not be knowledgeable about their individual soldiers' strengths and weaknesses, and would lack a complete picture of where all the parts fit together.

Right now in Tibet, the army was a jigsaw puzzle without a design.

K ASIM WALKED FROM the truck and approached the C-130 radio operator. "What have you got from inside?" he asked.

"We have another plane circling out of sight of the Chinese deployment, capturing their signals and bouncing them here," the operator said. "Right now, most of the communications pertain to laying fuel dumps on the road north. The tanks are outrunning the fuel supply."

"Have you heard from the tail?" Kasim asked.

The operator, a Chinese American formerly employed by the Defense Intelligence Agency and now attached to the CIA proprietary airline supplying the C-130, scanned his notes. "As of nineteen thirty Zulu time, the rear of the convoy had passed through Naggu."

"They're making good time," Kasim noted. "At this speed, they will pass through Amdo before eleven p.m. and then another two hours or so and they will make the border with Tsinghai Province."

The operator stared at a classified satellite photograph and compared it with a detailed Defense Mapping Agency map. "The pass at Basatongwula Shan will slow them some; it's riddled with steep mountains and tight turns. The altitude is almost sixty-one hundred meters."

"Twenty thousand feet," Kasim said. "That's high. The border's about two hundred fifty miles from Lhasa," Kasim noted, "and our reports state these are the older Type Fifty-nine tanks. That gives them a range of two hundred seventy miles on a tank of diesel, or about a hundred more if they have the external fuel tanks mounted."

The operator nodded. "I've been watching the progress. The Type Fifty-nine on a road can top out around fifty kilometers an hour or thirty-plus miles an hour. Normally, however, they cruise at something like twenty miles an hour."

"What are you saying?" Kasim asked.

The operator smiled and reached for a pack of cigarettes. He tapped one from the pack, lit it with a Zippo lighter, then took a drag. Blowing out the smoke, he answered.

"What I'm saying is that these boys are running at nearly full speed no matter what the cost in fuel usage. They will need to stop in Amdo and fill the tanks so they can make the pass. Then they'll have a run downhill that will take them to Kekexili for the next stop."

"So when they reach there sometime around breakfast Easter day," Kasim said, "they will be four hundred miles from Lhasa, with a twenty-thousand-foot pass in between them and us."

"Sounds about right," the operator said.

"Thanks for the help," Kasim said.

A line of Vietnamese air force airmen carried the last of the crates aboard the C-130. Hanley stood off to the side, talking to the Vietnamese general in charge of the arrangements. Kasim watched as Hanley handed the man an envelope, then the two shared a laugh. Hanley shook the general's hand, then walked over to the C-130.

"Mr. Hanley," Kasim said, "I have a plan."

THE GULFSTREAM G550 carrying Cabrillo and the Golden Buddha landed at Amritsar, India, and Cabrillo and the icon were flown in a helicopter the rest of the way to Little Lhasa, near Dharamsala in the northern Himachal Pradesh region of northern India.

The aide quickly ushered him in to his meeting with the Dalai Lama.

"Your Holiness," Cabrillo said as he entered and bowed his head slightly.

The Dalai Lama stood silently, staring at Cabrillo for a full minute. Then he smiled.

"You are a good man," he said at last. "Langston told me—but I needed to be sure for myself."

"Thank you, sir," Cabrillo said. "These are the papers that we re-covered from inside the Buddha," he said, handing them to the Dalai Lama's aide. "I'll need them transcribed before my meeting with the Russians."

"Copy them and translate them into English," the Dalai Lama or-dered his aide. "Mr. Cabrillo will need to leave again shortly."

The Dalai Lama motioned to a long couch, where Overholt was already seated. Cabrillo sat on the end and the Dalai Lama slipped between the two men. "So explain the plan," he said.

"I believe the Russians will support your bid to regain your country. They will offer the muscle to deter the Chinese from making an assault once we gain control of Lhasa, in return for the rights to develop what you claim those documents represent: the vast oil reserves of the Hima-layas."

"Their location's known only to us," said the Dalai Lama. "In those documents. So—your president got them to the border by offering them the aid package," the Dalai Lama said, "but to fight, they need more."

"Exactly," Cabrillo said.

"And you?" the Dalai Lama asked. "Your company? What were you hired to do?"

"We were hired to steal the Golden Buddha and to pave the way for your return. Once you are back inside Tibet, our obligation would, by the contract wording, end."

"So I would be left—how do you say it?—high and dry," the Dalai Lama said.

"Hard to say," Cabrillo admitted, "and this has bothered me and my associates."

"Why?" the Dalai Lama said. "Are you not mercenaries? Once your obligation is over, don't you just blend into the night?"

Cabrillo thought for a minute how to answer this question. He paused and thought as the Dalai Lama waited. "It's a little more complex than that, Your Holiness. If we did what we did just for money, we would have all retired by now. It's more involved than that. In the past, most of us worked for one government agency or another, and we were compelled by Congress, or public opinion, to do things we knew or felt were wrong. We don't do those things anymore. We were formed to make a profit, that's for sure, but as much as we like the money, we are also cognizant of the chances that arise for us to somehow right the wrongs of others."

"You are speaking of Karma," the Dalai Lama said. "Something I am most aware of."

Cabrillo nodded. "We have decided that to leave you alone to fight the Chinese would be wrong. The solution came to us when we realized the significance of the papers inside the Golden Buddha."

"And I assume your company will profit from such a deal?" the Dalai Lama asked.

"Is that bad?" Cabrillo asked.

"Not necessarily," the Dalai Lama said, "but explain more."

Ten minutes later, Cabrillo was finished.

"I'm impressed," the Dalai Lama said, "now let me explain mine."

Another five minutes passed as the Dalai Lama spoke.

"Brilliant," Cabrillo said when the Dalai Lama had finished.

"Thank you," the Dalai Lama said, "but to sway the vote will take funds—will you bear the cost?"

"We made a little money on a side deal," Cabrillo said, thinking of the $100 million in bearer bonds. "So the costs are not a problem."

Overholt had remained silent as the two spoke. Now he interjected. "If you can pull this off," he said eagerly, "the president will kiss you."

"Mr. Cabrillo," the Dalai Lama said, "this gives us both an opportunity to keep the bloodshed down, while at the same time offering our actions a legitimacy that is indisputable. If you can make this happen, I will agree to your deal as offered."

"Thank you, Your Holiness," Cabrillo said.

"Good luck, Mr. Cabrillo," the Dalai Lama said. "May Buddha bless your mission."

After a short meeting with Overholt, Cabrillo collected the translated pages and maps, then climbed back in the helicopter and was flown back to Amritsar. President Putin had been promised the meeting would be worth the effort. Cabrillo would not fail to deliver.

JUST AFTER MIDNIGHT, the C-130 carrying the members from the Corporation landed in Thimbu, Bhutan, and the plane was surrounded by a dozen Philippine Special Forces soldiers. Off to the side, the eight Bell 212 helicopters were aligned in a row, with ten feet separating each ship.

A large domed hangar was nearby, with the door open and light spilling out onto the runway. Carl Gannon walked from inside and extended his hand to Eddie Seng. "They tell me you're in charge until the chairman arrives," he said. "Let me show you around."

The others followed Seng and Gannon inside the hangar. "I've managed to scrounge up radios and have established a link with the *Oregon*," he said, pointing to a wooden table with a computer and a stack of papers. "The latest data is on top."

Alongside the table were several corkboards displaying maps of Tibet, satellite weather images and other documents. A chalkboard was erected on an easel, where Seng could make notes and draw the plans, as well as a large plastic-covered map showing the city of Lhasa that was taped to a piece of plywood and sat atop another table.

Off to the side, milling around an area with a large coffeepot, small refrigerator, and cardboard boxes containing food, were the eighteen mercenary pilots. Murphy made his way to the coffee, poured a cup and greeted an old friend. "Gurt," he said, "you old dog."

Gurt, a mid-fifties blond-haired man with a crew cut and a gold tooth in front, smiled.

"Murphy," he said, flashing the tooth, "I thought this might be something you'd be involved in. It had the smell of a Corporation operation."

The men continued visiting while Seng flipped through the information Gannon had amassed. Five minutes later, he called everyone to sit in the rows of folding wooden chairs arranged in front of the boards. The pilots ambled over and took seats behind the Corporation crew. Seng glanced at the assembled group before speaking.

"For those of you who don't know me," he said easily, "my name is Eddie, Seng. Please call me Seng and not Eddie so there is no confusion. I will be commander in charge of this operation until the time that our chairman, Juan Cabrillo, arrives in the theater."

The group nodded.

"The breakdown of flight operation will be as follows. Six of the helicopters will be tasked with offensive operations, one for the chairman when he arrives, one for medical. We will draw the assignments out of a hat on who is assigned to what, to be fair. Each of the helicopters will carry one member of our team, and the pilots will be required to fly this person anywhere he requests. Gentlemen, we will potentially be under fire and in harm's way for the next twenty-four to forty-eight hours. If this is not what you signed up for, let me know now so you can be replaced. If not, I want you to understand that as pilots you will be answering to the team member aboard. If you hesitate or refuse to comply with a request, you will be replaced by one of our team that is qualified in helicopter operations, and you will forfeit your second half payment. Any questions?"

Gurt raised his hand. "When do we receive our first half?"

"Ah . . . a real pilot," Seng said, "The answer is, as soon as we are finished here. Everyone okay with that?"

Heads nodded.

"If you have personal property or letters to loved ones or wish us to transfer the funds to another party if something happens to you," Seng noted, "please see either Gannon or Crabtree."

Gannon and Crabtree raised their hands.

"Now, are there any other business matters before I explain the operation?"

The hangar was silent.

"Good, then," Seng said. "Here's the plan."

THE GULFSTREAM G550 was at forty-one thousand feet racing toward Moscow as Cabrillo talked over a secure satellite telephone to the *Oregon*. "Go over them again," he said as he scrawled notes on a yellow pad. "Okay, I've got them."

The line was silent as Cabrillo studied the list.

"And Halpert set up the main corporate entity in Andorra."

"Correct," Hanley said.

"Lucky break," Cabrillo said, "but then, by looking at this list, the Dalai Lama is a lucky one too. If this had been scheduled last year, I don't know if we could have pulled it off."

"Isn't that the truth?" Hanley said.

"Here's how I see it," Cabrillo said. "Of the fifteen members of the

United Nations Security Council, we have three of the five permanent members: the United States, the United Kingdom and Russia. China is obviously not going to vote our way, and France is currently trying to sell whatever they can to the Chinese, so they'll probably vote with them so as not to upset any deals they have in progress. The remaining ten will be tricky—we need to pull six out of the ten to give us the nine we need for the resolution. Let me go over it with you. Afghanistan we're not going to get—even with the U.S. involvement a few years ago, there are still too many pockets of anti-Buddhist revolutionaries for their leaders to risk voting with us. Sweden is and will always be pacifistic, at least at the start, as will Canada. Cuba receives too much aid from China to risk voting our way, not to mention they almost always vote the opposite of the U.S."

"Sounds about right," Hanley said.

"That leaves us Brunei, Laos, Qatar, Andorra, Kiribati and Tuvalu."

"Correct," Hanley said.

"It's blind luck that we have two tiny South Pacific nations on the Security Council at the same time," Cabrillo said.

"It's like a couple of years ago, when Cameroon and Guinea were both members at the same time," Hanley said. "It happens."

"Each country in the United Nations has one vote," Cabrillo said, "but this is the first time I really considered the impact."

"Same here," Hanley said.

Cabrillo thought for a moment. "I know the emir of Qatar," he said. "If we offer him a favor later, he'll order his people to vote the way we want. What have we got coming up?"

Hanley thought for a moment. "Nothing right now, but that can change. The last time he went in with us, he made something like eighty million. If we call in the past favor and dangle something ahead, you got the vote."

"You're right," Cabrillo said. "I'll take care of dealing with him."

"Good," Hanley said. "Laos should be easy. They're Buddhist, and the general wants his car."

"Offer him several," Cabrillo said.

"Where are we funding this from?" Hanley asked.

"We're going to try to use around half of the hundred million windfall for everything."

"Easy come easy go," Hanley said. "Brunei should be ours. The country is fifteen percent Buddhist and the sultan can't risk alienating his constituents."

"Plus we saved his brother's life a couple of years ago," Cabrillo added.

"Andorra," Hanley said, "what about them?"

"Good thing Halpert set up the new company there," Cabrillo said. "What's their GDP?"

Hanley scanned through an almanac and found the information. "It's around one point two billion."

"Once the oil comes online," Cabrillo noted, "we'll be bringing another twenty percent to the table. If someone explains that to their ambassador, he'd be stupid not to see his way to giving us their vote. Money talks—plus this is the right thing to do, anyway."

"I agree," Hanley said.

"That just leaves the little guys," Cabrillo said. "Kiribati and Tuvalu."

"Kiribati's GDP is sixty million," Hanley said. "Tuvalu's is even less. It's something like eight million split up over ten thousand citizens. Put two to a room, and one of the major Las Vegas hotels could house the entire country."

Cabrillo was silent for a moment.

"Call Lowden in Colorado and have him start buying cars for the general. Next, send Halpert to Andorra to explain the impact our company will have on their economy. I'll take care of the emir of Qatar and the sultan of Brunei."

"And the little guys?"

"Truitt's free, isn't he?" asked Cabrillo.

"Yes, he is."

"Get him on a jet with a stack of bearer bonds."

"You want him to buy the votes?" Hanley asked.

"Exactly."

39

THE STORM THAT brought the torrential rains to Macau had turned into spring snow by the time it crossed Russia. Had it not been night, Cabrillo would have seen that Moscow was covered in a wet blanket of white that rounded the edges of buildings and quieted the sounds. Peering from the windows of the Gulfstream as the pilots shut down the engines, he could see a trio of black Zil limousines with police escorts front and rear. Holding a fax that had arrived from Overholt only minutes before, he slid the document into the file and then unbuckled his seat belt and rose. The copilot was unlatching the door as he walked forward.

"Do you men need anything?" Cabrillo asked.

"I think we're okay, boss," the copilot said. "We'll just refuel and await your return."

Cabrillo nodded and waited as the step was lowered. "Wish me luck," he said as he stepped down onto the snow-covered tarmac.

A tall man in a thick, dark blue wool coat was standing a few feet from the Gulfstream. His head was covered by a fur Cossack cap and his breath made puffs of mist as he exhaled. He approached Cabrillo while removing a glove and offered his hand. Cabrillo shook it, then the man motioned to the middle limousine.

"I'm Sergei Makelikov," the man said as the driver opened the door, "special assistant to President Putin."

Cabrillo followed the man into the rear of the limousine. "Juan Cabrillo, chairman of the Corporation."

The door was closed, and a few seconds later the police cars started away from the Gulfstream followed by the trio of limousines. "The president is very interested in hearing what you have to say," Makelikov noted. "May I offer you a drink, perhaps vodka, or some coffee?"

"Coffee, please," Cabrillo said.

Makelikov reached for a silver-plated thermal carafe and poured the contents into a red mug with the crest of the Russian republic on the side. He handed it to Cabrillo.

"How was your flight?"

The streets were deserted at this late hour. The procession roared down the road toward central Moscow, followed by a cloud of snowflakes. Cabrillo sipped the coffee.

"No problems," Cabrillo said, smiling.

"Cuban cigar?" Makelikov asked.

"Don't mind if I do," Cabrillo said as he selected one from the box Makelikov held.

Trimming the end with a tool from inside the box, Cabrillo leaned over for a light from Makelikov. "We'll be there shortly," the Russian noted. "In the meantime, perhaps you would like to hear some music."

He motioned to a CD player and a stack of discs. They were all jazz.

"I see you know my taste in music," Cabrillo said.

"We know a lot about you," Makelikov said easily, "and that is why President Putin is staying up late to see you."

Cabrillo nodded and smiled. "Great cigar."

Makelikov lit one and puffed. "It is, isn't it?"

Cabrillo slid a CD into the player and the men relaxed and listened.

Fourteen minutes later the procession slid to a stop in front of a row of town houses near Gorky Park. Makelikov waited until the driver opened the door, then he stepped out onto the snow-covered sidewalk.

"One of the president's hideaways," he said as Cabrillo climbed out. "We can talk here in private."

The two men headed up the walkway to the steps and climbed up to the door, where Makelikov nodded at a Russian army sergeant. He saluted and swung the door open. Makelikov and Cabrillo walked inside.

"Mr. President," Makelikov said loudly, "your visitor has arrived."

"I'm in the living room," a voice said from a room to the right.

"Let me take your coat," Makelikov said, helping Cabrillo out of his overcoat. "Go on in—I'll join you in a few minutes."

Cabrillo walked into the living room. The room was fitted and furnished like the library of an expensive gentleman's club. Dark wood paneling, the walls were covered with paintings of hunting scenes and birds. Along the right wall was a fireplace containing a roaring wood fire. A pair of high-backed red leather chairs framed the fireplace, with a couch just behind them closer to the door. A thick red carpet atop the inlaid wood floors led almost to the fireplace hearth. Two brass lamps on each side of the couch cast pools of light in the otherwise dark room. President Putin's back was to Cabrillo as he stoked the fire. Finishing, he stood up and turned.

"Mr. Cabrillo," he said, smiling, "come in and have a seat."

Cabrillo slid into the red leather chair to the left of the fireplace, while Putin took the right.

"Back when I was with the KGB, I had quite a file on you," Putin said.

"And me you," Cabrillo said in Russian.

Putin nodded, then looked directly into Cabrillo's eyes. "Your Russian is much better than my English."

"Thank you, sir," Cabrillo said.

Putin nodded. "I assume you have done a recent psychological profile on me," he said. "Did it hazard a guess as to how I would respond?"

"It doesn't take a team of psychologists," Cabrillo said, "to know you'll say yes."

"Then why don't you tell me what I'm agreeing to," Putin said, smiling.

Cabrillo nodded, then opened the file he had brought. "Sir," he said, "we've been commissioned to put the Dalai Lama back in power. We think we've worked out a solution that can benefit everyone. We just need some Russian muscle."

"Explain," Putin said.

Cabrillo handed over the document Overholt had faxed to the Gulfstream. "This is a classified satellite image of potential oil reserves inside Tibet. We recently recovered ancient documents that list thousands of oil seeps in the northern region."

"From the Golden Buddha that your company stole in Macau?" Putin asked.

"Your intelligence is good," Cabrillo said.

Putin studied the image and nodded. "Yes, it is," he said.

"The preliminary estimates place the reserves in the neighborhood of fifty billion barrels."

"That's an expensive neighborhood," Putin said. "About half of the reserves in Kuwait, or around five percent of the world's known reserves."

"It's potentially an elephant field," Cabrillo agreed. "Even if it is less, we believe it is definitely larger than the field on the north slope of Alaska."

"That would put it in the top twenty of all known fields," Putin noted.

"Exactly, sir," Cabrillo said.

"However, right now, the Chinese have control of the field and they don't even know of its existence," Putin said, "so you want us to remove them from Tibet."

"Not exactly, sir," Cabrillo said. "What we are proposing is that Russia join in a consortium to develop the field. Fifty percent to Tibet, forty percent to your country."

"And the other ten percent?"

"The other ten percent will be owned by my company," Cabrillo said, "for putting it all together."

"Nice tip," Putin said, smiling, "but you are asking me to commit my forces for a profit. As soon as the casualties start pouring in, my citizens will smell a rat."

Cabrillo nodded slowly. Then he set the hook.

"Then we make a deal with China," he said easily. "Jintao wants out anyway—his economy is tanking and his increasing oil imports are accelerating his problems. You make a diplomatic mission to China and offer him half of the production at a cost of fifteen dollars a barrel for the next ten years, and I think he'll take it and back down."

Putin laughed. "Brilliant."

"There's one more thing," Cabrillo said slowly.

"Yes?"

"We need your UN vote in the Security Council meeting Monday," Cabrillo said.

"You're going to legitimize the coup?" Putin asked.

"We think we can pull the votes," Cabrillo agreed.

"A lot could go wrong," Putin said, "but it could work. What exactly would Russia need to do to participate?"

"First we need your troops to enter Mongolia," Cabrillo said. "I understand the Mongolian government would okay the incursion. That draws the Chinese farther from Tibet. Second, I would need as many crack paratroops as you can field to enter the country as soon as the Dalai Lama returns and we stabilize the situation. The Dalai Lama has agreed to invite Russia to provide security until the situation stabilizes.

The invitation will be announced to the world community, so the fallout other than from China should be small. Third, we need you to make the diplomatic approach to China with the oil offer—it has been made clear to me the United States wants no direct involvement in the liberation of Tibet."

"I have spoken to your president," Putin said. "He mentioned the need for secrecy."

"Good," Cabrillo said. "Next, I need that vote in the UN. If we can hold off the Chinese until the vote comes in and the peacekeepers arrive, then the Russian troops will be relieved."

Putin rose from the chair and stoked the fire. "So Russia invests no money, only muscle."

"The company that will develop the oilfield has already been formed," Cabrillo said. "All I need is your signature on this document that has already been signed by the Dalai Lama, and your word you will do what we have discussed, and we can proceed."

Makelikov entered the room just as Putin placed the stoker back in the rack. He stepped over to Cabrillo, took the document and read it quickly.

"Sergei," he said, "bring me a pen."

"I'LL SWAP YOU," Gurt said to one of the other mercenary pilots, "if you don't mind."

"What did you draw?" the other pilot asked.

"Medevac," Gurt said.

"I'll gladly switch," the pilot said. "Mine looks to be the most dangerous mission."

"I've worked with Murphy before," Gurt said. "Plus I have more high-altitude flying time than you. I don't mind."

"Be my guest," the pilot said. "Flying a load of explosives north is not my idea of a good time."

"I'll make sure it's okay with Seng," Gurt said, walking off.

*   *   *

"THE FASTEST WAY to get you there," Hanley said, "is to drop you in Singapore, then have you flown by jet to Vanuatu. From there we'll switch you to a turboprop STOL that can land at the smaller airfields on Kiribati and Tuvalu."

Truitt nodded.

"We need those votes," Hanley said quietly. "Do whatever it takes to make that happen."

"Not to worry," Truitt said. "Even if it takes a river of grease, by Monday vote time they will be ours."

Later that night, the *Oregon* passed the breakwater and entered the port, and Truitt boarded the waiting jet for the nine-hour flight to the South Pacific. He would arrive on Easter morning.

40

THE ZIL LIMOUSINE slid to a stop in front of the Gulfstream G550. Cabrillo climbed out, clutching a folder containing the documents, and made his way up the ramp without hesitating. The copilot immediately retracted the ramp and fastened the door. Then he shouted toward the cockpit.

"We're good to go."

Instantly, the pilot engaged the igniters, and a few seconds later the jet engines began to spool up. Cabrillo made his way to a seat and fastened the belt as the copilot started for the cockpit.

"We received your telephone call, sir," the copilot said over his shoulder as he slid into his seat. "The course is all plotted and we've received preliminary clearance."

"What's the distance?" Cabrillo asked.

"Straight through, it's about thirty-four hundred miles," the copilot said. "The winds are favorable, so we estimate six hours' flight time."

The Gulfstream started taxiing toward the runway.

"Easter morning seven a.m.," Cabrillo said.

"That's the plan, sir," the copilot said.

S OMETIMES IT ALL comes down to a few. A few minutes, a few
strokes of luck, a few people.

At this instant, it was two. Murphy and Gurt. Two men, one helicopter with extra fuel pods and a load of explosives would form the
advance team for the liberation of Tibet.

They lifted off just after 4 A.M. under the waning light of a quarter
moon.

Once Gurt had the Bell 212 at an altitude of one thousand feet above
ground level and in a steady forward flight, he spoke into the headset.

"Our mission," he said, "seems fairly impossible."

"Is it the altitude of the pass?" Murphy asked. "Or the lack of fuel
for the return flight that concerns you the most?"

"Neither," Gurt said. "It's missing Sunday service and the chicken
dinner afterward."

Murphy reached behind his seat and retrieved a small pack. Unzip-
ping it, he removed a single can and a small blue-covered book. "Spam
and a Bible," he said.

"Excellent," Gurt noted. "I can proceed, then."

"Will there be anything else?" Murphy asked.

"Only one more thing," Gurt said.

"What's that?"

"Keep your eyes on the road," Gurt said. "I don't want to get lost."

"Not to worry," Murphy said. "The *Oregon* is running the command and control. This operation will run like a well-oiled sewing machine."

"I would have felt better," Gurt said, pointing out a herd of deer
underneath that were lit by the moon, "had you said *like a computer.*"

Murphy was staring at the instruments. "We're a little hot," he said. "Take it down a notch."

Gurt made the adjustment. They continued north.

A T ABOUT THE same instant that the Bell 212 carrying Murphy and Gurt crossed into Tibetan airspace, Briktin Gampo was steering the two-and-a-half-ton truck along a rutted dirt road. Locating the spot his *Dungkar* cell leader had marked, he slowed and pulled to a stop.

Gampo was on the flats just below Basatongwula Shan in an open meadow ringed by stunted trees. Climbing from the truck, he walked around to the rear and removed several metal tubes and felt them. They were cold to the touch. Remembering what he had been told, Gampo pulled a small fuel oil stove from the rear, moved a distance away, then erected the legs. Once the stove was assembled, he removed some tent poles and slid them inside an off-white canvas tent and hoisted the apparatus into the air. Once the tent was secure, he lit the stove, brought the tubes inside to keep them warm, then went back to the rear of the truck and removed a radio, a folding chair and a fur to cover himself while he waited.

Then he switched on the radio and began to listen.

Outside the tent, thousands of stars flickered against the black sea of deep space. A cold wind blew down from the mountain. Gampo pulled the fur closer around his neck until the tent warmed. Then he patiently waited for the hours to pass.

O N THE *OREGON*, Hanley was staring at the wall of flat-screen monitors. Suddenly, the satellite feed of the Russian troop concentration near Novosibirsk began to display a thermal image of tanks being started. At the same instant, the secure telephone began to ring.

"We're a go," Cabrillo said.

"I have confirmation over the satellite," Hanley told him. "The Russian tanks are warming."

"Link my computer to the *Oregon*'s data banks," Cabrillo ordered. "I want to monitor the situation from here until I arrive."

Hanley nodded to Stone, who typed in commands on his computer keyboard.

"Signal's going out," Stone said a minute later.

In the Gulfstream G550, Cabrillo stared at his laptop. Suddenly the screen erupted with a burst of light, then went dark, then slowly began to glow again. The screen split into six separate blocks, each duplicating what Hanley was seeing.

"I've got it," Cabrillo said.

"Mr. Chairman," Hanley said, "call the ball."

"Proceed as planned," Cabrillo said, "and link me up with Seng."

"You got it," Hanley said.

E DDIE SENG WAS pacing back and forth inside the hangar in Thimbu, Bhutan. Occasionally he would return to the table where the computer screen showed the pulsing red dot that marked the progress of the helicopter carrying Murphy and Gurt. Then he would walk around the hangar again like a caged lion.

He answered his telephone before the second ring.

"Eddie," Cabrillo said, "we're a go."

"Yes, sir," Seng said. "We have a team already flying north—I took the liberty, knowing we could call them back if necessary."

"Good job," Cabrillo said. "Max?"

"I'm on the three-way," Hanley said from the *Oregon*.

"Send Seng the latest data showing the airport near Lhasa."

"It's being transmitted now."

Seng walked over to the printer. A few seconds later, it began to spit out documents.

"It's coming across now," Seng noted.

"Okay," Cabrillo said, "you have your playbook and the latest intelligence."

"Yes, sir," Seng said.

"Now go take Gonggar Airport," Cabrillo said.

"You got it, boss," Seng said eagerly.

F IVE A.M. THE early-morning hours when drunks sweat and nightmares grow ugly.

A cold wind was blowing across the runway at Gonggar Airport, located fifty-nine miles from Lhasa. A pair of Chinese transport planes sat on the far end of the runway along with three helicopters. The other Chinese aircraft inside Tibet had been called north in support of the tank column.

Gonggar Airport was as deserted as a cemetery on a weekday.

A single janitor swept the chipped concrete floor in the crude main terminal. Taking a break to smoke a hand-rolled cigarette, he stepped outside and stood where a wall shielded him from the wind. The limited troops on duty at the airport were sleeping. They were not due to rise for another hour.

A sound came up the valley. It was a whoosh, like a well-thrown football. Then a stark white-colored craft raced past at thirty feet above the tarmac. The strange object sped to the end of the airport, then made an arcing turn and lined up for a pass. Suddenly, twin streams of fire erupted from the sides and a pair of missiles streaked toward the parked transport planes.

The Predator had found her prey.

I N THE HANGAR in Bhutan, Lincoln stared at the image from the Predator's onboard cameras. Steering the Predator into another arcing turn, he lined up in front of the helicopters and flicked the trigger. Then he made another turn to see the results.

The cargo planes were ablaze. The helicopters would join them in a second.

At the same instant, 160 yards from the edge of the field, nearly one hundred *Dungkar* troops slid out from under white tarps that blended with the snow on the ground. Screaming a war cry, they raced toward the terminal. Dressed in black robes with ceremonial knives in their belts and handguns and rifles that had been smuggled into the country only days before, they swarmed like locusts into predetermined positions. From the south came the thumping sound of seven helicopters approaching. As the helicopter carrying Seng popped up to the plateau, he could see the fires from the Predator's attack burning bright in the early morning.

Then, as if a divine light was making its way to earth, a series of red light sticks began to flicker on the tarmac. The *Dungkar* were sending the message it was safe to land.

"Land inside the box," Seng said to the pilot.

"Will do," the pilot said, starting his descent.

Seconds after the helicopter landed, Seng climbed from the front while King made his way from the rear. Seng quickly walked to the terminal, where he met up with the leader of the *Dungkar*. At the same time, King motioned to the troops for help, and then began to unload crates of rifles and ammunition from the cargo area.

"What have you got?" Seng asked the man, who was no more than thirty.

"The hangars over there," the man said, pointing, "contain one fighter plane, one cargo plane and a pair of attack helicopters. The hangar next door must be for repairs—there is a helicopter disassembled and the fuselage of an observation plane with the engine removed."

Cabrillo had asked the Dalai Lama to make sure the *Dungkar* officers he picked were able to speak English. There was no time for his team to learn Tibetan and less time for misunderstanding.

"Where did you go to school?" Seng asked.

"Arizona State, sir," the man said eagerly. "Go, Sun Devils."

"Good," Seng said. "I'm sure you're glad to be home—now, let's see if we can keep it that way. First, I want a couple of your men to work with the guy coming in on that helicopter." He pointed to another Bell, just touching down twenty yards away. "We need to rig these buildings with charges to burn them if necessary."

"I'll put a dozen of my best men on it," the man said eagerly.

"How many Chinese have you captured?" Seng asked.

"Less than a dozen, sir," the man said. "One of mine dead—two of theirs."

The airport was a bedlam of activity. The fires burned at the far end of the field against the tapestry of the early morning, and the sound of the landing helicopters added a surreal element to the quiet air. All at once, solitude had become a salvo.

"Listen carefully," Seng said to the leader of the *Dungkar* forces, "this comes from the Dalai Lama himself. There will be no brutality or mistreatment of the prisoners—make sure your men know this clearly. Once this is all said and done, we're returning whatever prisoners we capture to China—my company doesn't want to hear of any atrocities whatsoever. This is a coup d'etat, not an ethnic cleansing. Are we clear on that?"

"Company, sir?" the man asked. "Aren't you United States troops?"

"We're from the States," Seng said, "at least most of us, but we are a private firm now working under the direction of your leader. If you and the other *Dungkar* do what we order, in the next twenty-four to forty-eight hours, there will be a free Tibet once again."

"You've done this sort of thing before?" the man asked in amazement.

"There's no time for chitchat," Seng snapped. "You all do exactly what you're ordered and this will go as smoothly as possible."

"Yes, sir."

"Good," Seng said. "Bring the highest-ranking prisoner to the main terminal and have him seated in a chair and guarded. We'll be setting

up operations there in the next several minutes—then I want to speak
to him."

The man shouted orders in Tibetan. The *Dungkar* soldiers lined up
in rows. He explained what Seng had relayed, then ordered six sergeants
to the forefront. Then one group led by a sergeant went off to round
up the prisoners. Another split off to the helicopter Kasim had left.

"Hali," Seng shouted, "take these men and wire the other hangars
to blow if we need to."

Kasim motioned to the troops and raced back to the helicopter.

The Bell that had carried Seng and King to the airfield was now
unloaded. King motioned for it to lift off. The pilot ascended to one
thousand feet over the field and then began to fly in large lazy circles.
Two more touched down, and Crabtree and Gannon climbed out.

"What's your name?" Seng shouted to the leader of the *Dungkar*.

"Rimpoche, Pache Rimpoche."

Gannon and Crabtree raced over.

"Carl," Seng said, "this is General Rimpoche. Tell him what you
need."

Gannon walked a few feet away to where they could hear better
and explained. Rimpoche summoned a sergeant and a dozen men raced
off.

"I need the supplies unloaded and taken inside," Crabtree said to
Seng, who pointed to Rimpoche.

"General Rimpoche," he said, motioning to the man, "will take care
of it."

Seng unclipped a portable radio from his belt and switched it on,
then spoke.

"Airport is under our control," he said to Hanley on the *Oregon*.
"What do you see?"

Hanley studied the satellite image on the screen before answering.
"No troop movement yet—but if they do come, it will be from the road
that enters from the east. There is what looks like a bridge about three-

quarters of a mile toward Lhasa. Control that, and you'll be able to make a stand if necessary."

"No planes or helicopter activity?" Seng asked.

"None," Hanley said. "Anything not on the ground there is far to the north. Even if they called them back now, you have an hour or so."

"Good," Seng said as Meadows walked up. "Reach me by portable if the situation changes."

"We're on full alert," Hanley said. "It all comes down to the next few hours."

Seng clipped the radio back on his belt and turned to Meadows. "Bob, take fifty troops and your weaponry down that road," he said, pointing. "There's a bridge we need to control."

"Who's in charge from their side?" Meadows asked.

"General Rimpoche," Seng said, pointing to the man.

At that instant, three trucks slowly drove in front of the terminal and were motioned to stop by Gannon. At the same time, Tom Reyes walked over.

"General?" Seng shouted.

Rimpoche approached. "Yes?"

"I need four of your best men, crack shots and fearless."

Rimpoche turned and shouted out names to the cluster of troops. Four men emerged from the crowd. Not one of the men was over five feet six. Dripping wet, not one of them could have weighed over 150 pounds.

"Do any of them speak English?" Seng asked.

"All of them do a little," Rimpoche said.

"Tell them this," Seng said. "They will be going into Lhasa with two of my men to capture a very important man. They need to do *exactly* what my men tell them—without hesitation."

Rimpoche translated.

As soon as he had finished, the four men shouted "Huh" and stomped one foot on the tarmac.

"You have your file?" Seng asked Reyes.

"Yes, sir," Reyes said.

King was a short distance away, removing a long black case from a crate. "Okay, Larry," Seng shouted, "you and Tom can go do your thing."

Holding a set of night-vision goggles, King walked over. "Let's do it," he said.

Reyes motioned to the four Tibetans, who were eagerly waiting. "We're going to grab someone, and we're going to do it with a minimum of shooting—do you men understand?"

"I speak fair English," one of the soldiers said. "I'll translate."

He reiterated what Reyes had said, then turned. "Which helicopter?"

"This way," Reyes said, leading them back to the helicopter he had just climbed off. King followed the four Tibetans, and once they were seated inside, the helicopter lifted off and headed into the center of town.

"Who are they after?" Rimpoche asked.

"The chairman of the Tibet Autonomous Region, Legchog Zhuren."

The last helicopter was on the ground, and Huxley walked over.

"This is our medical officer," Seng said to Rimpoche. "Poll your troops and see if any of your men have any experience as doctors or nurses—if so, we need them to work with Julia here. Right now, however, we need that helicopter unloaded and the contents carried inside the terminal. Ms. Huxley will be setting up a field hospital immediately. If any of your men were injured or wounded, she'll treat them shortly."

Rimpoche shouted orders and men raced to the helicopter to unload. Adams and Gunderson were standing to the side, waiting for Seng to finish. He turned and smiled.

"You two go see what the Chinese have that we can use," Seng said. "I need to interrogate a prisoner."

The two pilots ambled off toward the hangars. Seng walked inside to where a Chinese air force lieutenant was sitting in a chair in the middle of the terminal with four fierce-looking Tibetan soldiers surrounding him.

41

"DAMN NICE SCENERY," Murphy noted, glancing out the window. "Like Alaska on steroids."

Gurt was watching the altitude gauge as they climbed higher toward the imposing ridge of mountains just ahead. The sun had yet to peek over the horizon, but her coming was heralded by the pink glow being cast over the rugged terrain.

"We could probably claim the helicopter altitude record," Gurt said.

"I don't think so," Murphy said. "Some guy went to twenty-four thousand feet a couple of years ago to perform a Himalayan rescue."

"I read about that," Gurt said, "but that was in a Bell 206. And it had special rotor blades."

"You sound a little worried," Murphy said.

"Not worried," Gurt said, "just apprehensive."

He pointed out the front windshield at the wall approaching. The trees were petering out as they drew nearer. Now there was only the black and gray of rocks streaked with tendrils of snow and ice that dripped down the sides of the imposing mountain like rivulets of ice cream on a child's hand. A gust of wind buffeted the helicopter, blowing it sideways. Clouds started to appear around the Bell. Gurt stared at the gauge again.

It read eighteen thousand feet and climbing.

T HE HELICOPTER CARRYING Reyes, King and the *Dungkar* forces came in twenty feet above the ground and approached Lhasa from the south. The sound from the Lhasa River helped cover the noise as the pilot landed on a small spit of sand in the river just east of what the Chinese referred to as Dream Island, formerly an idyllic picnic spot now replaced by tacky Chinese shops and karaoke bars.

"Unload the crates," Reyes shouted to the *Dungkar*.

As soon as the crates were unloaded and King had exited, they all raced a short distance away and crouched down to avoid the blast of sand from the rotor wash as the helicopter quickly lifted off and raced downriver. Once the helicopter was out of sound and sight, Reyes opened a small satchel and removed a parabolic dish for listening. Quickly switching it on, he listened for the sound of alarms in the city. He heard only the sound of the river.

Nodding, he whispered to one of the Tibetans, "Look."

Prying a crate open, he pointed. It was a box of Tibetan flags, which had long ago been banned by the Chinese oppressors. The flags featured a snow lion with red and blue rays. The man bent down and touched the pile gingerly, and when he rose to look at Reyes, his eyes were filled with tears.

"We need to carry all these crates across the river," Reyes said to the Tibetan, "and stash them. Then you and the others need to follow me and King to Zhuren's house."

"Yes," the Tibetan said eagerly.

"We'll need one of you to guard the flags and one man to go with

Mr. King. The other two of you," Reyes said quietly, "will enter the house with me."

The Tibetan nodded, then began to whisper orders to his men.

Five minutes later, they were all safely across the river and walking toward the Barkhor area of Lhasa. King and his Tibetan helper peeled away from the group and made their way to the tallest building near the home of the Chinese government official. The streets were empty except for a few Tibetan merchants who were sweeping the square in preparation of setting up shop. Taking the steps two at a time, King and his helper made their way to the rooftop, where they took up position. Once he was in place, King reached into his bag, removed a small bottle of oxygen, and then took a few deep breaths. He then offered the bottle to the Tibetan, who smiled but shook his head no. Then he scanned the area through his scope.

The home of Legchog Zhuren was an ornate affair whose front faced south onto Barkhor Square. Just to the east of the house lay the Jokhang, a temple built sometime in the seventh century. The Jokhang, the most revered religious building in Lhasa, featured dozens of statues, a variety of gold artwork and some thirty chapels.

King watched as Reyes passed in front of the Jokhang. He stopped for a second and raised a closed fist into the air. Then Reyes, followed by two Tibetans, made his way down an alley between the temple and the chairman's house and passed out of view.

King pushed the button on a silver-plated stopwatch, set the time for one minute, and watched.

When the stopwatch read fifteen seconds, King reached into his satchel and removed a hollowed-out ram's horn and handed it to the Tibetan.

"When I say," he told him, "start blowing, and don't stop until I tell you to, or we're dead."

The man nodded eagerly and took the horn. King took another breath of oxygen and checked the stopwatch. Five seconds. He glanced at the guards patrolling the walkway outside Zhuren's house. There

were two outside the wrought-iron gate, two more just outside the front
door sitting on chairs. He lined up his shots.

"Now," he said loudly.

The horn erupted with the sound of a cat under a vacuum cleaner.

Like wraiths appearing above a graveyard, the square was suddenly
filled with four dozen *Dungkar* warriors. They had posed as shopkeepers and early-morning walkers, and had hidden inside drums containing
spices and seeds. They screamed war cries and raced toward the gate
leading up to the chairman's home. On the front porch, one of the
guards was roused from a half sleep by the sound of the horn and the
approaching horde. He stood up and reached for a bell near the front
door. But before he could reach it to sound the alarm, he heard a sharp
crack. As if in a dream, he stared in amazement as his hand and arm
from the elbow dropped onto the porch.

Then he screamed as blood erupted from the stump like a geyser.

At the same time, the *Dungkar* reached the pair of guards outside
the gate; they were dead before they could comprehend what was happening, their throats slit like pigs at slaughter.

Swiveling around, the front-door guard stared in horror at the advancing *Dungkar*. His partner started to speak, but a second later his
head was blown off his shoulders. It landed on the porch with a thud,
the lips still straining to answer a signal from an impulse now dead.
The first *Dungkar* raced up the steps with his sword held in front. The
guard tried to reach for his handgun, but with no hand he had no
chance.

The sword ran through his middle and pinned him to the wooden
door like some macabre Christmas wreath. He mouthed a few words
before dying, but only blood seeped from inside. The force of the guard
slamming into the door burst the lock.

The door swung open and the *Dungkar* raced inside.

*   *   *

A ROUND THE REAR of the house the scene was less violent. The single guard at the door off the kitchen had been asleep. His dereliction of duty would save his life. Reyes crept up, hit him with a stun gun, then had one of the Tibetans bind his mouth, wrists and legs with duct tape before he had a chance to do anything. Then Reyes popped open the lock with a pick and made his way inside. He and the Tibetans were halfway up the stairs leading to Zhuren's bedroom before the horn sounded.

Then Reyes saw them.

There were three unarmed men at the top of the landing. He reached for his holstered .40 handgun, but before he could snap off a round, a Tibetan houseboy appeared from behind and lopped a leather garrote over the men's heads and pulled tight. Their heads slammed together, then their legs began to kick as the houseboy tightened the cord. Reyes motioned for one of the men following to help, then raced past to Zhuren's door. Stopping for a second to line himself up, he slammed his polished black boot at a point just above the doorknob. The door burst open and he stepped inside. The man in the bed slowly started to rise while rubbing his eyes, then he reached toward the nightstand. Reyes fired a round into the headboard above the man's head and the room filled with the smell of spent gunpowder.

"I wouldn't," Reyes said, "if I were you."

"I CAN'T SEE much," Gurt admitted.

The clouds had closed in as they neared the top of the pass. Snow and sleet raked across the windshield of the Bell. The 212 was slowly ascending, but barely making any forward movement at all. They were flying blind on the edge of the helicopter's performance envelope.

"I've got a road," Murphy suddenly shouted, "on the port side."

Gurt spotted the black stripe against the white background. A movement of vehicles across the terrain had displaced most of the snow, leaving only dirt and rock.

"What's that?" Gurt said, straining to see.

"I think it's a column of tanks," Murphy said.

"I'll go to one side," Gurt said, "and stay in the cloud cover."

Along the side of the road, a Chinese tank commander was watching several of his soldiers repair a tread that had come loose. He heard the helicopter in the distance, so he climbed inside and called his superior on the radio.

"No idea," his superior reported, "but you'd better find out what it is."

Popping his head out of the hatch, the tank commander shouted down to his men, then he began to pass rifles out of the hatch. Two minutes later, the soldiers were hiking up the road away from their disabled tank.

"THERE'S THE CREST," Murphy shouted. "Find a spot to touch down."

Gurt played with the collective, but at this altitude he had little control. "Hold on," he shouted.

The landing was more a controlled crash than a touchdown. The 212 came down hard on the skids, but they held. Murphy was already unsnapping his safety harness.

"Driver," he said, smiling, "just keep her running—I'll only be a minute."

Opening the door, he stepped out and a few feet back and opened the cargo door. Then he removed a pair of snowshoes, which he attached to his feet. Pulling another coat over the one he was already wearing, he began to dig in a crate, placing the items he needed into a backpack.

"Hold down the fort," he shouted to the front of the helicopter. "I'm going to set the charges."

Gurt nodded, then watched as Murphy disappeared into the blowing snow. Then he began to play with his radio. He found little to hear, so he switched back to the regular frequency.

"SHERPA, SHERPA, SHERPA, this is the *Oregon*, over."
In the control room, Eric Stone looked at Hanley with worry.
"That's the fifth time, nothing."

"Sherpa, Sherpa, Sherpa, this is the *Oregon*, over."

"*Oregon*, this is Sherpa," Gurt answered. "Read you eight by eight."

There was a two-second delay as the signal bounced off the ionosphere and down to the ship.

"Where are you?" Hanley said, taking the microphone.

"We're on site," Gurt reported. "Your man just left for the appointment."

"We just intercepted a communication from the bad guys," Hanley said. "Someone heard you go over and they've been asked to investigate."

"This is not good, *Oregon*," Gurt said quickly. "I have no way to reach Murphy and warn him. Plus, it's going to take us some time to lift off."

"Okay," Hanley said, "we can send a signal to Murph's beeper— we'll tell him to return to where you are. In the meantime, keep a close eye for anyone approaching. If they do, you take to the air."

"Send a message to Murphy to withdraw," Hanley said to Stone, who quickly punched the commands into his keyboard.

"My visibility is around thirty to forty feet," Gurt said, "and I'm not leaving Murph—no way."

"No, we don't want you to—" Hanley started to say.

"*Oregon*," Gurt shouted over the radio. "There are Chinese troops coming through the snow."

Murphy was bent over, placing the charges in the snow, when his beeper chirped. He finished attaching the detonation cord, then rose up and removed the beeper from his pocket.

"Damn," he said, flipping the switch open so the charge could be remotely detonated. Then he pulled his M-16 around from his back on its sling and began heading back in the direction of the helicopter.

Gurt reached behind his seat and felt for a handgun in a rack. The Chinese troops were struggling through the thick snow, making slow but steady progress toward the Bell. They were holding rifles, but they had yet to take a shot.

Murphy stumbled along as fast as one could run on snowshoes. While he ran, he was folding out a grenade launcher. Reaching over his shoulder into the pack, he removed a rocket-propelled grenade and started fitting it into the launcher. He was on a sloping ridge, racing down, when he first caught sight of the Chinese troops. They were twenty-five feet from the Bell. Murphy estimated his angle and fired a grenade. It went over the heads of the Chinese troops and exploded. They flopped on their bellies in the deep snow.

"What the—" Gurt started to say as he turned and saw Murphy approaching in the distance.

Adding fuel to the turbine, Gurt tried to lift off. Nothing. Murphy was twenty feet away now and racing toward the helicopter. The first few Chinese troops began to rise from the snow and shoulder their rifles. Gurt started firing the handgun from the window. A couple seconds later, Murphy's M-16 opened up.

Ten feet now. Gurt reached across and opened the copilot's door. Murphy paused in his firing, removed his pack, placed it gingerly behind his seat and climbed inside, holding the M-16 in his lap. Gurt was firing the handgun and fiddling with the collective at the same time.

"Morning," Murphy said when there was a moment of quiet. "Anything exciting happen while I was away?"

"We have no lift," Gurt said before squeezing off a few rounds. "I'll need to milk the cyclic to get us off the ground."

The Chinese troops had stopped advancing. Now they were digging in to make their kill shot.

Murphy slipped between the seats into the rear and yanked open both cargo doors. "Quit firing and take us up, Gurt. I'll handle these boys."

Milking the cyclic is bad for helicopters. It consists of jamming the cyclic from side to side while pumping up and down on the collective. It can create lift when there is none—but it can also easily cause the mast that supports the rotor to bump against other parts of the helicopter. Then you run the risk of a nick or a fracture in the mast.

Lose the mast and you've lost the helicopter.

The firefight had erupted so quickly that the Chinese tank commander had little time to rally his men. Now that he'd had a few minutes to prepare and his troops were dug in to the snow, he began to shout orders that would concentrate the fire in the right direction.

Gurt slammed the cyclic from one side to the other and the 212 began to rise slowly.

Right at that instant, the Chinese commander screamed for his men to advance, and the front line rose. At the same time, Murphy triggered the grenade and it left the launcher with a whoosh and a burning smell that filled the cabin. The round landed six feet in front of the lead soldier and exploded. Murphy followed that up with a complete clip from the M-16. He replaced the clip and prepared to fire again.

Just then, Gurt got the Bell off the ground and struggled to turn away from the firefight.

They were a hundred feet away from the Chinese troops when Murphy blew through the second clip and the bloody snow where the Chinese troops lay began to fade in the distance. He quickly replaced the clip, set the M-16 to one side and reached for the remote detonator.

The C-6 erupted with a force equivalent to ten thousand pounds of TNT. A slab of snow was ripped from the side of the hill and raced down the slope, covering the Chinese troops. Then the slide raced across the road with a wall of snow and ice twenty feet high. In sympathy, smaller slides broke loose from the opposite hillside from the shock wave that trembled through the rock and soil. These slides added another eight to ten feet to the mess already created. The few Chinese troops still living after the firefight were buried beneath the wall of snow.

42

THE PILOT OF the Gulfstream stared at his navigation screen carefully. The route he was taking did not allow much margin for error. He was flying above a small corridor of Indian airspace that jutted between Bangladesh and Nepal. The surface area was but twenty miles in width at the smallest point. The land below was hotly contested by all three countries.

Slowly he steered the Gulfstream in a sweeping turn to the left.

"Sir," he shouted to the rear cabin, "we're through the worst of it."

The Gulfstream was now above the wider strip of land between Nepal and Bhutan.

"How long until we reach Tibetan airspace?" Cabrillo asked.

The pilot stared at the GPS screen. "Less than five minutes."

Juan Cabrillo should have been bone-tired, but he was not. He stared out the window at the mountainous terrain below. The rising sun was blanketed in a glow of pinks and yellows. Tibet was directly ahead. He reached for the secure telephone and dialed.

I N BEIJING, HU Jintao was awakened early. The actions in Barkhor Square had not gone unnoticed. Jintao quickly rose from his bed, washed his face, and went downstairs, still dressed in his nightclothes.

"What's the situation?" he asked a general without preamble.

"It's all fluid, Mr. President," the general admitted, "but the Russian tank column has started moving into Mongolia. Their ambassador assures us the movement is just an exercise between their country and Russia. However, at the speed they are moving, they could enter China across the Altai Mountains into the Tarim Basin anytime in the next few hours."

"What about aircraft?" Jintao asked.

"They have several paratroop units at the staging area inside Russia," the general said. "Our satellites have detected transport planes moving on the tarmac. As of right now, nothing has left the ground."

Jintao turned to the head of foreign relations. "We don't currently have any dispute with Russia," he said. "What possible reason would they have to launch an attack on our border?"

"At the moment, our relations are peaceful."

"Most odd," Jintao said.

"The Russian ambassador has asked for a meeting at ten A.M. this morning," the man added. "The request came overnight through a priority channel."

"Did he disclose the nature of his request?" Jintao asked.

"No," the foreign relations head said.

Jintao stood quietly for a moment, thinking.

"Mr. President," the general said, "there's more. We just received reports from the capital of Tibet that a protest has formed in one of the main squares inside the city."

"What's the chairman of the region say?" Jintao asked.

There was a pause before the general answered. "Well, Mr. President, that's the problem. We have been unable to reach Chairman Zhuren."

"D AMN, GURT," MURPHY said. "That was close."

"I think one of the rounds hit a hydraulic line that controls our forward pitch. As for me, I was hit in my left shoulder."

"How bad is it?" Murphy said quickly.

"She'll fly," Gurt noted, "but it'll be a little hairy."

"I mean you, Gurt," Murphy thundered. "How bad are you hit?"

Gurt was steering the Bell down the slope leading off the pass through a thick cloud cover. The helicopter's nose was pointed down and both men's bodies were tight against the seat harnesses.

"Hang on," Gurt said. "I'll lean forward so you can check."

Gurt moved his upper torso away from the seat back and Murphy leaned over and looked. Then he reached over with his hand and felt around. A second later he pulled a flattened slug from inside the foam of the seat.

"The round passed clean through and was stopped by the metal back plate on the seat," Murphy noted, "but you're losing blood."

"It wasn't hurting until now," Gurt disclosed. "I think I was on such an adrenaline high I didn't really notice it much."

"I'm going to need to bind the wound," Murphy said. "Hold on a minute—let me make a call."

He reached for his portable radio and called the *Oregon*.

"W EDGE IT IN there," Gunderson said, "but make sure the spent cartridges have a way to blow out the side door. I don't want any live rounds cooking off inside the cargo area."

The *Dungkar* soldier assisting Gunderson nodded. Ten minutes earlier, they had yanked a rapid-firing antiaircraft gun from its mount on the border of Gonggar Airport. Now they were fitting it to the cargo plane to make a crude gunship. The soldiers worked quickly, as did those at the other end of the hangar.

George Adams watched as the *Dungkar* troops filled the fuel tank on the attack helicopter. For the last ten minutes, he had climbed around inside the ship in an effort to determine the controls and weapons systems. At this instant, he was convinced that he could probably fly the bird—making the weapons perform as desired was a little iffier.

"Welcome to the *Dungkar* Air Force," Gunderson said, walking over. "We fly, you die."

"How's it going over there?" Adams said, smiling.

"I'm not sure," Gunderson admitted. "We have the weapon lodged in the rear and supported with enough planks to build a barn—if it doesn't fly out the opposite side the first time we light it up, we should be okay. How about you?"

"My Chinese is a little rusty," Adams said. "About as rusty as an iron ship on the bottom of the ocean. But I think I can pilot this beast."

Gunderson nodded. "Let's make a pact, old buddy," he said, smiling.

"What's that?" Adams asked.

"When we get up there," Gunderson said, "let's not shoot each other down."

He turned and started to walk back to the cargo plane. "Good luck," he said over his shoulder.

"You too," Adams answered.

Right then the door started to rise, and sunlight and cold air swept into the hangar. A minute later the attack helicopter was wheeled onto the tarmac and a motorized cart was attached to the front of the cargo plane to pull it onto the runway.

*   *   *

B ARKHOR SQUARE WAS rapidly filling with Tibetans. The crude
human telegraph system that operates in time of crisis was working overtime. Four blocks away, a platoon of Chinese soldiers were
attempting to make their way by armored personnel carrier from their
barracks to the square after receiving a call that there was action at the
chairman's home.

Tibetans clogged the streets and the going was slow.

"Piper, Piper, this is Masquerade."

"Masquerade, this is Piper, we read."

"Request immediate extraction," Reyes said. "We have the target."

"State point of extraction, Masquerade."

"Spot one, one, primary, Piper. Spot one three, secondary HH."

"Acknowledge extraction coordinates, Masquerade, they are inbound in three."

Upon receiving the order, the helicopter that had delivered them to
the river lifted from the ground at a spot ten miles between Lhasa and
Gonggar Airport, where the pilot had been waiting. Once he had the
helicopter in forward flight, the pilot stared at a map listing the extraction points they had arranged, and glanced at the note he had scribbled
on a pad attached to the clip on his knee. He flew fast and low toward
Barkhor Square.

I N LITTLE LHASA, the Dalai Lama waited inside the communications
room near a bank of radios. In the last few minutes, his network of
spies inside Tibet had begun to report the progress. So far, at least, the
operation appeared to be going flawlessly.

He turned to an aide-de-camp. "Are the preparations completed for
our trip home?" he asked.

"As soon as word comes from Mr. Cabrillo, Your Holiness," he
said. "We can have you there in two hours by jet."

The Dalai Lama thought for a moment. "Once we take off," he
asked, "how long will it be until we are over Tibet?"

"Half an hour," the man noted, "give or take."

"I am going to the temple now to pray," the Dalai Lama said, rising. "Keep watch on the situation."

"Yes, Your Holiness," the aide said.

C HUCK GUNDERSON WAS helping George Adams strap himself into the attack helicopter. None of the Chinese helmets inside the hangar were large enough to fit his head, so he was using his own personal headset, plugged into the radio for communications. He was squeezed into the seat like a fat girl in spandex.

"They don't make these for big guys like us," Adams joked.

"You should see mine," Gunderson said. "The Chinese still believe in quantity over quality. My cockpit looks like I'm back in World War Two. I keep expecting Glenn Miller music to start playing over the radio."

"Look at this dashboard," Adams said as Gunderson finished and stood upright on the ladder. "It's got more metal that a fifty-seven Chevy."

Just then, Eddie Seng walked over quickly. You need to get airborne and clear the runway. Cabrillo just called. He's five minutes out."

Gunderson pushed down on the Plexiglas shield over Adams's head and held it as he fastened it in place. Then he thumped the top and gave Adams a thumbs-up sign. Climbing back down the ladder, he motioned for the Tibetan helpers to wheel it out of the way. He began walking with Seng toward the cargo plane as he heard the igniters in the turbine engine of the attack helicopter begin to wind up.

"Mr. Seng," Gunderson said, "what's the latest?"

"I interrogated the Chinese lieutenant that was the ranking officer here," Seng said. "He was not able to get word to Beijing before we captured his forces."

"So for now," Gunderson said, reaching the door of the cargo plane, "we don't need to worry about an attack from Chinese fighters from outside the country?"

"If the Russians do their job and keep the Chinese on their toes," Seng said, "your role right now seems to be to provide close air support for the *Dungkar* forces."

"I'll do what I can," Gunderson said, climbing into the side door of the cargo plane.

"Good," Seng said, patting the side of the plane. "Now get to work—the boss is coming."

At just that second, Adams pulled the collective and the Chinese helicopter lifted from the ground. The helicopter wobbled a little as Adams fought to get the feel, then it moved forward, broke through the ground effect, and headed in the direction of Lhasa.

Gunderson walked up the slope to the cockpit, slid into his seat, then began the engine-starting procedure. Once the pair of engines were running smoothly, he glanced back to the four *Dungkar* soldiers manning the gun in the rear.

"Okay, men," he shouted over the noise of the engines, "I'll tell you when and where to direct the fire. For right now, we're just taking a little flight."

That sounded simple enough—but not one of the Tibetans had ever been inside a plane before.

ON BOARD THE *Oregon*, Hanley stood above the microphone and talked in a clear voice.

"I just sent word to your contact," he said. "Watch for red strobes as your signal."

"Same spot as we had first planned?" Murphy asked.

"Yes," Hanley said. "Now as far as Gurt is concerned, we talked to Huxley. You need to apply direct pressure to the wound as soon as possible."

"Do you have us on satellite surveillance?" Murphy asked.

"Yes," Hanley said, staring at the screen. "You're about five minutes from the rendezvous point."

"We'll report back once we land," Murphy said.

The radio went dead. Hanley dialed Seng and waited while it rang.

B RIKTIN GAMPO CHECKED to make sure the strobes were flashing, then stared up at the sky. The clouds were low, almost a fog, but from second to second they would shift, revealing patches of open air. In the distance he could hear a helicopter approaching. He walked back inside, stirred a pot of tea on the stove, then went back out to await the arrival.

"I see one," Murphy said, pointing.

In the last few minutes, Gurt's face had turned ashen. Murphy could see beads of sweat on his forehead, and his hand controlling the helicopter was shaking.

"Hold on," Murphy said, "we're almost there."

"I'm starting to see black on the edges of my eyes," Gurt said. "You might need to guide me on where to land."

T HE SOUND OF the cargo plane lifting off was loud. Eddie Seng was forced to yell into the telephone. "How bad is it?" he asked Hanley.

"We don't know," Hanley said, "but we should dispatch someone now—the flight north takes a couple of hours. If the support is not needed, we can call it back."

"Got it," Seng said.

Then he walked toward the makeshift clinic to see if Huxley had found anyone trained in nursing to fly along. Five minutes later, he had a helicopter refueled, a Tibetan soldier with a limited nursing background, and supplies in the air.

* * *

"Y OU'RE CLOSE ENOUGH, Gurt," Murphy said, "and you're about twelve feet above the ground."

Gurt started to descend, then vomited across the dashboard of the Bell. "In case I can't, when that gauge reads green," he said, wiping the sleeve of his flight suit across his mouth, "flick these three switches down. That will shut down the turbines."

Six feet above the ground in a slow descent, Gurt paused and hovered for a second, then took her the rest of the way to the ground. As soon as the helicopter settled on the skids, he slumped over in the harness and sat unmoving.

Murphy started to unsnap him from the belt as he waited for the helicopter to cool, then turned the engines off and waited for the rotor to stop spinning. Then he quickly climbed from his seat and raced around to the pilot's door. With Gampo's help, they carried Gurt inside the tent.

Then Murphy began to cut off his flight suit with a knife.

The cloth was saturated by blood and the wound was still leaking.

"S IR," THE PILOT of the Gulfstream said, "we're on final approach."

Cabrillo stared out the window. Smoke was still rising from the burning wreckage at the far end of Gonggar Airport. The sun was over the horizon and he could just catch sight of Lhasa sixty miles distant. Staring up the aisle, through the open cockpit door and out the windshield, he could see a lumbering silver plane some seventy feet above the runway climbing out and away. On the ground were several trucks driving down the road away from the airfield.

They were a hundred feet above the runway and two hundred yards downwind. Two minutes later, the tires touched the tarmac with a squeal. The pilot taxied off the runway near the terminal and stopped. The turbines were still spinning when Cabrillo climbed out.

C HAIRMAN ZHUREN HAD tape across his eyes and his wrists were taped behind his back. The dark-haired man that had burst into his bedroom was pulling him quickly along. Zhuren could hear a noisy crowd of people nearby. Then distant gunfire rang out from a few blocks away.

The thumping of a distant helicopter grew louder.

King watched through the scope as Reyes led Zhuren through the crowd. He could see Reyes ordering the *Dungkar* soldiers with him to clear the people away from the landing zone. Turning, he glanced from his perch a few blocks away to where the armored personnel carriers were approaching. Crowds of Tibetans were trying to stop them but they were being felled by bursts of machine-gun fire. The lead APC was coming down a narrow street, with Tibetans fleeing from the front. He watched as it ran over the fallen body of a Tibetan freedom fighter. It flattened the body like a frog on a train track.

Reaching into his bag, he removed a belt of ammunition containing armor-piercing rounds and slid them into the .50. The helicopter was just about to touch down when he started firing.

Ten shots in seven seconds. Ten more for good measure.

The lead APC ground to a halt. The ones to the rear stopped also.

The sound of the helicopter was loud in Zhuren's ears. He felt himself being pulled from inside and pushed from outside into a seat, then he felt someone slide in next to him. He sniffed the air. It was the dark-haired man, the man who had yanked him from safety into the unknown.

The helicopter lifted off.

"They will hover above us and we'll climb inside," King said to his *Dungkar* assistant.

"Mr. Sir," the Tibetan said, "can I stay?"

"What's your plan?" King asked.

The Tibetan pointed to where his countrymen were swarming over the disabled APC.

The helicopter was almost to the rooftop. King reached into his satchel and removed a black cloth bag. "These are hand grenades," he said. "Do you know how they work?"

"Pull the metal thing and run?" the *Dungkar* said, smiling.

"You got it," King said, "but keep your people back when you use them—these will shred a human like cheese in a grater."

The helicopter was above the rooftop and lowering down. The Tibetan grabbed the bag and started for the ladder down.

"Thank you, sir," the *Dungkar* soldier shouted.

"Good luck," King shouted as a pair of hands from inside the helicopter reached for him and he stepped up onto the skid, then ducked down and climbed inside.

"How's things?" Reyes shouted after the door was closed and the helicopter had turned back toward Gonggar Airport.

"You know what they say," King said wearily. "We do more before lunch than most people do all day."

43

"M R. SENG," CABRILLO said, "excellent job so far."

A cold wind was blowing from the north. It bore the scent of forests and glaciers, aviation fuel and gunpowder. Cabrillo zipped the leather jacket he was wearing tighter around his neck, then reached in his rear pocket and removed a carefully folded white handkerchief and dabbed his nose, which was running.

"Thank you, sir," Seng said. "Here's the most current situation report. Murphy and the contract pilot managed to get the charges placed and cause the avalanche at the pass. Any Chinese armor is now effectively immobilized. Even if they decided to ignore the Russian advance and try to return to Lhasa now, their only route would cost them at least forty-eight hours of transit time, and that is *if* the weather holds."

"Problems with that operation?" Cabrillo asked.

"The contract pilot, one Gurt Guenther, was hit by small-arms fire," Seng said. "The extent of his injuries is unknown."

"You've dispatched backup?"

"A relief helicopter with Kasim aboard is en route," Seng said, "but they made it to the fuel stop and managed to land, so Guenther might not be too critical. The way it stands now is that if Murphy's team can fly themselves out, we can call back Kasim."

"Good," Cabrillo said. "We might just need him here."

"Speaking of the weather," Seng said, "we are going to catch a late spring storm this afternoon, then it will clear for tomorrow and the next few days. The estimate is two to three inches of snow, and for the temperature to go below freezing before a slow warming trend."

"The weather has the same impact on us as on the Chinese," Cabrillo said, "but it is a possible advantage for the *Dungkar* forces. We'll score it in Tibet's favor."

From far in the east came the sound of an approaching helicopter. Cabrillo stared in the distance and tried to make out which type it was.

"That's one of ours, sir," Seng said. "It contains Reyes, King and Legchog Zhuren."

"Excellent."

The two men started walking closer to the terminal. Zhuren would end up there soon enough.

"We have managed to field an attack helicopter liberated from the Chinese and piloted by Mr. Adams. Also a cargo plane we modified into a gunship with Gunderson at the controls, as well as the rental Bells and the Predator."

"An excellent air armada for the newly resurrected Tibetan military," Cabrillo said.

"Everything else in the plan has taken place at the correct time," Seng said, "but there is one problem that has arisen. I discovered it when questioning a captured Chinese lieutenant."

"What?" Cabrillo asked.

"Because the Chinese troops in Tibet have always been outnumbered," Seng said, "if they were overrun—and I mean a Broken Arrow situation, no hope at all—the plan called for them to gas the Tibetan rebels with an airborne paralyzing agent."

"The drums must be marked with some symbols," Cabrillo said. "We'll just call Washington and receive recommendations for how to disable it."

"That's the problem," Seng said loudly over the sound of the helicopter hovering to land. "The lieutenant doesn't know where it was stored. He only knows it exists."

Cabrillo reached into his coat pocket and removed a Cuban cigar. Biting off the end, he spit the plug to the side, then reached for a Zippo lighter with the other hand and did a single-hand light. He puffed the cigar to life before speaking.

"I have a feeling, Mr. Seng, it's going to be a long day."

M URPHY WAS ANGRY. Gampo had left him alone in the tent with a weak and bleeding Gurt. If this was the way the feared *Dungkar* reacted to blood, they'd lose this war before it ever started. The *Oregon* was sending help, but even at the fastest cruising speed the Bell could fly, that would be hours away. Gurt, his friend and fellow warrior, was growing weaker by the minute. His skin was an ugly gray and he was drifting in and out of consciousness.

Just then the flap of the tent was pulled back and Gampo entered.

He was carrying a handful of long-bladed grass clippings in one hand and what looked like a wet dirt clod in the other, and under his chin was a chunk of meat from some unspecified beast.

"Where the hell did you go?" Murphy said.

"Stir the fire in the stove," Gampo said quietly, setting down the grass and mud, "then add these to the fire," he added, removing a leather pouch with powdered minerals inside. "We need a good amount of smoke inside the tent. Once you have that done," he said, pointing to the meat, "cook that in with the tea and make me a meat broth."

Murphy stared at Gampo as if he were crazy.

But the Tibetan was already busy cleaning and bandaging Gurt's wound, so Murphy did as he was told. Two minutes later, the tent was filled with a smoke that smelled somewhat like cinnamon cloves washed in lemon. Three more minutes and Gampo stood upright and stared at Murphy. Then he motioned to help him prop Gurt up. The grass and mud had dried into a pair of oblong bandages front and rear. They adhered to his skin like plaster of paris laced with glue. Gurt's eyes began to flicker open and he drew a few deep breaths.

"Give him the broth of the bear," Gampo said. "I'll go gas up your flying ship."

JUST ACROSS THE border of Russia and Mongolia, General Alexander Kernetsikov was breathing deeply of the diesel-smoke-tinged air. After leaving Novosibirsk, his tank column had blown through the Altai Region like a top-fueler down a drag strip. Kernetsikov was riding in the lead tank with his head out of a forward hatch. He was wearing a helmet with a headset so he could communicate with his other officers, and a uniform with enough ribbons to decorate a Christmas tree. In his mouth was an unlit Cuban cigar. In his hand was a GPS that he was using to track the column's speed.

The distance to the Tibet border was five hundred miles. They were traveling at thirty-five miles per hour.

Kernetsikov stared overhead as a flight of fighters crisscrossed high in the air above. Then he called his intelligence officer over the radio to learn what was new. The weather was due to change to snow sometime in the next few hours. Other than that, all was the same.

IN MACAU, SUNG Rhee was reaching the end of his patience.

Marcus Friday had learned that his plane had been found and had ordered it to return to pick him up and fly him out of the city. Stanley Ho was still angry about the theft of his priceless Buddha. The later discovery that the one Friday had recovered was fake just added to his rage.

After the Chinese navy had realized that the cargo ship they had illegally stopped on the high seas had nothing to do with the incident in Macau, they had broadened their circle of observation and tracked the *Oregon* to Vietnam.

Po had made a few calls to a friend he knew in the Da Nang police department and learned that a C-130 had left Da Nang for Bhutan. A few more calls and some wired bribes had led him to a rumor that the group that had stolen the statue was on their way to Tibet.

Po was a Chinese police officer and Tibet was a Chinese region, so Po had decided to follow the trail. Flying from Macau to Chengdu, he had arrived on the last flight in Gonggar yesterday evening. By the time he'd arrived at the office of the Public Security Bureau, Tibet's police force, it was closed. So he'd checked into a hotel and waited for morning.

This morning was chaotic in Lhasa, but he'd managed to meet with the chief of police and requisitioned half a dozen men to help his investigation before the street fighting escalated. By now, he'd figured out which of the band members had been the ringleader. The memory of Cabrillo's face on the tape from the single security camera that had worked had burned a hole in his brain that only death or insanity would erase.

Po set out to see if he could find his target—he had no idea of the impending war.

As Po and the other policemen loaded into a large six-passenger truck to scour Lhasa, the Chinese military officers were beginning to realize the gravity of the situation. They started to assemble to exert control over the city and crush the rebel forces.

The *Dungkar* started their plan in motion as well.

TIME WAS OF the essence and Cabrillo had none to spare. For a man that had been yanked from sleep, bound and transported south to the airport under guard, Legchog Zhuren was surprisingly belligerent. Cabrillo had first tried to appeal to Zhuren's sense of goodness, asking him just to explain the procedure for the poison gas and where the stockpiles were located, but Zhuren had spit in his face and puffed up his chest.

It was obvious that goodness was not a quality Zhuren cherished.

"Tape him," Cabrillo said.

Up until this second, Cabrillo had tried to show respect by allowing Zhuren to simply sit in the chair in front of him—now it was time to learn what he needed, and for that the Chinese leader would need to be secured. Seng and Gannon wrapped his arms and legs with duct tape and secured him to the chair.

"Prepare the juice," Cabrillo said to Huxley.

"What are you—" Zhuren started to say.

"I asked you nice," Cabrillo said, "to help me save both the Chinese in Tibet as well as the Tibetan nationals. You didn't seem to want to cooperate. We have a little serum that will help to loosen your tongue. Trust me, you'll tell us everything, from your first conscious memory to the last time you had sex. The only problem is this:

We cannot always get the dosage right. Too much and we erase your memory like a wet cloth across a chalkboard. Usually we gradually increase the dosage to try and avoid that—but you're a prick, so I think we'll bypass that step."

"You're lying," Zhuren said in a voice showing fear.

"Ms. Huxley," Cabrillo said, "twenty cc's in the lieutenant's arm, please."

Huxley walked over to where the Chinese army lieutenant was still bound to his chair. She squirted some of the liquid in the air until she had the correct amount, then with her other hand wiped an alcohol swab across his upper arm, then plunged the needle into a vein. Cabrillo watched the second hand of his watch as fifteen seconds passed.

"Name and where you were born, please," Cabrillo said.

The lieutenant rattled off the information like his tongue was on fire.

"What is the total troop strength inside Lhasa?"

"There were eighty-four hundred approximate troops," the lieuten-ant said. "Just over six thousand were sent north toward Mongolia. That leaves around twenty-four hundred. Of those, some two hundred fifty were sick or injured. The remaining troops are Company S, Com-pany L—"

"That's enough," Cabrillo said.

"I don't mind," the lieutenant said, smiling. "We have the following armor. Four T-59—"

"That's fine," Cabrillo said.

Zhuren stared at the lieutenant in horror.

"Ms. Huxley," Cabrillo said slowly. "Prepare one hundred cc's."

Zhuren started talking and it was nearly a half hour before he fin-ished.

Cabrillo was scanning the notes of Zhuren's disclosures. He turned to Seng, pointed out a spot on the map, and then examined a satellite photograph of the area.

"I want to lead this one myself," he said slowly. "I'll need a dozen men, air cover and some way to destroy the gas."

"Sir, I inventoried the hangar," Gannon said. "There were a pair of fuel-air cluster bombs in the ordnance room."

"That should do it," Cabrillo said.

S TANLEY HO MIGHT own a mansion in Macau and bear all the earmarks of legitimacy, but the fact was that he was really only one step away from street-level thug. Once he realized that Winston Spenser had screwed him on the Golden Buddha, his every waking min-ute since had been used in scheming to settle the score. It was not just that Spenser had ripped him off—that was one thing. It was the fact that he had dealt with Spenser so many times in the past. That Spenser had smiled in his face, then stabbed him in the back. To Ho, that meant that Spenser had been toying with him, that all the art dealer's good-natured ass-kissing and pandering had been merely a prelude to the big screw. Ho had been treated like a dupe—and he hated that most of all.

Ho had personally gone down to the Macau immigration office to bribe the clerk. That had given him a list of everyone who had exited the country the day after the robbery. With that in hand, it had just been a case of eliminating all the improbabilities until Ho had gotten down to just three people. Then he had sent three men hired from the local triad leader to Singapore, Los Angeles, and Asunción, Paraguay. The first two had been washes; the parties had been observed and disqualified and the men were called back. Ho was starting to think that maybe he'd need to expand the search, that he had somehow eliminated Spenser from the first cut by accident. He was beginning to think this would take longer than he'd planned.

Just then his fax started printing and a picture came across.

Ho was staring at the photograph when his telephone rang.

"Yes or no?" a voice with a rough Chinese accent asked.

Ho stared a second longer, then smiled. "His hands and his head," he said quietly. "Pack them in ice and overnight them."

The telephone went dead in his ear.

P ARAGUAY IN GENERAL and Asunción in particular is more European feeling than South American. The massive stone buildings and extensive parks with fountains scream Vienna, not Rio. Spenser tossed some feed purchased from a machine nearby toward the pigeons, then wiped the cold sweat from his forehead.

The fact is, a man who commits a crime is never free—even if it seems he pulled it off.

The abiding knowledge of his infraction is never far from his mind and it weighs on his psyche, and holding it inside only makes it worse. Only the sociopath feels no remorse—the events happened to another, if they ever happened at all.

Spenser brushed the last of the feed from his hand, watched as the birds fought over the morsels, then stood up. It was late afternoon. He decided to return to his anonymous hotel and nap before going out for a late dinner. Tomorrow he would start looking for a house to rent and begin to rebuild his life. Tonight, his plan was to eat, sleep and try to forget.

The art dealer was not a stupid man. He knew Ho would scour the earth for him.

Right now, however, Spenser was just trying to put that all out of his mind. He had a few days at least, he thought, before the trail here might be detected, if it ever was. That would give him time to move out of the capital into the countryside. There, he would eventually make friends who could help warn him if people started poking around. And hide him, if they came too close.

At this instant in time, however, his guard was down and he was weary. Tomorrow he could worry—tonight he would have a fine Argentine steak and an entire bottle of red wine. Crossing through the park, he started down the cobblestone street leading up the hill toward the hotel.

The sidewalk was deserted; most people were taking their midday break. That gave him comfort. He was humming, "I Left My Heart in San Francisco" as he strolled along. Halfway up the block, he saw the awning leading to the street from his hotel.

Spenser was still humming when a side door onto the sidewalk swung open and a garrote was slipped over his head and he gagged over his verse.

With lightning speed the triad killed and dragged Spenser inside a garden at the rear of a home facing the street. The occupants of the home were out of town, but that was of little matter to the killer—had they been unfortunate enough to be home, he would have killed them too.

Four days passed before the remains of Spenser's body were found. It was minus the hands and the head, but the arms had been carefully folded across his chest and the Canadian passport tucked into his belt.

44

T RUITT STARED AT the water as the turboprop made a final approach for landing at the Kiribati capital city of Tarawa. The water was a light sapphire color, with coral reefs clearly visible beneath
the surface. Fishermen in small canoes and outboard-motored crafts
plied the waters, while a black-hulled tramp steamer was tied alongside
the dock at the main port.

It looked like a scene out of *South Pacific*.

The plane was not crowded, just Truitt, a single chubby male islander who had yet to stop smiling, and a load of cargo in the rear. The
inside of the cabin smelled like salt, sand and the aroma of light mold
that seemed to permeate everything in the tropics. It was hot inside the
plane, and humid, and Truitt dabbed a handkerchief to his forehead.

The pilot lined up for a landing on the dirt strip, then eased the
plane down.

A bump, the feeling of the brakes slowing the aircraft to a crawl,

then a slow taxi to the concrete-block terminal building. Truitt watched
out the window as the plane stopped in front of the terminal, then felt
a rush of humid, flower-scented air as the pilot walked back and lowered
the door. The islander climbed down first and walked toward a woman
holding a pair of smiling children in her arms, while Truitt grabbed his
overnight bag from the seat behind. Then he rose and walked down the
steps. The presidents of Kiribati and Tuvalu were waiting.

THE ATTORNEY HIRED by Halpert sat on the rear deck of the
spacious mountain chalet. In the distance, across a meadow with
a stone fence marking the borders and a haystack leaving no doubt as
to the purpose of the land, a dark-haired man adjusted a portable
propane-fueled heater, then sat down in a chair across the table.

Marc Forne Molne, the head of government of Andorra, was kindly
but direct.

"You may relay to your principals that I sincerely appreciate the
investment in my country—we always welcome finding a home for fine
companies. However, the simple fact is this: Even if they had not chosen
to base their operations here, our vote would have gone toward a free
Tibet."

Molne rose again and adjusted the flame higher. "Opposition
against tyranny and oppression is an Andorran legacy."

Molne brushed a drop of water from his hands. "You tell your men
they have our vote. And you also tell them if they need anything else,
they need but ask."

The attorney rose from his chair. "Thank you, sir," he said. "I will
report back to them immediately."

Molne motioned with his hand and a butler appeared out of nowhere.

"Show this man to my office," he ordered. "He needs to use the
telephone."

* * *

T WO HOURS LATER, Truitt had forged an agreement. A pair of trusts, one for each nation. Because the population of Kiribati was just over 84,000, they received $8.4 million. Tuvalu, with a population of 10,867, received $1.1 million. Another $5.5 million was dedicated for development of eco-tourism on the two chains of islands. To promote tourism, the two countries decided on a series of small island resorts where the natives would act as guides, scuba-diving masters and overseers.

The planned stilt homes would be self-service. The tourists could clean their own rooms.

Truitt caught the last flight out on Easter day.

H ANLEY WAS STARING at a satellite image of Tibet as he spoke on the telephone.

"You're sure, Murph?" he asked. "He's fit to fly?"

"It was like magic," Murphy said over the secure line. "Gurt looks better than before he was shot. He's outside doing repairs on the chopper as we speak."

"Hold on," Hanley said from the *Oregon*. "I'll call off the cavalry."

Reaching for a scrambled radio, he called the rescue helicopter. "Stop where you are," Hanley said, "and wait. If my fuel calculations are correct, you should have more than half tanks right now. Wait until you see the other Bell pass nearby, then follow her home to Gonggar."

"Understand," the pilot answered. "What's the ETA?"

"They're about an hour away," Hanley noted, "but I'll monitor the situation and report to you when they are near."

"We're touching down now," the pilot said, "and standing by."

* * *

I N WASHINGTON, D.C., hands-off was becoming hands-on.

Langston Overholt sat in a room off the Oval Office, waiting for the president to reappear. Truitt had notified Hanley of his successful mission. Hanley had faxed the details to Cabrillo in Tibet. Once that was done, he had telephoned Overholt and reported the news.

Overholt then made his way to the White House to report to the president.

"For someone who was supposed to be outside the loop," the president said, entering the room, "I'm as wrapped up in this as a kitten in a yarn ball."

It was early morning in Washington, and the president had been preparing for bed when he had been summoned. He was dressed in gray sweatpants and a blue T-shirt. He was drinking a glass of orange juice.

He stared at Overholt, then grinned. "You must know I stay up late and watch *Saturday Night Live*."

"Don't all politicians, sir?" Overholt asked.

"Probably," the president said. "It was always the rumor that it cost Gerald Ford the election."

"How did it go, sir?" Overholt asked.

"Qatar was a gimme," he said easily. "Me and Mr. al-Thani are old friends. Brunei was not such a pushover. The sultan needed a few concessions—I gave them, and he agreed."

"I'm sorry we needed to involve you, sir," Overholt said. "But the contractors were short of both men and time."

"Have you got the last vote?" the president asked. "Is Laos in the bag?"

Overholt glanced at his watch before answering. "Not yet, sir," he said, "but we will have it in about fifteen minutes."

"I'll instruct the ambassador to the United Nations to call for a special vote in the morning," the president said. "If your guys can hold down the fort for six hours or so, we're home free."

"I'll notify them immediately, sir," Overholt said, rising.

"Good," the president said. "Then I'm going to catch a few hours of shut-eye."

A Secret Service agent led Overholt down the elevator and into the secret tunnel. Twenty minutes later he was in his car and on his way back to Langley.

T HE WHITE 747 cargo plane slowed to a stop at the end of the runway in Vientiane, then taxied over to a parking area and shut down the engines. Once everything was shut down, the pilot began the process of raising the entire nose cone in the air, opening up the immense cargo area. Once the nose was in the air, cargo ramps were attached to a slot in the open front of the fuselage.

Then, one by one, cars were driven out onto the tarmac.

The first was a lime-green Plymouth Superbird with a hemi-engine. The second, a 1971 Ford Mustang Boss 302 in yellow with the shaker hood, rear slats over the window and the quarter-mile clock in the dashboard. The third was a 1967 Pontiac GTO convertible, red with a black interior, red-line tires and air conditioning. The last was a 1967 Corvette in Greenwood green, with the factory speed package and locking rear differential.

The man who carefully removed the cars from inside the 747 was of medium height with thick brown hair. As soon as the last car, the Corvette, was on the runway, he reached into the glove box, removed a letter, then climbed out and lit up a Camel filter.

"You must be the general," he said to a man approaching followed by a dozen soldiers.

"Yes," the general said.

"I'm Keith Lowden," the man said. "I was told to give you this."

The general scanned the letter, folded it and placed it in his rear pants pocket. "These all original?"

"They are," Lowden said. "The serial numbers all match."

Lowden then motioned to the general to walk over to the Superbird and started explaining the car, the documentation and the rare options. By the time Lowden had finished with the second car, the Boss 302, the general stopped him.

"You want—" he started to say just as Lowden's cell phone rang.

"Sorry," Lowden said as he answered. He listened for a minute, then turned to the general.

"They want to know if it's a deal," he said, placing his hand over the telephone.

The general nodded his head in the affirmative.

"He said okay," Lowden said.

A second later he hung up the telephone and turned back to the general. "Now, what were you about to ask me?"

"I was wondering if you had time to spend the night here in my country," the general said, "so we might talk about the cars."

"I don't know," Lowden said, smiling. "This country have any beer?"

"Some of the best," the general said, smiling back.

"Good," Lowden said. " 'Cause you can't talk cars when you're thirsty."

P O AND HIS team were searching throughout Lhasa, but they had yet to turn up a single U.S. or European citizen. The six members of his team were all Tibetan, and Po didn't care for them much. First of all, like most people, he hated traitors—and any way you sliced it, Tibetans that worked for the PSB had sold out to the Chinese. In the second part, the men appeared lazy; they did the questioning in a hap-hazard fashion and didn't seem to be committed to finding the people Po was seeking. Thirdly, for being members of the country's crack police service, they didn't seem to have much training in police procedures.

Po, for his part, had little choice, so he doubled his own efforts and hoped for the best.

* * *

"THE SON-OF-A-BITCHES," CABRILLO said angrily, "it's like putting an atomic bomb in the Vatican."

Zhuren had just given them the site of the poison gas. It was in Potala, the home of the Dalai Lama, and one of the most sacred of structures in all of Tibet. The Chinese plan was evil, but ingenious. Potala sat on a hill outside of town; if one waited until the winds were right, you could blanket Lhasa in a matter of minutes.

Seng nodded, then reached for his beeping radio. "Go ahead, *Oregon*," he said.

"Is Cabrillo there with you?"

"Hold on," Seng said, handing him the radio.

"Juan," Hanley said quickly, "we have the votes. All you need to do is keep it together for another few hours and help will be on the way."

"What's the latest on the Russians?" Cabrillo asked.

"They're five hours from the Mongolian-Tibetan border," Hanley said, staring at the large monitor on the wall, "give or take."

"Call and have them slow the tank column down," Cabrillo said. "If they reach the border before the vote, we could have World War Three on our hands."

"I'll do it," Hanley said. "Now, what's happening on the ground?"

"I just found out the Chinese have one last trick up their sleeve," Cabrillo said. "A doomsday gas."

"Do you know the location and type?" Hanley said.

Cabrillo rattled off the chemical composition.

"We'll get to work here figuring out how to render the gas inert," Hanley said.

"Good," Cabrillo said. "That frees me up to pinpoint the exact location."

"Somehow," Hanley said, "I knew you were going to say that."

45

THE *OREGON* WAS surging into the Bay of Bengal in preparation for the team's extraction. Word of the street fighting in Lhasa had reached the news media. Television crews, newspaper and magazine reporters, and radio teams were making final preparations to enter the country. To maintain the veil of secrecy necessary for the Corporation to conduct business, they needed to be away from Tibet before the reporters appeared.

So far the plan had worked like clockwork, but there was still a wild card to contend with.

The Russian ruse had successfully tied up the Chinese army far to the north, but the risk now was from the Chinese air force. If Beijing ordered squadrons of bombers and fighter planes to attack the country, the results would be catastrophic. The *Dungkar* forces had limited means to wage ground-to-air warfare. Carpet bombing of Lhasa would result in heavy losses.

The only hope was if the news media could shine the beacon of truth on China.

If the world could be shown via television that the Tibetans had overthrown their oppressors on their own and that the control of Tibet was in the hands of the people and their divine leader the Dalai Lama, then any bombing by China would be taken for what it was—a senseless act of brutality. The ensuing worldwide condemnation would be a burden even China could not bear.

Hanley placed a call to Bhutan and ordered the C-130 to prepare to evacuate his team.

"CLIMBER ONE," MURPHY said, "to Rescue."

Gurt was steering the Bell 212 above a mountain plain with jagged peaks to each side. Several miles in the distance, the rescue helicopter was visible on the ground. As Murphy watched through his binoculars, the rotor blade started to spin, then gain speed until it was just a blur.

"Rescue One," the radio squawked. "We have visual and will follow along."

Murphy watched as the helicopter lifted into a high hover, then slowly began to move forward. Passing to one side, Murphy craned his head to the rear and confirmed they were in formation behind and to one side.

"How are you feeling?" he said over the intercom to Gurt.

"My shoulder feels like I've been kicked by a mule," he noted, "but all in all, I'm not doing too bad."

"I'd like to know what Gampo gave you," Murphy said.

"Some ancient Tibetan potion," Gurt said, staring at the gauges. "I just hope it lasts."

"I spoke to the *Oregon*," Murphy said. "One of the backup pilots will fly you back to Bhutan."

"Heck of a deal," Gurt said. "I thought I was a goner."

"Me too, old buddy," Murphy said quietly. "Me too."

FOR THE CHINESE, the battle for Lhasa was all but over. They had lost the initiative when King stopped the movement of the armored column. From that point on, the *Dungkar* forces had been seized by a rage that showed no boundaries.

Teams under the leadership of General Rimpoche had spread out through Lhasa, rounding up Chinese troops in their barracks and elsewhere. The war for the motor pool was bloody, but after forty minutes of fierce fighting, the *Dungkar* had taken control.

"This was all the red paint available in town," a *Dungkar* warrior said as he slid to a stop inside the fenced yard of the motor pool.

General Rimpoche was sitting in the passenger seat of a Chinese jeep with a bloody bandage wrapped around his lower leg. A red-hot chunk of shrapnel from a fragmentary grenade had hit him as he was leading the last charge in the battle.

"Mark the captured armored personnel carriers and the three remaining tanks with the Dalai Lama's symbol," he said, coughing, "then alert our forces that these vehicles are under our control."

The man scurried off to fulfill the request while at the same time his aide approached.

"I've found a dozen men with at least basic knowledge of how to drive," the aide said. "We can have the vehicles on the streets of the city as soon as they are painted."

"Good," Rimpoche said. "We need to show we're in control."

Right at that instant, he heard a helicopter approaching from Gonggar. He watched as it passed overhead and headed for Potala.

DETECTIVE PO AND his Tibetan underlings had just escaped a mob of Tibetans intent on capturing them. Po was now on the outskirts of Lhasa at the east end of the city. More and more he was considering his mission a failure. Either there was no one answering the description of the people he sought, or the Tibetans he and his men had questioned were lying. But the situation went deeper than that. In the last half hour, Po had felt the tide turn.

More and more he was feeling like the hunted, not the hunter.

His last call to the Public Security Bureau had gone unanswered, and although it might be a figment of his imagination, he was thinking the Tibetans assigned to help him had begun eyeing him differently.

Right then, a helicopter flew overhead and slowed to touch down on the flats below Potala.

"Stop the truck," Po ordered.

The driver slowed and stopped. The helicopter was only two hundred yards away and the skids had just touched the ground. Straining to watch with his binoculars, Po waited until the dust from the rotor wash had cleared and the occupants climbed out. The leader of the group was wearing a helmet, and he was pointing out a spot on the palace grounds to the other men who had climbed out. At that instant, Po saw the man remove a portable telephone from his belt. Then he removed the helmet to hear.

Po stared through the binoculars. The man's hair was worn in a short blond crew cut, but his face was familiar. Po watched.

"YOU'RE SURE, MAX?" Cabrillo asked.

"I just received confirmation," said Hanley, a thousand miles away on the *Oregon*.

"Good, I'm going in," Cabrillo said.

"The media is on their way," Hanley said, "and the Dalai Lama has already left India. Both are due to arrive in Lhasa in just over an hour. We need you all out of there posthaste. I've dispatched the C-130 from Thimbu, and Seng is rounding everyone up. Just get this done—and get out of there."

"All I can say is that you'd better have some beer on board that plane," Cabrillo said, laughing.

"Bet on it," Hanley said.

T HE SMILE. THE smile was the same as that of the man on the tape. Po slid the binoculars back in the case and turned to the driver. "To Potala."

"F LY THE CARGO to that level and unload it," Cabrillo said, pointing to a stark white center section of the palace, "then start searching. I'll meet you on the courtyard that abuts the taller section."

The *Dungkar* in charge of the detail nodded.

"I'm going to take the stair and search the lower levels," Cabrillo said, removing a small portable oxygen tank from inside the helicopter and strapping it on his back. He attached a nose clip, turned on the flow of oxygen, then started up the stairs.

A few minutes later, the helicopter lifted off the flats and dropped off the *Dungkar* and cargo. Four minutes later, the truck carrying Po and the Public Security Bureau members slid to a stop at the bottom of the stairs. Po unholstered his pistol and, followed by the others, started up the stairs. Cabrillo disappeared out of sight in the first structure bordering the stairs.

The helicopter, now empty, parked on the flats near the truck.

The pilot noticed the truck and radioed the *Oregon*.

"It has markings from the Public Security Bureau," he said.

"I'll call Cabrillo," Hanley said, "but I wouldn't worry about it right now. We're receiving sporadic radar returns here. We have yet to determine the source. Watch overhead."

*   *   *

G EORGE ADAMS HAD stopped and refueled the Chinese attack helicopter twice. Chuck Gunderson still had half a tank. For the most part, their mission so far had been quiet. Gunderson had been called in to monitor the fighting at the motor pool, but the *Dungkar* had gained control fast enough that they never needed his makeshift gunship. Adams had yet to locate a clear target to fire upon. In the last twenty minutes, the situation had changed—other than a few pockets of small-arms fire in the city, it appeared that Lhasa was now firmly under *Dungkar* control. Both men could see the transformation clearly from the air—the war was almost over.

"Gorgeous George, this is Tiny," Gunderson said over the radio.

"Hey, Chuckie," George said, "you as bored as I am?"

"I'm telling you—" Gunderson started to say.

"This is Climber One," Murphy said. "A trio, meaning three, Chinese fighters just blew past me and Rescue One. We are fifty miles out of Lhasa inbound for Gonggar."

"All Corporation members, this is the *Oregon*," Hanley said. "We have detected three Chinese fighters inbound from the northern theater. Assume them as unfriendly. Prepare to take cover. All offensive forces report in now."

"Predator, ready," Lincoln said from his remote station in Bhutan.

"Attack One, ready," Adams said.

"Gunship One, ready," Gunderson said.

"I'm sorry, people," Hanley said. "They must have slipped in low under the radar. We now have intermittent returns and expect arrival in minutes."

The three fighters roared down the canyon from the north toward Lhasa.

C ABRILLO WAS IN a large prayer room with small rooms to each side. He was searching each room one at a time, but the going was slow. Po and his team had made it up the stairs. Po paused outside the door with his pistol in the air and peered inside. Then, seeing no one, he crept inside. Cabrillo was searching through a large stack of wooden crates in a storeroom. His attention was focused on locating the poison gas, so he was unaware that Po and his men were outside. The crates contained scrolls, old textbooks and documents. Wiping his hands, he walked out.

Po was standing outside the door with his pistol trained on Cabrillo's chest. The six members of the Public Security Bureau carried rifles, which they pointed at him as well.

Cabrillo smiled. "Morning, men," he said easily. "Just changing the filters in the furnace. This old palace can get a mite drafty when it snows."

"I'm Detective Ling Po from the Macau Constabulatory, and you're under arrest for theft and murder."

"Murder?" Cabrillo said quietly. "I didn't kill anyone."

"Your little Buddha theft and the subsequent escape left three Chinese citizens dead."

"Do you mean when the Chinese navy attacked my boat?" Cabrillo said. "They started it."

Right at that instant, the first fighter plane passed over Lhasa, and all hell broke out.

MURPHY'S WARNING GAVE Adams and Gunderson just enough time to prepare. Adams clung to the side of a mountain west of Lhasa, pointing his tail boom toward the fighters. Gunderson clung to the mountains on the east side with the mini-gun ready to fire. The Predator was in a slow orbit over Gonggar, ready to protect the area.

The fighters passed over Lhasa and unleashed their chain guns, killing scores of Tibetans, then they continued toward the airport. A minute or so later, the fighters neared Gonggar and the antiaircraft guns opened fire. Flying through flak, the lead fighter pilot passed over the airport, then made a sweeping left turn back toward Lhasa. Slowly a helicopter appeared against the mountain. Then a puff of smoke and a flaming spear emerged from under the fuselage.

Adams watched the video camera and made adjustments as the missile streaked toward the fighter. He'd aimed for the main fuselage. What he hit was a wing. The pilot ejected and Adams saw a chute open.

In a textbook maneuver, the second fighter pilot had broken right. He was racing back toward Lhasa when a target showed on his radar scope off his left wing. Before he could react, a Chinese cargo plane appeared. Confused for a second by the appearance of a seemingly friendly force, the pilot hesitated firing.

"Open up," Gunderson shouted to the rear.

The Tibetan gunner let loose with a volley that stitched the side of the fighter like a shotgun blast to the gut of a duck. The man kept firing even after the plane passed from view.

"I think you got him," Gunderson shouted back. "Hold off."

Gunderson made a sweeping turn and caught a glimpse as the flaming wreckage spun into a mountain. There was no ejection, no salvation.

As soon as the third fighter realized they were being fired upon, he made a steep climb straight up in the air. The Predator was hot on his tail.

"Fire four," Lincoln said over the radio as he blew off all his remaining missiles at once.

The jet raced into the heavens, but the lighter and smaller missiles were faster.

The Tibetans on the ground watched as the white contrail from the jet made a straight line up into the sky. Two sets of twin tendrils of steam followed. Then, high over Lhasa, a fireball erupted. The three fighters would fight no more.

"GO SEE WHAT that was," Po ordered one of the Tibetans.

The man walked out and stared down at the city, then

walked back inside. "Planes attacking," was all he said when he returned.

"That's the Chinese retaking the city," Po said. "In a few minutes—"

Just then Cabrillo's telephone rang. So he answered it.

"Excuse me," he said to Po, holding his hand over the receiver.

"Right," Cabrillo said. "Okay, good. No, not yet, there has been a slight snag. There is a Macau policeman here that's—"

Po slid his pistol in his holster and batted the telephone to the floor.

"You shouldn't have done that," Cabrillo said. "I didn't buy the extended warranty."

Po was enraged. His control was slipping and he needed it back now.

On the *Oregon*, Hanley was still listening to the open line.

"Against the wall," Po said, dragging Cabrillo against a stone wall, then stepping back.

Cabrillo stood there, the realization of what was happening slowly dawning.

"What do you think, Po" he spat. "That you're judge, jury and executioner?"

"Men," Po said, "line up."

The Tibetans formed a firing line, their rifles at their shoulders.

On the *Oregon*, Eric Stone was next to Hanley, listening in. "Sir," he said, "what can we do?"

Hanley raised his hand to quiet him.

"On behalf of the Macau authorities," Po said, "I have heard your admission of guilt and find you guilty of murder. Your sentence is death by firing squad, at this time and place."

Stone looked in horror at Hanley, whose face remained impassive.

"Do you have any last words or pleas?" Po asked.

"Yes," Cabrillo said. "I ask that you stop this nonsense immediately—there is a deadly gas somewhere in this palace, and if I don't find it soon, we all will die."

"Enough of your lies," Po thundered. "Men, prepare to fire."

Cabrillo brushed his hand along his crew-cut hair, then smiled and winked.

"Fire," Po shouted.

A volley of shots rang out and the prayer room was filled with the scent of gunpowder.

"THERE THEY ARE," the leader of the *Dungkar* detail said. Three stainless-steel canisters were marked with Chinese symbols. The *Dungkar* erected the apparatus to burn off the gas, then started to dress in gas masks and rubber gloves. The gas had been right where Zhuren had said.

"Has anyone seen the American?" the *Dungkar* leader asked.

The answer came back negative.

"Slowly and carefully start to destroy the gas," the leader said. "I'm going downstairs to report."

THE SMOKE CLEARED and Cabrillo was still standing. One of the Public Security Bureau officers reached over and took Po's handgun from his holster. Then he did a quick pat-down search to look for other weapons.

"You missed," Cabrillo said, wiping a fleck of blood off his cheek from where a chip of stone had struck.

Stone looked over at Hanley, who smiled. "The Tibetans are with us," he explained. "They have been all along."

Stone raised his arms in the air in exasperation. "No one tells me anything," he said.

Cabrillo was walking over to pick up his telephone when the *Dungkar* leader burst into the room. He stared at the scene in shock. Against the far wall was a large outline of a man that had been made by the bullets striking the stone. Five PSB officers were standing with rifles, while a lone PSB officer was placing another man in handcuffs.

"We found the gas," the *Dungkar* blurted out. "We're burning it off now."

Cabrillo bent down and retrieved the telephone. "Max," he said, "did you hear that?"

"I did, Juan," Hanley said. "Now get the hell out of there."

Cabrillo folded the telephone in half and slid it in his pocket. "Norquay, I assume?" he asked the leader of the PSB officers.

"Yes, sir," the officer answered.

"Assist the *Dungkar* with the destruction of the gas," Cabrillo said. "Then secure Potala. General Rimpoche will be in contact with you soon—thanks for your help."

Norquay nodded.

"To a Free Tibet," Cabrillo shouted.

"To a Free Tibet," the men answered.

Cabrillo began walking toward the door.

"Sir?" Norquay said, "there's just one more thing."

Cabrillo paused.

"What do you want us to do with him?" Norquay said, motioning to Po.

Cabrillo smiled. "Let him go."

Cabrillo reached for the door handle. "But take his uniform and papers. He's just too emotional to be a policeman."

Then Cabrillo walked out the door, climbed down the steps and boarded the helicopter. Five minutes later he was back at Gonggar Airport. Ten minutes later he and his team were airborne in the C-130. They passed the fleet of leased helicopters in the air, headed for Bhutan, and the pilot of the C-130 wagged his wings. The helicopters returned the good-bye by flicking on their landing lights.

Then the team settled in for the short flight. Soon they'd be back on the *Oregon*.

46

IN BEIJING, NEWS of the events in Tibet was filtering in, and a hurried meeting was held.

President Jintao was direct. "What are our options?" he asked.

"We could send bombers to hit Lhasa," the head of the Chinese air force said. "Then ready paratroopers for a later assault."

"But that leaves us short on the Mongolian border," Jintao noted. "What's the latest intelligence on the Russian movements?"

The head of Chinese intelligence was a short man with a pronounced belly. He adjusted his glasses before speaking. "The Russian forces are enough for them to sweep down and flank our troops that are currently still headed down the pass into Qinghai Province. If they supported their efforts with air power, we could lose both Qinghai and Xinjiang Provinces, basically the entire western frontier."

"That would give them control of our secret advanced weapons facilities at Lop Nur, plus a good portion of our space program," Jintao said wearily.

"I'm afraid so, sir," the head of intelligence noted.

"Okay—" Jintao started to say before his aide rushed into the room and walked over and whispered in his ear.

"Gentlemen," President Jintao said, "continue discussions—I have an emergency meeting. The Russian ambassador is insisting we talk and has arrived ahead of his scheduled meeting."

The Russian ambassador was waiting in an outer office. He rose as Jintao walked into the room. "Mr. President," he said solicitously, "I apologize for moving up the time of our meeting, but the president of my country insisted I see you immediately."

"Do you come bringing a declaration of war?" Jintao asked directly, motioning the Russian to take a seat on a couch near a window with a view of the outer gardens.

The Russian ambassador sat on the left end of the couch, Jintao farther down on the right.

"No, Mr. President," the Russian ambassador said, straightening his suit pants. "I come with a business offer that can put an end to the tension between our countries, as well as placing your economy on solid footing again."

Jintao stared at his watch before answering. "You have five minutes."

The Russian ambassador explained it all in four.

"So you are convinced you can pull a UN Security Council vote?" Jintao said after he was through.

"We can," the Russian said.

"What do we get if we go along with the vote?" Jintao asked. "If China votes to go along."

The Russian ambassador smiled. "World peace?"

"I was thinking of a larger percentage of the field."

Two minutes later, the Russian had his offer.

"Mr. President," he said, "allow me to make a telephone call."

"Tell them I want your armored column stopped immediately," Jintao said, "confirmed by satellite reconnaissance."

Eight minutes later, the new percentages would be confirmed and the Russian armored column would grind to a halt. Further negotiations would continue right up until the UN vote.

A T THE SAME instant the Russian ambassador was calling Moscow, the C-130 containing the Corporation team was crossing into India. Off the right wing the jet carrying the Dalai Lama home passed. The pilot of the jet wagged his wings and the pilot of the C-130 reciprocated.

Less than an hour later, the team reached Calcutta, India, and was met by the Corporation's amphibious airplane. Within minutes of the C-130 touching down, the crew was being flown out to the ship.

By sundown on March 31, the *Oregon* was steaming south in the Bay of Bengal.

On the deck, Hanley and Cabrillo watched the setting sun.

"I got a call from Overholt after you left Calcutta," Hanley said.

"I'm sure it was the usual," Cabrillo said. "Rah, rah, good job. The check is in the mail."

"He did mention that, and a wire transfer that Halpert has already confirmed."

"What else?" Cabrillo asked.

"He has another job for us," Hanley said.

"Where?" Cabrillo asked.

"The land of the midnight sun, Mr. Chairman," Hanley said. "The Arctic Circle."

Cabrillo sniffed the salt air, then began walking for the hatch inside. "Come on, you can explain over dinner."

"It had better be dinner and drinks," Hanley said. "I haven't had a cocktail since Cuba."

"Cuba," Cabrillo said wearily. "Seems like years ago."

EPILOGUE

THERE EXIST SNIPPETS of history etched into the fabric of time and so perfectly formed that they may never be duplicated. Seemingly scripted by a power with perfect timing and blessed with scenes that know no bounds, these moments exist to be captured on film, to be remembered and cherished for centuries to come.

These snippets do not happen often. They are as rare as the perfect turn on skis, as delightful as homemade ice cream in the hot sun. They exist to remind man there is hope. They exist to show promise. They exist for generations yet unborn.

The Dalai Lama's return to Lhasa was one of these events.

April 1, 2005, dawned with clear skies and no wind. The snow-capped mountains surrounding the city appeared to be close enough that one could run his fingertip across the sharp crests. The very air in Lhasa seemed alive with energy. It filled the lungs of the faithful with a hope silent for decades and soothed and cooled the fires of war.

"Unbelievable," a reporter for a Los Angeles newspaper said quietly.

It was an image from Shangri-la. Potala Palace was glistening like a mirage in the mind of a complicated man. The hillside surrounding the palace was covered with a flowing field of red and blue blooming flowers that spilled down the hill in a waterfall of color. One thousand Buddhist monks in yellow robes filled the steps from top to bottom like a colored strip of DNA molecules. On the lower buildings, parts of the green roofs were visible, adding contrast, while the white rocks of the structure seemed to have been scrubbed clean of dirt as a result of the cloak of oppression being lifted. High overhead a hawk circled lazily on the warming air.

The chosen one was coming home.

Nearly a mile away, on the large flat meadow below Potala, a monk stepped over to a six-foot-tall gong suspended from a dark, carved wooden frame. He glanced at the Dalai Lama, who was sitting atop a gold gilded throne chair. The throne chair was topped with a fringed silk awning, supported by wooden poles at the corners and held aloft by six stout monks who walked in unison with the throne chair.

The six monks chanted a single-word chant and the wood-and-leather hammer struck the gong.

The sound of the gong filled the air. One, two, until it sounded three times. And then the procession started forward. The Ngagpa, carrying the symbolic wheel of life, led the column. Directly behind the Ngagpa were Tibetan horsemen, their steeds decorated with ceremonial blankets whose intricate needlepoint depicted scenes from Tibetan history. The horsemen wove their mounts back and forth in a choreographed display of precision. In their hands were triangular flags attached to long bronze staffs that were capped with fluted tops. To the rear of the horsemen were two dozen archers with bows at parade rest against their shoulders. They marched in perfect harmony. Next came a dozen porters carrying cages filled with songbirds that chirped a song of freedom and happiness. The porters were followed by fifty-five monks from the Dalai

Lama's home monastery at Namgyal. They chanted in a single voice and carried in their hands the sacred texts.

Next were more horsemen, four dozen in total, who were also musicians. They played their flutes and stringed instruments while they steered their mounts with their knees. The horse-mounted musicians were followed by monks from the Tsedrung Order, who represented the government of Tibet, followed by children waving thin, pointed, ornately colored flags that danced through the air like kites without tails.

To the rear of the children was another group of horsemen with serious faces, dressed in Tibetan army uniforms of green cloaks and red hats. They steered their horses a few feet forward, then stopped. A few more feet, then a pause again. These soldiers carried the Tibetan Seals of State. Just to the rear of the soldiers carrying the Seals of State were ten simple monks, barefoot and dressed in yellow robes. The ten monks were humming loudly.

The Golden Buddha came next. It sat on a plain wagon pulled by a single horse.

Only a few feet behind the Golden Buddha was the throne chair containing the Dalai Lama.

Two hundred thousand Tibetans lined the procession route leading to Potala. They massed on both sides of the cleared path through the meadow. The day they had prayed and hoped for over these last decades was finally here—and they allowed their joy to wash across the land. As soon as the Golden Buddha appeared, the crowd went wild.

A roar erupted, and the faithful prostrated themselves onto the hard soil, then began to chant as one.

The Dalai Lama began passing through the crowd and witnessed the tears of joy on the cheeks of the faithful. The sight filled him with happiness, duty and honor, and it caused him to smile.

Following the throne chair were members of the Dalai Lama's inner cabinet, the Kasag. Next came the Kusun Depon, the Dalai Lama's bodyguards, dressed in their black padded suits and carrying their curved swords. Following the bodyguards was the commander in chief of the Tibetan army, the Mak-chi, and a platoon of soldiers.

The Mak-chi and the soldiers were dressed in their ceremonial uniforms consisting of blue trousers and yellow tunics covered in gold braid. They marched in slow and perfect cadence, with their boots making a timed thumping sound as they struck the soil. Next were the Dalai Lama's religious tutors and teachers, as well as family and friends.

At the rear of the procession came a wagon with a tiger in a cage, followed by a single horseman holding a thirty-foot-tall staff flying the formerly outlawed Tibetan flag. The parade was both magisterial and magnificent. It was based on two thousand years of tradition and strengthened by fifty-five years of exile.

The procession continued toward Potala.

A T THE BASE of the eighty-foot-tall foundation wall of Potala, four hundred laborers had worked eight hours the night before to build a series of stone steps leading from the edge of the meadow to the top of the wall. As soon as the first of the procession reached the lowest step, they parted to each side, like the flow of water in a stream being split by a boulder, then took their positions alongside the temporary stairway.

Once the Golden Buddha reached the base of the steps, the ten monks walked over, formed a ladder with their arms, then carried the Buddha up the steps and placed it on the top of the wall. Then they descended the stairway as the throne chair containing the Dalai Lama slowed and stopped at the base. On a signal from the Dalai Lama, the monks carrying the throne chair bowed down on their knees, then swiveled to the side. Holding the throne chair only inches above the ground, they waited until the Dalai Lama climbed off the chair onto the thick woven carpet that lay upon the ground. Breathing a sigh of relief as the weight was removed from the chair, the monks waited until the Dalai

Lama started up the stairs, then they set the throne chair upon the ground and rose to their feet.

With a soul seeped in tradition and divinely inspired, the Dalai Lama ascended the stairway.

Reaching the top, he slowly turned and stared out at the crowd. The mass of humanity stretched across the meadow and onto the surrounding hillsides. He bowed his head, then closed his eyes for a moment. Then he spoke.

"I have missed you," he said simply.

The crowd, so subdued only seconds before, once again erupted into cheers.

Twenty minutes would pass before it quieted down enough for the Dalai Lama to speak again.